THE OTHER QUEEN

Philippa Gregory is an established writer and broadcaster for radio and television. She holds a PhD in eighteenth-century literature from the University of Edinburgh. She has been widely praised for her historical novels, including *Earthly Joys, Virgin Earth, A Respectable Trade, The Queen's Fool, The Virgin's Lover, The Constant Princess, The Boleyn Inheritance, The Other Queen*, as well as her works of contemporary suspense. *The Other Boleyn Girl* was adapted for BBC television and is now a major film, starring Scarlett Johansson, Natalie Portman and Eric Bana. Philippa Gregory lives in the North of England with her family and welcomes visitors to her website PhilippaGregory.com

By the same author

PHILIPPA GREGORY

THE OTHER QUEEN

HARPER

HarperCollins*Publishers*
77–85 Fulham Palace Road,
Hammersmith, London W6 8JB

www.harpercollins.co.uk

This paperback edition 2011
1

Copyright © Philippa Gregory Ltd 2011

Philippa Gregory asserts the moral right to
be identified as the author of this work

Mary Queen of Scots' letter featured on the endpapers is used by
permission of the National Archives, ref. SP51/1

A catalogue record for this book
is available from the British Library

ISBN: 978 0 00 792606 0

Typeset in Minion by Palimpsest Book Production Limited,
Falkirk, Stirlingshire
Printed and bound in Great Britain by
Clays Ltd, St Ives plc

MIX
Paper from
responsible sources
FSC® C007454

FSC
www.fsc.org

For Anthony

1568, Autumn, Chatsworth House, Derbyshire: Bess

Every woman should marry for her own advantage since her husband will represent her, as visible as her front door, for the rest of his life. If she chooses a wastrel she will be avoided by all her neighbours as a poor woman; catch a duke and she will be Your Grace, and everyone will be her friend. She can be pious, she can be learned, she can be witty and wise and beautiful; but if she is married to a fool she will be 'that poor Mrs Fool' until the day he dies.

And I have good reason to respect my own opinion in the matter of husbands having had three of them, and each one, God bless him, served as stepping stone to the next until I got my fourth, my earl, and I am now 'my lady Countess of Shrewsbury': a rise greater than that of any woman I know. I am where I am today by making the most of myself, and getting the best price for what I could bring to market. I am a self-made woman – self-made, self-polished and self-sold – and proud of it.

Indeed, no woman in England has done better than me. For though we have a queen on the throne, she is only there by the skill of her mother, and the feebleness of her father's other stock, and not through any great gifts of her own. If you kept a Tudor for a breeder you would eat him for meat in your second winter. They are poor weak beasts, and this Tudor queen must make up her mind to wed, bed and breed, or the country will be ruined.

If she does not give us a bonny Protestant boy then she will abandon us to disaster, for her heir is another woman: a young woman, a vain woman, a sinful woman, an idolatrous Papist woman, God forgive her errors, and save us from the destruction she will bring us. Some days you hear one story of Mary Queen of Scots, some days another. What you will never, never hear, even if you listen a hundred times, even when the story is told by her adoring admirers, is the story of a woman who consults her own interest, thinks for herself, and marries for her best advantage. But since in this life a woman is a piece of property, she does well to consider her improvement, her sale at the best price and her future ownership. What else? Shall she let herself tumble down?

A pity that such a foolish young woman should be foisted on me and my household, even for a short stay, while Her Majesty Elizabeth the Queen decides what is to be done with this most awkward guest. But no house in the kingdom can be trusted to entertain and – yes – secure her like mine. No husband in England could be trusted with such a Salome dancing on his terrace but mine. Only my household is run with such discipline that we can accommodate a queen of royal blood in the style that she commands and with the safety that she must have. Only my newly wedded husband is so dotingly fond of me that he is safe under the same roof as such a temptress.

No-one knows of this arrangement yet; it has been decided in secret by my good friend Secretary William Cecil and by me. As soon as this hopeless queen arrived in rags at Whitehaven, driven from Scotland by her rebellious lords, Cecil sent me a short note by an unknown messenger to ask if I would house her, and I sent him a one-word reply: yes. Yes indeed! I am honoured by Cecil's faith in me. From such trust comes great challenges, and from great challenges come great rewards. This new world of Elizabeth's is for those who can see their chances and take them. I foresee honours and riches if we can host this royal cousin and keep her close. Cecil can rely on me. I shall guard her and befriend her, I shall house and feed her, I shall treat her royally and honourably and keep her safe as a little bird in the nest till the moment of his choosing, when I will hand her over intact to his hangman.

1568, Autumn, Hampton Court: George

I am nobody's agent. I am no bought opinion. I am no hired blade. I am neither Cecil's spy nor executioner. I wish to God that I were not here in London, on this bad business, but home at Chatsworth House with my darling innocent wife Bess, in the simple country and far away from the conspiracies and perils of court. I can't say that I am happy. I can't say that I like this. But I will do my duty – God knows that I always do my duty.

'You have been summoned for nothing but to order the death of Mary Queen of Scots,' Thomas Howard hisses in my ear as he catches up with me in a gallery at Hampton Court. They have closed the shutters for cleaning and the place is shadowy in the early-evening dusk. The portraits on the walls seem to show pale-faced listeners leaning forward to hear as Howard takes my arm to warn me of dangers that I already fear.

'We are to throw suspicion on her. Nothing else. Don't deceive yourself. Cecil decided that this queen was a threat to the kingdom, from the moment of her birth. She may think that she has escaped her enemies in Scotland to sanctuary in England; but she has just exchanged one danger for another. Cecil has decided that she must die. This is his third attempt to convict her. We are to be his hangmen, without opinions of our own.'

I look down at Howard; he is a small man, well-dressed and neat with a well-trimmed black beard and bright dark eyes. Today he is almost dancing with fury at the queen's minister. We all resent Cecil, all us old lords; but it rubs Howard worse than any other. He is the queen's cousin, the head of the Howard family, he is the Duke of Norfolk, he would expect to be her chief advisor – but she depends on Cecil and always has done.

'I have been appointed by the queen herself to inquire into the conduct of her cousin the Queen of Scots. I am no hangman,' I say with quiet dignity. A man goes past, and hesitates as if to listen to our conversation.

Howard shakes his dark head at my naivety. 'Elizabeth may want the Queen of Scots' name cleared. But William Cecil is not notorious for his soft heart. He wants the Protestant faith to rule Scotland as England, and the Catholic queen to lie in jail, or in her coffin. Either suits him equally well. He will never agree that she is guilty of nothing and must be restored to her throne.'

I cannot argue against Howard's irritable righteousness. I know that he is speaking only the truth. But he is speaking it too loud and too clear for my liking. Anyone could be behind the tapestry screens, and though the stranger has strolled on, he must have heard some of this.

'Hush,' I say and draw him to a seat so that we can whisper. At once we look like conspirators, but the whole court looks like conspirators or spies these days. 'What can we do?' I ask him quietly. 'Cecil has called this inquiry to hear the evidence against the Scots queen, to judge whether she should be restored to her throne, whether she is fit to rule. What can we do to make sure that she is treated justly?'

'We have to save her,' Howard says firmly. 'We have to declare her innocent of murdering her husband, and we have to restore her to her throne in Scotland. We have to accept her claim to be Elizabeth's heir. She must be confirmed as heir to the throne of England when . . .' He breaks off. Not even Howard dares mention the death of his cousin the queen. 'When the time comes. Only the confirmed inheritance of Mary Stuart will give us the safety of knowing our next monarch. We have a right to know the heir. We have to fight her cause as if it were our own.'

He sees my hesitation. A couple of men go by and look curiously at the two of us. I feel conspicuous and get to my feet.

'Walk with me,' Howard says. 'And listen. We have to fight her cause as if it were our own because it *is* our own. Say that we let Cecil imprison her, or trump up a charge of murder and accuse her. What do you think happens then?'

I wait.

'What if next he decides that *I* am a danger to the kingdom? What then? What if after me, he names you?'

I try to laugh. 'He is hardly likely to accuse you, or me. We are the greatest men in England. I am the greatest landowner north of the Trent and you are the queen's own cousin and a duke.'

'Yes. And that is why we are in danger. We are his rivals for power. He will destroy anyone who challenges him. Today the Queen of Scots faces his tribunal. Tomorrow it could be me, or any that have dared to challenge him: Percy, Dacre, Sussex, Arundel, Dudley, the Northern lords, you. He has to be stopped,' Howard says, his voice a low rumble in my ear. 'Wouldn't you stop him if you could?'

'It can't be done,' I say cautiously. 'The queen is free to choose her own advisors, and she trusts him like no other. He has been at her side since she was a young princess. What could we accuse him of?'

'Stealing Spanish gold! Pushing them to the brink of war! Making an enemy of France! Driving half the country towards treason with his constant suspicion and spying on people who want nothing more than to worship in the old way! Look at the court! Have you ever been at court before and felt yourself so fearful? It is filled with spies and plots.'

I nod. It is undeniable. Cecil's fear of Papists and his hatred of foreigners stalk England.

'This last idiocy of his is the worst,' Howard says furiously. 'That a ship should take refuge from bad weather in our port and be seized! He makes us a nation of pirates and the seas unsafe for our shipping.'

I can't disagree. The Spanish treasure ship was blown into Plymouth expecting sanctuary, and Cecil, the son of a poor man, could not resist the gold it carried. He stole the gold – simple as that. And now the Spanish are threatening a blockade of trade, even war, if we do not pay it back. We are utterly in the wrong, all because Cecil is utterly in the wrong; but he has the ear of the Queen of England.

Howard masters his irritation with some difficulty. 'Please God we never see the day when you come to me and say I was right to fear him and we should have defended ourselves, but now it is too late and one of our own is on trial for some trumped-up charge. Please God he does not pick us off one by one and we too trusting to defend ourselves.' He pauses. 'His is a rule of terror. He makes us afraid of imaginary enemies so we don't guard ourselves against him and against our government. We are so busy watching for foreigners that we forget to watch our friends. Anyway, you keep your counsel and I'll keep mine. I'll say no more against Cecil for now. You will keep this close? Not a word?'

The look he gives me persuades me, more than any argument. If the only duke in England, cousin to the queen herself, should fear his own words being reported to a man who should be little more than a royal servant, it proves that the servant has become over-mighty. We are all growing afraid of Cecil's knowledge, of Cecil's network of intelligencers, of Cecil's growing silent power.

'This is between the two of us,' I say quietly. I glance around to see that no-one is in earshot. It is amazing to me that I, England's greatest earl, and Howard, England's only duke, should fear eaves-droppers. But so it is. This is what England has become in this tenth year of Elizabeth's reign: a place where a man is afraid of his own shadow. And in these last ten years, my England seems to have filled with shadows.

1568, Winter, Bolton Castle: Mary

I refuse, I utterly refuse to wear anything but my own gowns. My beautiful gowns, my furs, my fine lace collars, my velvets, my petticoats of cloth of gold were all left behind in Holyroodhouse, dusted with scented powder and hung in muslin bags in the wardrobe rooms. I wore armour when I rode out with Bothwell to teach my rebel lords a lesson, but it turned out I was neither teacher nor queen, for they beat me, arrested me and hunted Bothwell down for an outlaw. They imprisoned me and I would have died in Lochleven Castle if I had not escaped by my own wits. Now, in England, they think I am brought so low as to wear hand-me-downs. They think I am sufficiently humbled to be glad of Elizabeth's cast-off gowns.

They must be mad if they think that they can treat me as an ordinary woman. I am no ordinary woman. I am half divine. I have a place of my own, a unique place, between the angels and nobles. In heaven are God, Our Lady and Her Son, and below them, like courtiers, the angels in their various degrees. On earth, as in heaven, there are the king, the queen and princes; below them are nobles, gentry, working people and paupers. At the very lowest, just above the beasts, are poor women: women without homes, husbands, or fortune.

And I? I am two things at once: the second highest being in the world, a queen; and the very lowest: a woman without home, husband, or fortune. I am a queen three times over because I was born Queen of Scotland, daughter to King James V of Scotland, I was married to the Dauphin of France and inherited the French crown with him, and I am, in my own right, the only true and legitimate heir to the throne of England, being the great-grandniece to King Henry VIII of England, though his bastard daughter, Elizabeth, has usurped my place.

But, *voilà!* At the same time I am the lowest of all things, a poor woman without a husband to give her a name or protection, because my husband the King of France lived for no more than a year after our coronation, my kingdom of Scotland has mounted an evil rebellion against me and forced me out, and my claim to the throne of England is denied by the shameless red-haired bastard Elizabeth who sits in my place. I, who should be the greatest woman in Europe, am reduced so low that it is only her support that saved my life when the Scots rebels held me and threatened my execution, and it is her charity that houses me in England now.

I am only twenty-six years old and I have lived three lifetimes already! I deserve the highest place in the world and yet I occupy the lowest. But still I am a queen, I am a queen three times over. I was born Queen of Scotland, I was crowned Queen of France, and I am heir to the crown of England. Is it likely I will wear anything but ermine?

I tell my ladies-in-waiting, Mary Seton and Agnes Livingstone, that they can tell my hosts, Lord and Lady Scrope of Bolton Castle, that all my gowns, my favourite goods and my personal furniture must be brought from Scotland at once and that I will wear nothing but my own beautiful clothes. I tell them that I will go in rags rather than wear anything but a queen's wardrobe. I will crouch on the floorboards if I cannot sit on a throne under a cloth of estate.

It is a small victory for me as they hurry to obey me, and the great wagons come down the road from Edinburgh bringing my gowns, my bureaux, my linen, my silver, and my furniture; but I fear I have lost my jewels. The best of them, including my precious black pearls, have gone missing from my jewel chests. They are the finest pearls in Europe, a triple rope of matched rare black pearls, everyone knows they are mine. Who could be so wicked as to profit from my loss? Who would have the effrontery to wear a queen's pearls robbed from her ransacked treasury? Who would sink so low as to want them, knowing they had been stolen from me when I was fighting for my life?

My half-brother must have broken into my treasure room and stolen them. My false brother, who swore to be faithful, has betrayed me; my husband Bothwell, who swore he would win, is defeated. My son James, my most precious son, my baby, my only heir, whom I swore to protect, is in the hands of my enemies. We are all forsworn, we are all betrayers, we are all betrayed. And I – in one brilliant leap for freedom – am somehow caught again.

I had thought that my cousin Elizabeth would understand at once that if my people rise against me in Scotland, then she is in danger in England. What difference? *Rien du tout!* In both countries we rule a troublesome people divided in the matter of religion, speaking the same language, longing for the certainties of a king but unable to find anyone but a queen to take the throne. I thought she would grasp that we queens have to stick together, that if the people pull me down and call me a whore then what is to stop them abusing her? But she is slow, oh God! She is so slow! She is as sluggish as a stupid man, and I cannot abide slowness and stupidity. While I demand safe conduct to France – for my French family will restore me to my throne in Scotland at once – she havers and dithers and calls for an inquiry and sends for lawyers and advisors and judges and they all convene in Westminster Palace.

To judge what, for God's sake? To inquire into what? For what is there to know? *Exactement!* Nothing! They say that when my husband, the fool Darnley, killed David Rizzio, I swore vengeance and persuaded my next lover the Earl of Bothwell to blow him out of his bed with gunpowder and then to strangle him as he ran naked through the garden.

Madness! As if I should ever allow an assault on one of royal blood, even for my own vengeance. My husband must be as inviolable as myself. A royal person is sacred as a god. As if anyone with half a wit would commission such a ridiculous plot. Only an idiot would blow up a whole house to kill a man when he could easily smother him with a quiet pillow in his sottish sleep! As if Bothwell, the cleverest and wickedest man in Scotland, would use half a dozen men and barrels of gunpowder, when a dark night and a sharp knife would do the deed.

Finally, and worst of all, they say that I rewarded this incompetent assassination by running off with the assassin, the Earl of Bothwell, conceiving children in adulterous lust, marrying him for love, and declaring war against my own people for sheer wickedness.

I am innocent of this, and of the murder. That is the simple truth and those who cannot believe it have made up their minds to hate me already for my wealth, for my beauty, for my religion, or because I was born to greatness. The accusations are nothing but vile slander, *calomnie vile.* But it is sheer folly to repeat it word for word, as Elizabeth's inquiry intends to do. Utter idiocy to give it the credence of an official inquiry. If you dare to say that Elizabeth is unchaste with Robert Dudley or any other of the half-dozen men who have been named with her through her scandalous years, starting with her own stepfather Thomas Seymour when she was a girl, then you are dragged before a justice of the peace and your tongue is slit by the blacksmith. And this is right and proper. A queen's reputation must be untouched by comment. A queen must seem to be perfect.

But if you say that *I* am unchaste – a fellow queen, anointed just as she is, and with royal blood on both sides that she lacks – then you can repeat this in Westminster Palace before whoever cares to come by to listen, and call it evidence.

Why would she be such a fool as to encourage gossip about a queen? Can she not see that when she allows them to slander me she damages not just me, but my estate, which is exactly the same as her own? Disrespect to me will wipe the shine off her. We should both defend our state.

I am a queen, different rules apply for queens. I have had to endure events as a woman that I would never even name as a queen. I would not stoop to acknowledge them. Yes, I have been kidnapped, I have been imprisoned, I have been raped – but I will never, never complain of it. As a queen my person must be inviolate, my body is always holy, my presence is sacred. Shall I lose that powerful magic for the benefit of moaning on about my injuries? Shall I trade majesty itself for the pleasure of a word of sympathy? Would I prefer to command, or do I long to whimper about my wrongs? Shall I order men, or shall I weep at the fireside with other injured women?

Of course. The answer to this is simple. *Bien sûr.* No-one must ever pity me. They can love me or hate me or fear me. But I shall never let anyone pity me. Of course, when they ask me, did Bothwell abuse you? I will answer nothing, not at all, never a word. A queen does not complain that she has been ill-treated. A queen denies that such a thing could happen. I cannot be robbed of myself, I cannot mislay my own divinity. I may be abused but I will always deny it. Whether I am seated on a throne or wearing rags, I am still a queen. I am no commoner who has to hope for the right to wear velvet or live out his life in homespun. I am above all degree of ordinary men and women. I am ordained, I am chosen by God. How can they be so dense as not to see it? I could be the worst woman in the world and I would still be queen. I could romp with a dozen Italian secretaries, a regiment of Bothwells, and write them all love poems, and I would still be queen. They can force me to sign a dozen abdications and lock me in prison forever but I will still be queen and anyone who sits on my throne will be a usurper. *Je suis la reine.* I am queen till death. It is not an office, it is not an occupation, it is an inheritance of blood. I am queen while the blood flows through my veins. So I know. So everyone knows. So even they know, in their faithless hearts, the fools.

If they want rid of me there is only one way; but they will never dare to take it. If they want rid of me they will have to sin against the order of heaven. They will have to defy the God-given chain of being. If they want rid of me they will have to behead me.

Think of that!

The only way I cease to be Dowager Queen of France, Queen of Scotland, and the only true heir to the throne of England is when I am dead. They will have to kill me if they want to deny me my throne. And I wager my title, my fortune and my life that they will never dare to do that. To lay violent hands on me would be the same as throwing down an angel, a sin like crucifying the Christ again. For I am no ordinary woman, I am a sanctified queen, I am seated above every mortal; only the angels are my superiors. Mortals cannot kill such a being as me. I am anointed with holy oil, I am chosen by God. I am untouchable. They can fear me and they can hate me, they can even deny me. But they cannot kill me. Thank God, I am at least safe in this. I will always be safe in this.

1568, Winter, Chatsworth: Bess

I have news from my husband the earl, of the inquiry at Westminster. (I am still newly wed, I love to say 'my-husband-the-earl'.) He writes to me almost daily to tell me of his discomfort, and in return I send him news of his children and mine, home-baked pies and the best Chatsworth cider. He says he has been secretly shown letters of the most damning evidence, love letters from the married queen to the married Earl of Bothwell urging him to kill her husband, poor young Lord Darnley, telling him that she is on fire with lust for him. Wanton poems, promises of nights of pleasure, French pleasures are especially mentioned.

I think of the judges – my husband, young Thomas Howard, his friend the Earl of Sussex and old Sir Ralph Sadler, Robert Dudley and my good friend William Cecil, Nicholas Bacon, Sir Thomas Percy, Sir Henry Hastings, and all the others – reading this nonsense with shocked faces, trying to believe that a woman planning to murder her husband by packing his cellars with gunpowder would spend the very night before the explosion, at her husband's sickbed, writing love poetry to her accomplice. It is so ridiculous that I wonder they are not laughed out of court.

But these are honest thoughtful highly respected men. They do not ask: what would a real woman do in such circumstances? They are not in the habit of considering the nature of any real woman.

They look only at the evidence that is laid before them. And bless me – what a lot of evidence has been produced! What a lot of effort has been put into blackening her name! Someone, somewhere, has gone to a good deal of time and trouble: stealing her letters, copying her hand, writing them in French and then translating them into Scots and English, putting them into a special casket monogrammed with her initials (in case we thought that they had been written by some other Mary Stuart), and then having them discovered, amazingly badly hidden, in her private rooms. This Someone's work is thorough and extremely convincing. Everyone who has seen the letters now believes that the young queen is an adulterous whore who murdered her young English husband for lust and revenge.

Now I might have an idea who this clever Someone would be. Actually, everyone in England would have a pretty good idea who this Someone might be. And it is rare that he does not have his way. This poor queen will find herself hopelessly outmatched by this Someone, who plans for the long term and plays a long game. She may find that if he does not catch her in his net this time, he will make another with a finer mesh, and again and then again, until she cannot escape.

This time though, it cannot be done; she has wriggled free. The greatest witness against her is her own bastard half-brother, but since he has seized the regency in her absence and holds her baby son as a hostage, not even a courtroom of highly respected men can bring themselves to believe a word that he says. His hatred of her is so obvious and his faithlessness so offensive that not even the judges appointed by Cecil can stomach him. The judges, including my husband, the earl, are all men who pride themselves on their loyalty. They look askance at a subject who is grossly treacherous. They do not like the behaviour of the Scots queen but they like the behaviour of her Scots lords even less. My bet is that they will rule that she has been ill-treated by her people and must be restored to her throne. Then the Scots can deal with their queen as they wish, and we cannot be blamed.

1568, Winter, Hampton Court: George

My queen, Elizabeth, is more generous and more just than anyone can imagine. With so much suspicion now raised and expressed against her cousin, she has ordered that the slanderous letters shall be kept secret forever, and she will restore her cousin to her kingdom. Elizabeth will not hear another word against her cousin, she will not have her name dragged through the mud. She is generous and just in this; we could never have reached a fair judgement without listening to the most terrible scandal, so Elizabeth has silenced both scandal and defence.

But even though she is a monarch of such justice and wisdom I find I am a little perturbed that I am summoned to see her.

She is not on her brown velvet throne embroidered with pearls and diamonds in the Paradise room, though there are, as ever, dozens of men waiting about, hoping to catch her attention when she comes out for company before dinner. The strangers to Hampton Court Palace examine the exquisite musical instruments that are scattered on tables around the room, or play draughts on the ebony boards. Those who are old hands at court idle in the window bays, concealing their boredom at the delay. I see Cecil, watchful as ever. Cecil, dressed in black like some poor clerk, is talking quietly with his brother-in-law Nicholas Bacon. Behind them hovers a man I don't know, but who is now admitted into their councils, a man who wears his hat pulled down over his eyes as if he does not want to be recognised. And behind him, another new man, Francis Walsingham. I don't know who these men are, nor where they belong, to which great families they are allied. To tell truth, most of them don't have family – not as I understand such a thing. They are men without background. They have come from nowhere, they belong nowhere, they can be recruited by anyone.

I turn away as the queen's lady-in-waiting Lady Clinton comes out through the grand double doors from the queen's inner chamber, and when she sees me, speaks to the guard, who stands aside and lets me in.

There are more guards than usual, at every doorway and every gate to the castle. I have never seen the royal palace so heavily manned. These are bitterly troubled times, we have never needed such protection before. But these days there are many men – even Englishmen – who would carry a knife and strike down their own queen if they could. There are more of them than anyone could have dreamed. Now that the other queen, the one that they call the true heir, is actually in England, the choice between the Protestant princess and the Catholic rival is set before every man, and for every Protestant in the land today there are two secret Papists, probably more. How are we to live, when we are divided among ourselves, is a question I leave to Cecil, whose unending enmity to Catholics has done so much to bring this about, and to make a bad situation so much worse.

'Is Her Grace in good spirits today?' I ask in an undertone to her ladyship. 'Happy?'

She understands me well enough to give me a quick sideways smile. 'She is,' she says. She means that the famous Tudor temper is not unleashed. I have to admit I am relieved. The moment that she sent for me I was afraid I would be scolded for letting the inquiry reach no damning conclusion. But what could I do? The terrible murder of Darnley and her suspicious marriage to Bothwell, his probable killer, which appeared as such a vile crime, may not have been her fault at all. She may have been victim rather than criminal. But unless Bothwell confesses everything from his cell, or unless she testifies to his wickedness, no-one can know what took place between the two of them. Her ambassador will not even discuss it. Sometimes I feel that I am too frightened even to speculate. I am not a man for great sins of the flesh, for great drama. I love Bess with a quiet affection, there is nothing dark and doomed about either of us. I don't know what the queen and Bothwell were to each other; and I would rather not imagine.

Queen Elizabeth is seated in her chair by the fireside in her private chamber, under the golden cloth of estate, and I go towards her and sweep off my hat and bow low.

'Ah, George Talbot, my dear old man,' she says warmly, calling me by the nickname she has for me, and I know by this that she is in a sunny mood, and she gives me her hand to kiss.

She is still a beautiful woman. Whether in a temper, whether scowling in a mood or white-faced in fear, she is still a beautiful woman, though thirty-five years of age. When she first came to the throne she was a young woman in her twenties and then she was a beauty, pale-skinned and red-haired with the colour flushing in her cheeks and lips at the sight of Robert Dudley, at the sight of gifts, at the sight of the crowd outside her window. Now her colour is steady, she has seen everything there is to see, nothing delights her very much any more. She paints on her blushes in the morning, and refreshes them at night. Her russet hair has faded with age. Her dark eyes, which have seen so much and learned to trust so little, have become hard. She is a woman who has known some passion but no kindness; and it shows in her face.

The queen waves her hand and her women rise obediently and scatter out of earshot. 'I have a task for you and for Bess, if you will serve me,' she says.

'Anything, Your Grace.' My mind races. Can she want to come to stay with us this summer? Bess has been working on Chatsworth

House ever since her former husband bought it, for this very purpose – to house the queen on her travels to the North. What an honour it will be, if she plans to come. What a triumph for me, and for Bess's long-laid plan.

'They tell me that your inquiry against the Scots queen, my cousin, failed to find anything to her discredit. I followed Cecil's advice in pursuing the evidence till half my court was turning over the midden for letters, and hanging on the words of maids spying at bedroom doors. But there was nothing, I believe?' She pauses for my confirmation.

'Nothing but gossip, and some evidence that the Scots lords would not publicly show,' I say tactfully. 'I refused to see any secret slanders as evidence.'

She nods. 'You would not, eh? Why not? Do you think I want a dainty man in my service? Are you too nice to serve your queen? Do you think this is a pretty world we live in and you can tiptoe through dry-shod?'

I swallow on a dry mouth. Pray God she is in a mood for justice and not for conspiracy. Sometimes her fears drive her to the wildest of beliefs. 'Your Grace, they would not submit the letters as evidence for full scrutiny, they would not show them to the Queen Mary's advisors. I would not see them secretly. It did not seem to be . . . just.'

Her dark eyes are piercing. 'There are those who say she does not deserve justice.'

'But I was appointed judge, by you.' It is a feeble response, but what else can I say? 'I have to be just if I am representing you, Your Majesty. If I am representing the queen's justice, I cannot listen to gossip.'

Her face is as hard as a mask and then her smile breaks through. 'You are an honourable man indeed,' she says. 'And I would be glad to see her name cleared of any shadow of suspicion. She is my cousin, she is a fellow queen, she should be my friend, not my prisoner.'

I nod. Elizabeth is a woman whose own innocent mother was beheaded for wantonness. Surely, she must naturally side with a woman unjustly accused? 'Your Grace, we should have cleared her name on the evidence that was submitted. But you stopped the inquiry before it reached its conclusions. Her name should be free of any slur. We should publish our opinions and say that she is innocent of any charge. She can be your friend now. She can be released.'

'We will make no announcement of her innocence,' she rules. 'Where would be the advantage to me in that? But she should be returned to her country and her throne.'

I bow. 'Well, so I think, Your Grace. Your cousin Howard says she will need a good advisor and a small army at first to secure her safety.'

'Oh, really? Does he? What good advisor?' she asks sharply. 'Who do you and my good cousin nominate to rule Scotland for Mary Stuart?'

I stumble. It is always like this with the queen, you never know when you have walked into a trap. 'Whoever you think best, Your Grace. Sir Francis Knollys? Sir Nicholas Throckmorton? Hastings? Any reliable nobleman?'

'But I am advised that the lords of Scotland and the regent make better rulers and better neighbours than she did,' she says restlessly. 'I am advised that she is certain to marry again, and what if she chooses a Frenchman or a Spaniard and makes him King of Scotland? What if she puts our worst enemies on our very borders? God knows her choice of husbands is always disastrous.'

It is not hard for a man who has been around the court for as long as I have to recognise the suspicious tone of William Cecil through every word of this. He has filled the queen's head with such a terror of France and Spain that from the moment she came to the throne she has done nothing but fear plots and prepare for war. By doing so, he has made us enemies where we could have had allies. Philip of Spain has many true friends in England and his country

20

is our greatest partner for trade, while France is our nearest neighbour. To hear Cecil's advice you would think one was Sodom and the other Gomorrah. However, I am a courtier, I say nothing as yet. I stay silent till I know where this woman's indecisive mind will flutter to rest.

'What if she gains her throne, and marries an enemy? Shall we ever have peace on the northern borders, d'you think, Talbot? Would you trust such a woman as her?'

'You need have no fear,' I say. 'No Scots army would ever get past your Northern lords. You can trust your old lords, the men who have been there forever. Percy, Neville, Dacre, Westmorland, Northumberland, all of us old lords. We keep your border safe, Your Grace. You can trust us. We keep armed and we keep the men levied and drilled. We have kept the Northern lands safe for hundreds of years. The Scots have never defeated us.'

She smiles at my assurance. 'I know it. You and yours have been good friends to me and mine. But do you think I can trust the Queen of Scots to rule Scotland to our advantage?'

'Surely, when she goes back she will have enough to do to re-establish her rule? We need not fear her enmity. She will want our friendship. She cannot be restored without it. If you help her back on her throne with your army, she will be eternally grateful. You can bind her with an agreement.'

'I think so,' she nods. 'I think so indeed. And anyway, we cannot keep her here in England; there is no possible argument for keeping her here. We cannot imprison an innocent fellow queen. And better for us if she goes back to Edinburgh, than runs off to Paris to cause more trouble.'

'She is queen,' I say simply. 'It cannot be denied. Queen born and ordained. It must be God's will that she sits on her throne. And surely, it is safer for us if she can bring the Scots to peace than if they are fighting against each other. The border raids in the North have been worse since she was thrown down. The border raiders fear no-one, now that Bothwell is far away in prison. Any rule is better than none. Better the queen should rule than no rule at all. And surely, the French or the Spanish will restore her if we do not? And if they put her back on the throne we will have a foreign army on our doorstep, and she will be grateful to them, and that must be far worse for us.'

'Aye,' she says firmly, as if she has made a decision. 'So think I.'

'Perhaps you can swear an alliance with her,' I suggest. 'Better to deal with a queen, you two queens together, than be forced to haggle with a usurper, a new false power in Scotland. And her half-brother is clearly guilty of murder and worse.'

I could not have said anything that pleased her more. She nods and puts her hand up to caress her pearls. She has a magnificent triple rope of black pearls, thick as a ruff, around her throat.

'He laid hands on her,' I prompt her. 'She is an ordained queen and he seized her against her will and imprisoned her. That's a sin against the law and against heaven. You cannot want to deal with such an impious man as that. How should he prosper if he can attack his own queen?'

'I will not deal with traitors,' she declares. Elizabeth has a horror of anyone who would challenge a monarch. Her own hold on her own throne was unsteady in the early years, and even now her claim is actually not as good as that of the Queen of Scots. Elizabeth was registered as Henry's bastard and she never revoked the act of parliament. But Mary Queen of Scots is the granddaughter of Henry's sister. Her line is true, legitimate and strong.

'I will never deal with traitors,' she repeats. She smiles, and at once I see again the pretty young woman who came to the throne with no objection at all to dealing with traitors. She had been the centre of all the rebellions against her sister, Mary Tudor, but was always too clever to be caught. 'I want to be a just kinswoman to the Scots queen,' she says. 'She may be young and foolish and she has made mistakes that are shocking beyond words – but she is my kinswoman and she is a queen. She must be well treated, and she must be restored. I am ready to love her as a good kinswoman and see her rule her country as she should.'

'There speaks a great queen and a generous woman,' I say. It never hurts with Elizabeth to slather on a bit of praise. Besides, it is earned. It will not be easy for Elizabeth to resist the terrors that Cecil frightens her with. It will not be easy for her to be generous to a younger and more beautiful kinswoman. Elizabeth won her throne after a lifetime of plotting. She cannot help but fear an heir with a claim to the throne, and every reason to conspire. She knows what it is like to be the heir excluded from court. She knows that when she was the heir excluded from court she spun one plot after another, murderous rebellions that nearly succeeded in destroying her half-sister and bringing down the throne. She knows what a false friend she was to her sister – it will be impossible for her to trust her cousin who is, just as she was, a young princess impatient of waiting.

She beams at me. 'So, Talbot. This brings me to your task.'

I wait.

'I want you to house the Scots queen for me, and then take her back to her kingdom when the time is right,' she says.

'House her?' I repeat.

'Yes,' she says. 'Cecil will prepare for her return to Scotland; in the meantime, you shall house her and entertain her, treat her as a queen, and when Cecil sends you word, escort her back to Edinburgh, and return her to her throne.'

It is an honour so great that I can hardly catch my breath at the thought of it. To be host to the Queen of Scotland and to return her to her kingdom in triumph! Cecil must be sick with envy; he has no house half as grand as Bess's at Chatsworth, though he is building like a madman. But not fast enough, so she will have to come to us. I am the only nobleman who could do the task. Cecil has no house and Norfolk, as a widower, has no wife. No-one has a grand house and a well-loved loyal reliable wife like Bess.

'I am honoured,' I say calmly. 'You can trust me.' Of course, I think of Bess, and how thrilled she will be that Chatsworth will house a queen at last. We will be the envy of every family in England, they will all want to visit us. We shall have open house all the summer, we shall be a royal court. I shall hire musicians and masquers, dancers and players. We will be one of the royal courts of Europe – and it will all be under my roof.

She nods. 'Cecil will make the arrangements with you.'

I step backwards. She smiles at me, the dazzling smile that she gives to the crowds when they call out her name: the Tudor charm at full meridian. 'I am grateful to you, Talbot,' she says. 'I know you will keep her safe in these troubled times, and see her safely home again. It will only be for the summer and you will be richly rewarded.'

'It will be my honour to serve you,' I say. 'As always.' I bow again and walk backwards and then out of the presence chamber. Only when the door is closed and the guards before it cross their halberds once more do I allow myself to whistle at my luck.

1568, Winter, Bolton Castle: Mary

My faithful friend, Bishop John Lesley of Ross, who has followed me into exile, saying that he cannot stay at home in comfort beside an empty throne, writes to me in our secret code from London. He says that although Elizabeth's third and final inquiry in Westminster Palace could find nothing against me, yet the French ambassador has not yet been told to prepare for my journey to Paris. He is afraid that Elizabeth will find an excuse to keep me in England for another week, another month, God only knows how long; she has the patience of a tormentor. But I have to trust to her friendship, I have to rely on her good sense as a cousin and a fellow queen. Whatever my doubts about her – a bastard and a heretic though she is – I have to remember that she has written to me with love and promised her support, she has sent me a ring as pledge of my safety forever.

But while she hesitates and considers, all this while, my son is in the hands of my enemies, and his tutors are Protestants. He is two years old; what they tell him of me, I cannot bear to imagine. I have to get back to him before they poison him against me.

I have men and women loyal to me, waiting for my return, I cannot make them wait forever. Bothwell, imprisoned in Denmark on a ridiculous charge of bigamy, will be planning his own escape, thinking ahead to setting me free, determined that we shall be reunited on the throne of Scotland. With or without him I have to get back and claim my throne. I have God's hand of destiny on my life, I was born to rule Scotland. I cannot refuse the challenge to win back my throne. My mother gave her life to keep the kingdom for me, I shall honour her sacrifice and pass it on to my heir, my son, her grandson, my little boy, James, Prince James, heir to Scotland and to England, my precious son.

I cannot wait to see what Elizabeth will do. I cannot wait for her slowly to act. I don't know if my son is safely guarded, I don't even know if he is well-nursed. His false uncle, my half-brother, has never loved him; what if he has him killed? I left him with trustworthy guardians in Stirling Castle; but what if they are besieged? I dare not sit here quietly and wait for Elizabeth to forge a treaty with my enemies that sends me on parole to France, or orders me to hide in some convent. I have to get back to Scotland and enter the battle for my throne once more. I did not escape from Lochleven Castle to do nothing. I did not break free from one prison to wait quietly in another. I have to be free.

Nobody can know what this is like for me. Certainly not Elizabeth, who was practically raised in prison, under suspicion from the age of four. She is a woman trained to a cell. But I have been mistress of my own great rooms since I was a girl of eleven in France. My mother insisted I should have my own rooms, my own presence chamber, my own entourage; even as a child I had the ordering of my own household. Then as now, I cannot bear to be constrained; I must be free.

The ambassador bids me keep up my courage and wait for his news. But I cannot just wait. I cannot have patience. I am a young woman in the very prime of my health and beauty and fertility. They have left me to celebrate my twenty-sixth birthday in prison. What do they think they are doing to me? What do they think I will endure? I cannot be confined. I must be free. I am a queen, I was born to command. They will find that I am a dangerous and untamed prisoner. They will find that I will be free.

1568, Winter, Chatsworth House: Bess

Cecil's clerk writes to tell me that Mary Queen of Scots is not to come to us at Chatsworth, where I could entertain her as she deserves: in a great house with a beautiful park and everything done as it should be. No, she is to come to Tutbury Castle in Staffordshire: one of our poorest properties and half-derelict, and I have to turn my life upside down to make this ruin fit for a queen in the middle of winter.

'If your lord and husband could only have been prevailed on to see all the evidence against her, she could have been returned to Scotland in disgrace already,' Cecil writes, sweet as an unripe apple, in a postscript. 'Then we would all have been able to rest easy this Christmastide.'

There is no need for Cecil to reproach me. I warned my lord that the inquiry was a sham and a show, as close to life as are the mummers dressed in motley at Christmas. I told him that if he chose to become a player in this scene of Cecil's devising then he must follow the playscript word by word. He was not invited there to improvise. He should have found the verdict that Cecil wanted. But he would not. If you hire an honourable man to do dirty work you will find the work honourably done. Cecil chose the wrong lord when he chose my husband to supervise the disgrace of the Scots queen. And so Cecil has no scandal, and no dishonoured queen, and I have no husband at home, and I have to clean and rebuild a derelict castle in the middle of winter.

Cecil says: 'I am sorry that you have to house this Athalia; but I hope it will not be for long, for certainty, she will follow the destiny of her namesake.'

This obviously means something to Cecil, who has the benefit of a man's education, but for a woman such as me, the daughter of a farmer, it is as opaque as a code. Fortunately, my darling son Henry is staying with me, on a brief holiday from his place at court. His father, my second husband, Cavendish, left me with instructions and an income to get him educated like a gentleman, and I sent him, and then his two brothers, to school at Eton.

'Who is Athalia?' I ask him.

'Obscure,' he replies.

'So obscure that you don't know the answer?'

He smiles lazily at me. He is a handsome boy and he knows that I dote on him.

'So, my Mama-Countess. What is the information worth to you? We live in a world where all intelligence is for sale. You pay me well enough to report the gossip from court. I am your spy in the house of your friend Robert Dudley. Everyone has an informant and I am merely one of many of yours, I know. What will you pay me for the fruits of my education?'

'I have paid for it once already in your tutors' fees,' I reply. 'And they were dear enough. Besides, I think you don't say because you don't know. You are an ignoramus and my money was wasted on your education. I hoped to buy myself a scholar and all I have is an idiot.'

He laughs. He is such a handsome boy. He has all the disadvantages of a rich boy. Even though he is my own darling, I can see it clearly. He has no idea that money is hard to earn, that our world is filled with opportunity and also danger. He has no idea that his father and I went to the limits of the law and beyond to make the fortune that we would lavish on him and on his brothers and sisters. He will never work as I do, he will never worry as I do. To tell the truth, he has no idea of either work or worry. He is a well-fed boy, whereas I was raised with hunger – a hunger for everything. He takes Chatsworth for granted as his pleasant home, his due; whereas I have put my heart and soul here, and I would sell my heart and soul to keep it. He will be an earl if I can buy him an earldom, a duke, if I can afford it. He will be the founder of a new noble family: a Cavendish. He will make the Cavendish name a noble one. And he will take it all, as if it came easily, as if he had to do nothing but smile as the sun warmly smiles on him; bless him.

'You misjudge me. I do know, actually,' he says. 'I am not such an idiot as you think. Athalia is in the Old Testament. She was a queen of the Hebrews and she was accused of adultery and killed by the priests, so as to free her throne so that her son Joash could become king.'

I can feel my indulgent smile freeze on my face. This is no matter for jokes. 'They killed her?'

'They did indeed. She was known to be unchaste, and unfit to rule. So they killed her and put her son in her place.' He pauses. His dark eyes gleam at me. 'There is a general view, I know vulgar, Mama, but a general view, that no woman is fit to rule. Women are by nature inferior to men and it goes against nature if they so much as try to command. Athalia was – tragically for her – only typical.'

I raise a finger to him. 'Are you sure of that? Do you want to say any more? Would you like to expound further on female inability?'

'No! No!' he laughs. 'I was expressing the vulgar view, the common error, that is all. I am no John Knox, I don't think you are all a monstrous regiment of women, honestly, Mama, I do not. I am not likely to think that women are simple-minded. I have been brought up by a mother who is a tyrant and commander of her own lands. I am the last man in the world to think that a woman cannot command.'

I try to smile with him but inwardly I am perturbed. If Cecil is naming the Scots queen as Athalia then he means me to understand that she will be forced to let her baby son take the throne. Perhaps he even means that she will die to make way for him. Clearly, Cecil does not believe that the inquiry cleared her of the murder of her husband and of adultery with his killer. Cecil wants her publicly shamed and sent away. Or worse. Surely he cannot dream that she could be executed? Not for the first time I am glad that Cecil is my friend; for he is certainly a dangerous enemy.

I send my son Henry, and my dear stepson Gilbert Talbot, back to court and tell them that there is no point staying with me, for I have work to do; they might as well see in the Christmas season in comfort and merriment in London, for I can provide neither. They go willingly enough, revelling in each other's company and in the adventure of the ride south. They are like a pair of handsome twins, alike in age – seventeen and fifteen – and in education, though my boy Henry, I must say, is far and away naughtier than my new husband's son, and leads him into trouble whenever he can.

Then I have to strip my beautiful house, Chatsworth, of hangings and tapestries and carpets, and ship linen by the cartload. This Queen of Scots is to come with a household of thirty persons and they will all have to sleep somewhere, and I know full well that Tutbury Castle has no furniture nor comfort of any kind. I command my Chatsworth chief steward of the household, the grooms of the servery and of the buttery and the master of horse at the stables to send food and trenchers, knives, table linen, flagons and glassware by the wagon-load to Tutbury Castle. I command the carpentry shop to start making beds and trestle tables and benches. My lord uses Tutbury no more than once a year, as a hunting lodge, and the place is barely furnished. Myself, I have not ever been there, and I am only sorry that I have to go there now.

Then, when Chatsworth is in chaos from my orders and the wagons are stuffed with my goods, I have to climb on my own horse with my teeth gritted at the stupidity of this journey, and at the head of my own wagons I ride south-east for four hard days across inhospitable country on roads that are frosty in the morning and thick with mud by midday, through fords which are swollen with freezing floods, starting at wintry dawn and ending in the early dark. All this, so that we can get to Tutbury and try to put the place into some kind of order before this troublesome queen arrives to make us all unhappy.

1568, Winter, Hampton Court: George

'But why does the queen want her taken to Tutbury Castle?' I ask William Cecil, who of all men in England always knows everything, he is a tradesman of secrets. He is the very monopolist of secrecy. 'Chatsworth would be more fitting. Surely the queen wants us to house her at Chatsworth? To be honest, I have not been to Tutbury myself in years; but you know that Bess bought Chatsworth with her previous husband and brought it as her dowry to me, and she has made it very lovely.'

'The Scots queen won't be with you for long,' Cecil says mildly. 'And I would rather have her in a house with a single entrance by a guardhouse, which can be well-guarded, than have her gazing out of fifty windows over beautiful parkland and slipping out of half a dozen doors into the gardens.'

'You don't think we might be attacked?' I am shocked at the very thought of it. Only later do I realise that he seems to know the grounds of Tutbury Castle, which is odd, since he has never visited. He sounds as if he knows it better than I do myself, and how could that be?

'Who knows what might happen, or what a woman like her will take into her head to do, or what support she can attract? Who would have thought that a score of educated noblemen, clearly instructed and advised, with well-trained witnesses and perfect evidence, would sit down to inquire into her behaviour, see the most scandalous material ever written, and then rise up, having decided nothing? Who would have thought that I would convene a tribunal three times over, and still be unable to get a conviction? Are you all so besotted with her?'

'A conviction?' I repeat. 'You make it sound like a trial. I thought it was a conference? You told me it was an inquiry.'

'I fear our queen has been ill-served in this.'

'But how?' I ask. 'I thought we did what she wanted. She stopped the inquiry herself, saying that it was unjust to the Queen of Scots? Surely she has cleared the Scots queen of any wrongdoing? Surely you should be glad? Surely our queen is glad that we held a thorough inquiry but could find nothing against her cousin? And that being so, why should our queen not invite Queen Mary to live with her at court? Why should she come to us at all? Why should they not live as cousins in harmony, queen and heir? Now that her name is cleared?'

Cecil chokes on a laugh that he cannot silence, and claps me on the shoulder. 'You know, you are the very man to keep her safe for us,' he says warmly. 'I think you are the most honourable man in England, indeed. Your wife is right to caution me that you are a man of utter honour. And the queen will be indebted to you for your good guardianship of her dear cousin. I am sure that all of us are as glad as you are that the inquiry cleared the Scots queen's name, and now we know that she is innocent. You have proved her innocent, thank God. And we will all have to live with the consequences.'

I am troubled, and I let him see it. 'You did not want her cleared of blame?' I say slowly. 'And you want her at Tutbury, and not held with honour at Chatsworth?' I have a sense of something amiss. 'I have to warn you: I will only deal with her fairly, Master Secretary. I will have to beg an audience and ask our queen what she intends.'

'Nothing but good,' he says smoothly. 'As I do. As you do. You know that the queen is going to invite you to become a member of the Privy Council?'

I gasp. 'Privy Council?' This has been a long time coming. My family name commends me; but I have had to wait a long time for this moment, it is an honour that I have yearned for.

'Oh yes,' he says with a smile. 'Her Majesty trusts you so well. Trusts you with this task, and others that will follow. Will you serve the queen without question?'

'I always do,' I say. 'You know, I always do.'

Cecil smiles. 'I know. So guard the other queen and keep her safe for us until we can return her safely to Scotland. And make sure you don't fall in love with her, good Talbot. They say she's quite irresistible.'

'Under my Bess's nose? And us married less than a year?'

'Bess is your safeguard as you are ours,' he says. 'Give her my warmest wishes and tell her that when she next comes to London she must break her journey at my house. She will want to see the progress I am making with it. And if I am not mistaken she will want to borrow some of my plans; but she may not steal my builders. Last time she came I found her in deep conversation with my plasterer. She was tempting him away to flower her hall. I swore I would never trust her with one of my artisans again, she poaches them, she truly does. And I suspect her of putting up wages.'

'She will give up her building projects while she is caring for the queen,' I tell him. 'Anyway, I think she must have finished the work on Chatsworth by now. How much work does a house need? It is good enough now, surely? She will have to give up her business interests too, I shall have my stewards take over her work.'

'You'll never get her to hand over her farms and her mines, and she'll never finish building,' he predicts. 'She is a great artificer, your new wife. She likes to build things, she likes property and trade. She is a rare woman, a venturer in her heart. She will build a chain of houses across the country, and run your estates like a kingdom, and launch a fleet of ships for you, and found a dynasty of your children. Bess will only be satisfied when they are all dukes. She is a woman whose only sense of safety is property.'

I never like it when Cecil talks like this. His own rise from clerk to lord has been so sudden, on the coat-tails of the queen, that he likes to think that everyone has made their fortunes from the fall of the church, and that every house is built with the stone of abbeys. He praises Bess and her mind for business, only to excuse himself. He admires her profits because he wants to think that such gains are admirable. But he forgets that some of us come from a great family that was rich long before the church lands were grabbed by greedy new men; and some of us have titles that go back generations. Some of us came over as Norman noblemen in 1066. This means something, if only for some of us. Some of us are wealthy enough, without stealing from priests.

But it is hard to say any of this without sounding pompous. 'My wife does nothing that does not befit her position,' I say, and Cecil gives a little laugh as if he knows exactly what I am thinking.

'There is nothing about the countess and her abilities that does not befit her position,' he says smoothly. 'And her position is very grand indeed. You are the greatest nobleman in England, Talbot, we all know that. And you do right to remind us, should we ever make the mistake of forgetting it. And all of us at court appreciate Bess's good sense, she has been a favourite amongst us all for many years. I have watched her marry upwards and upwards with great pleasure. We are counting on her to make Tutbury Castle a pleasant home for the Queen of Scots. The countess is the only hostess we could consider. No-one else could house the Queen of Scots. Any other house would be too mean. No-one but Bess would know how to do it. No-one but Bess could triumph.'

This flattery from Cecil should content me; but we seem to be back to Bess again, and Cecil should remember that before I married her she was a woman who had come up from nothing.

1568, Winter, Bolton Castle: Mary

It is to be tonight. I am going to escape from Bolton Castle, their so-called, *soi-disant*, 'impregnable' Yorkshire castle, this very night. Part of me thinks: I dare not do this; but I am more terrified of being trapped in this country and unable to go either forward or back. Elizabeth is like a fat ginger cat on a cushion, she is content to sit and dream. But I must reclaim my throne; and in every day of my exile, the situation grows worse for me. I have castles holding out for me in Scotland and I must get relief to them at once. I have men ready to march under my standard, I cannot make them wait. I cannot let my supporters die for lack of my courage. I have Bothwell's promise that he will escape from Denmark, and return to command my armies. I have written to the King of Denmark, demanding Bothwell's freedom. He is my husband, the consort of a queen, how dare they hold him on the word of a merchant's daughter who complains that he promised marriage? It is nonsense, and the complaints of such a woman are of no importance. I have a French army mustering to support me, and promises of Spanish gold to pay them. Most of all, I have a son, a precious heir, *mon bébé, mon chéri*, my only love; and he is in the hands of my enemies. I cannot leave him in their care: he is only two years old! I have to act. I have to rescue him. The thought of him without proper care, not knowing where I am, not understanding that I was forced to leave him, burns me like an ulcer in my heart. I have to get back to him.

Elizabeth may dawdle; but I cannot. On the last day of her nonsensical inquiry I received a message from one of the Northern lords, Lord Westmorland, who promises me his help. He says he can get me out of Bolton Castle, he can get me to the coast. He has a train of horses waiting in Northallerton and a ship waiting off Whitby. He tells me that when I say the word he can get me to France – and as soon as I am safe at home, in the country of my late husband's family, where I was raised to be queen, then my fortunes will change in an instant.

I don't delay, as Elizabeth would delay. I don't drag my feet and puzzle away and put myself to bed, pretending illness as she does whenever she is afraid. I see a chance when it comes to me and I take it like a woman of courage. 'Yes,' I say to my rescuer. '*Oui,*' I say to the gods of fortune, to life itself.

And when he says to me: 'When?', I say, 'Tonight.'

I don't fear, I am frightened of nothing. I escaped from my own palace at Holyrood when I was held by murderers, I escaped from Linlithgow Castle. They will see that they can take me but they cannot hold me. Bothwell himself said that to me once, he said: 'A man can take you; but you cling to your belief that he can never own you.' And I replied: 'I am always queen. No man can command me.'

The walls of Bolton Castle are rough-hewn grey stone, a place built to resist cannon; but I have a rope around my waist and thick gloves to protect my hands and stout boots so that I can kick myself away. The window is narrow, little more than a slit in the stone, but I am slim and lithe, and I can wriggle out and sit with my back to the very edge of the precipice, looking down. The porter takes the rope and hands it to Agnes Livingstone and watches her as she ties it around my waist. He makes a gesture to tell her to check that it is tight. He cannot touch me, my body is sacred, so she has to do everything under his instruction. I am watching his face. He is not an adherent of mine, but he has been paid well, and he looks determined to do his part in this. I think I can trust him. I give him a little smile and he sees my lip tremble with fear for he says, in his rough northern accent, 'Dinnae fret, pet.' And I smile as if I understand him and watch him wind the rope around his waist. He braces himself and I wriggle to the very brink and look down.

Dear God, I cannot see the ground. Below me is darkness and the howl of air. I cling to the post of the window as if I cannot let it go. Agnes is white with fear, the porter's face steady. If I am going to go, I have to go now. I release the comfort of the stone arch of the window, I let myself stretch out on to the rope. I step out into air. I feel the rope go taut and terrifyingly thin, and I start to walk backwards, into the darkness, into nothingness, my feet pushing against the great stones of the walls, my skirt filling and flapping in the wind.

At first, I feel nothing but terror; but my confidence grows as I take step after step and feel the porter letting out the rope. I look up and see how far I have come down, though I don't dare to look below. I think I am going to make it. I can feel the joy at being free growing inside me until my very feet tremble against the wall. I feel sheer joy at the breath of the wind on my face, and even joy at the vast space beneath me as I go down; joy at being outside the castle when they think I am captive, cooped up in my stuffy rooms, joy at being in charge of my own life again, even though I am dangling at the end of a rope like a hooked trout, joy at being me – a woman in charge of her own life – once more.

The ground comes up underneath me in a dark hidden rush and I stagger to my feet, untie the rope and give it three hard tugs and they pull it back up. Beside me is my page, and Mary Seton, my life-long companion. My maid-in-waiting will come down next; my second lady-in-waiting, Agnes Livingstone, after her.

The sentries at the main gate are careless, I can see them against the pale road, but they cannot see us against the dark of the castle walls. In a moment there is to be a diversion – a barn is to be fired, and when they hurry to put out the fire, we will run down to the gate where horses will come galloping up the road, each rider leading a spare, the fastest for me, and we will be up and away, before they have even realised we are gone.

I stand quite still, not fidgeting. I am excited and I feel strong and filled with the desire to run. I feel as if I could sprint to Northallerton, even to the sea at Whitby. I can feel my power flowing through me, my strong young desire for life, speeding faster for fear and excitement. It beats in my heart and it tingles in my fingers. Dear God, I have to be free. I am a woman who has to be free. I would rather die than not be free. It is true: I would rather die than not be free.

I can hear the soft scuffle as Ruth, my maid, climbs out of the window and then the rustle of her skirts as the porter starts to lower her. I can see the dark outline of her quietly coming down the castle wall, then suddenly the rope jerks and she gives a little whimper of fear.

'Sshh! Sssh!' I hiss up at her, but she is sixty feet above me, she cannot hear. Mary's cold hand slips into mine. Ruth isn't moving, the porter is not letting her down, something has gone terribly wrong, then she falls like a bag of dusters, the rope snaking down from above her as he drops it, and we hear her terrified scream.

The thud when she hits the ground is an awful sound. She has broken her back, for sure. I run to her side at once, and she is moaning in pain, her hand clamped over her mouth, trying, even at this moment, not to betray me.

'Your Grace!' Mary Seton is tugging at my arm. 'Run! They are coming.'

I hesitate for a moment, Ruth's pale face is twisted with agony, now she has her fist thrust in her mouth, trying not to cry out. I look towards the main gate. The sentries, having heard her scream, are turned questingly towards the castle, a man runs forward, shouts to another, someone brings a torch from the sconce at the gateway. They are like hounds spreading out to scent the quarry.

I pull my hood up over my head to hide my face, and start to duck backwards into the shadows. Perhaps we can get around the castle and out of a back gate. Perhaps there is a sally-port or somewhere we can hide. Then there is a shout from inside the castle, they have raised the alarm in my chambers. At once the night is ablaze with the bobbing flames of torches and 'Hi! Hi! Hi!' they bellow like hunters, like beaters driving the game before them.

I turn to one side and then the other, my heart thudding, ready to run. But now they have seen us silhouetted by their torches against the dark walls of the castle, and there is a great bellow of 'View halloa! Here she is! Cut her off! Run round! Here she is! Bring her to bay!'

I can feel my courage drain from me as if I am bleeding to death, and I am icy. The taste of defeat is like cold iron in my mouth, like the bit for an unbroken filly. I could spit the bitter taste. I want to run and I want to throw myself face down on the ground and weep for my freedom. But this is not the way of a queen. I have to find the courage to push back my hood and stand straight and tall as the men come running up and thrust their torches in my face so they can see what they have caught. I have to stand still and proud, I have to be seen to be a queen, even dressed like a serving woman in a black travelling cape. I have to enact being a queen so they do not treat me as a serving woman. There is nothing more important now, at this moment of my humiliation, than preserving the power of majesty. I am a queen. No mortal man may touch me. I have to make the magic of majesty all alone, in the darkness.

'Je suis la reine,' I say, but my voice is too quiet. I can hear it tremble with my distress. I stand taller and lift up my chin, I speak louder. 'I am the Queen of Scotland.'

Thank God they don't grab me, nor put so much as one hand

on me. I think I would die of shame if a common man were to abuse me again. The thought of Bothwell's hand on my breast, his mouth on my neck, makes me burn even now.

'I warn you! You may not touch me!'

They form a circle around me with their bowed-down torches, as if I am a witch that can be held only by a ring of fire. Someone says that Lord Talbot, the Earl of Shrewsbury, is coming. He was at his dinner with Sir Francis Knollys and Lord Scrope, and they have told him that the Scots queen was running away like a thief in the night, but she is caught now.

And so that's how he first sees me, when he comes at a stumbling run, his tired face scowling with worry. He sees me standing alone, in a black cape with my hood pushed back from my face so that everyone can recognise me and know that they may not put a hand on me. A white-faced anointed queen of the blood. A queen in every way, showing the power of defiance, a queen in the authority of her stance, a queen in everything but the ownership of her thrones.

I am a queen at bay.

1568, Winter, Bolton Castle: George

They have her ringed with torches, like a witch held in by fire, ready for burning. As I run up, my breath is coming hard and my chest is tight, my heart is pounding from the sudden alarm, I sense the stillness around her as if they are all frozen by an enchantment. As if she were a witch indeed and the mere sight of her has turned them all to stone. Her hand holds back her hood from her face and I can see her dark hair, cropped jagged and short as an urchin's, the white oval of her face and her dark luminous eyes. She looks at me, unsmiling, and I cannot look away. I should bow, but I cannot bow. I should introduce myself, at this, our first meeting; but I am lost for words. Someone should be here to present me, I should have a herald to announce my titles. But I feel as if I am naked before her: it is just her, and just me, facing each other like enemies across the flames.

I stare at her and take in every aspect of her. I just stare and stare like a schoolboy. I want to speak to her, to introduce myself as her new host and her guardian. I want to seem an urbane man of the world to this cosmopolitan princess. But I gag on words, I can find neither French nor English. I should reproach her for this wanton attempt at escape; but I am struck dumb, as if I am powerless, as if I were horrified by her.

The blazing torches give her a crimson halo, as if she were a burning saint, a fiery saint of red and gold; but the sulphurous smell of the smoke is the very stink of hell. She looks like a being from unearthly regions, neither woman nor boy, a gorgon in her cold forbidding beauty, a dangerous angel. The sight of her, ringed with fire, strange and silent, fills me with wordless terror as if she were some kind of portent, a blazing comet, foretelling my death or disaster. I am most afraid, though I don't know why, and I stand before her and I can say nothing, like an unwilling disciple terrified into adoration; though I don't know why.

1568–9, Winter, Tutbury Castle: Bess

Mary, this most troublesome queen, delays as long as she can. Someone has told her that Tutbury Castle is no fit place for a queen of the blood and now Her Grace refuses to come here, and demands to be sent to her good cousin's court, where she knows well enough that they are celebrating the twelve days of Christmas with feasts and dancing and music, and at the heart of it all will be Queen Elizabeth, with a light heart and light feet, darting around and laughing because the Scots, the greatest threat to the peace of her country, are all falling out amongst themselves, and the greatest rival to her power, the other Queen of England, their queen, is a prisoner without plans for release. Or honoured guest, as I believe I am to call her, as I set about making Tutbury something more than a rapidly improvised dungeon.

I must say that Mary Queen of Scots is not the only one who would rather be at Hampton Court this Christmas season, and can find little joy in the prospect of a long cold winter at Tutbury. I hear from my friends who send me all the gossip that there is a new suitor for Elizabeth's hand, the Austrian archduke who would ally us with Spain and the Hapsburgs, and Elizabeth is beside herself with the sudden surging of lust for her last chance to be a wife and a mother. I know how the court will be: my friend Robert Dudley will be smiling but guarded – the last thing he wants at court is a rival to his constant courtship of the queen. Elizabeth will be in a fever of vanity, every day will bring new pretty things to her rooms, and her women will rejoice in the spoil of her cast-offs. Cecil will manage everything to the outcome of his choosing, whatever that may be. And I should be there, watching and gossiping with everyone else.

My son Henry, at service in Robert Dudley's household, writes me that Dudley will never allow a marriage which would displace him from Elizabeth's side, and that he will oppose Cecil as soon as that old fox shows his hand. But I am for the marriage – any marriage. Pray God that she will have him. She has left it as late as any woman dare, she is thirty-five, dangerously old to give birth to a first child; but she will have to grit her teeth and do it. We have to have a son from her, we have to have an heir to the throne of England. We have to see where we are going.

England is a business, an estate like any other. We have to be able to plan ahead. We have to know who will inherit and what he will get, we have to foresee what he will do with his inheritance. We have to see our next master and know what his plans will be. We have to know whether he will be Lutheran or Papist. Those of us living in rebuilt abbeys and dining off church silver are especially anxious to know this. Please God this time she settles on this suitor, marries him, and gives us a new steady Protestant master for the trade of England.

Elizabeth is a hard mistress to serve, I think, as I command the carpenters to mend the gaps in the floorboards. This would have been our first Christmas at court, for me and my lord the earl. Our first Christmas as newlyweds, the first Christmas I would have been a countess at court, where I should have sparkled like a snowflake and taken great joy in settling old scores from my newly raised position. But instead, the queen allowed my husband the earl only a couple of days with me before dispatching him to Bolton Castle to fetch the Scots Queen while I set to work on this hovel.

The more I repair this half-ruined wreck of a house the more ashamed of it I am, though God knows it is no fault of mine. No house of mine would ever fall into disrepair like this. All of my

properties – most of which came to me through the good management of my second husband, William Cavendish – were renovated
and rebuilt as soon as we acquired them. We never bought anything
without improving it. Cavendish prided himself on parcelling
together plots of land and swapping one farm for another till he
made a handsome estate, which I would then run at a profit. He
was a careful man, a great businessman, an older man, over forty
when he married me, his bride of nineteen.

He taught me how to keep an accounts book for our household,
and make it up every week, as faithfully as reading a sermon on
Sunday. When I was little more than a girl, I used to bring my household book to him like a child with her schoolwork, and he would
go through it with me on a Sunday evening, as if we were saying
our prayers together, like a pious father and daughter, our heads
side by side over the book, our voices murmuring the numbers.

After the first month or so, when he saw that I had such an apti-
tude and such a love for the figures themselves, as well as the wealth
they represented, he let me see the accounts book for the small
manor he had just bought, and said that I could keep it too, to see
if I would manage it well. I did so. Then, as he bought more properties, I took care of them. I learned the wages of field labourers as
well as housemaids, I learned how much we should pay for cartering
as well as for washing the windows. I started to run his farms as I
ran our house and I kept the books for them all the same.

He taught me that it means nothing to own land or money as
the old lords own their estates and waste them from one generation
to another. Wealth means nothing at all if you do not know, to the
last penny, what your fortune is. You might as well be poor if you
do not know what you have. He taught me to love the order of a
well-kept accounts book and how the bottom of the page at the end
of each week should show the balance between money coming in
and money going out; so that you know, and know to a penny,
whether you are ahead in the world or behind.

Cavendish told me that this is not how the great lords do it. Many of their stewards do not even keep the books like this, the new way, with receipts and expenses put side by side for comparison, and this is why, at the end of the day, we will do better than them. He told me that they treat their houses and their lands and their tenants and their fortunes as if they were all a great mass that cannot be calculated. So – since this is what they believe – they never try to calculate their wealth. They inherit and pass it on wholesale, without inventory. They lose and gain without keeping account. They have no idea whether a townhouse should rent out at a greater profit than a wheatfield. When they are taxed they guess at what they are worth, when they borrow money they cannot calculate their fortune. When they are paid a huge sum in war, or inherit treasure on marriage, they tumble it into their strongroom and never even list it. Whereas we, the new men and women who have risen so recently, we look at every field, at every trade, at every ship, and we see that it pays for itself.

Slowly, as Cavendish and I added property and houses to our fortune, each one chiselled from the dying body of the old church, I created new books, a new one for each new estate, each one showing a good balance of profit on rents, or sale of wool, or hay or corn or wheat or iron ore, or whatever goods each land could bring to us. Slowly I learned the prices of trees standing in a forest and the value of timber when they were felled. Slowly I learned to estimate the price of wool on a sheep's back or the profits to be made from a flock of geese at Christmas. My husband Cavendish hired good reliable men who had served the monks in the abbeys and the nuns in the nunneries and knew how lands should yield good rents and revenue, and I set myself to learn from them. Soon it was my task to read the accounts brought to me by the stewards of our growing estates, I was overseer as well as house manager. Soon it was I who knew to the last penny that our properties were well-run and our wealth was increasing.

None of this happened overnight, of course. We were married ten years, we had our children – eight of them, bless them all, and bless the good husband who gave them to me, and the fortune to endow them. He rose high in the favour of the court. He served first Thomas Cromwell and then directly the king. He served in the Court of Augmentations, that prime position, and travelled the country valuing the church properties and turning them over to the Crown, as one after another proved to be unfit for the work of the Lord and better closed down.

And if it happened that the houses that were the richest, and the most profitable, were the first to attract the attention of godly reform, then it was not for us to question the mysterious ways of Providence. If they had been good men they would have been good stewards of the wealth of the Lord and not squandered the church's fortune: encouraging the poor in idleness, and building churches and hospitals of excessive beauty. Better for God that poor stewards be replaced by those who knew the value of money and were ready to set it to work.

Of course my husband bought on his own account. God knows, everyone in England was buying land on his own account, and at the most desperate prices. It was like the herring fleet coming in, all at once. We were like fishwives on the harbour wall, revelling in a glut. We were all mad to get our hands on our share of the old church lands. It was a banquet of land-grabbing. No-one questioned William as he valued for the Crown and then bought and sold for himself. It was expected by everyone that he should supplement his fees by trading on his own account, and besides, he took no more than was customary.

How did he do it? He valued land low in his own favour, sometimes for the benefit of others. Sometimes he received gifts, and sometimes, secret bribes. Of course! Why not? He was doing the king's work and furthering the reform of the church. He was doing God's work in expelling corrupt priests. Why should he not be richly rewarded? We were replacing a rotten old church with one in the true image of His son. It was glorious work. Was my husband not on God's own work, to destroy the old bad ways of the Papist church? Was he not absolutely right, directed by God Himself, to take wealth away from the corrupt Papal church and put it into our hands, who would use it so much better? Is that not the very meaning of the sacred parable of the talents?

And all the while I was his apprentice, as well as his wife. I came to him a girl with a burning ambition to own my own property and to be secure in the world. Never again would I be a poor relation in the house of a richer cousin. He taught me how I could do it. God bless him.

Then I told him that the Chatsworth estate was for sale, near to my old home of Hardwick in Derbyshire, that I knew it well and it was good land, that the original owner was my cousin but he had sold it to spite his family, that the new owner, frightened by claims against the freehold, was desperate for a sale, that we could make a sharp profit if we were not too particular at taking advantage of a fool in trouble. William saw, as I did, the profit that could be made from it, and he bought it for me at a knockdown price, and swore it would be the greatest house in the North of England, and it would be our new home.

When the new queen, Mary Tudor, came to the throne – and who would have thought she could defeat the good Protestant claimant, my friend Jane Grey? – they accused my poor Cavendish of defrauding his office, of taking bribes, and of stealing land from the Holy Roman Catholic church – which now rose again from the dead like Jesus Himself. Shameful accusations and frightening times: our friends held in the Tower for treason, dearest little Jane Grey facing death for claiming the throne, the reformation of religion utterly reversed, the world turned upside down again, the cardinals returned and the Inquisition coming. But the one thing that I was sure of, the one thing that comforted me through all the worry, was the knowledge that he would know to a penny how much he had stolen. They might say that his books at the palace did not account for the huge fortune he had made, but I knew that he would know; somewhere there would be accounts that would show it all, good and clear, theft and profit. When he died, my poor husband Cavendish, still under suspicion of theft, corruption, and dishonest accounting, I knew that he would make his accounts in heaven, and St Peter (who I supposed would be restored also) would find them exact, to the last penny.

In his absence, it fell to me, his widow, all alone in the world, to defend my inheritance on earth. He had left me everything in my own name, God bless him, for he knew I would keep it safe. Despite every tradition, custom and practice which makes widows paupers and men the only heirs, he put every penny in my name, not even in trust, not to a kinsman. He did not favour a man, any man, over me, his wife. He gave it wholly to me. Think of that! He gave everything to me.

And I swore that I would not betray my dearest Cavendish. I swore, with my hand on his coffin, that I would keep the sacks of gold under the marriage bed, the lands that I had inherited from him, the church candles on my tables and the pictures on my walls, and that I would show my duty to him, as his good widow, by fighting to prove their title as my own. He left his fortune to me; I owed it to him to see that his wishes were honoured. I would make sure that I kept every-thing. I made it my sacred duty to keep everything.

And then, thank God the claims against me were cut short by another royal death. God Himself preserved my Protestant fortune. Queen Mary the Papist would have clawed back all the church lands if she could have done. She would have had monasteries rebuilt and abbeys re-dedicated, and certainly everything taken back from good officers who were only doing their duty – but God quickly took her to Himself and she died before she could dispossess us all, and the new ruler was our Elizabeth.

Our Elizabeth, the Protestant princess who knows the value of good property as well as the rest of us, who loves, as we do, peace, the land, and a reliable currency. She understands well enough the price of our loyalty to her. We will all be good Protestants and loyal subjects if she will leave us with our stolen Papist wealth, and make sure that no Papist ever gets the throne and threatens our fortunes again.

I had placed myself close to her from the earliest years, both by calculation and preference. I was raised in a Protestant household, in service to the great Lady Frances Grey, I was companion to Lady Jane Grey, and I served a God who recognises hard work. I was at Hatfield when my friend Robert Dudley himself brought the news that the old queen was dead and Elizabeth was the heir. I was at her coronation as a beautiful and wealthy widow (God bless my husband Cavendish for that) and my next husband, Sir William St Loe, was her chief butler of England. I caught his eye on the night of her coronation dinner and knew that he looked at me and saw a pretty woman of thirty, with great lands that marched temptingly beside his own. Dearest Cavendish had left me so prosperous that perhaps I could have made a deal for an even better husband. Sir John Thynne of Longleat was mentioned as one, and there were others. But to tell truth, William St Loe was a handsome man and I liked him for himself. Also, although Sir John has Longleat, which is a house any woman could covet, William St Loe's lands were in my home country of Derbyshire and that made my heart beat faster.

With him as my husband, and a good Protestant queen on the throne, I knew there would be no questioning the history of a pair of gold candlesticks that once stood on an altar and now my best table. No-one would worry about some three hundred handsome silver forks, a couple of dozen golden ewers, some exquisite Venetian glass, and chests of gold coins which suddenly appeared in the accounts of my household goods. Surely, to the Protestant God whom we all worship and adore, no-one would trouble a loyal widow who has done nothing but love things of beauty that have come her way? There would be no great anxiety about lands that had once belonged to the church and now belong to me. And nor should there be. 'Thou shalt not muzzle the ox that treads the corn,' my Cavendish used to say to me and some-times, only half in jest, 'the Lord helps them who help themselves.'

But neither of us – I swear to Our Lady – neither of us, at our most acquisitive, would have taken Tutbury Castle even as a gift. It will cost more to put right than it would to pull down and start again. I can just imagine my Cavendish looking it over and saying to me: 'Bess, beloved, a castle is a very fine thing, but where is the profit in it?' And the two of us would have ridden away to a better investment: something that we could buy cheap and make better.

When I remember Cavendish, I have to marvel at my new husband, the earl. His family have owned half of England for centuries, and leased this property of Tutbury forever; but they have let it get so run down that it is no good for them, nor for any fool that might have taken it off their hands. Of course, my husband the earl has no mind for detail, he has never had to trouble himself with the vulgar questions of profit and loss. After all, he is a nobleman, not a merchant like my Cavendish. He is not on the rise as my Cavendish had to be, as I was then proud to be. My husband the earl has such great lands, he has so many people as servants and tenants and dependants, that he has no idea what profit he makes and what are his costs. Cavendish would have been sick to his heart to do business like this; but it is the noble way. I don't do it myself; but I know enough to admire it.

Not that there is anything wrong with Tutbury village. The road that winds through it is broad enough and well-enough made. There is a moderately good ale house and an inn that once was clearly a church poorhouse in the old days before someone put in their bid and seized it – though looking at it and the fields around it, I doubt there was a great profit. There are good farms and fertile fields and a river that runs deep and fast. It is low-lying land, not the countryside I love: the steep hills and low valleys of the Derbyshire Peaks. It is all rather flat and dull and Tutbury Castle sits atop its own little mound like a cherry on a pat of syllabub. The road to the castle winds up this little hill like a path up a midden and at the top is a handsome gateway built of good stone and an imposing tower which makes you hope for better; but you are soon disappointed. Inside the curtain wall to the left is a small stone house which all but leans against the damp wall, with a great hall below and privy rooms above, a kitchen and bakehouse on the side. These, if you please, are to be the apartments of the Queen of Scots, who was born in the Castle of Linlithgow and raised in the Chateau of Fontainebleau and may well be a little surprised to find herself housed in a great hall which has next to no daylight in winter and is haunted by the lingering stink of the neighbouring midden.

On the opposite side of the courtyard are the lodgings for the keeper of the castle, where I and my lord are supposed to huddle in a part-stone, part-brick building with a great hall below and lodgings above and – thank God – at least a decent fireplace big enough for a tree at a time. And that is it. None of it in good repair, the stone outer wall on the brink of tumbling into the ditch, the slates loose on every roof, crows' nests in every chimney. If the queen takes herself up to the top of the tower at the side of her lodgings she can look out over a country as flat as a slab of cheese. There are some thick woods and good hunting to the south but the north is plain and dull. In short, if it were a handsome place I would have pressed my lord to rebuild it and make a good house for us. But he has taken little interest in it and I have none.

Well, I am taking an interest now! Up the hill we toil with my good horses slipping and scrabbling in the slush and the wagoners shouting, 'Go on! Go on!' to get them to strain against the traces and haul the carts up the hill. The castle doors are open and we stumble into the courtyard and find the entire household, mouths agape, in dirty clothes, the spit boys without shoes, the stable lads without caps, the whole crew of them looking more like they had just been freed from a Turk's galley than the staff of a nobleman's house, waiting to serve a queen.

I jump down from my horse before anyone has the wit to come and help me. 'Right, you scurvy knaves,' I say irritably. 'We have to get this place in order by the end of January. And we are going to start now.'

1569, January, on the journey from Bolton Castle to Tutbury Castle: George

She is a plague and a headache and a woman of whims and fancies, she is a nightmare and a trouble-maker and a great, great queen. I cannot deny that. In every inch of her, in every day, even at her most troublesome, even at her utterly mischievous, she is a great, great queen. I have never met a woman like her before. I have never even seen a queen such as her before. She is an extraordinary creature: moody, mercurial, a thing of air and passion, the first mortal that I have ever met that I can say is indeed truly divine. All kings and queens stand closer to God than ordinary men and women; but this is the first one in my experience who proves it. She is truly touched by God. She is like an angel.

I cannot like her. She is frivolous and whimsical and contrary. One day she begs me to let her gallop over the fields to escape the drudgery of plodding along the muddy road (I have to refuse); then the next she is too ill and too weary to move. She cannot face the cold, she cannot tolerate the icy wind. Her health is fragile, she has a persistent pain in her side. I believe she is frail as any weak woman. But if so, how did she find the courage and the strength to come down the walls of Bolton Castle on a rope? Or ride for three days from a bitter defeat at Langside, Scotland, to Whitehaven, England, three days of dining on nothing but oatmeal, with her hair cropped short as a boy's for disguise? Riding hard and sleeping rough, with rough soldiers as her companions? What powers can she draw on, that we mere mortals cannot have? It has to be God Himself who gives her this tremendous power and her female nature that undermines her strength with natural delicacy.

I must say, she does not inspire me either to love, or to deep loyalty. I would never trust her with my oath – as I have trusted my own queen. This one is quicksilver: she is all fire and light. A queen who wants to hold her lands needs to be more of the earth. A queen who hopes to survive the hatred that all men naturally have for women who contradict God's law and set themselves up as leaders has to be a queen like a rock, a thing of the earth. My own queen is rooted in her power. She is a Tudor with all their mortal appetites and earthly greed. My queen Elizabeth is a most solid being, as earthy as a man. But this is a queen who is all air and angels. She is a queen of fire and smoke.

On this journey (which feels as if it will last forever) she is greeted all along the road by people turning out to wave to her, to call their blessings down on her; and it makes a hard journey ten times longer. It amazes me that in midwinter, they would leave their firesides to wait all day at the crossroads of the cold lanes for her small train to come by. Surely they must have heard the scandals about her? Every drinker in every ale house in the kingdom has smacked his lips over the rumours which have somehow spilled out from the inquiries into her character; and yet I have to send orders ahead of us, wherever we go, that they are not to ring the church bells for this queen's entry into their village, they are not to bring their babies for her blessing, they are not to bring their sick for her to touch against the King's Evil, they are not to cut green branches and throw them down in the road before her as if she were riding in triumph: as blasphemous as if she were Jesus going into Jerusalem.

But nothing I say prevents them. These Northern superstitious feckless people are besotted with this woman, who is so far removed from them that they might as well love the moon. They honour her as if she were more than a queen, more than an ordinary woman whose reputation is already shadowed by gossip. They honour her as if they knew better than me – as if they knew a higher truth. As if they know her to be, indeed, the angel that she resembles.

It is a matter of faith, not wisdom. These are a stubborn people who don't agree with the changes that our queen – Elizabeth – has introduced into their churches. I know that they keep the old faith as best they can, and they want a priest in the pulpit and the Mass said in the old ways. Half of them still probably hear the Mass behind closed doors on a Sunday and none the wiser. They would rather have their faith and their God and their sense of Our Lady watching over all of them than obey the new ever-changing laws of the land. The whole of the North has always been determinedly unimpressed by the reform of religion, and now that this other queen is riding down their lanes, they are showing their true colours: their loyalty to her, their constancy to their faith. They are hers, heart and soul, and I do not know if Cecil had considered this when he ordered me to move her to Tutbury. I don't know if he understands how little sway Queen Elizabeth, and her faith, has in these northern counties. Perhaps he should have taken her further south? But perhaps everywhere she goes she will be passionately loved? There are Papists, God knows, everywhere in England, perhaps half the country believes that this is our true queen, and the other half will love her when they see her.

This queen, as equally famous for her piety as she is notorious for her lust, wears a rosary at her belt and a crucifix at her throat where I sometimes see her blush rise; she flushes pink like a girl. The Pope himself prays for her by name as she rides through mortal peril. At the worst moments, when we are half-mobbed by a crowd of people quietly whispering blessings on her, I am afraid they would prefer her on the throne and the church unreformed and unchanged than all the benefits that Queen Elizabeth has brought them.

Because these are not people like my Bess – middling people who saw their chance and snatched at profits in the times of change; these are the poor who used to go to the abbey for their hurts and their fears, who liked the priest coming to them for their deathbeds and christenings. They don't like the churches pulled down, the sanctuaries made unsafe, the nuns with their healing hospitals driven away. They don't know where to pray, now that the shrines have been destroyed, they don't know who will help them now they cannot light a candle for a saint. They don't understand that holy water is not holy any more, that the stoops are dry. They don't know where they can claim sanctuary now that the abbeys are closed, they don't know who will feed them in time of need now that the abbey kitchens are destroyed, and the kitchen fires gone cold. Barren women cannot go on pilgrimage to a sacred well, sick men cannot hobble to a shrine. They know themselves to be bereft. Undeniably, they have been robbed of much that made their lives happier. And they think that this exquisite other queen, dressed in black with a veil of white, as seductive as a novice nun, will bring back all the good things for them, and they crowd around her and tell her that good times will come again, that she must wait, as they will wait for her, until I have to shout at the guard to push them away.

Perhaps it is no more than the trivial matter of her beauty. People are so foolish over a beautiful woman, they attribute all sorts of magic to her for nothing more than the set of her dark eyes and the thickness of her dark eyelashes. They come to the roadside to stare for curiosity and then they stay and call blessings on her in the hopes of seeing her smile. She raises her hand in thanks; I have to say, she does have extraordinary grace. She smiles at each and every one of them as a private greeting. Everyone who sees her is besotted: hers for life. She has such a presence that nobody ever asks me which of the women in the travelling cloaks in the queen. She is slim like a thoroughbred horse; but tall, tall as a man. She carries herself like a queen and every eye is drawn to her. When she rides by, there is a whisper of admiration like a breeze, and this adoration has blown around her all her life. She carries her beauty like a crown and she laughs and gives a little shrug at the constant admiration she attracts, as if it is a cloak that someone has dropped: ermine, around her pale shoulders.

They throw evergreen leaves down on the road before her since they don't have flowers in this wintry season. At every stop someone presses pots of honey and preserves on us for her pleasure. The women bring out rosaries for her to touch as if she were a saint, and I have to look the other way, for the rosaries themselves are against the law now. Or at any rate, I think so. The laws change so often I can't always keep up. My own mother had a rosary of coral, and my father had a candle lit before a marble crucifix every day of his life; but Bess keeps these hidden in our treasure room now, jumbled up with the icons her previous husband stole from the abbeys. Bess treats them all as profitable goods. She does not think of them as sacred, Bess does not think of anything as sacred. This is the new way.

But when we pass a roadside shrine where a statue or a crucifix once stood, there is now a candle new-set and burning with a brave little light as if to say that the statue may be broken and the crucifix thrown down; but the light on the road and the flame in the heart still burn. She insists on pausing before these empty shrines to bow her head and I cannot hurry her because there is something about her in prayer . . . something about the turn of her head, as if she is listening as well as praying. I cannot make myself interrupt these brief communions though I know that when people see her, it just encourages Papacy and superstition. I can see that these little prayers strengthen her as if someone – who? Her mother? Her lost husband? Perhaps even her namesake, the very Mother of God? – is speaking to her in the silence.

How should I know? I am a man who simply follows my king. When my king is a Papist, I am a Papist. When he is a Protestant, I am a Protestant, if he became a Mussulman I suppose I would do so too. I don't think of these things. I have never thought of these things. I pride myself in being a man who does not think about such things. My family do not struggle for their faith, we remain faithful to the king and his God is our God. But when I see her face illuminated by the candle from a roadside icon and her smile so rapt . . . well, in truth, I don't know what I see. If I were foolish like the common people I would think I see the touch of God. I would think I see a woman who is as beautiful as an angel, because she is an angel, an angel on earth, as simple as that.

Then she laughs in my face some evenings, feckless as the girl she is. 'I am a great trial to you,' she says, speaking French. 'Don't deny it! I know it and I am sorry for it. I am a great trouble to you, Lord Shrewsbury.'

She cannot pronounce my name at all. She speaks like a Frenchwoman; you would never know that her father was a Scot. She can say 'the earl' well enough. She can manage 'Talbot'; but 'Shrewsbury' utterly defeats her. She puckers up her mouth into a kissing pout to attempt it. It comes out 'Chowsbewwy' and it is so funny that it almost makes me laugh. She is charming; but I remember that I am married to a woman of great worth and I serve a queen of solid merit.

'Not at all,' I say coldly, and I see her girl's smile falter.

1569, January, on the journey from Bolton Castle to Tutbury Castle: Mary

Bothwell,

They are moving me to a new castle, Tutbury, near Burton-on-Trent. I shall be the guest of the Earl of Shrewsbury but I am not free to leave. Come as soon as you can get free.

Marie

I keep my head down and I ride like a nun on her way to Mass but everywhere I go, I am taking in everything. I ride as Bothwell the tactician taught me to ride: constantly on the lookout for ambush, for opportunity, for danger, mapping the land in my mind as he would. This England is my kingdom, my inheritance, and these Northern lands will be my especial stronghold. I don't need secret letters from my ambassador, the good Bishop John Lesley of Ross, to tell me that half the country is mine already, longing to be rid of the tyranny of the usurper, my cousin Elizabeth; for everywhere I go, I see that the common people want to go back to the old ways, the good ways, they want the church restored and a queen that they can trust on the throne.

If it were the common people alone I would take their praise and their gifts and smile my thanks and know that they can do nothing; but it is so much more than them. At every stop on the road, when the wine comes in for dinner, a server drops a message into my lap or palms me a note. Shrewsbury is a hopeless guardian, bless him. He watches the door but forgets all about the windows. Half a dozen lords of England have sent me assurances that they will never let me be held captive, that they will never let me be sent back to Scotland as a prisoner, that they have vowed to set me free. They will make Elizabeth honour her word to restore me to my throne, or they will challenge her in my name. There is a conspiracy against Elizabeth smouldering, like a fire in heather, spreading, hidden at the very roots. In hesitating to restore me to my throne she has gone too far for her court to support. They all know that I am her only legitimate heir; and they all want me to be secure of my kingdom in Scotland and assured of my inheritance in England. This is nothing more than simple justice, this is my right; and the English nobility as well as the commoners want to defend my right. Any English queen of any sense would make this clear for me, clear for her lords, clear for her country. Any queen of any sense would name me as her heir and put me back on the throne of Scotland and order me to bide my time until her death. If she would treat me fairly like this, I would honour her.

For many of them Elizabeth is a pretender to the throne, a Protestant bastard who has played on her Tudor-red hair and my absence to put herself where I should be. All of Europe and half of England accept that I am the true heir, descended in a straight and legitimate line from King Henry VII, whereas she is an acknowledged bastard, and worse: a known traitor to the queen who went before her, the sacred Mary Tudor.

It is a tricky path I have to tread. No-one would blame me if I escaped from this compulsory hospitality. But everyone, even my own family, even Elizabeth's enemies, would condemn me if I raised a riot in her kingdom. She too would be within her rights to accuse me of troublemaking, even treason, if I made a rebellion against her; and I dare not risk that. These lords must be led on to free me, for I must be free. But they must do it of their own choice. I cannot encourage them to rebel against their crowned sovereign. In truth: nor would I. Who believes more strongly than I that an anointed queen should reign? A legitimate sovereign cannot be questioned.

'But is *she* a legitimate sovereign?' Mary Seton, my companion, asks me slyly, knowing that she is only repeating my old words back to me, as we rest one evening in a poor inn on the road to Tutbury.

'She is,' I say firmly. 'At any rate, when we are in her lands and with no power of our own, we will treat her as such.'

'The child of Anne Boleyn, conceived outside wedlock when the king was married to a Catholic princess,' she reminds me. 'Declared a bastard by her own father, and that law never revoked. Not even by her . . . as if she is afraid to ask the question . . . Heir to the throne only because the king named her on his deathbed, after his son, after his legitimate daughter, the desperate last words of a frightened man.'

I turn away from her to the fire and push the most recent note, a promise of help from Mary's faithful brother, Lord Seton, to the back of the logs and watch it burn. 'Whatever she is, whatever her mother was, even whatever her father – even if he was Mark Smeaton a singer – nonetheless she is an anointed queen now,' I say firmly. 'She found a bishop who could bring himself to crown her, and as such she is sacred.'

'All but one of her bishops refused. The whole church but one Judas denied her. Some of them went to prison rather than crown her. Some of them died for their faith, and died denying her. They called her a usurper, a usurper on your throne.'

'*Peut-être.* But she is on it now, and I will never, never be a party to overthrow an ordained queen. God has allowed her to be queen, for whatever reason. She has been anointed with sacred oil, she has the crown on her head and the orb and sceptre in her hand. She is untouchable. I shall not be the one to throw her down.'

'God has made her queen but not authorised her to be a tyrant,' Mary observes quietly.

'Exactly,' I say. 'So she may rule her kingdom but she may not tyrannise over me. I will be free.'

'Amen to that,' Mary says devoutly. I look at the scrap of paper falling to ash in the red heart of the embers.

'I will be free,' I repeat. 'Because, in the end, no-one has the power to imprison me. I was born, bred, crowned, anointed, and wed to a king. No-one in Christendom is more a queen than I. No-one in the world is more of a queen than I. Only God Himself is above me. Only He can command me, and His command is that I must be free and take my throne.'

1569, Winter, Tutbury Castle: Bess

We do it. I do it. By using the men I have brought from Chatsworth
– good men who have served me well, who know how I like things
done – by using the hard-working women that I recruit from Tutbury
and train into doing things my way, by scattering around the handsome things I have brought from Chatsworth, by patching and nailing
and cleaning and thatching as best we can. By hanging tapestries
over damp plaster, by lighting fires in blocked chimneys and burning
out vermin, by glazing some windows and blocking up others, by
curtaining doorways and hammering down loose floorboards; in
the end we make a place that, if not fit for a queen, cannot be – of
itself – grounds for complaint. The queen herself, Queen Elizabeth,
sends me goods from the Tower for the extra comfort of her cousin.
Second-rate I have to say, but anything which makes these dark
empty rooms look a little less like a dungeon and more like a house
must be regarded as a vast improvement.

It is a great job of work that I and my workmen have done. I don't
expect thanks for it, a nobleman like my husband the earl thinks that
houses build themselves, sweep their own floors, and furniture strolls
in and arranges itself. But I take a pleasure and a pride in my work.
Others in this kingdom build ships and plan ventures far away, raid
like pirates, discover new countries and bring back wealth. My work
is closer to home. I build, I establish, I run at a profit. But whether

it is Sir Francis Drake's work or mine, it is alike; it is all in the service of the Protestant God, and my clean floor and the gold in my purse both honour His Holy Name.

The waiting, the feverish preparation, the arrival of the queen's own goods all build to a sense of such anxiety that when the lad I have posted at the top of the tower yells out: 'I see them! They are coming!' the whole household takes to their heels as if they feared a Spanish invasion instead of one young queen. I can feel my stomach lurch as if I had the flux, and I take off the sacking I have tied at my waist to protect my gown, and I go down to the courtyard to greet this unwanted guest.

It is snowing again, just a flurry, but she has her hood pulled forward over her head to shield herself from the bitter weather, so all I see at first is a big horse and a woman huddled in cloaks in the saddle. My husband is riding at her side and I have an odd, actually, a very odd feeling, when I see him lean towards her as the horses halt. He inclines towards her, as if he would save her the least discomfort or trouble, he looks as if he would spare her the cold wind if he could; and I have a moment when I think that in our businesslike courtship, our well-advised marriage and our cheerful consummation in the big marital bed, that he has never yearned towards me as if he thinks I am fragile, as if he desires to protect me, as if I need protection.

Because I am not. Because I don't. And I have always been proud of this.

I shake my head to clear such folly and I go briskly forward. My Chatsworth master of horse is holding her horse's head, and my steward is holding her stirrup. 'Welcome to Tutbury, Your Grace,' I say.

It is odd to say 'Your Grace' to a young woman again. Elizabeth has been the only queen in England for ten years. She and I have grown old together, I am forty-one, she is thirty-five years old now; and here is a young woman, in her mid-twenties, with an equal claim to the title. She is a queen in her own right in Scotland, she is heir to the throne of England, some would even argue she is the true Queen of England. There are two queens in England now: the one who holds the throne by our good will, and the other one who probably deserves it; and I am in the odd position of being in the service of them both.

My husband the earl is down from his horse already, and he turns to her without even greeting me – as he should do, as is right and proper, though it feels a little odd to me, a newly wed wife. She reaches both arms out to him and he lifts her down from the saddle. Watching the thoughtless ease they have in this embrace reminds me that he has probably lifted her down every noon and night for the ten days of this journey. She must be light as a child, for he swings her down easily, as if in a dance. I know that I would be more of a weight for him. She turns to greet me while still in his arms, one hand casually on his shoulder, as she extends her other hand in the soft leather glove, and I curtsey low.

'Thank you,' she says. Her voice is musical, she speaks English like a Frenchwoman – that accent which is the very sound of perfidy and glamour to honest English ears. 'I thank you for your welcome, Lady Shrewsbury.'

'Please come in,' I say, hiding my smile at her pronunciation of Shrewsbury, which is really ridiculously affected. She sounds like an infant learning to talk with her 'Chowsbewwy'. I gesture towards her lodgings. An anxious glance from my husband asks me if the place is habitable and I give him a little nod. He can trust me. I am a partner in this venture, as I am a partner in this marriage. I shall not fail him, nor he me.

There is a fire in her great hall and she goes towards it and sits herself in the big wooden chair that is drawn close to the blaze for her comfort. Since the wind is in the east the chimney will not blow back a buffet of wood-smoke, please God, and she must admire the table before her, which is spread with a fine Turkey carpet and my best gold abbey candlesticks. The tapestries on the walls are of the very best, woven by nuns, thank God for them, and in her bedroom she will find the bed curtains are of cloth of gold and the coverlet of the richest red velvet which once graced the bed of a most senior churchman.

Everywhere is bright and warm, lit by the great square wax candles that are hers by right of being a queen, and in the sconces against the stone walls there are torches burning. She puts back the hood of her cape and I see her for the first time.

I gasp. I can't help myself. Truly, I gasp at the most beautiful woman I have ever seen in my life. She has a face like a painting, as an artist might draw. She has the face of an angel. She has thick black hair, cropped like a boy's, but sparkling at the front now with melting snow. She has dark arched eyebrows and eyelashes so long they sweep her cheeks. Her eyes are dark, dark and clear, and her skin is like porcelain, white and smooth without a single flaw. Her face is perfect like the carving of an angel, a serene heartless face; but what makes her remarkable, unlike anyone I have ever seen before, is her charm. She turns a smile on me and suddenly she is luminous, like a shaft of sunlight, like a sparkle on water, she is like some beautiful thing that makes your heart lift for the mere joy of it. Like the swoop of a swallow in flight which makes you feel glad to be alive. Her smile is like that, is my first foolish thought, her smile is like the swoop of a swallow in flight in midsummer dusk. My second thought is that Queen Elizabeth will hate her like poison.

'This is a most kind welcome,' she says in French, then sees my frown as I can't understand her and she says in hesitant English: 'You are kind, thank you.' She holds out her hands to the blaze and then she stands up. Quietly, her lady-in-waiting comes forward and unties the furs at her neck and slips off her wet cloak. She nods her thanks. 'Lady Shrewsbury, may I present my ladies-in-waiting? This is Lady Mary Seton, and here is Lady Agnes Livingstone,' she says, and the women and I curtsey to each other and I nod to one of my servants to take the wet cloak away.

'May I offer you some refreshment?' I say. I left Derbyshire when I was a girl and I have studied my speech ever since; but even so my voice seems too loud, uncouth in the room. Damn it, I have lived in the greatest houses of the land. I have served Queen Elizabeth and I count Robert Dudley and William Cecil as my personal friends, but I could bite my tongue when I hear the words come out of my mouth clotted with the Derbyshire burr. I flush with embarrassment. 'Would you like a glass of wine or a mulled ale against the cold?' I ask, taking extra care with my speech and sounding now stilted and false.

'Now, what do you like?' She turns to me as if she is truly interested in my tastes.

'I'd have a glass of mulled ale,' I say. 'I brought it from my brewhouse at Chatsworth.'

She smiles. Her teeth are small and sharp, like a kitten's. '*Parfait!* Let's have that then!' she says, as if this is to be a delightful treat. 'Your husband, his lordship, has told me you are a great manager of your houses. I am sure that you have everything that is the very best.'

I nod to the groom of the servery and know that he will bring everything. I smile at George, who has thrown off his own travelling cloak and is standing at the fireside. We both of us will stand until she invites us to sit, and seeing George, an earl in his own house, standing like a lad before his master, I realise for the first time that we have not allowed a guest into our house but rather that we have joined the court of a queen, and that from now on everything will have to be done as she wishes, and not how I prefer.

1569, Winter, Tutbury Castle: Mary

'And what d'you think of my lady Bess?' Mary Seton asks me, speaking French for greater discretion, a hint of malice in her voice. 'Is she as you expected? Worse?'

Now they are gone and we are alone in these pitiful little rooms I can lean back in my chair and let the pain and exhaustion seep through my body. The ache in my side is especially bad tonight. Mary kneels at my feet and unties the laces on my boots and gently pulls them off my cold feet.

'Oh, I heard so much about what a woman of sense she is and what a grand manager of business that I was expecting a Florentine banker at the very least,' I say, turning the criticism.

'She won't be like Lady Scrope at Bolton Castle,' Mary warns me. She puts my boots to dry at the fireside and sits back on her heels. 'I don't think she has any sympathy for you and your cause. Lady Scrope was a good friend.'

I shrug. 'Her ladyship thought I was the heroine of a fairytale,' I say irritably. She was one of those who sees me as a queen of ballads. A tragic queen with a beautiful childhood in France and then a lonely widowhood in Scotland. A balladeer would describe me married to the beautiful weakling Darnley, but longing for a strong man to rescue me. A troubadour would describe me as doomed from the moment of my birth, a beautiful princess born under a dark star. It doesn't matter. People always make up stories about princesses. It comes to us with the crown. We have to carry it as lightly as we can. If a girl is both beautiful and a princess, as I have been all my life, then she will have adherents who are worse than enemies. For most of my life I have been adored by fools and hated by people of good sense, and they all make up stories about me in which I am either a saint or a whore. But I am above these judgements, I am a queen. 'I expect no sympathy from her ladyship,' I say bitterly. 'She is my cousin the queen's most trusted servant, as is the earl. Otherwise we would not be housed by them. I am sure she is hopelessly prejudiced against me.'

'A staunch Protestant,' Mary warns me. 'Brought up in the Brandon family, companion to Lady Jane Grey, I am told. And her former husband made his fortune from the ruin of the monasteries. They say that every bench in her house is a pew.'

I say nothing; but the small incline of my head tells her to go on.

'That husband served Thomas Cromwell in the Court of Augmentations,' she continues softly. 'And made a fortune.'

'There would be a great profit in the destruction of the religious houses and the shrines,' I say thoughtfully. 'But I thought it was the king who took the profit.'

'They say that Bess's husband took his fee for the work, and then some more,' she whispers. 'He took bribes from the monks to spare their houses, or to undervalue them. That he took a fee for winking when treasure was smuggled out. But then he went back later and threw them out anyway, and took all the treasure they thought they had saved.'

'A hard man,' I observe.

'She was his sole heir,' she tells me. 'She had him change his will so that he disinherited his own brother. He did not even leave money to his children by her. When he died he left every penny of his ill-gained wealth to her, in her name alone, and set her up as a lady. It was from his springboard that she could vault to marry her next husband, and she did the same with him: took everything he owned, disinherited his own kin. At his death he left it all to her. That is how she got enough wealth to be a countess: by seducing men and taking them from their families.'

'So – a woman of few scruples,' I remark, thinking of a mother disinheriting her own children. 'A woman who is the greater power in the household, who has things done to her own advantage.'

'A forward woman,' Mary Seton says disapprovingly. 'Without respect for her husband and his family. A crowing hen. But a woman who knows the value of money.' She is thinking as I am – that a woman who does not scruple to make her fortune from the destruction of the church of God can surely be bribed to look the other way just once, for just one night.

'And him? The Earl of Shrewsbury?'

I smile. 'D'you know, I think he is all but untouchable? All he seems to care for is his own honour and his dignity; and of all men in England, he must be safe in that.'

1569, Winter, Tutbury Castle: Bess

'How much are we being paid for her?' I ask George as we take a glass of spiced wine seated either side of our bedroom fire. Behind us the maids are turning down our bed for the night.

He gives a little start and I realise that I am, once again, too blunt. 'I beg your pardon,' I say quickly. 'Only I need to know for my book of accounts. Is the court to pay us a fee?'

'Her Majesty the Queen graciously assured me that she will meet all the costs,' he says.

'All of them?' I ask. 'Are we to send her a note of our expenses, monthly?'

He shrugs his shoulders. 'Bess, dearest wife . . . this is an honour; to serve is a privilege that many seek but only we were chosen. The queen has assured me that she will provide. Of course we will benefit from our service to her. She has sent goods from her own household for her cousin, has she not? We have the queen's own furniture in our house?'

'Yes,' I say hesitantly, hearing the pride in his voice. 'But really, it is only some old things from the Tower. William Cecil wrote to me that Queen Mary's household is supposed to be thirty people?'

My husband nods.

'She has come here with at least sixty.'

'Oh,' he says. 'Has she?'

For some reason, known only to men and in this instance a nobleman, he has ridden at the head of a train of a hundred people for ten days and failed to notice.

'Well, they don't all expect to be housed here, I suppose?'

'Some of them have gone to the ale house in the village; but her household – companions, retainers, servants and the grooms – are under our roof, and they are all eating and drinking at our expense.'

'She has to be served as a queen,' he says. 'She is a queen to her fingertips, don't you think, Bess?'

It is undeniable. 'She is a beauty,' I say. 'I always thought they must be exaggerating when they spoke of her as the most beautiful queen in the world; but she is all of that, and more. She would be beautiful if she were a commoner, but the way she carries herself and her grace . . .' I hesitate. 'Do you like her very much?'

The gaze he turns to me is totally innocent, he is surprised by the question. 'Like her? I hadn't thought. Er, no, she is too . . .' He breaks off. 'She is troubling. She is challenging. Everywhere we go she has been a centre for treason and heresy. How can I like her? She has brought me nothing but difficulty.'

I hide my pleasure. 'And do you have any idea how long she will stay with us?'

'She will go home to Scotland this summer,' he says. 'The inquiry has cleared her of any wrongdoing; our queen is certain that there is nothing against her. Indeed, she seems to have suffered much injustice. And her lords put themselves utterly in the wrong by holding her prisoner, and making her abdicate her throne. We cannot tolerate this in a neighbour. To throw down a queen is to overthrow the natural order. We dare not let them do it. It is to go against the order of God. She has to be restored and the rebels punished.'

'Will we escort her home?' I ask. I am thinking of a royal progress to Edinburgh, of the castles and the court.

'Our queen will have to send an army to secure her safety. But the lords have agreed to her return. Her marriage to Bothwell will be annulled and they will bring her husband Lord Darnley's murderers to trial.'

'She will be queen in Scotland again?' I ask. 'Despite Cecil?' I try to keep the doubt from my voice but I shall be very surprised if that arch plotter has an enemy queen in his hands and quietly sends her home in comfort, with an army to help her.

'What has Cecil to do with it?' he asks me, deliberately obtuse. 'I don't think that Cecil can determine who is of royal blood, though he thinks to command everything else.'

'He cannot want her restored to power,' I say quietly. 'He has worked for years to put Scotland under English command. It has been the policy of his life.'

'He cannot prevent it,' he says. 'He has no authority. And it will be something then, my Bess, for us to be the dearest friends of the Queen of Scotland, don't you think?'

I wait for the two girls to finish turning down the bed, curtsey and leave the room. 'And of course, she is heir to England,' I say quietly. 'If Elizabeth returns her to Scotland she is acknowledging her as queen and her cousin, and so it is to acknowledge her as the heir. So she will be our queen here, one day, I suppose. If Elizabeth has no child.'

'God save the queen,' George says at once. 'Queen Elizabeth, I mean. She is not old, she is healthy she is not yet forty. She could yet marry and have a son.'

I shrug. 'The Queen of Scots is a fertile woman of twenty-six. She is likely to outlive her cousin.'

'Hush,' he says.

Even in the privacy of our bedroom, between two loyal English subjects it is treason to discuss the death of the queen. Actually, it is treason to even say the words 'death' and 'queen' in the same sentence. We have become a country where words have to be watched for betrayal. We have become a country where you can hang for grammar.

'Do you think the Scots queen is truly innocent of the murder of Lord Darnley?' I ask him. 'You saw the evidence, are you sure she was not guilty?'

He frowns. 'The inquiry closed without a decision,' he says. 'And these things are not a matter for women's gossip.'

I bite my tongue on an irritable reply. 'It is not for gossip that I ask you,' I say respectfully. 'It is for the safety and honour of your house.' I pause. He is listening now. 'If she is the woman that they say – a woman who would murder her husband in cold blood and then marry the man who did the deed for her own power and safety – then there is no reason to think that she would not turn against us, if it was in her interest to do so. I don't want my cellars packed with gunpowder one dark night.'

He looks aghast. 'She is a guest of the Queen of England, she will be restored to her own throne. How can you think that she would attack us?'

'Because if she is as bad as everyone says, then she is a woman who will stop at nothing to gain her way.'

'There is no doubt in my mind that Lord Darnley, her own husband, was in a plot against her. He had joined with the rebel lords and was guided by her half-brother, Lord Moray. I think together they planned to throw her down and imprison her and put him as king consort on the throne. Her half-brother would have ruled through Darnley. He was a weak creature, they all knew that.'

I nod. I knew Darnley from a boy, a boy horridly spoiled by his mother, in my opinion.

'The lords loyal to the queen made a plot to kill Darnley, Bothwell probably among them.'

'But did she know?' I demand. It is the key question: is she a husband-killer?

He sighs. 'I think not,' he says fairly. 'The letters that show her ordering the deed are certainly forgeries, the others are uncertain. But she was in and out of the house while they were putting the gunpowder in the cellar, surely she would not have taken the risk if she had known of the danger. She had planned to sleep there that night.'

'So why marry Bothwell?' I demand. 'If he was one of the plotters? Why reward him?'

'He kidnapped her,' my loyal husband says quietly, almost in a whisper. He is so ashamed by the shame of the queen. 'That seems certain. She was seen to be taken by him without her consent. And when they came back to Edinburgh he led her horse by the bridle so that everyone could see she was his captive and innocent of a conspiracy with him.'

'Then why marry him?' I persist. 'Why did she not arrest him as soon as she was safe in her castle and throw him on the scaffold?'

He turns away, he is a modest man. I can see his ears going red from a blush. He cannot meet my eyes. 'He did not just kidnap her,' he says, his voice very quiet. 'We think he raped her and she was with child by him. She must have known herself to be utterly ruined as a woman and a queen. The only thing she could do was to marry him and pretend that it was by consent. That way at least she kept her authority though she was ruined.'

I give a little gasp of horror. A queen's person is sacred, a man has to be invited to kiss her hand. A physician is not allowed to examine her, whatever her need. To abuse a queen is like spitting on a holy icon; no man of conscience would dare to do it. And for the queen to be held and forced would be like having the shell of her sanctity and power broken into pieces.

For the first time, I feel pity for this queen. I have thought of her so long as a monster of heresy and vanity that I have never thought of her, little more than a girl, trying to rule a kingdom of wolves, forced in the end to marry the worst of them. 'Dear God, you would never know to look at her. How does she bear it? It is a wonder that her spirit is not broken.'

'So you see, she will be no danger to us,' he says. 'She was a victim of their plotting, not one of the plotters. She is a young woman in much need of friends and a place of safety.'

There is a tap at the door to tell me that my private household is assembled in our outer chamber, ready for prayers. My chaplain is already among them. I have household prayers said every night and morning. George and I go through to join them, my head still spinning, and we kneel on the cushions that I have embroidered myself. Mine has a map of my beloved Derbyshire, George's shows his family crest, the talbot. All of my household, from pageboy to steward, kneel on their cushions and bow their heads as the chaplain recites the prayers for the evening. He prays in English so that everyone may speak to God together in language that we all understand. He prays for the kingdom of God and for the kingdom of England. He prays for the glory of heaven and the safety of the queen. He prays for my lord and for me and for all these souls in our care. He thanks God for the gifts we enjoy, as a result of Elizabeth on the throne and the Protestant bible in the churches. This is a godly Protestant household and twice a day we thank God who has rewarded us so richly for being His people, the best Protestants in Christendom. And so we remind everyone – me as well – of the great rewards that come from being a godly Protestant household in the direct charge of a Protestant God.

This is a lesson that the Catholic queen may learn from me. We Protestants have a God who rewards us directly, richly, and at once. It is by our wealth, our success and our power that we know that we are the chosen. Who can doubt God's goodness to me, when they see my house at Chatsworth, now three storeys high? Who, if they saw my accounts books with the figures marching so strongly down to the bottom line, could doubt that I am one of the chosen, one of the specially favoured Children of God?

1569, Spring, Tutbury Castle: George

I am surprised to have no instructions yet from the queen to prepare for the journey to Scotland, though I look for a command every day. I had expected by now to have been ordered to prepare a great escort to take the Queen of Scots home. In the absence of any message, the days go on, the weather improves, and we are starting to live together as a household, a royal household. It is a great honour and I have to remind myself not to become overproud of the good management of my wife and the lineage of my guest. She seems to be enjoying her visit with us, and I cannot help but be glad that we are her hosts in England. What benefits may flow from this friendship I would not stoop to calculate, I am not a paid companion. But of course, it goes without saying, that to be the trusted and most intimate friend of the next Queen of England has to be an advantage, even to a family already well established.

I receive a note, not from the queen herself, but from Cecil, who tells me that we must hold the other queen for only a few days longer while the Scots negotiate for her safe return to her kingdom and her throne. Then she will leave. The Scots have agreed that they will have her back as queen and she will return to her country with honour, this very month.

The relief for me is tremendous. Even though I know that our inquiry cleared her, and the queen herself is defending her cousin's name, I was anxious for her. She is so young, and without advisors. She has neither father nor husband to defend her, and she has such enemies ranged against her! And the more time I spend with her the more I hope for her safety, even for her success. She has a way – I have never known such a woman before – she has a way of making everyone feel that they would like to serve her. Half of my household is openly in love with her. If I were a bachelor, or a younger man, or a fool outright, I would say that she is enchanting.

The same messenger from London brings me a packet from Thomas Howard, Duke of Norfolk, and I open it slowly. He has such a passionate opposition to the growing power of Cecil, to the fearful England that Cecil is making, that I think this may be the invitation to be part of some plot against the Secretary of State. If he is inviting me to join against Cecil I will be hard put to refuse him. Indeed, in honour, I think I cannot refuse him. The man has to be curbed if not stopped outright and we lords are the ones who will have to do it. For a moment I consider going to find Bess so that we can read his letter together. But then curiosity is too much for me and I open it. A sealed package falls from the inside, into my hands with this note:

Shrewsbury, please convey this letter to the Queen of Scots. It is a proposal of marriage from me and has the blessing of all the other lords. I trust to your discretion. I have not yet told Her Grace the Queen of my intention; but Leicester, Arundel and Pembroke all think this a good solution to the current difficulty, returning her to her throne with an English connection and preventing a foreign husband. It was suggested by the Scots lords themselves, as a way to guarantee her safe return with a reliable Protestant Englishman at her side. I hope she will marry me. I believe it to be her safest route, indeed her only route,

Norfolk.

I think I had better take this to Bess.

1569, Spring, Tutbury Castle: Bess

Our days have fallen into a rhythm dictated by the queen, who rules this castle as her own palace, as I suppose she should. In the morning she prays and hears Mass in her own way with her secretary who, I imagine, is an ordained priest. I am supposed not to know, and so I do not ask, though I am required to give him four square meals a day and fish on Friday.

I have made sure that my household know that they are not to join nor even to listen to the heresies that take place behind the closed doors of her lodgings, and so I hope to confine the confusion and distress that always follows the rule of Rome to her rooms. But once she has done with heretical mutterings, and taken her breakfast in her rooms, she likes to ride out accompanied by my husband the earl. She has ten horses that are taking up ten loose boxes in our stables, and are feeding well on our oats. She rides with my lord and his guard in the morning while I go to the small parlour that I have set aside for my business and I meet with the stewards of all my houses and ventures who report to me either by letter or, when there is trouble, in person.

This is a system of my own devising, based on my first lessons from my dear Cavendish with the housekeeping books. Each manor, each house has its own book, each has to meet its own costs. By treating each parcel of land as a separate kingdom I make sure that they each make money. It may seem obvious – but this is unique. I know no other landlord who does it. Unlike me, my lord's stewards who work in the old ways bundle all their accounts together, use land as security against loans for cash, endow it, buy it, sell it, mortgage it and entail it away on heirs. At best they can always keep my lord's treasure room rich with cash; but at worst they never know what is earned and what is borrowed and what is owed. Badly handled, a whole fortune can slip through the fingers of a landlord and go out of the family altogether. They can never know if they are in profit or loss, there is a continual exchange of land into debt, into cash, and back to land again. The value of the land changes, even the value of the currency changes, and this is beyond their control – they can never know for sure what is happening. This is the way that the nobility run their business, grandly but vaguely; whereas I run mine like a poor woman's household and know to a penny what I am worth at the end of every week. Of course, they start with an enormous fortune. All they have to do is not to squander their wealth, whereas I started from nothing and nothing is easily counted. But a landlord like me – a newcomer – has to watch every penny and every acre, has to be alert to every change. It is a different view of the land, and my view is a novelty. Never before was there a landlord in England like me. Never in the world, for all I know, was there a woman in business like me.

Only a trader at his stall, only a cobbler at his last, would understand the pleasure I have at knowing the cost of things, and the profit from things, and the balancing of the books. Only a woman who has been poor would know the heartfelt sense of relief that comes from looking at the household accounts books and seeing a profit. There is nothing that warms my heart more than knowing that I am safe in my house, with cash in my treasure room, with land at my doorstep, and my children endowed or well married. Nothing in the world is better for me than the sense that I have money in my purse and that no-one can rob me.

This should be a strength of course, but it means that any loss strikes me hard. For within the first week of having the Scots queen as our guest, I have a letter from the Lord Treasurer's office telling me that we will be paid fifty-two pounds a week for hosting the Queen of Scots. Fifty-two pounds! A week!

After my initial dismay I cannot say that I am surprised. Anyone who has served at court knows that Queen Elizabeth is as mean with her money as when she was a bankrupt princess. She was brought up as a girl who was sometimes heir, sometimes pauper, and it has left her with a terrible habit of penny pinching. She is as bad as I am for keeping watch over a groat. She is worse than me, for it is her trade as queen to be generous; whereas it is my trade as a subject to turn a profit.

I look at the letter again. I calculate that she is offering us about a quarter of what we are paying out at present for the pleasure of housing and entertaining our guest. They, in London, have calculated that this queen will be served with thirty people and have a stable of six horses. In truth she has a household of double that number as well as a good hundred of trouble-makers and admirers and followers who have settled in Tutbury and nearby, but visit us constantly, especially at mealtimes. We are not housing a guest with a retinue, we are housing a full royal court. Clearly, the Treasury will have to pay us more. Clearly, this Scots queen's companions will have to be sent back to their homes. Clearly, I shall have to persuade my husband to make these unwanted announcements, since no-one else can tell the two queens that their arrangements are unworkable. My difficulty is that George will not like to do this, being a lord who has never had to deal with money, and never in his life drawn up an accounts sheet. I doubt I can even make him understand that we can barely afford this; not now, not for this month, certainly not till midsummer.

In the meantime I will have to send to my steward at Chatsworth and tell him to take some of the smaller pieces of silver down to

London and sell them for cash. I cannot wait for the rents at quarter day; I have to buy things in Tutbury and pay extra servants, and for this I need more coin than I earn. I could laugh at my own sense of loss when I write to him to sell half a dozen silver plates. I have never used them but they are mine, hoarded away in my own treasure room. To sell them for their value as scrap is as painful to me as a personal loss.

At midday the hunting party comes home. If they have killed on the hunt then the meat goes straight to the kitchens and is an essential addition to the provisioning of this great household. We dine altogether in my lodgings, on this sunny side of the courtyard, and in the afternoon the queen often sits with me in my presence chamber for the light is better for sewing, and the room brighter, and her women can sit with mine and we can all talk.

We talk as women always do: inconsequentially but with enthusiasm. She is the greatest needlewoman I have ever met, she is the only woman I have ever known whose ability and love of sewing matches mine. She has wonderful pattern books that arrive, travel-stained but intact, from Edinburgh Castle and she falls on them like a child and shows me the pictures and explains them to me. She has patterns for Latin inscriptions and classical designs that all mean different things. They are beautiful and all carry hidden meanings, some of them secret codes, and she says that I can copy them out.

Her designer joins our household after a few days – he had been left behind at Bolton Castle. He sets to work for us both, drawing up designs, and I watch him as he sketches freehand on canvas the wonderful symbolic flowers and heraldic beasts as she commands him. She can say to him, 'And put an eagle over it all,' and his chalk arcs like a child scribbling in the sand and suddenly, there is an eagle! With a leaf in its beak!

It is a great thing, I think, to have an artist such as this man in your train. She takes him quite for granted, as if it were natural that a man of great talent, a truly fine artist, should do nothing but sketch designs for her to sew. I think of King Henry using Hans Holbein to draw designs for his masques which would be broken up the day after the dance was done, and employing great musicians to write songs for his chamber or the way that the poets spend their talents writing plays for Queen Elizabeth. Truly, these are the luxuries of kings. Of all of the riches that have surrounded this spoilt young woman from childhood, this employment of such a gifted man gives me the best sense of what her life has been like until now. Everything she has had around her has been supreme, the best of the very best; everyone who works for her, or follows in her train, is the most talented or charming or skilled. Even the design for her embroidery must be a work of art before she will touch it.

Together we work on a new cloth of estate for her. It will hang over her chair to proclaim her royalty. Her *tapissier* has already started stitching the dark red background. In gold curly script the letters will say: *'En Ma Fin Est Ma Commencement'*.

'What does that mean?' I ask.

She is seated on the best chair, between the window and the fire. I am on a lower chair, though this is my own room in my own house, and our ladies-in-waiting are on stools and benches near the windows for the light.

'It was my mother's motto,' she says. 'It means: "in my end is my beginning". I have been thinking of it in these troubled days, and decided to take it as my own. When I lost my husband and was no longer Queen of France then I began my life as Queen of Scotland. When I fled from Scotland my new life in England begins. Soon, another phase of my life will start. I will return to my throne, perhaps I shall re-marry. In every end is a new beginning. I am like a queen of the sea, I am a queen of tides. I ebb, but I also flow. One day I shall cease to be queen on earth of any kingdom and be a queen in heaven over all kingdoms.'

I scowl at my women, whose heads bob up like rabbits at this unseemly and papistical assurance.

'Should you like to do the gold lettering?' she offers. 'The silk is such a pleasure to work with.'

Despite myself, my hands go out to touch it. The silk is very fine, I have never worked with anything so beautiful, and I have loved needlework with a passion for all my life. 'How is it so smooth?'

'It is spun gold,' she says. 'Real gold thread. That is why it glitters so. Do you want to sew with it?'

'If you wish,' I say, as if I don't much mind.

'Good!' she says, and she beams as if she is genuinely delighted that we will work together. 'You will start at that end and I shall start at this and bit by bit we shall come closer and closer together.'

I smile in reply, it is impossible not to warm to her.

'And at the end we shall meet in the middle, head to head and the greatest of friends,' she predicts.

I draw up my chair and the fine fabric loops from her lap to mine. 'Now,' she says quietly, when we are settled with our gold thread. 'Do tell me all about my cousin the queen. Have you been much to her court?'

Indeed, I have. I don't boast but I let her know that I have been a senior lady-in-waiting at the queen's court, at her side from the earliest of days of her reign, her friend when she was nothing more than a princess, friends with her friends, loyal informant to her advisor.

'Oh, so you must know all her secrets,' she says. 'Tell me all about her. And tell me about Robert Dudley. Was she really so desperately in love with him as they all said?'

I hesitate at that. But she leans forward to engage me. 'Is he still so very handsome?' she whispers. 'She offered him to me, you know, in marriage, when I first came to Scotland. But I knew she would never part with him. She is lucky to have such a loyal lover. It is a rare man who can love a queen. He has devoted his life to her, has he not?'

'Forever,' I say. 'From the moment she came to the throne and formed her court. He came to her then and he has never left. They have been hand in glove for so long that they finish each other's sentences, and they have a hundred secret jokes, and sometimes you see her just glance towards him, and he knows exactly what she is thinking.'

'Then why does she not marry him, since he is free?' she asks.

'She made him an earl so that she could propose him for me. If he was good enough for me he must be more than good enough to marry her.'

I shrug. 'The scandal . . .' I say very quietly. 'After his wife's death. The scandal has never gone away.'

'Can she not defy the scandal? A queen of courage can live down a scandal.'

'Not in England,' I say, thinking: and probably not in Scotland either. 'A queen's reputation is her crown, if she loses one she loses the other. And Cecil is against him,' I add.

She widens her eyes. 'Cecil commands her in even this?'

'He does not rule her,' I say carefully. 'But I have never known her go against his advice.'

'She trusts him with everything?'

I nod. 'He was her steward when she was a princess with few prospects. He managed her small fortune and he saw her through the years when she was under suspicion of treason by her half-sister Queen Mary. He kept her safe. He guided her away from the rebels whose plans would have destroyed her. He has always stood by her; she trusts him as a father.'

'You like him,' she guesses from the warmth in my voice.

'He has been a true friend to me also,' I say. 'I have known him since I was a young woman living with the Grey family.'

'Yet I hear he is ambitious for his own family? Building a great house, seeking alliances? Matching himself with the nobility?'

'Why not?' I ask. 'Does not God Himself command us to use our talents? Does not our own success show that God has blessed us?'

She smiles and shakes her head. 'My God sends trials to those He loves, not wealth; but I see that your God thinks like a merchant. But of Cecil – does the queen always do as he commands?'

'She does as he advises,' I temper. 'Most of the time. Sometimes she hesitates so long that she can drive him quite wild with impatience, but generally his advice is so good and their strategy is so long-planned that they must agree.'

'So he is the one who makes her policy? He decides?' she presses.

I shake my head. 'Who knows? They meet in private.'

'This is a matter of some importance to me,' she reminds me. 'For I think he is no friend of mine. And he was an inveterate enemy to my mother.'

'She usually follows his advice,' I repeat. 'But she insists that she is queen in her own country.'

'How can she?' she asks simply. 'I don't know how she dares to try to rule without a husband. A man must know best. He is in the very shape of God, he has a superior intelligence. All else aside, he will be better educated, he must be better taught than any woman. His spirits will be more courageous, his determination more constant. How can she dream of ruling without a husband at her side?'

I shrug. I cannot justify Elizabeth's independence. Anyway, everyone in the country would agree with her. It is God's will that women are subject to men, and Elizabeth herself never argues against it. She just does not apply it to herself. 'She calls herself a prince,' I say. 'As if being royal exceeds being a woman. She is divinely blessed, she is commanded by God to rule. Cecil acknowledges her primacy. Whether she likes it or not, she is set above everyone – even men – by God Himself. What else can she do?'

'She could rule under a man's instruction,' she says simply. 'She should have found a prince or a king or even a nobleman who could be trusted with the good of the country and married him, and made him King of England.'

'There was no-one . . .' I begin defensively.

She makes a little gesture with her hand. 'There were dozens,' she says. 'There still are. She has just got rid of the Hapsburg courtier, has she not? In France we heard all about them. We even sent our own candidates. Everyone believed that she would find a man that she could trust with the throne and then England would be safe. He would rule and make treaties with other brother kings. Treaties that could be based on the word of an honourable man, not on the changeable views of a woman; and then she could have conceived sons to come after him. What could be more natural and right? Why would any woman not do that?'

I hesitate, I cannot disagree. It is what we all thought would happen. It is what Queen Mary Tudor, Elizabeth's half-sister, tried to do, obedient to her wisest advisors. It is what this Scots queen did. It is what parliament went down on their knees to beg Elizabeth to do. It is what everyone hopes will happen even now, praying that it is not too late for Elizabeth to have a baby boy. How should a woman rule on her own? How did Elizabeth dare such a thing? And if she does, if she continues on this unnatural course: how shall she secure her succession? Very soon it will be too late. She will be too old to have a child. And however great the achievement of a reign, what is the use of a barren throne? What use is a legacy if there is no-one to inherit? What will become of us if she leaves the kingdom in turmoil? What becomes of us Protestant subjects under a Papist heir? What of the value of my property then?

'You are a much-married woman, are you not?' The queen peeps at me.

I laugh. 'The earl is my fourth husband, God bless and keep him,' I say. 'I have been so unlucky to be widowed three times. Three good men I have loved and lost, and mourned each one.'

'So you, of all people, cannot believe that a woman is best left alone, living alone, with only her fortune, and neither husband nor children nor home?'

In truth, I cannot. I do not. 'For me, there was no choice. I had

88

no fortune. I had to marry for the good of my family and for my own future. My first husband died when we were both children and left me with a small dowry. My second husband was good to me and taught me how to run a household and left me his estate. My third husband even more so. He left me his houses and all his lands entirely to me, in my own name, so that I could be a fit wife to the earl, Shrewsbury, who has given me my title, and greater wealth than I could ever have dreamed of when I was nothing more than the daughter of a poor widow at Hardwick.'

'And children?' she prompts me.

'I have borne eight,' I say proudly. 'And God has been good to me and I have six still living. My oldest daughter, Frances, has a babe in arms, they called her Bessie for me. I am a grandmother as well as a mother. And I expect to have more grandchildren.'

She nods. 'Then you must think as I do, that a woman who makes herself a barren spinster is flying in the face of God and her own nature, and cannot prosper.'

I do think this; but I am damned if I would say it to her. 'I think the Queen of England must do as she prefers,' I declare boldly. 'And not all husbands are good husbands.'

I am speaking at random, but I score such a hit at her that she falls silent and then to my horror I see that she has looked away from her sewing and there are tears in her eyes.

'I did not mean to offend you,' she says quietly. 'I know full well that not all husbands are good husbands. Of all the women in the world I would know that.'

'Your Grace, forgive me!' I cry out, horrified by her tears. 'I did not mean to distress you! I was not thinking of you! I did not mean to refer to you or your husbands. I know nothing of your circumstances.'

'You must be unique then, for every ale house in England and Scotland seems to know everything about my circumstances,' she snaps, brushing the back of her hand across her eyes. Her lashes are wet. 'You will have heard terrible things about me,' she says steadily. 'You will have heard that I was an adulteress against my husband with the Earl of Bothwell, that I urged him to murder my poor husband, Lord Darnley. But these are lies. I am utterly innocent, I beg you to believe me. You can watch me and observe me. Ask yourself if you think I am a woman that would dishonour herself for lust?' She turns her tear-stained beautiful face to me. 'Do I look like such a monster? Am I such a fool as to throw honour, reputation and my throne away for the pleasure of a moment? For a sin?'

'Your life has been much troubled,' I say weakly.

'I was married as a child to the Prince of France,' she tells me. 'It was the only way to keep me safe from the ambitions of King Henry of England, he would have kidnapped me, and enslaved my country. I was brought up as a French princess, you cannot imagine anything more beautiful than the French court – the houses and the gowns and the wealth that was all around me. It was like a fairy-tale. When my husband died it all ended for me in a moment, and then they came to me with the news that my mother had died too; and I knew then that I would have to go home to Scotland and claim my throne. No folly in that, I think. No-one can reproach me for that.'

I shake my head. My women are frozen with curiosity, all their needles suspended and their mouths open to hear this history.

'Scotland is not a country that can be ruled by a woman alone,' she says, her voice low but emphatic. 'Anyone who knows it knows that to be true. It is riven with faction and rivalry and petty alliances that last for the length of a murder and then end. It is barely a kingdom, it is a scatter of tribes. I was under threat of kidnap or abduction from the first moment that I landed. One of the worst of the noblemen thought to kidnap me and marry me to his son. He would have shamed me into marriage. I had to arrest him and execute him to prove my honour. Nothing less would satisfy the court. I had to watch his beheading to prove my innocence. They are like wild men, they respect only power. Scotland has to have a merciless king, in command of an army, to hold it together.'

'You cannot have thought that Darnley . . .'

She chokes on an irresistible giggle. 'No! Not now! I should have known at once. But he had a claim to the English throne, he swore that Elizabeth would support him if we ever needed help. Our children would be undeniable heirs of England from both his side and mine; they would unify England and Scotland. And once I was married I would be safe from attack. I could not see otherwise how to protect my own honour. He had supporters at my court when he first arrived, though later, they turned against him and hated him. My own half-brother urged the marriage on me. And yes – I was foolishly mistaken in him. He was handsome and young and everyone liked him. He was charming and pretty-mannered. He treated me with such courtesy that for a moment it was like being back in France. I thought he would make a good king. I judged, like a girl, on appearances. He was such a fine-looking young man, he was a prince in his bearing. There was no-one else I would have considered. He was practically the only man I met who washed!' She laughs and I laugh too. The women breathe an awed giggle.

'I knew him. He was a charming young man when he wanted to be.'

She shrugs her shoulders, a gesture completely French. 'Well, you know. You know how it is. You know from your own life. I fell in love with him, *un coup de foudre*, I was mad for him.'

Silently, I shake my head. I have been married four times and never yet been in love. For me, marriage has always been a carefully considered business contract, and I don't know what *coup de foudre* even means, and I don't like the sound of it.

'Well, *voilà*, I married Darnley, partly to spite your Queen Elizabeth, partly for policy, partly for love, in haste, and regretted it soon enough. He was a drunkard and a sodomite. A wreck of a boy. He took it into his stupid head that I had a lover and he lighted upon the only good advisor I had at my court, the only man I could count on. David Rizzio was my secretary and advisor, my Cecil if you like. A steady good man that I could trust. Darnley let his bullies into my private rooms and they killed him before my very eyes, in my chamber, poor David . . .' She breaks off. 'I could not stop them, God knows I tried. The men came for him and poor David ran to me. He hid behind me; but they dragged him out. They would have killed me too, one of them held a pistol against my belly, my unborn son quickening as I screamed. Andrew Kerr his name was – I don't forget it, I don't forgive him – he put the barrel of his pistol to my belly and my little son's foot pressed back. I thought he would shoot me and my unborn child inside me. I thought he would kill us both. I knew then that the Scots are beyond ruling, they are madmen.'

She holds her hands over her eyes as if to block out the sight of it even now. I nod in silence. I don't tell her that we knew of the plot in England. We could have protected her; but we chose not to do so. We could have warned her, but we did not. Cecil decided that we should not warn her, but leave her, isolated and in danger. We heard the news that her own court had turned on her, her own husband had become corrupt, and it amused us: thinking of her alone with those barbarians. We thought she would be forced to turn to England for help.

'The lords of my court killed my own secretary in front of me, as I stood there trying to shield him. Before me – a Princess of France.' She shakes her head. 'After that it could only get worse. They had learned their power. They held me captive, they said they would cut me in pieces and throw my body in bits from the terrace of Stirling Castle.'

My women are aghast. One of them gives a little sigh of horror and thinks about fainting. I scowl at her.

'But you escaped?'

At once she smiles a mischievous grin, like a clever boy. 'Such an adventure! I turned Darnley back to my side and I had them lower us out of the window. We rode for five hours through the night, though I was six months pregnant, and at the end of the road, in the darkness, Bothwell and his men were waiting for us and we were safe.'

'Bothwell?'

'He was the only man in Scotland I could trust,' she says quietly. 'I learned later he was the only man in Scotland who had never taken a bribe from a foreign power. He is a Scot and loyal to my mother and to me. He was always on my side. He raised an army for me and we returned to Edinburgh and banished the murderers.'

'And your husband?'

She shrugs. 'You must know the rest. I could not part from my husband while I was carrying his child. I gave birth to my son and Bothwell guarded him and me. My husband Darnley was murdered by his former friends. They planned to kill me too but it happened I was not in the house that night. It was nothing more than luck.'

'Terrible, terrible,' one of my women whispers. They will be converting to Papacy next out of sheer fellow feeling.

'Yes indeed,' I say sharply to her. 'Go and fetch a lute and play for us.' So that gets her out of earshot.

'I had lost my secretary and my husband, and my principal advisors were his murderers,' she said. 'I could get no help from my family in France, and the country was in uproar. Bothwell stood by me, and he had his army to keep us safe. Then he declared us married.'

'Were you not married?' I whisper.

'No,' she says shortly. 'Not by my church. Not in my faith. His wife still lives, and now another one, another wife, has thrown him into prison in Denmark for breach of promise. She claims they were married years ago. Who knows with Bothwell? Not I.'

'Did you love him?' I ask, thinking that this is a woman who was once a fool for love.

'We never speak of love,' she says flatly. 'Never. We are not some romantic couple writing poetry and exchanging tokens. We never speak of love. I have never said one word of love to him nor he to me.'

There is a silence, and I realise she has not exactly answered me. 'And then?' one of my entranced half-wit women whispers.

'Then my half-brother and his treacherous allies called up their army to attack Bothwell and me with him; and Bothwell and I rode out to battle together, side by side, as comrades. But they won – it is as simple as that. Our army drained away as we delayed. Bothwell would have fought at once and we might have won then; but I hoped to avoid bloodshed of kin against kin. I let them delay us with talks and false promises and my army slipped away. We made an agreement and Bothwell got away. They promised me safe conduct but they lied. They held me as a prisoner, and I miscarried my twins, two boys. They made me abdicate while I was ill and broken with grief. My own half-brother claimed my throne, the traitor. He sold my pearls, and they have my son . . . my boy . . .' Her voice, which has been low and steady, wavers now for the first time.

'You will see him again, for sure,' I say.

'He is mine,' she whispers. 'My own son. He should be raised as a Prince of Scotland and England. Not by these heretical fools, not by the murderers of his own father, men who believe neither in God nor king.'

'My husband says that you will be restored to your throne this very summer, any day now,' I say. I do not add that I think him mistaken.

She lifts her head. 'I shall need an army to get back my throne,' she says. 'It is not a question of simply riding back to Edinburgh. I shall need a husband to dominate the Scots lords and an army to hold them down. Tell Elizabeth when you write to her that she must honour her kinship to me. She must restore me. I shall be Queen of Scotland again.'

'Her Majesty doesn't take advice from me,' I say. 'But I know she is planning for your restoration.' Even if Cecil is not, I think.

'I have made mistakes,' she concedes. 'I have not judged very well for myself, after all. But perhaps still I may be forgiven. And at least I do have a son.'

'You will be forgiven,' I say earnestly. 'If you have done anything wrong, which I am sure . . . and anyway, as you say, you do have a son, and a woman with a son is a woman with a future.'

She blinks back the tears and nods. 'He will be King of England,' she breathes. 'King of England and Scotland.'

I am silent for a moment. It is treason to speak of the queen's death, it is treason to speculate about her heir. I shoot a hard look at my women who are all, wisely, eyes down on their sewing now and pretending they cannot hear.

Her mood shifts, as quickly as a child's. 'Ah, here I am becoming as morbid as a Highlander!' she cries out. 'Lady Seton, ask a page to come and sing for us and let's have some dancing. Lady Shrewsbury here will think herself in prison or in mourning!'

I laugh, as if we were not in truth in prison and bereft, and I send for wine and for fruit, and for the musicians. When my lord comes in before dinner he finds us in a whirl of dancing and the Scots queen in the middle, calling the changes and laughing aloud as we get all muddled up and end opposite the wrong partners.

'You must go right! Right!' she calls out. '*Gauche et puis à gauche!*' She whirls around to laugh at him. 'My lord, command your wife! She is making a mockery of me as a dancing tutor.'

'It is you!' he says, his face reflecting her joy. 'No! No! Truly it is you. You shall not accuse the countess, indeed you shall not. *Gauche* means left in English, Your Grace! Not right. You have been commanding them the wrong way round.'

She screams with laughter and falls into my arms and kisses me the French way, on both cheeks. 'Ah, pardon, Lady Bess! Your husband is right! I have been teaching you all wrong. I am a fool not to speak your difficult language. You have a most poor master of dance. But tomorrow I shall write to my family in Paris and they shall send me a dancing teacher and some violinists, and he will teach us all and we shall dance beautifully!'

1569, Spring, Tutbury Castle: George

I draw Bess to one side before dinner and tell her. 'Our guest is to leave us. She is to be returned to Scotland. I heard from Cecil himself today.'

'Never!' she exclaims.

I cannot restrain a knowledgeable nod. 'As I said,' I remind her. 'The queen said she should be restored to her throne and the queen honours her own word. We will take her back to Scotland. She will return in triumph. And we will be there with her.'

Bess's eyes gleam. 'This will be the making of us. Good God, she might give us a massive estate on the borders. She will have acres to give away, she will have miles.'

'The recognition we deserve,' I correct her. 'And perhaps, a token of her thanks. But the messenger brought me something else.' I show her the sealed package and Norfolk's letter. 'Should I give it to her, d'you think?'

'What does it say?'

'How should I know? It is sealed. He wrote to me that it is a proposal of marriage. I can hardly pry into a courtship.'

'With her you can. You have not lifted the seal and re-sealed it?'

Sometimes, my Bess shocks me. 'Wife!' I have to remember that she was not born into this position. She has not always been, as she is now, a countess and a Talbot.

She drops her gaze, penitent at once. 'But my lord, should we not know what the Duke of Norfolk is writing? If you give her the letter you are condoning whatever he says.'

'All the other lords condone it. They support it.'

'The other lords were not personally commanded by the queen to guard her,' she remarks. 'The other lords are not here, handing over secret letters.'

I feel deeply uneasy. Queen Mary is a guest under my roof, I can hardly spy on her.

'Does he say that Cecil knows?' she asks.

'He wouldn't confide in Cecil,' I say irritably. 'Everyone knows that Cecil hopes to rule everything. His ambition is unbearable. A Howard would hardly apply to William Cecil for permission to marry.'

'Yes, but I do wonder what Cecil thinks,' she muses.

I am so annoyed by this that I can hardly reply. 'My lady, it does not matter a fig to me what Cecil thinks. It does not matter to Howard what Cecil thinks. It should not matter to you what Cecil thinks. He is little more than the queen's steward, as he always has been. He should not presume to advise those of us who are lords of the realm, and have been for generations.'

'But, husband, the queen listens to Cecil more than any other. We should take his advice.'

'A Talbot would never apply to such as William Cecil for advice,' I say grandly.

'Of course, of course,' she soothes me, finally understanding that I am obdurate. 'So give me the package for now, and I will return it to you after dinner and you can give it to her then.'

I nod. 'I cannot spy on her, Bess,' I say. 'I am her host, I stand in a position of honour and trust with her. I cannot be her jailor. I am a Talbot. I cannot do anything that is at all dishonourable.'

'Of course not,' she says. 'Leave it all to me.'

We go in to dinner happily enough and for once the queen eats well, her sickness has passed and she has had a merry day, riding with me and sewing with Bess, and then dancing. After dinner Bess goes out for a little while on household business while the queen and I play cards. When Bess comes back into the presence chamber she calls me to one side, and says that she thinks I am right, and that the queen should have her letter.

I am deeply relieved at her agreeing with me. I cannot be under the cat's paw in this marriage. Bess will have to learn that I must be master in my house. She can act as if she is the manager of everything, just as she likes; I never stand in her way. But she must know that the steward is not the master. She can be my wife and the keeper of my house but she can never be head of the household. We are the Talbots, I am a Privy Councillor, I am the Earl of Shrewsbury. I cannot do anything dishonourable.

I am glad that Bess has come to see reason. I cannot withhold letters to a queen, and a guest in my household. Norfolk is a nobleman, he knows where his duty lies. I cannot sink to the level of a Cecil and spy on those who are my friends and family.

1569, Spring, Tutbury Castle: Mary

After dinner, which we eat together in the great hall of the Shrewsburys' lodgings, the earl asks if he may speak with me for a moment and we step across to a window as if to look out over the little courtyard where there is a well, a patch of garden growing herbs, and a few servants lazing about. Good God, this is a poor, ugly little place.

'I have very good news for you,' he says, looking down on me kindly. 'I have heard this afternoon from William Cecil. I am very pleased to say that I am commanded to make arrangements for you to return to Scotland. You are to be restored to your throne.'

For a moment his warm face blurs before my eyes. I cannot see clearly. Then I feel his gentle hand under my elbow. 'Are you faint?' he asks. 'Shall I call Bess?'

I blink. 'I am so relieved,' I say, heartfelt. 'I am just so relieved. It is as if . . . Good God, my lord. You have brought me the best news I have ever had. My heart . . . my heart . . .'

'Are you ill?'

'No,' I say wonderingly. 'I think I am well for the first time since you have known me. My heart has stopped aching. The pain is going. I can hope for happiness again.'

He is beaming down at me. 'I too am so glad,' he says. 'I too. It is as if a shadow has lifted from England, from me . . . I shall arrange for a guard and the horses to escort you to Scotland. We could leave within the month.'

I smile at him. 'Yes, do. As soon as we can. I cannot wait to see my son, I cannot wait to be back in my true place. The lords will accept me, and obey me? They have given their word?'

'They will receive you as queen,' he assures me. 'They acknowledge that the abdication was unlawful and forced. And there is something else which should give you greater safety there.'

I wait. I turn my head and smile at him, but I take care not to appear too eager. It is always good to go slowly with shy men; they are frightened by a quick-witted woman.

'I have received a letter addressed to you,' he says in his awkward way. 'It comes from the Duke of Norfolk, Thomas Howard. Perhaps you are expecting it?'

I incline my head, which could mean 'yes' or 'no', and I smile up at him again.

'I am at a loss as to know what I should do,' he continues, more to himself than to me. 'It is your letter. But it has come to me.'

I keep a steady smile. 'What is your question?' I ask pleasantly. 'If it is my letter?'

'It is the content,' he says heavily. 'I cannot in honour deliver a letter which contains unsuitable material. But I cannot, in honour, read a letter which is addressed to another. Especially to a lady. Especially to a queen.'

I swear I could take his troubled face in my hands and kiss away his frown. 'My lord,' I say gently. 'Let me resolve this.' I put out my hand. 'I shall open it and read it before you. You shall see the letter yourself. And if you think it was not fit for me to see, then you can take it back and I will forget it, and no harm will be done.' I am burning up to see this letter, but he would never know it from my steady hand and sweet patient smile.

'Very well,' he agrees. He hands it over and steps to one side, puts his hands behind his back like a sentry on duty and raises himself up on his toes in his embarrassment at having to be guardian and host, all at once.

I see at once that the seal has been lifted and re-sealed. It has been done with great care but I have been spied on for all my life; not much escapes me. I give no sign that I know my letter has been opened and read by someone else, as I break the seal and unfold the paper.

Dear God, it takes all my long years of training as a French princess to keep my face completely still and calm. In my hands I have a letter of such importance that the words dance before my eyes as I read it and read it again. It is very brief. It is, I think, my pass of safe conduct to guarantee I shall get me out of this bailey on a midden, and back to my throne, and my son, and my freedom. Ross said that this would come, and I have been hoping. It is a proposal of marriage. It is my chance for happiness once more.

'You know what he says?' I ask Lord Shrewsbury's discreetly turned back.

He swings round. 'He wrote to me in a covering letter that he was proposing marriage,' he says. 'But he has not asked permission of the queen.'

'I don't need her permission to marry,' I snap. 'I am not her subject, she has no command over me.'

'No, but he does. Anyone who is close kin to the throne has to have permission from the queen. And are you not married already?'

'As your inquiry proved, my marriage to Lord Bothwell was forced and invalid. It will be annulled.'

'Yes,' he says uncertainly. 'But I did not know that you had rejected the Lord Bothwell.'

'He forced the marriage,' I say coldly. 'It was made under duress. It is invalid. I am free to marry another.'

He blinks at this sudden clarity and I remember to smile. 'I think this a great solution to our difficulties,' I say cheerfully. 'Your queen would certainly be confident of me, with her own cousin as my husband. She could be certain of my affection to her and to her country. She could depend on the loyalty of such a husband. And Lord Howard can help me return to my throne in Scotland.'

'Yes,' he says again. 'But still.'

'He has money? He says he is a wealthy man? I will need a fortune to pay soldiers.' I could laugh to see Shrewsbury's delicacy around the sensitive subject of wealth.

'I can hardly say. I have never thought about it. Well – he is a man of substance,' he finally admits. 'I suppose it is fair to say that he is the greatest landowner in the kingdom after the queen. He owns all of Norfolk and he has great estates in the North too. And he can command an army, and he knows many of the Scots lords. They trust him, a Protestant, but there are those of his family who keep to your faith. He is, probably, the safest choice of any to help you to keep your throne.'

I smile. Of course I know that the duke owns all of Norfolk. He commands the loyalty of thousands of men. 'He writes that the Scots lords themselves suggested this marriage to him?'

'I believe they thought it would give you . . .'

A man to rule over me, I think bitterly.

'A partner and steady counsellor,' says Shrewsbury.

'The duke says that the other peers approve the idea?'

'So he wrote me.'

'Including Sir Robert Dudley? The queen's great friend?'

'Yes, so he says.'

'So if Robert Dudley gives his blessing to this proposal, then the queen's approval will certainly follow? Dudley would never involve himself with anything that might displease her.'

He nods. These Englishmen are so slow you can almost hear their brains turning like mill-wheels grinding. 'Yes. Yes. That is almost certainly so. You are right. That is true.'

'Then we may assume that although the duke has not yet told his cousin the queen of his plans, he will do so soon, with the confidence that she will be happy for him, and that all the lords of her realm and mine approve the marriage?'

Again he pauses to think. 'Yes. Almost certainly, yes.'

'Then perhaps we have here the solution to all our troubles,' I say. 'I shall write to the duke and accept his proposal, and ask him what he plans for me. Can you see that the letter is delivered for me?'

'Yes,' he says. 'There can be nothing wrong in you writing a reply to him, since all the lords and Dudley know . . .'

I nod.

'If William Cecil knew, I would be happier in my own mind,' he says almost to himself.

'Oh, do you have to ask his permission?' I ask as innocently as a child.

He flares up, as I knew he would. 'Not I! I am answerable to none but the queen herself. I am Lord High Steward of England. I am a member of the Privy Council. There is no man placed over me. William Cecil has no power over my doings.'

'Then what William Cecil knows and what he approves are alike indifferent to us both.' I give a little shrug. 'He is no more than a royal servant, is he not?' I see his eager nod. 'Just the queen's secretary of state?'

Emphatically, he nods again.

'Then how should his opinion affect me, a queen of the blood? Or you, a peer of the realm? And I shall leave my lord Norfolk when he thinks that the time is right to tell the servants of the queen, Cecil among them. His Grace the duke must be the judge of when he makes an announcement to the servants.'

I stroll back to my seat near the fire and take up my sewing. Bess glances up when I take my seat. My hands are trembling with excitement but I smile calmly, as if her husband was talking of the weather and the chance of hunting tomorrow.

Thank God, thank God who has answered my prayers. This is the way to get me quickly and safely back to my throne in Scotland, back to my son, and with a man at my side who can be trusted by his own ambition, and by the power of his family to guard my safety in Scotland and ensure my claims in England. The queen's own cousin! I shall be married to Elizabeth's cousin and our sons shall be Stuart children and Tudor kin.

He is a handsome man, his sister Lady Scrope promised me as much when I was with her at Bolton Castle. They said then that the Scots lords who were loyal to me would approach him and ask him if he would take up my cause. They said he would be smuggled into the garden of Bolton Castle so that he could see me. They said that if he saw me he would be certain to fall in love with me, and determine at once to be my husband and King of Scotland. Such nonsense, surely! I wore my best gown and walked in the garden every day, my eyes down and my smile thoughtful. At least I do know how to be enchanting, it was my earliest lesson.

He must be a fair man – he was judge at the inquiries and he will have heard every bad thing they said against me; but he has not let it stand in his way. He is a Protestant, of course, but that is only to the good when it comes to dealing with the Scots, and with pressing my claims to inherit England. Best of all, he is used to dealing with a woman who is queen. He was raised as kin to Elizabeth, who was a princess and heir to the throne. He will not bully me like Bothwell, nor envy me like Darnley. He will understand that I am queen and that I need him to be a true husband, an ally, a friend. Perhaps for the first time in my life I will find a man who can love me as a woman and obey me as a queen. Perhaps for the first time I will be married to a man I can trust.

Good God, I could dance for joy! Seated demurely on my chair I can feel my toes tapping in my silk slippers for sheer pleasure. I knew that I would rise from this defeat, I knew that in my end would be my beginning. What I did not expect was that it would come so easily and so sweetly and so soon.

1569, Spring, Tutbury Castle: Bess

To William Cecil,

Dear Sir,

Please find enclosed a copy of a letter sent by the Duke of Norfolk to our
guest. The letter was given to her by my husband with the seals unbroken
and neither he nor she knows that I have had sight of it and copied it for
you. I would appreciate your discretion in this matter, as you can be sure
of mine.

Your friend,

Bess

1569, Spring, Tutbury Castle: Mary

Husband Bothwell,

The queen's own cousin, Thomas Howard, Duke of Norfolk, has proposed marriage to me and promises to use his fortune and army to restore me to my throne in Scotland. Should we be blessed with children they will be doubly heirs to the throne of England from my line and his. Of course, in order to marry him I have to be free from my vows to you, so please apply for an annulment of our marriage at once, on the grounds that it was forced on me, and I will do so too. I continue to demand your freedom from the King of Denmark. He will have to free you when I am restored as queen and we will meet again in Scotland.

I am, as I always will be,

Your,

Marie

1569, April, Tutbury Castle: Bess

Word comes from Cecil that the queen is to prepare for her journey to Scotland. First we are all to be released from this imprisonment at Tutbury. He says that at last we can take the queen to a palace which is fit to house her, where we can live as a noble household and not as a straggle of gypsies in the shelter of a ruin.

Everything is to change. The queen is to enjoy greater freedom, she can see visitors, she can ride out. She is to live as a queen and not as a suspect. Cecil even writes me that the cost of her keep will be settled, the arrears paid to us and our claims will be met promptly in future. We are to give her the honour and the hospitality that a queen deserves, and she is to set off for Edinburgh later in this month and be restored by midsummer.

Well, I concede I was mistaken. I thought Cecil would never let her go; but I was wrong. I thought he would keep her in England and have one trumped-up inquiry after another until he had found or forged enough evidence to imprison her for life. I thought she would end her days in the Tower in a long miserable imprisonment. But I was wrong. He must have another plan in mind. He was always too deep to predict, those of us who are his friends and allies have to keep our wits sharp just to follow him. Who knows what he intends now?

Perhaps it is the marriage with Norfolk, perhaps he has come to think that a queen of royal blood, a queen anointed by God, cannot be kept forever under house arrest. Or perhaps my lord is right and Cecil is losing ground in the counsels of Queen Elizabeth. His star which has been rising for so long may be in eclipse. Perhaps all the other lords who have resented his influence will have their way, and my old friend Cecil will have to bow to their authority again, just as he did when we were both young and on the rise. My son Henry, serving at court in the Dudley household, writes to me that he thinks this is the case. He says that twice recently Cecil clashed with a nobleman and came off worse both times. The scandal of the Spanish gold has hurt him badly; even the queen acknowledges that he was mistaken and we will have to repay to the Spanish the bullion that Cecil stole.

'Even so, retain your friendship with him, as I will,' I write cautiously to Henry in reply. 'Cecil plays a long game and the queen loves those who protected her as princess.'

My whole household is to move to my husband's great palace at Wingfield with the Scots queen, and she is radiant at the chance of getting away from Tutbury. Nothing is too much trouble for her, she arranges her own household's packing into wagons, her own goods, clothes, and jewels are ready to go at dawn. Her pet birds are in their boxes, she swears her dog will sit on anyone's saddlebow. She will ride ahead with my husband, the earl; as usual, I am to follow with the household goods. I shall trail behind them like their servant. I shall ride in the mud churned up by the hooves of their horses.

It is a beautiful morning when they set off, and the spring birds are singing, larks rising into the warm air as they go over the moor. It starts to rain by the time I have the baggage train packed and ready to go and I pull my hood up over my head, mount my horse, and lead the way out of the yard and down the muddy hill.

We go painfully slow. My husband the earl and the queen can canter on the grassy verges, and he knows the bridleways and short cuts through woods and leads her splashing through streams. They will have a pleasant journey through the country with half a dozen companions. They will gallop on the high moors and then drop down to the shaded paths beside the rivers where the trees make an avenue of green. But I, fretting about the wagons and the household goods, have to go as slowly as the heaviest cart can lumber along the muddy lanes. When we lose a wheel, we all halt for several hours in the rain to make repairs, when a horse goes lame we have to stop and take it from the shafts, and hire another at the next village. It is hard labour and I might begrudge it if I had been born and raised as a lady. But I was not born a lady; I was born and raised as a working woman and I still take great joy in doing hard work, and doing it well. I don't pretend to be a lady of leisure. I have worked for my fortune and I take a pride in it. I am the first woman in my family to rise from poverty by my own efforts, actually I am the first woman in Derbyshire to own great property in my own right. I am the first woman that I know to use my own judgement to make and keep a fortune. This is why I love the England of Elizabeth: because a woman like me, born as low as me, can make and keep my own fortune.

The last few miles of the journey to Wingfield follow the course of the river. It is evening by the time we get there and at least the rain has lifted. I am wet through; but at any rate I can put back my hood and look around me at the most beautiful approach to my lord's favourite house. We ride along the floor of the valley, with moorhen scuttering away into the water of the river, and lapwing calling in the evening sky, then we round the corner and see, across the water meadows, the beautiful palace of Wingfield, rising above the trees, like a heavenly kingdom. The marshes lie beneath it with mist coiling off the waters, I can hear the croaking of frogs and the booming of the bittern. Above the water is a thick belt of trees, the ash coming green at last, the willows whispering in thick clumps. A throstle thrush sings, its warble sharp against the dusk, and there is a whisper of white like a ghost as a barn owl sweeps past us.

This is a Talbot property, belonging to my husband, inherited from his family, and I never see it without thinking how well I have married: that this palace should be one of the great houses that I may count as my home. It is a cathedral, it is an etching of stone against sky. The high arched windows are traceries of white stone, the turrets ethereal against the evening sky, the woods like billowing clouds of fresh green below it, and the rooks are cawing and settling for the night as we ride up the muddy track towards the house and they throw open the great gates.

I had sent half my household ahead of us to prepare, so that when the queen and my husband the earl rode in together, hours earlier, they arrived in afternoon sunshine and to a band of musicians. When they entered the great hall there were two huge fires either end of the room to warm them, and the servants and the tenantry lined up, bowing. By the time I arrive, at dusk, with the rest of the household furniture, the valuables, and the portraits, gold vessels and other treasures, they are already at dinner. I go in to find them seated in the great hall, just the two of them at the high table, she in my husband's place, her cloth of estate over her throne, thirty-two dishes before her, my husband seated on an inferior chair just below her, serving her from a great silver tureen, collected from an abbey, with the abbot's own golden ladle.

They do not even see me when I enter at the back of the hall, and I am about to join them, when something makes me hesitate. The dirt from the road is in my hair and on my face, my clothes are damp, I am muddy from my boots to my knees, and I smell of horse sweat. I hesitate, and when my husband the earl looks up from his dinner I wave and point towards the great stairs to our bedchamber, as if I am not hungry.

She looks so fresh and so young, so pampered in her black velvet and white linen, that I cannot bring myself to join them at the dining table. She has had time to wash and change her clothes; her dark hair is like a swallow's wing, sleek and tucked up under her white hood. Her face, pale and smooth, is as beautiful as a portrait as she looks down the hall and raises her white hand to me and smiles her seductive smile. For the first time in my life, for the first time ever, I feel untidy; worse, I feel . . . old. I have never felt this before. All through my life, through the courtships of four husbands, I have always been a young bride, younger than most of their household. I have always been the pretty young woman, skilled in household arts, clever at managing the people who work for me, neat in my dress, smart in my clothes, remarkable for wisdom beyond my years, a young woman with all her life before her.

But tonight, for the first time ever, I realise that I am not a young woman any more. Here, in my own house, in my own great hall, where I should be most at ease in my comfort and my pride, I see that I have become an older woman. No, actually not even that. I am not an older woman: I am an old woman, an old woman of forty-one years. I am past childbearing, I have risen as high as I am likely to go, my fortunes are at their peak, my looks can now only decline. I am without a future, a woman whose days are mostly done. And Mary Queen of Scots, one of the most beautiful women in the world, young enough to be my daughter, a princess by birth, a queen ordained, is sitting at dinner, dining alone with my husband, at my own table, and he is leaning towards her, close, closer, and his eyes are on her mouth and she is smiling at him.

1569, May, Wingfield Manor: George

I am waiting with the horses in the great courtyard of the manor when the doors of the hall open, and she comes out, dressed for riding in a gown of golden velvet. I am not a man who notices such things, but I suppose she has a new gown, or a new bonnet, or something of that nature. What I do see is that in the pale sunshine of a beautiful morning she is somehow gilded. The beautiful courtyard is like a jewel box around something rare and precious, and I find myself smiling at her, grinning, I fear, like a fool.

She steps lightly down the stone stairs in her little red leather riding boots, and comes to me confidently, holding out her hand in greeting. Always before, I have kissed her hand and lifted her into the saddle without thinking about it, as any courtier would do for his queen. But today I feel suddenly clumsy, my feet seem too big, I am afraid the horse will move away as I lift her, I even think I may hold her too tightly or awkwardly. She has such a tiny waist, she is no weight at all, but she is tall, the top of her head comes to my face. I can smell the light perfume of her hair under her golden velvet bonnet. For no reason I feel I am growing hot, blushing like a boy.

She looks at me attentively. 'Shrewsbury?' she asks. She says it: 'Chowsbewwy?' and I hear myself laugh from sheer delight at the fact that still she cannot pronounce my name.

At once her face lights up with reflected laughter. 'I still cannot say it?' she asks. 'This is still not right?'

'Shrewsbury,' I say. 'Shrewsbury.'

Her lips shape to make the name as if she were offering me a kiss. 'Showsbewy,' she says and then she laughs. 'I cannot say it. Shall I call you something else?'

'Call me Chowsbewwy,' I say. 'You are the only person ever to call me that.'

She stands before me and I cup my hands for her booted foot. She takes a grip of the horse's mane, and I lift her, easily, into the saddle. She rides unlike any woman I have ever known before: French-style, astride. When my Bess first saw it, and the manilla pantaloons she wears under her riding habit, my wife swore that there would be a riot if she went out like that. It is so indecent.

'The Queen of France herself, Catherine de Medici, rides like this, and every Princess of France. Are you telling me that she, and all of us, are wrong?' Queen Mary demanded, and Bess blushed scarlet to her ears and begged pardon and said that she was sorry but it was odd to English eyes, and would the queen not ride pillion, behind a groom, if she did not want to go sidesaddle?

'Because this way, I can ride as fast as a man,' Queen Mary said, and that was the end to it, despite Bess's murmur that it was no advantage to us if she could outride every one of her guards.

From that day she has been riding on her own saddle, astride like a boy, with her gown sweeping down on either side of the horse. She rides, as she warned Bess, as fast as a man, and some days it is all I can do to keep up with her.

I make sure that her little heeled leather boot is safe in the stirrup, and for a second I hold her foot in my hand. She has such a small high-arched foot, when I hold it I can feel an odd tenderness towards her. 'Safe?' I ask. She rides a powerful horse, I am always afraid it will be too much for her.

'Safe,' she replies. 'Come, my lord.'

I swing into the saddle myself and I nod to the guards. Even now, even with the plans for her return to Scotland in the making, her wedding planned to Norfolk, her triumph coming at any day now, I am ordered to surround her with guards. It is ridiculous that a queen of her importance, a guest in her cousin's country, should be so insulted by twenty men around her whenever she wants to ride out. She is a queen, for heaven's sake; she has given her word. Not to trust her is to insult her. I am ashamed to do it. Cecil's orders, of course. He does not understand what it means when a queen gives her word of honour. The man is a fool and he makes me a fool with him.

We clatter down the hill, under the swooping boughs of trees, and then we turn away to ride alongside the river through the woods. The ground rises up before us and we come out of the trees when I see a party of horsemen coming towards us. There are about twenty of them, all men, and I pull up my horse and look back at the way we have come and wonder if we can outride them back to home, or if they would dare to fire on us.

'Close up,' I call sharply to the guards. I feel for my sword but of course I am not wearing one, and I curse myself for being over-confident in these dangerous times.

She glances up at me, the colour in her cheeks, her smile steady. She has no fear, this woman. 'Who are these?' she asks, as if it is a matter of interest and not hazard. 'We can't win a fight, I don't think, but we could outride them.'

I squint to see the fluttering standards and then I laugh with relief. 'Oh, it is Percy, my lord Northumberland, my dearest friend, and his kin, my lord Westmorland, and their men. For a moment I thought that we were in trouble!'

'Oh, well met!' Percy bellows as he rides towards us. 'A lucky chance. We were coming to visit you at Wingfield.' He sweeps his hat from his head. 'Your Grace,' he says bowing to her. 'An honour. A great honour, an unexpected honour.'

I have been told nothing of this visit, and Cecil has not told me what to do if I have noble visitors. I hesitate, but these have been my friends and my kin for all my life; I can hardly make them strangers at my very door. The habit of hospitality is too strong in me to do anything but greet them with pleasure. My family have been Northern lords for generations, all of us always keep open house, and a good table for strangers as well as friends. To do anything else would be to behave like a penny-pinching merchant, like a man too mean to have a great house and a great entourage. Besides, I like Percy, I am delighted to see him.

'Of course,' I say. 'You are welcome as ever.' I turn to the queen and ask her permission to present them. She greets them coolly with a small reserved smile and I think that perhaps she was enjoying our ride and does not want our time together interrupted.

'If you will forgive us, we will ride on,' I say, trying to do whatever she wants. 'Bess will make you welcome at home. But we won't turn back just yet. Her Grace values her ride and we have just come out.'

'Please, don't change your plans for us. May we ride with you?' Westmorland asks her, bowing.

She nods. 'If you wish. And you may tell me all the news from London.'

He falls in beside her and I hear him chattering to entertain her, and occasionally the ripple of her laughter. Percy brings his horse alongside mine and we all trot briskly along.

'Great news. She is to be freed next week,' he says to me, a broad smile spread across his face. 'Thank God, eh, Shrewsbury? This has been an awful time.'

'So soon? The queen is going to free her so soon? I heard from Cecil only that it would be this summer.'

'Next week,' he confirms. 'Thank God. They will send her back to Scotland next week.'

I nearly cross myself, I am so thankful at this happy ending for her; but I cut short the gesture and instead put my hand out to him and we shake hands, beaming. 'I have been so concerned for her . . . Percy, you have no idea how she has suffered. I have felt like a brute to keep her so confined.'

'I don't think a faithful man in England has slept well since that first damned inquiry,' he says shortly. 'Why we did not greet her as a queen, and give her safe haven without asking questions, God knows. What Cecil thought he was doing, treating her like a criminal, only the devil knows.'

'Having us sit as judges on the private life of a queen,' I remind him. 'Making all of us attend such an inquiry. What did he want us to find? Three times her enemies brought the filthy letters in secret and asked the judges to read them in secret and make a verdict on evidence that no-one else could see. How could anyone do such a thing? To such a queen as her?'

'Well, thank God you did not, for your refusal defeated Cecil. The queen always wanted to be fair to her cousin, and now she finds a way out. Queen Mary is saved. And Cecil's persecution is thrown back to the Lutherans where it belongs.'

'It is the queen's own wish? I knew she would do the right thing!'

'She has opposed Cecil from the very beginning. She has always said that the Queen of Scots must have her throne again. Now she has convinced Cecil of it.'

'Praise be. What's to happen?'

He breaks off as she has pulled up her horse ahead of us, and turned to call to me. 'Chowsbewwy, can I gallop here?'

The track ahead of her is even, grassy and rises steadily uphill. My heart is always in my mouth when she thunders off like a cavalry charge but the going is firm and she should be safe. 'Not too fast,' I say, like a worried father. 'Don't go too fast,' and she waves her whip like a girl, wheels her horse, and takes off like a mad thing with her guards and Westmorland trailing behind her, hopelessly outpaced.

'Good God!' exclaims Percy. 'She can ride!'

'She's always like this,' I say, and we let our horses go after her for a long breathless gallop until she pulls up and we all come tumbling up to her side, and find her laughing with her hat blown askew and her thick dark hair falling down.

'That was so good!' she says. 'Chowsbewwy, did I frighten you again?'

'Why can you not ride at a normal pace?' I exclaim and she laughs again.

'Because I love to be free,' she says. 'I love to feel the horse stretch out and the thunder of his hooves and the wind in my face and knowing we can go on and on forever.'

She turns her horse for she cannot go on and on forever, or at least not today, and leads the way back to the castle.

'I have prayed every night to see her restored to her own again,' I say quietly to my friend Percy; and I hope he cannot hear the tenderness in my voice. 'She is not a woman who can be confined in one place. She does indeed need to be free. It is like mewing up a falcon to keep her in one small place. It is cruel. I have felt as if I were her jailor. I have felt that I was being cruel.'

He shoots a sideways look at me, as if considering something. 'But you would never have let her go,' he suggests in an undertone. 'You would never have turned a blind eye if someone had come to rescue her.'

'I serve Queen Elizabeth,' I say simply. 'As my family have served every King of England since William of Normandy. And I have given my word as an English nobleman. I am not free to turn a blind eye. I am honour bound. But it does not stop me caring for her. It does not stop me longing to see her as she should be – free as a bird in the sky.'

He nods and compresses his lips on his thought. 'You have heard she is to marry Howard, and they will be restored to Scotland together?'

'She did me the honour of telling me. And Howard wrote to me. When did the queen give the marriage her blessing?'

Percy shakes his head. 'She doesn't know yet. She flies into such a temper over the marriages of others that Howard is waiting to pick his time to tell her. Dudley says he will broach it when the time is right but he is delaying too long. There are rumours, of course, and Norfolk has had to deny it twice already. He'll probably tell her on the summer progress. Dudley has known from the beginning, he says he'll introduce the idea gently. It makes sense for everyone, it guarantees her safety when she is back on her throne.'

'What does Cecil think of it?'

He shoots me a quick hidden smile. 'Cecil knows nothing of it, and there are those who think that Cecil can steep in his ignorance until the matter is signed and sealed.'

'It would be a pity if he advised against it. He is no friend of Howard's,' I say cautiously.

'Of course he is no friend of Howard's, nor yours, nor mine. Name me one friend of Cecil's! Who likes or trusts him?' he demands bluntly. 'How should any of us befriend him? Who is he? Where does he come from? Who even knew him before she made him steward of everything? But this is the end for Cecil's power,' Percy says in a low voice to me. 'Howard hopes to drive him out, this is all part of the same plan. Howard hopes to rid us of Cecil, of his enmity to the Spanish, and to save the Scots queen from his spite, and to see him reduced at court, perhaps thrown out altogether.'

'Thrown out?'

'Thomas Cromwell rose greater and Thomas Cromwell was stripped of his badge of office by a Howard at a Privy Council meeting. Don't you think such a thing could happen again?'

I try to check my smile at this but it is no good. He can see my pleasure in the very thought of it.

'You like him no more than the rest of us!' Percy says triumphantly. 'We will have him thrown down, Shrewsbury. Are you with us?'

'I cannot do anything which would conflict with my honour,' I start.

'Of course not! Would I suggest such a thing? We are your brother peers. Howard and Arundel and Lumley and the two of us are all sworn to see England in the hands of her proper rulers again. The last thing we want to do is to demean ourselves. But Cecil pulls us down in every direction. The penny-pinching he wants at court, the enmity to the Scots queen, the persecution of anyone but the strictest of Puritans, and –' he drops his voice '– the endless recruitment of spies. A man cannot so much as order a meal in a London tavern without someone sending the bill of fare to Cecil. He'll have a spy in your own household, you know, Talbot. He knows everything about all of us. And he gathers the information and draws it together and waits to use it, when the time suits him.'

'He could have nothing on me,' I say staunchly.

Percy laughs. 'When you refused to name the Scots queen as a whore at his inquiry?' he jeers. 'You were his enemy from that moment. He will have a folder of papers with your name on it, gossip from the backstairs, rumours from bad tenants, envy from your debtors, and when the time suits him, or when he wants you humbled, he will take it to the queen and tell her she cannot trust you.'

'She would never . . .'

'He will have your personal servants in the Tower within the day, and a confession racked out of them that you are Queen Mary's secret admirer.'

'No servant of mine . . .'

'No man in the world can resist the rack for long, nor the press, nor the iron maiden. Do you know that they tear out men's finger-nails now? They hang them from their wrists. There is not a man in the kingdom that can bear such pain. Every suspect says whatever he tells them to say within three days.'

'He would not use such things on honest men . . .'

'Shrewsbury, he does. You don't know how it is in London now. There is no-one can stop him. He uses what means he likes, and he tells the queen that these are such dangerous times as need dangerous measures. And she is so fearful and so persuaded by him that she lets him do his dirty business as he wishes. He has a whole army of secret men who do his bidding and know everything. Men are arrested in the night and taken to the Tower or to hidden houses and not a justice of the peace gives a warrant. It is all on Cecil's say-so.

'Not even the Star Chamber orders these arrests, the queen does not sign for them, no-one but Cecil authorises them. It is all done in secret, on his word alone. The queen trusts him and his crew of informers and torturers, and the prisoners stumble out of the Tower sworn to report to Cecil for the rest of their lives. He is making a Spanish Inquisition on innocent Englishmen. Who can say that he won't start to burn us? He is destroying our freedoms. He is the enemy of the lords and of the people alike and we must stop him. He will destroy us, he will destroy the queen. A man truly loyal to the queen must be Cecil's enemy.'

The horses stretch their necks as we go up the hill to the manor, and I loosen my reins and say nothing.

'You know I am right,' he says.

I sigh.

'She will make him a baron.'

My horse flinches as I jerk on the reins. 'Never.'

'She will. She pours wealth on him and she will pour honours too. You can expect him to ask for your stepdaughter's hand in marriage for his son. Perhaps the queen will request that you marry your Elizabeth to the dwarf Robert Cecil with his hump back. Cecil will grow great. He will have a title to match your own. And we will none of us be safe to speak our minds in our own homes. He is making us a kingdom of spies and suspects commanded only by himself.'

I am so shocked that I cannot speak for a moment.

'He has to be stopped,' Percy says. 'He is another Wolsey, another Cromwell. Another upstart who has come from nothing by slavish drudgery. He is a bad advisor, he is a dangerous voice in her counsels. And like both of them he will be thrown down by us lords if we act together. He has to be thrown down before he becomes over-mighty. I swear to you he is a danger to the commonwealth of England. We cannot allow him to be made a lord of the realm.'

'A baron? You are certain she is going to make him a baron?'

'She pays him a fortune. We have to stop him, before he becomes too great.'

'I know it,' I say heavily. 'But a baron!'

The queen is already through the gateway. Someone else will have to help her down from the saddle, I cannot hurry to get there in time to be the one to lift her and hold her.

'You will dine with us?' I ask. I cannot see who is holding her horse and who is lifting her down. 'Bess will be glad to see you.'

'Cecil will know we have been here,' he says. 'Be warned.'

'Surely, I can invite a guest to dinner in my own house,' I exclaim. 'The queen will dine apart from us in her own rooms. There is no danger. What business is it of Cecil's?'

'Everything is his business in England today,' he replies. 'Within four days he will know we have been here; and everything we say at dinner will be reported to him, word for word. We are prisoners just as much as she is, when he spies on us at our very table. Do you know the name of his spy in your household? He will have one, at least: he will probably have two or three.'

I think of my own wife and her affection for Cecil. 'Bess trusts him,' I say. 'He would not put spies on her. He would never put a spy in Bess's household.'

'He spies on everyone,' he insists. 'You and Bess, as us. He must fall. We have to bring him down. Do you agree? Are you with us?'

'Yes,' I say slowly. 'Yes. Let us have the Queen of England advised by her peers again, and not by a man born to be a servant, supported by spies.'

Slowly Percy puts out his hand. 'You are with us,' he says. 'You swear?'

'I am with you,' I say. 'He cannot be a baron. I cannot see him ennobled, it is wrong. It goes against the very grain. I will bring Cecil down with you. Us lords together. We will be lords of the realm again, together.'

1569, May, Wingfield Manor: Bess

'They can't dine here,' I say flatly.

My husband the earl raises his eyebrows at me and I realise that my anxiety has put the twang of Derbyshire back in my voice. 'I am sorry, my lord,' I say rapidly. 'But they cannot dine here. You should not have ridden with them. You should have told them to ride on by. You should have brought her straight home as soon as you saw them.'

He looks at me as I might look at a recalcitrant maid. 'These are my friends,' he says carefully. 'Fellow lords of England. Of course my door is open to them. I would be shamed not to welcome them to my home. My door is always open to them.'

'I don't think that Cecil . . .'

His face darkens. 'Cecil does not have the command of my house, of any of my houses,' he says. 'I shall entertain my friends as I wish and my wife will show her good will to them.'

'It's not a matter of good will,' I say. 'It is not even a matter of my obedience. It is a matter of the safety of the Queen of Scots. What is to prevent them passing information to her? What is to prevent them plotting with her? What is to stop them riding off with her?'

'Because they are my guests,' he says carefully, as if I am too stupid to comprehend normal speech. 'It is a matter of honour. If you can't understand this, you understand nothing about me and my world. Bess, your third husband St Loe was a gentleman even if the others were not. You must know that no gentleman would plot against another while breaking his bread?'

'They are probably besotted with her,' I say, irritably. 'Like half the fools in England.'

'She is to marry the Duke of Norfolk,' he says, his voice very calm and measured in contrast to my sharp tone. 'She is to marry him and return to her kingdom as queen. Her future is assured, there is no need for her to plot and escape.'

'Perhaps,' I say doubtfully.

'She will be restored. Percy told me himself. It has been agreed with the Protestant lords of Scotland. She is to guarantee their safety and that of the Protestant faith. In turn she will take the Mass in private. The Protestant lords of Scotland are prepared to have her back if she is a married woman, as a queen with a king consort of their own faith, of undeniable nobility, fortune and strength. They believe that Thomas Howard will bring a safe alliance with England and will make a great king consort for Scotland. They planned this with Howard last year at York. And they think he will keep her in order and get another son on her.'

I am silent, thinking quickly. 'And has our queen agreed to all this?'

His hesitation tells me everything.

I knew it! I knew no-one had dared to tell her. She hates weddings and marriage and anything that takes her court away from her. To tell the truth, she hates not to be the centre of attention and a bride on her wedding day must rival even the Queen of England. And I swear on my life that she would never agree to see her own cousin Thomas Howard jumped up to be a rival king! Howard has always been a difficulty for her, she has never loved him as a cousin, she has always envied him his pride and his lands. She will never want to see him raised up so high. She will begrudge him his throne.

I would put money on it – she would rather see him dead at her feet than have a son of his inherit her throne. This is a jealous queen, she never wants anyone else to gain wealth or power. She has to be supreme. She would never let her cousin, her young cousin, over-reach her. From the moment I saw Howard's letter of proposal I knew she would forbid the marriage as soon as she learned of it.

'She will never allow it,' I say bluntly. 'And Cecil will never support anything which will make Howard King of Scotland. Cecil and Howard have been rivals for power for years. Neither Cecil nor Elizabeth will let Howard leap up to greatness. Neither of them could stomach him as a king.'

'Cecil will not rule this kingdom forever,' my husband says, surprising me with his authority. 'The days of the steward in the master's chair are done.'

'You cannot say that.'

'Yes, Bess, I can.'

'Cecil is far more than a steward. He has planned every part of Elizabeth's reign, he has guided everything she has done. He is more than a servant. He has made England as it is today. He is her guide. Half of what she thinks has been taught to her by him.'

'No, he is not. And soon he will not be even that.'

1569, May, Wingfield Manor: Mary

The lord of Westmorland gave me a bundle of messages from London as we rode out together, and whispered the news as we rode home.

Thank God, I am saved, my future has never looked brighter. My marriage to Thomas Howard will go ahead. My ambassador, Bishop Lesley, is drawing up the agreement. The Scots lords will accept Thomas Howard as king and will restore me to my throne with him at my side. And he is a fertile man of only thirty years, he has children already. There is no doubt in my mind but we will have children together, another son for the throne of Scotland, a daughter for me to love. Howard has agreed to forward money from the Spanish to me. They will smuggle gold coin to him, he will send it on to me. I am glad of this, it is a good test of him. If he will handle Spanish gold for me then it proves him, it proves his love for me. Also, once he receives letters in cipher from Spain and handles gold directed to me, then he has taken his first step in my cause and he will find that one step leads to another. He is no fool, he must have thought of this. He must be determined to be my husband, to be King of Scotland, and I am glad of this.

A woman once married to Bothwell could never tolerate a half-hearted man. Actually, a woman married to Bothwell will be spoiled for any other. God knows, I love his ambition. I love how he sees his opportunities. I love how he goes like an arrow to the heart of any matter. I have never known a man so brave, he would risk anything to achieve his goal. I remember the night that I ran from Edinburgh after Rizzio was killed. Darnley was with me, more like a frightened child than a husband, and we rode through the darkness, desperate to get away from the Scots lords who had killed Rizzio and would have killed me too. I remember the leap of terror I felt when we turned a corner and I saw four horsemen, blocking our way, huge across the dawn sky.

Darnley shouted, 'Save yourselves!' and spurred off into the moorland. But I rode forward and then I recognised Bothwell, waiting for me, a safe castle behind him, a spare horse beside him, coming down the road to greet me, ready to fight anyone to take me to safety.

He, who was never gentle, lifted me gently down from my horse and carried me in his arms into the castle, up the stairs to a bedroom and laid me on the bed. He, who was never tender, washed my face and my hands, and pulled off my riding boots. He, who was a known killer, untied the front of my gown and laid his ear to my rounded belly to listen for the heartbeat, smiled up at me, and said, 'It is all right. I swear it. He is unhurt, I can hear him. I can feel him move. He is alive, a strong little king for Scotland.' And I, who never loved him, put my hand down to touch the thick black curls of his hair and said: 'Thank God you are faithful.'

'Thank God you came to me,' he replied.

Better for me that I don't think of him. Better for me that I never think of him at all.

But it is good that Howard is ambitious too.

Westmorland has other news to whisper on our ride. Philip of Spain stands my friend, he has declared that I must not be held any longer as a prisoner. My ambassador is in touch with the Spanish ambassador, who has a network of conspirators in England poised to free me if I do not go to Scotland this month. I will regain my Scottish throne by agreement; but Elizabeth should be warned. I have powerful friends and half of England would rise for me if I summoned them, and Spain is building an armada of ships. Elizabeth dare not delay any longer. The Spanish will insist I am fairly treated. The Spanish intend that I shall be Queen of England and the heretic Elizabeth to be thrown down altogether.

I wait till I am alone in my room to open my letters. The one from Bishop Lesley is in code, I shall work on it in the morning, but there is a note from Thomas Howard written in French, and a ring. The sweet man, the tender-hearted man! He has sent me a ring for our betrothal and I slip it on my hand and admire it. It is a diamond, a wonderful stone, cut square, and it shines with a fiery whiteness. It is good enough for a queen, it is good enough for me. I put it to my lips and kiss it for his sake. This man is going to save me, this man is going to restore me to my kingdom, this man is going to love me and for the first time in my life I will have a lover who has the strength of a man and the breeding of an equal. Not a boy prince, not a half-devil like Bothwell. I shall be loved by a husband who has spent his life at courts, who is kin to the monarchs of England, and who wants me and loves me as a woman as well as a queen.

I am glad that this has all been done by me, without even the smallest help from Elizabeth. She is a fool. If she had taken my part when I first came to England she could have sponsored this marriage and restored me to my throne and I would have been forever in her debt. I would have loved her as her cousin twice over. We would have been friends for life. As it is, I will never forgive her. When I am on my throne again she will know that she has an enemy on her border, and that my friends are the Spanish who support me and the French who are my kin, the Northern lords who have been faithful and the Papists of England who wait for me to inherit and for the good days to come again. My new husband will come to see her as a reluctant friend and an unreliable cousin. I will prevail upon him to forget his loyalty to her and think only of himself and me.

We will make a powerful royal couple and together we will free Scotland and make alliances with the great Papist powers. Then she will be sorry that she treated me with suspicion, then she will be sorry not to have treated me like a sister. Then she will sit alone in one of her cold palaces and know that everyone has left her to go to the court of her heir.

I go to my desk and write a letter to my betrothed to thank him for his ring and promise my love and fidelity. This is going to be a courtship at a distance, my letters are going to have to keep his attention until he can meet me. I promise him my heart, my fortune. I assure him of my love for him. I want to make him fall passionately in love with me by letter. I must seduce him with every word. I shall write letters which amuse and intrigue him, I shall make him laugh and I shall prompt his desire. I shall feel truly safe only when I know he has fallen in love with me and wants me for desire as well as ambition.

I go to bed early. To tell the truth, even with my letters and my diamond ring, I am burning with secret resentment. I feel excluded from the dinner this evening, and I am deeply offended at Bess, the countess from nowhere, sitting at the high table with my friends Northumberland and Westmorland, and music playing and good wine being served, when I am here, practically alone with Mary and Agnes and only a dozen courtiers. I am accustomed to being the greatest lady in the room. In all my life I have always been the centre of every occasion, never before have I been the one left out. Before I go to bed at midnight I slip out of my rooms and go to the head of the stairs. In the great hall below the candles are still burning, and they are all still making merry. It is an outrage that I should not be invited, it is ridiculous that there should be dancing and I should not be there. I will not forget this exclusion, I will not forgive it. Bess may think it is her triumph but it is the upsetting of the proper order and she will regret it.

1569, June, Wingfield Manor: Bess

The Queen of Scots, waiting for the guard to escort her to Edinburgh, prevails upon me to walk with her in the gardens of Wingfield Manor. She knows nothing of gardening but she is a great lover of flowers and I tell her their names in English as we walk on the gravel paths between the low hedges. I understand why her servants and courtiers love her, she is more than charming, she is endearing. Sometimes she even reminds me of my daughter Frances whom I married to Sir Henry Pierrepoint and who now has my granddaughter, little Bessie. The queen asks me about my girl, and about my three boys and two other daughters.

'It is a great thing to have a large family,' she compliments me.

I nod. I do not even try to hide my pride. 'And every one shall marry well,' I promise. 'My oldest boy Henry is married already to my stepdaughter Grace Talbot, my husband's daughter, and my daughter Mary is married to my stepson Gilbert Talbot.'

The queen laughs. 'Oh, Bess! How clever of you to keep all the money in the family!'

'That was our plan,' I admit. 'But Gilbert is a wonderful boy, I could not hope for a better husband for my daughter, and he is such good friends with my boy Henry, they are at court together. Gilbert will be the Earl of Shrewsbury when my lord is gone and it is nice to think of my daughter inheriting my title, and being a countess and living here, like me.'

'I should so love to have a daughter,' she says. 'I should name her for my mother, I think. I lost my last babies. I had conceived twins, twin boys I should have had. But after the last battle, when they captured me, I lost my boys.'

I am aghast. 'Bothwell's children?'

'Bothwell's boys,' she says. 'Think what men they would have made! Twin boys, the sons of Bothwell and of Mary Stuart. England would never have slept soundly again!' She laughs, but there is a catch in her throat.

'Is that why you acknowledged the marriage to him?' I ask her very quietly. 'Because you knew you were with child?'

She nods. 'The only way to keep my reputation and my crown was to put a brave face on it, let Bothwell push the marriage through, and refuse ever to discuss it with anyone.'

'He should die for it,' I say fiercely. 'Men are hanged for rape in England.'

'Only if the woman dares to name her rapist,' she says drily. 'Only if she can prove that she did not consent. Only if a jury believes the word of a silly woman against a strong-minded man. Only if the jury does not believe in their hearts that all women are easily seduced and they say "no" but mean "yes". Even in England the word of a man takes precedence. Who cares what a woman says?'

I put out my hand to her. I cannot help myself. I was born a poor girl, I know how dangerous the world can be for an unprotected woman. 'Are you sure you can save your reputation and reclaim your throne? Can you go back to Scotland and be safe this time? Will they not hold this shame against you?'

'I am queen,' she says with determination. 'I shall annul the marriage to Bothwell and put it aside. I shall never mention it again and nor shall anyone else. It shall be as if it never happened. I shall return to Scotland as an anointed queen married to a great nobleman. That will be my safety and the rest of the scandals will be forgotten.'

'Can you decide what people say of you?'

'I am queen,' she says. 'One of the talents of a queen is to make the people think well of you. If I am really gifted and lucky, I will make the histories think well of me too.'

1569, August, Wingfield Manor: Mary

I love this summer. It is my first in England, my last too, for next summer I will be in Scotland again, my escort will come for me any day now. I laugh at the thought that then I shall be longing for this heat, and looking back on this as a golden season of leisure. It reminds me of my childhood in France, when I was a French princess and heir to the three thrones of France, England and Scotland, and in no doubt that I would inherit all three. We, the royal children of the privileged French court, used to spend the summer in the country and I was allowed to ride, and picnic, swim in the river, dance in the fields and hunt under the big yellow summertime moon. We used to row out on the river and fish from the boats. We used to have archery competitions in the cool of the morning and then celebrate with a winners' breakfast. My husband-to-be little Prince Francis was my playmate, my friend; and his father, the handsome King Henri II of France, was the hero of our days, the most handsome man, the most glamorous king, a charmer beyond all others. And I was his favourite. They called me *'mignonette'*. The beautiful princess, the most beautiful girl in France.

We were all indulged, we were all allowed anything that we wanted, but even among that richness and freedom the king singled me out as special. He taught me to amuse him, he taught me to delight him, he taught me – perhaps without knowing – that the most important skill a woman can learn is how to enchant a man, how to turn his head, how to swear him to her service, without him ever knowing he has fallen under her spell. He believed in the power of the women of the troubadours, and despite my tutors, and certainly despite his irritable wife, Catherine de Medici, he taught me that a woman can become the very pinnacle of a man's desire. A woman can command an army if she is their figurehead, their dream: always desirable, never attainable.

When he was dead, and his son was dead, and my mother was dead and I came to Scotland, quite alone, and quite desperate for advice as to how I would manage in this strange and savage country, it was his teaching that guided me. I thought I should be a queen that men could adore. I thought if I could be a queen that they could look up to, then we would find a way that I could rule them, and that they could gladly submit.

This time at Wingfield, knowing that my future is unfolding before me, knowing that I shall return to Scotland as acknowledged queen, is like being a girl again, with no equal for charm or beauty or wit, confident that my kingdom will be my own, that everything must always be perfect for me. And just as in France, I am admired and petted. Shrewsbury's servants cannot do enough for me. No luxury is too extravagant for me. And every day, when he comes to ride with me he brings me a little token: the little cup of mud of a swallow's nest, with two big pearls inside instead of eggs, a posy of roses with a gold chain twisted around the stems, a set of silver ribbons, a book of poems in French, scented leather gloves, a diamond brooch.

The terms of my return to Scotland are finally and fully agreed. William Cecil, once my sworn enemy, has changed his mind – who knows why? – and taken my side. He has negotiated for me with my half-brother, Lord Moray, and with Lord Maitland, and he has forged a good agreement that he is confident will hold. I am to return to Scotland as true and recognised queen. I am to be free to practise my faith. The country will be Protestant, as they say they prefer, but there will be no persecution of either Papists or Puritans. My son will be raised as a Protestant.

Some of this I will change when I am back on the throne. I have no intention of raising a heretic child destined for nowhere but hell. The lords who sign for my restoration now were my enemies only last year and I will have revenge. I have a list of the men who swore together to murder my husband and I will bring them to justice, they need not think that they will escape. Bothwell will be at my side and he will have his own scores to settle. But I can sign this agreement for now, with a clear conscience, since it restores me to the throne. The Holy Father will forgive me any agreement I make, as long as it serves the greater good of getting me back on my throne. Actually I would sign an agreement with the devil himself if it would get me back to the throne. Nothing is more important to me, to the Holy Church, and to the future of Scotland than I am returned.

Once restored to my throne, I can punish my enemies, and educate my people against heresy. Once there I can build my power with my friends and allies in England so that the moment Elizabeth dies, or when she faces invasion – and both are equally inevitable – then I am ready to move to take my second throne.

Cecil writes nothing about my betrothal with Howard; but he cannot be ignorant of it. I know that the Scots lords would never have agreed to have me back without a man at my side, they will have made my marriage a pre-condition of my return. They are so fearful of women in general and of me in particular that they would never rest until they had me wedded and bedded and sworn to wifely obedience. They would be in a terror that I would bring Bothwell down on them as king consort. They trust Thomas Howard in a way that they will never trust me, because he is a Protestant, because he is a man.

They will see. They will see their mistake. I will marry him and make him king consort; and they will still see that I shall have my own way, and I will still bring Bothwell down on them for my revenge.

I write faithfully to Thomas Howard, and my letters are as inviting and alluring as I can make them. Thank God, I know one thing: how to entice a man. I was not a French princess for nothing, I do know how to make a man fall in love, even at hundreds of miles' distance. I know how to lead him on, and draw back, come forward, make promises, renege, enchant, puzzle, confuse, seduce. I am irresistible in person, and I can be enchanting on paper. I write to him daily and I bring him onward and onward to ensure that he is mine.

As part of this campaign of seduction and compromise, I have embroidered for him a special cushion, which I think will amuse him. It shows a barren vine being pruned with a bill hook and he will know that I mean that the barren line of the Tudors can be cut down to let the new growth of our children take the throne. No-one can blame me for the design – though it is such a sharp slap at the spinster Elizabeth! – since it is a quotation from the Bible. What could be more tasteful and innocent? 'Virtue flourishes by wounding,' is the quotation that I have embroidered around the picture. Norfolk will see the slyest hint of treason in it, and if he has anything of a man about him he will be stirred by that provocative word 'wounding'.

Bess understood it at once, and was deliciously scandalised, and swore that I would not dare to stitch it when she first saw the design.

I dare! I dare anything! Let the barren vine be cut down. Let Elizabeth, the bastard, be struck down. I am a fertile woman of twenty-six, I have conceived nothing but boys. Howard is a man who has already fathered sons. Who can doubt that either my young son James, or our future sons – Stuart-Howards – will take Elizabeth's empty throne?

1569, August, Wingfield Manor: Bess

A note from Cecil delivered in secret reads:

> *No, you are not mistaken in my intentions, dear Bess. I am as like to install her on the throne of Scotland as I am to point a pistol at the heart of England and destroy everything I love.*
>
> *Every secret letter between her and our terrible enemies that comes to my hand convinces me of the greatness of the danger that she poses. How many letters elude me, only she will know, only the devil himself who directs her will know. Wait for news of her arrest for treason. C*

1569, August, Wingfield Manor: Mary

Oh God, I am a fool, a fool, and now a heartbroken fool. I am damned by my stars, and betrayed by my friends, and abandoned by my God.

This new blow is almost too much for me to bear. The pain in my side is so great that I can hardly bear to put my foot to the ground, it is like a knife in my side. It is Rizzio's wound bleeding from my own side. It is my stigmata.

Hamilton, my friend and spy in Scotland, writes to tell me that my half-brother Lord Moray has suddenly reneged on his agreement, and is now unwilling to let me return. He gives no reason, and indeed, there can be none except cowardice, greed and faithlessness. The English are on the brink of signing our treaty with him, I have already given my word. But he has suddenly broken off, at the very last minute. He has taken fright and says he will not have me back in the country. Saints forgive him! He is a false-hearted wicked man; but this last cruelty surprises me.

I should have known. I should have been prepared for his dishonesty. He is a usurper who drove me from my own throne, a bastard of my father's mistaken begetting, I should have guessed he would not want his true queen returned. What can I do but supplant and replace him and, as soon as I can, behead him?

The shock throws me into illness. I cannot stop myself from

crying. I take to my bed, and in rage and distress I write to Elizabeth that my brother is false through and through, a child conceived by mistake in lust, bad breeding coming out as dishonour. Then I remember that she too is a bastard of mistaken begetting, also occupying my throne, and I tear up the letter and painfully, slowly, forge something more dutiful and loving, and ask her, please, please, of her kindness, of her honour, to defend my rights as a fellow queen and as a sister, as the only woman in the world who can understand and sympathise with my plight.

Dear God, let her hear me and understand that she must, by the light of heaven, in all honour, help me. She cannot let me be thrown from my throne, thrown down to nothing. I am a queen three times over! I am her own cousin! Am I to end my life under house arrest, crippled with pain and weak with crying?

I take a sip of small ale from the cup by my bedside, I steady myself, it cannot be – it cannot be. God has chosen me and called me to be a queen; I cannot be defeated. I ring the bell for Mary Seton.

'Sit with me,' I say when she comes. 'This is a long night for me. My enemies are working against me and my friends do nothing. I have to write a letter.'

She takes a stool at the fireside and tucks a shawl around her shoulders. She will wait with me for as long as I need. Sitting up in my bed, despite the pain in my side, I write again, using our special cipher to urge my betrothed, the duke, to tell Elizabeth that we are agreed to marry, and that every lord in her own court supports this betrothal. I write sweetly and tenderly, urging him to be brave in this reversal of our fortunes. I never speak of my own well-being; I always speak of 'us'.

If he will only hold fast we will get our way. If he can only persuade Elizabeth to support this marriage and to support us, then the treaty will still go ahead. Moray may not like my return, especially with a strong husband at my side – but he cannot refuse if Elizabeth will only stand my friend. Dear God, if only she will do her duty and be a good cousin to Thomas Howard, a good cousin to me, then I shall be restored and our troubles will be over. Dear God, how can she not do the right thing by me? Any monarch in Europe would put out a hand to save me. Why not her?

Then I write to the only man in the world that I trust:

Bothwell,
Come, please please come.
Marie

1569, September, Wingfield Manor: George

Just when I have enough to worry about – the Scots queen ill with unhappiness and no explanation from court; my letters go unanswered because the court is on progress and my messenger has to chase around half of England to find them, and then is told that the queen is not doing business today, but he can wait – in the middle of all of this my steward comes to me with a grave face and says that a debt that I have carried for years has now fallen due and I have to pay two thousand pounds this Michaelmas Day.

'Well, pay it!' I say impatiently. He has caught me on my way to the stable and I am not in the mood for delay.

'That is why I have come to you, my lord,' he says uncomfortably. 'There are insufficient funds in the treasure house here at Wingfield.'

'Well, send to one of the other houses,' I say. 'They must have coin.'

He shakes his head.

'They don't?'

'It has been an expensive year,' he says tactfully. He says nothing more but this is the same old song that Bess sings to me – the expenditure on the queen and the fact that the court never reimburses us.

'Can we extend the debt for another year? Just to tide us over?' I ask. 'Till we get back to normal again?'

He hesitates. 'I have tried. The terms are worse, we would pay more interest, but it can be done. They want the woods on the south side of the river as security.'

'Do it then,' I decide quickly. I cannot be troubled with business, and this is a temporary difficulty until the queen repays us what she owes. 'Extend the debt for another year.'

1569, September, Wingfield Manor: Bess

I have a letter from my son Henry, an astute observer who reports to me. The court is on summer progress, which seems to have become a nightmare journey of suspicion and entrapment. The summers used to be the high point of the court year when we were all young and happy and in love and went hunting every day and dancing every night. Our fears have spoiled everything, we have destroyed our own joys ourselves, our enemies need do nothing. Nobody from beyond our borders needs to threaten us with destruction, we are already terrified of our own shadows.

Titchfield Palace,
Hampshire

Dear Mama,
The queen has long guessed of an agreement between Norfolk and the Queen of Scots and my lord Robert has just confessed it for them.
The duke, Thomas Howard, has denied his bride-to-be and the betrothal to the queen and now he has fled from the queen's presence, without permission, and everything is in uproar. They all say that he has gone to raise an army to rescue the other queen from your keeping. Lord Robert says that an army raised by him and led by her would be unbeatable as no-

one would take arms against Queen Mary. He says that against Norfolk and the Papists of England Elizabeth could not prevail and we will be ruined.

Lord Robert bids me tell you to ask the Scots queen to write to her cousin, confess the betrothal, and ask for forgiveness. He says she must also write to the duke and order him back to court to face the queen. Her Majesty is furious – as we all knew she would be – but without Norfolk here there is no-one to explain that this marriage is a good solution. He says that Norfolk must put a brave face on it to our queen, survive her anger, marry the Queen of Scots and take her home to Scotland.

Mama, I have to say that everyone here is very afraid that this is the start of a general uprising in support of your guest. I pray you to have a care of your own safety. It sounds very likely that an army could come against you to rescue her. Gilbert and I request that we may come home to you and my lord Papa, and help in the defence.

I remain your obedient son,

Henry

In a hastily scrawled postscript Robert Dudley has added:

The queen is beside herself at what looks like a conspiracy of her own two cousins against her. Bess, you must persuade your queen to reassure Elizabeth before she is seriously distressed, and we are all suspected of treason.

Yours aye,

Dudley

And burn this, Bess. There are spies everywhere. Sometimes I am even fearful for my own safety.

I go to the queen's apartments on the west side of the palace and find her listening to music. She has hired a new lute player who has recently joined the household at extra cost to me, and he is playing and singing for her. The music is very fine, which should give me some comfort for the bed, board and wages that I have to provide for him, his two servants and two horses.

When she sees my face she nods to him to be silent.

'Lady Shrewsbury?'

'Bad news from court,' I say baldly. And there! I see it! A flash across her face, instantly hidden, like a flare of torchlight in a shadowy room. She expects something, she is waiting for something to happen. There is a conspiracy indeed, and Dudley is wrong to think her innocent, and Cecil is right to alert the queen. Dear God, what if she is plotting war against us?

The smile she turns on me is utterly serene. 'Indeed, I am sorry to hear it. Tell me, is Her Grace the queen well?'

'She has learned of your proposed betrothal to the Duke of Norfolk,' I say flatly. 'And she is much distressed that he should have engaged himself without consulting her.'

She raises her eyebrows. 'Has he not done so yet?' she wonders.

'No,' I say shortly. 'And when she asked him for an explanation he left court without permission.'

She turns her eyes down as if in regret and then looks up again. 'He has gone away? Far?'

I nip my lip at irritation at this mummery, which may amuse her but does not entertain me. 'Robert Dudley suggests that you write to the queen and explain the betrothal, and that you write to the duke and persuade him to go back to court and reassure his queen and kinswoman.'

She lifts her face and smiles at me. 'I will certainly take Robert Dudley's advice,' she says sweetly. 'But my lord duke, Thomas Howard, will do as he thinks best. I cannot command him. I am his betrothed, his wife-to-be; not his master. I am not a wife who believes in ruling the roast. His own queen must command him; I cannot. Does she not order him back to court?'

'She orders him but he doesn't go,' I say curtly. 'And his staying away from court looks like a confession of guilt. Next thing they will be saying that he has run off to raise an army.'

Again, I see it, though her eyelashes flicker down to hide that flash of hope. So that is what she wants. She wants war, in the very heart of our court, in the very heart of our country. Dudley is mistaken; and Cecil is very right to fear her. Dear God, I am housing and humouring an enemy who will destroy us all. She hopes that Norfolk will lead an uprising. God damn her, she would see the peace of England broken to get her a husband and a throne.

'Don't even think it,' I warn her flatly. 'Thomas Howard would never raise an army against Elizabeth. Whatever he has written to you, whatever anyone has said to you, whatever you dream: don't think it. He would never lead out an army against the queen, and no-one would follow him against her.'

I speak very stoutly but I think she can hear the fear in my voice. The truth is that all of Norfolk and most of the east of England would turn out for the duke, whatever his cause, and all the north is solidly Papist and devoted to the Papist queen. But her beauty is impenetrable. I cannot tell what she is thinking as she smiles at me. 'God forbid,' she murmurs devoutly.

'And Your Grace,' I say more gently, as if she were my daughter, without good advice, and misunderstanding the powers that are ranged against her. 'You have to rely on the queen to restore you. If all goes well, the queen will overcome the Scots' objections and return you to your throne. The agreement is all but made. You can marry the duke then. Why not reassure the queen of your loyalty now, and wait for her to send you back to Scotland? You are close to your restoration. Don't put yourself at risk.'

She widens her eyes. 'Do you really think she will send me back in safety?'

'I am sure of it,' I lie. Then I check myself. There is something about her dark trusting gaze that makes me hesitate to lie. 'I think so, and in any case, the nobles will demand it.'

'Even if I marry her cousin and make him king?'

'I believe so.'

'I can trust her?'

Of course not. 'You can.'

'Despite my half-brother's treachery?'

I did not know she was getting news from Scotland; but I am not surprised.

'If the queen supports you, he cannot stand against you,' I say. 'So you should write to her and promise your loyal friendship.'

'And does Secretary Cecil now want me returned to my throne in Scotland?' she pursues sweetly.

I feel awkward, and I know I look awkward. 'The queen will decide,' I say weakly.

'I hope so,' she says. 'For my sake, for all our sakes. Because, Bess, don't you think, like your friend Robert Dudley, that she should have provided me with an army and sent me back to Scotland as soon as I arrived? Don't you think she should have honoured her promise to me at once? Don't you think she should have defended a fellow monarch at once? A fellow queen?'

In my discomfort, I say nothing. I am torn. She has a right to be returned to Scotland, God knows she has a right to be named as heir to the throne of England. She is a young woman with few friends and I cannot help but feel for her. But she is planning something, I know it. She has Norfolk dancing to her tune and what dance has she taught him? She has Robert Dudley in her set and most of the queen's court are tapping their feet to her song. How many dancers are learning her steps? What is the next movement she has choreographed for us all? Good God, she has me so frightened for myself and for my goods. God alone knows what men see in her.

1569, September, Wingfield Manor: George

I am one of the greatest men in England, who dares accuse me? What dare they say of me? That I have failed in my duty? Plotted against my own queen? Against my own country? Shall I be bundled into the Tower and accused? Shall I sit in a new inquiry, not as judge but as prisoner? Do they think to bring me to trial? Shall they forge statements against me? Will they show me the rack and tell me it would be better for me if I sign a document now?

There is wickedness abroad, God Himself knows it: omens and portents of bad days. A woman gave birth to a calf near Chatsworth, the moon was blood-red at Derby. The world will be turned upside down and men of family, men of honour, will be shamed. I cannot bear it. I run to find Bess with the letter, this damned insulting letter from Cecil, clenched in my hand. I am raging.

'I am betrayed! I am suspected! How could he think this of me? Even if he thought it, how dare he say it? How dare he write it to me?' I burst into the laundry room at Wingfield where she is at peace, surrounded by sheets, dozens of maids all around her, mending.

She takes one cool look and rises to her feet and whisks me out of the room to the gallery outside. Beautifully framed pictures, of anonymous saints and angels, smile down at us as if they were not at all perturbed to find themselves cut out from altarpieces by Bess's late husband to become nameless smiling faces in our gallery. I shall be like them, I know it, I shall be excised: cut away from my frame and nobody will know who I am.

'Bess,' I say brokenly. I could weep, I feel as weak as a child. 'The queen . . .'

'Which queen?' she asks quickly. She glances out of the window to the terrace where the Scots queen is walking with her little dog in the glow of late summer sunshine. 'Our queen?'

'No, no, Queen Elizabeth.' I do not even notice the power of what we have just said. We are become traitors in our own hearts and we do not even know. 'Dear God! No! Not her! Not our queen; Queen Elizabeth! Queen Elizabeth knows all about the betrothal!'

Bess's eyes narrow. 'How do you know?'

'Cecil says Dudley told her. He must have thought she would accept it.'

'She does not?'

'She has ordered Norfolk's arrest,' I say, clutching the letter. 'Cecil writes to me. Norfolk is accused of treason, the queen's own cousin, the greatest man in England, the only duke. He is fled to Kenninghall to raise an army of his tenants and march on London. Cecil says it is . . . it is . . .' I cannot catch my breath. Wordlessly I wave the letter. She puts a hand on my arm.

'What does Cecil say?'

I am choking on my words. 'He says the duke's betrothal is part of a treasonous plot by the Northern lords to rescue the queen. And we . . . and we . . .'

Bess goes white as the napkin in her hand. 'The betrothal was part of no plot,' she says rapidly. 'All the other lords knew as well as we . . .'

'Treason. The queen is calling it a treasonous plot. Norfolk is suspected, Throckmorton has been arrested. Throckmorton! Pembroke, Lumley, and even Arundel are confined to court, not allowed home, not allowed more than twenty-five miles from the court, wherever the court may be. Under suspicion of treason! Westmorland and Northumberland are ordered to London at once, on pain of . . .'

She gives a little whistle through her teeth, like a woman calling hens, and takes a few steps around as if she would lift the paintings off the walls and put them into hiding for safe-keeping. 'And us?'

'God knows what is going to happen to us. But half the court is under suspicion, all the lords . . . all my friends, my kinsmen . . . she cannot accuse us all . . . She cannot suspect me!'

She shakes her head, like a stunned ox struck by a hammer. 'And us?' she persists, as if she can think of nothing else.

'She has summoned the whole of the Council of the North, on pain of death, to court. She even suspects the Earl of Sussex, Sussex! She says she will question him herself. She swears that he shall tell her to her face what the Northern earls are planning. Cecil says that anyone who so much as speaks to the Queen of Scots is a traitor! He says that anyone who pities her is a traitor. But that is everyone. We all think the queen should be restored to . . .'

'And us?' she repeats in a whisper.

I can hardly bring myself to say it. 'We have to take Queen Mary back to Tutbury. The queen's orders. She thinks we cannot be trusted to keep her here. She says that we are unreliable. She suspects me.' The words hurt me even to say them. 'Suspects me. Me.'

'What of?'

Her words are like a knife. I don't even correct her speech, I am beyond improving her. 'Cecil writes that they know the Northern lords met her. They know that they came and dined with us and stayed overnight. Their visit was not authorised and now he tells me that we should not have let them in. He says I am guilty of negligence; if not worse. He dares to say such a thing to me. He says that he knows I passed Norfolk's letters to her and hers to him. He says I should not have done so. He all but accuses me of being hand in glove with Norfolk, he all but accuses me of plotting with him and

150

with the Northern lords to set her free. He calls them traitors, condemned to death, and says I am in league with them.'

Bess gives a little hiss, like a snake.

'He all but says I am guilty of treason.' The terrible word drops between us like a falling axe.

She shakes her head. 'No. He cannot say that we did not serve him. He was told. He knew everything that passed. We never gave her a letter that he didn't see. She never spoke with anyone but we reported it to him.'

I am in such a hurry to confess my faults that I do not hear what she is telling me. 'But Bess, you don't know. There was a conspiracy. There *is* a conspiracy. Not against the queen, God forbid. But against Cecil. Norfolk and the rest of us lords joined together against Cecil.' I am so distraught I can hear my voice tremble and I can't make it steady. 'It was nothing to do with the Scots queen. It was about bringing Cecil down. They came to me, and I swore to act with them. I said I would join with them to bring down Cecil. Westmorland and Northumberland invited me to join with them. I agreed. I said that Cecil should be humbled.'

Her sharp dark eyes fasten accusingly on my face. 'You plotted against Cecil!' she exclaims. 'You didn't tell me . . .'

'You know that I am no friend of his . . .'

'You can love him or you can hate him but don't tell me you joined a plot against him!'

'You don't understand.' I sound weak, even to my own ears.

'I know that one man rules England, one man advises the queen, and that man is Cecil. I know that my safety and your safety is that he must never doubt our loyalty to the queen and to him.'

I swallow on a dry mouth. I feel like retching. 'Us old lords . . .'

'Cocks on a dunghill,' she says, foul-mouthed as the farmer's daughter that she is. 'Old cocks on an old dunghill.'

'Us old lords, the true lords of England, feel that Cecil is over-reaching himself. We should advise the queen.'

'By putting the North into arms against her? By raising the east led by Norfolk? By calling out a rebellion of Papists? By overthrowing the safety and peace of the kingdom?'

'No, no,' I say hastily. 'That was never the plan. They never spoke to me of anything about that. We wanted to put Cecil into the place where he should be: steward to the queen, not her chief advisor, not chief counsellor to the throne. She should listen to her cousin, she should listen to us, she should be guided by us lords, the peers of the realm, the natural God-given leaders, the men that God has appointed to rule . . .'

Bess stamps her foot in temper. 'You have ruined us with this folly,' she spits at me, shrill as a shrew. 'I swear to God, my lord, you have judged most badly. You have overreached yourself. You may be able to tell the difference between supporting Howard and attacking Cecil, but Cecil will not. He will weave these single strands up into one thick rope of a plot and hang you all with it together.'

'You cannot know that.'

Her head rears up. 'Of course I know it. Anyone of any sense would know it! I know him. I know how he thinks. He is the only man who knows what England can be, who plans for this country. He is the only one who thinks, not of the old days, but of what will be, who looks forward and not back. The queen is guided by him night and day. Who could ever be such a fool as to think that the queen would ever go against him? She never has done! She has never gone against his advice! She is his creature. It is Cecil who rules. She sits on the throne but the power is with Cecil.'

'Exactly!' I chime in. 'He is overmighty.'

'Hear yourself! Yes! Think! You say it yourself! He is overmighty. So he is too mighty for you and those fools to pull down. Even acting together. And if he thinks you are against him he will destroy you. He will spin the queen a long yarn and hang the Northern lords for the treason of planning an uprising, punish Norfolk for the treason of this betrothal, and throw you into the Tower forever for being a part of both.'

'I knew nothing of either. All I joined with was a wish to see Cecil reduced. All I said was that I was with them to bring Cecil down.'

'Did you speak to the Northern lords of Norfolk's marriage to the Queen of Scots?' she demands, as passionately as a wife would force a husband to confess to a secret lover. 'When they visited that night? Did you agree with them that it would be a very good thing for Norfolk, and for yourselves, and a bad thing for Cecil? Did you say it would be good for her to take her throne in Scotland with him as her husband? Did you agree that the queen did not know of it? Did you say anything like that?'

'Yes,' I admit, as reluctantly as an unfaithful husband. 'Yes, I think I may have done.'

She throws down the napkin to the floor with the thread and the needle. I have never seen her careless with her work before. 'Then you have destroyed us,' she says. 'Cecil does not have to make it all one plot. Indeed, it is all different strands of the same plot. You passed her letters from Norfolk, you let her meet with the Northern lords, you spoke with them about the marriage, and you agreed to plot with them against the queen's advisor and against his policy.'

'What should I have done other?' I shout at her in my own fear. 'I am for England! Old England, as it was. My country, my old country! I don't want Cecil's England, I want the England of my father! What else should I have done but bring him down?'

The face she turns on me is like stone, if stone could be bitter. 'You should have kept me and my fortune safe,' she says, her voice quavering. 'I came to you with a good fortune, a great fortune, and it was yours by marriage, all yours. A wife can own nothing in her own name. A wife has to trust her husband with her wealth. I trusted you with mine. I trusted you to keep it safe. When we married, all my properties became yours, all you give me is a wife's allowance. I trusted you with my wealth, with my houses, with my lands, with my businesses. I gave them to you to keep them safe for me and my children. That is all I asked of you. To keep me and my fortune safe. I am a self-made woman. You promised that you would keep my fortune safe.'

'You shall have it all back under your own command,' I swear. I am furious with her, still thinking of money at a time like this. 'I shall free myself from this shadow on my name, I shall clear my name and the name of my house. And you shall have your own fortune back as your own again. You shall live apart in your own precious house and count your precious ha'pennies. And you shall be sorry, madam, that you and your great friend Cecil ever doubted me.'

Her face crumples at once. 'Oh, don't say it, don't say it,' she whispers. She comes to me and at the scent of her hair and the touch of her hand I open my arms and she falls into them, closes herself to me, cries against my chest, a weak woman after all.

'There,' I say. 'There, there.' Sometimes I ask too much of her. She is only a woman and she takes strange fearful fancies. She cannot think clearly like a man, and she has no education and no reading. She is only a woman: everyone knows that women have no steadiness of mind. I should protect her from the wider world of the court; not complain that she lacks a man's understanding. I stroke the smoothness of her hair and I feel my love for her from my bowels to my heart.

'I shall go to London,' I promise her quietly. 'I shall take you and the queen to Tutbury, and as soon as her new guardian arrives to replace me, I will go to London and tell the queen herself that I knew nothing of any plot. I am guilty of no plot. Everyone knew what I knew. I shall tell her that all I have ever done is to pray for the return of the England of her father. Henry's England, not Cecil's England.'

'Anyway Cecil knew, whatever he says now,' Bess declares indignantly, struggling out from my arms. 'He knew of this plot long before it was hatched. He knew of the betrothal as well as any of us, as soon as any of us. He could have scotched it in days, even before it started.'

'You are mistaken. He cannot have known. He learned of it only just now, when Dudley told the queen.'

She shakes her head impatiently. 'Don't you know yet that he knows everything?'

'How could he? The proposal was a letter from Howard to the queen, carried by Howard's messenger under seal. How could Cecil have learned of it?'

She steps back out of my arms and her glance slides away from me. 'He has spies,' she says vaguely. 'Everywhere. He has spies who will see all of the Scots queen's letters.'

'He can't have done. If Cecil knew everything, from the first moment, then why did he not tell me of it? Why not tell the queen at once? Why leave it till now, and accuse me of being an accomplice in a plot?'

Her brown eyes are hazy, she looks at me as if I were far, far away. 'Because he wants to punish you,' she says coolly. 'He knows you don't like him – you have been so indiscreet in that, the whole world knows you don't like him. You call him a steward and the son of a steward in public. You didn't bring him the result he wanted from the queen's inquiry. Then he learns that you are joined with Norfolk and the others in a plot to unseat him from his place. Then he knows that you encourage the queen to marry Norfolk. Then he learns that his sworn enemies, the Northern lords, Westmorland and Northumberland, have visited you and the queen, and been made right welcome. Why would you be surprised that now he wants to throw you down from your place? Do you not want to throw him down from his? Did you not start the battle? Do you not see that he will finish it? Have you not laid yourself open to accusation?'

'Wife!' I reprimand her.

Bess turns her gaze to me. She is not soft and weeping any more, she is critical and plain. 'I will do what I can,' she says. 'I will always do what I can for our safety and for our fortune. But let this be a lesson to you. Never ever work against Cecil. He commands England, he has a spy network that covers every house in the land. He tortures his suspects and he turns them to his service. He knows all the secrets, he sees everything. See what happens to his enemies? The Northern lords will go to the scaffold, Norfolk could lose his fortune, and we . . .' She holds up the letter. 'We are under suspicion at the very least. You had better make it clear to the queen and to Cecil that we know nothing of what the Northern lords planned, that they told us nothing, that we know nothing of what they are planning now; and make sure you say that Cecil had a copy of every letter that Norfolk ever sent, the moment that the Scots queen received it.'

'He did not,' I protest stupidly. 'How could he?'

'He did,' she says crisply. 'We are not such fools as to do anything without Cecil's permission. I made sure of it.'

I take a long moment to understand that the spy in my household, working for a man that I hate, whose downfall I have planned, is my beloved wife. I take another moment to understand that I have been betrayed by the woman I love. I open my mouth to curse her for disloyalty but then I stop. She has probably saved our lives by keeping us on the winning side: Cecil's side.

'It was you that told Cecil? You copied the letter to him?'

'Yes,' she says shortly. 'Of course. I report to him. I have done so for years.' She turns away from me to the window and looks out.

'Did you not think that you were being disloyal to me?' I ask her. I am exhausted, I cannot even be angry with her. But I cannot help but be curious. That she should betray me and tell me of it without the least shame! That she should be so bare-faced!

'No,' she says. 'I did not think I was being disloyal; for I was not disloyal. I was serving you, though you don't have the wit to know it. By reporting to Cecil I have kept us, and our wealth, safe. How is that disloyal? How does it compare to plotting with another woman and her friends against the peace of the Queen of England in your wife's own house? How does it compare to favouring another woman's fortune at the price of your own wife's safety? How does it compare to dancing attendance on another woman every day of your life, and leaving your own wife at risk? Her own fortune half-squandered? Her lands in jeopardy?'

The bitterness in her voice stuns me. Bess is still looking out of the window, her mouth full of poison, her face hard.

'Bess . . . wife . . . You cannot think I favour her above you . . .'

She does not even turn her head. 'What shall we do with her?' she asks. She nods to the garden and I draw a little closer to the window and see the Scots queen, still in the garden, with a cloak around her shoulders. She is walking along the terrace to look out over the rich woods of the river valley. She shades her eyes with her hand from the low autumn sun. For the first time I wonder why she walks and looks to the north, like this, every day. Is she looking for the dust from a hard-riding army, with Norfolk at their head, come to rescue her and then take her down the road to London? Does she think to turn the country upside down once more in the grip of war, brother against brother, queen against queen? She stands in the golden afternoon light, her cloak rippling behind her.

There is something in the set of her head, like a beautiful figure in a tableau, that makes one long for an army in the fields below her, an army to rescue her and take her away. Even though she is my prisoner I long for her escape. She is too fine a beauty to wait on a tower without rescue. She is like a princess in a child's fairy-tale, you cannot see the picture that she makes and not want to set her free.

'She has to be free,' I say unguardedly to Bess. 'When I see her like this, I know she has to be free.'

'She is certainly a trouble to keep,' she says unromantically.

1569, September, Tutbury Castle: Mary

Bothwell,
They are taking me to Tutbury Castle now. The Northern lords and Howard will rise for me on October 6th. If you can come, you shall command the army of the North and we will ride out in battle again with everything to win. If not, wish me luck. I need you. Come.
Marie

I swear by Our Lady, this is the last time that I will ever be taken back to this hateful prison of Tutbury Castle. I go quietly now, but this is the last time they will take me up this twisting road to this stinking prison where the sun never shines into my room and where the wind blows steadily and coldly over the flat fields. Elizabeth hopes that I will die of the cold and the damp here, or of disease from the fetid mists from the river; but she is wrong. I will outlive her. I swear I will outlive her. She will have to murder me if she wants to wear black for me. I will not weaken and die to convenience her. I will enter the castle now but I shall leave it at the head of my own army. We will march on London and I shall imprison Elizabeth and we shall see how long she lasts in a damp castle of my choosing.

They can rush me back here, they can march me all the way back to Bolton Castle if they like; but I am a queen of the tides and the current is flowing fast for me now. They will not keep me prisoner for more than another week. They cannot keep me. This is the end for the Shrewsburys, they do not know it yet but they are about to be destroyed. The Northern lords will come for me with Norfolk at their head. The date is set, it is to be October 6th, and I shall date my reign from that day. We will be ready, I am ready now. Then my jailors will be my prisoners and I shall treat them as I wish.

Norfolk will be calling up his tenants now, thousands will answer his call. The Northern lords will muster their great army. All the Shrewsburys achieve by bringing me here, to their most miserable dungeon, is to imprison me somewhere that I will be easy to find. Everyone knows that I am kept at Tutbury, everyone knows the road to the castle. The Northern army will come for me within weeks, and the Shrewsburys can choose whether to die in defence of their dirty castle, or surrender it to me. I smile at the thought of it. They will come to me and ask me to forgive them and to remember that they have always treated me kindly.

I respect the earl himself: no-one could fail to admire him; and I like Bess well enough, she is a good-hearted woman, though very vulgar. But this will be the end of them, perhaps the death of them. Anyone who stands in my way, between me and my freedom, will have to die. October 6th is the day and they must be ready, as I am ready: for victory or for death.

I did not choose this road. I came to Elizabeth in need, as a kinswoman imploring her help. She treated me as an enemy and now she treats her own lords and her own cousin as enemies. Everyone who thinks she is a great queen should note this: in triumph she was suspicious and ungenerous. In danger she is filled with panic. She has driven me to despair and she has driven them into rebellion. She will have no-one to blame but herself when they storm her castle and throw her into the Tower and put her on her mother's scaffold. She and her arch-advisor Cecil have such suspicious embittered minds that they have imagined their own undoing and so brought it about. Like fearful suspicious people always do: they have dreamed the worst and made it real.

I have a letter from my ambassador, the Bishop John Lesley of Ross, who is in London, watching the unravelling of Elizabeth's power. I found it tucked into my saddle when we mounted helter-skelter for the ride to Tutbury. Even in the terrified rush to get from Wingfield Manor to Tutbury Castle there was time for a loyal man to serve me. The Shrewsburys' own grooms are already turned to my side. Bess and her husband are betrayed in their own household. The place is full of spies, well-paid with Spanish gold, waiting to serve me. Lesley's note, scribbled in a mixture of French and code, tells me of panic in London, of Elizabeth in a frenzy of fear at hourly reports of an uprising which is breaking out all over the country.

The Northern lords are commanded to report to Elizabeth in London on pain of death, and they have defied her. They are summoning their men and as soon as they have an army they will come for you. They have confirmed the day as October 6th. Be ready.

Norfolk too is ready. He has disobeyed her command to attend court and fled to his house, Kenninghall, in Norfolk, to muster his army. All of the east of England will march for him.

The court has abandoned the progress and dashed back to London; now they are preparing Windsor Castle for a siege. The armed bands are being called out to defend London, but they cannot be mustered and armed in time. Half the citizens are hiding their goods and getting away from the City. The place is deserted at night, filled only with fear. The Spanish will have an army landed from the Netherlands within weeks to serve your cause, and they have sent gold through their banker Ridolfi, which I have passed to Norfolk to pay your soldiers.

Victory will be ours, it is a matter of weeks, Ross.

I scrunch up the letter and put it in my pocket, I will burn it as soon as we stop for dinner. I ride with my hands loose on the reins, hardly aware of the horse. I have a picture in my mind of Elizabeth, my cousin, rushing to Windsor Castle, looking around her court and seeing in every face the overly enthusiastic smile of betrayal. I know how it is. I have seen it myself. She will feel, as I felt at Holyrood, that there is no-one she can trust, she will know, as I knew at Dunbar, that her support is draining away and her followers are promising their loyalty even as they are abandoning her. Now she knows that even Dudley, her friend from childhood and her lover for years, has plotted with Norfolk to rescue me. Her own lover, her own cousin, and every lord of her Privy Council are all on my side. Every lord in her court wants to see me freed. The common people are mine heart and soul. She is utterly betrayed. When she came to the throne they called her 'our Elizabeth' and now she has lost their love.

I think of Shrewsbury riding gravely beside me, his hurrying forward to lift me down from the saddle, his quiet pleasure in my company at dinner, his little gifts and his constant courtesy. He is her sworn liegeman but I have won him over. I have won every lord in England to my side. I know it. I can see it in Shrewsbury and in every man in Bess's household. All of them long to set me free.

1569, October, Tutbury Castle: Bess

Half the things we need are left behind at Wingfield and I cannot buy fresh vegetables for love nor money in a radius of twenty miles. The countryside is exhausted and the men have run off to join the Northern army, which is mustering at Brancepath under the Earl of Westmorland, swearing loyalty to the Scots queen and a holy war for the Church of Rome. The country is on a war footing already and when I send my steward to market he says they will sell him nothing; he feels as if he is the enemy.

It is terrifying to think that out there, in the wilderness of the North, there are squires and gentry and lords calling their tenants together, mustering their friends, arming their followers and telling them to march under the banner of the five wounds of Christ to find me, to come to my house, to free my prisoner. I wake in the night at the slightest noise, in the day I am forever climbing to the castle wall to look out over the road, continually I see a cloud of dust and think it is them coming.

I have lived all my life as a private woman, on good terms with my neighbours, a good landlord to my tenants, a fair employer. Now I find myself at odds with my own people. I don't know who is a secret enemy, I don't know who would free the queen if they could, who would come against me if they dared. It makes me feel like a stranger in my own land, a newcomer in my own country. The people who I think of as my friends and neighbours may be on the other side, may be against me, may even be my enemies. My friends, even my kin, may take arms against me, may see me as a traitor to the true queen, my prisoner.

She herself is demure, like a novice in a convent, with an escape plan hidden in her sleeve, and my husband trustingly remarks to me: 'Thank God that she has not tried to break free. At least she knows nothing about the uprising.'

For the first time in my married life I look at him and I think: 'Fool'.

It is a bad moment when a wife thinks her husband a fool. I have had four husbands and I have had bad moments with all of them; but I have never before been married to a man whose stupidity could cost me my houses and my wealth.

I cannot bear it. I wake in the night and I could weep for it. No infidelity could be worse. Even with the most beautiful woman in Christendom under my roof I find I think more about whether my husband might lose my fortune than whether he might break my heart. A woman's heart can mend, or soften, or grow hard. But once you lose your house it is hard to get it back again. If Queen Elizabeth takes Chatsworth from us to punish my husband for disloyalty, I know that I will never set foot in it again.

All very well for him to plot against Cecil like a child with naughty friends, all very well to turn a blind eye to the Queen of Scots and her unending letters. All very well to delight in the company of a woman young enough to be his daughter, and her an enemy of the realm; but to go so far that now the court will not repay us what they owe! They are beyond arguing over the bills, they do not even reply to my accounts. To go so far that they might question our loyalty! Does he think of nothing? Does he not look ahead? Does he not know that a traitor's goods are at once, without appeal, forfeit to the Crown? Does he not know that Elizabeth would give her own rubies if she could take Chatsworth off me? Has he not given her that excuse with his stupid indiscretion with the Northern lords? Is he not exactly a fool? A wasteful fool? And wasting my inheritance as fast as his own? My children are married to his children, my fortune is in his care, will he throw everything away because he does not think ahead? Can I ever, ever forgive him for this?

I have been married before and I can recognise the moment when a honeymoon is over, when one sees an admired bridegroom for what he is: a mere mortal. But I have never before felt that my marriage was over. I have never before seen a husband as a fool and wished that he was not my lord and master, and that my person and my fortune were safe in my own keeping.

1569, October, Tutbury Castle: George

However long that I live, I will never forget this autumn. Every leaf that falls has stripped away my pride. As the trees have gone bare, I have seen the bones of my life revealed in darkness, in coldness, without the concealing shimmer of foliage. I have been mistaken. I have misunderstood everything. Cecil is more than a steward, far more. He is a landlord, he is a bailiff. He is bailiff of all England and I am nothing more than a poor copyholder who mistook his long life here, his family's home, his love of the land, for freehold. I thought I was a landowner here; but I find I own nothing. I could lose everything tomorrow. I am as a peasant – less, I am as a squatter on someone else's land.

I thought that if us lords of England saw a better way to rule this country than Cecil's unending readiness for war, Cecil's unending hatred of all Elizabeth's heirs, Cecil's unending terror of boggarts in shadows, Cecil's mad fear of Papists, then we could topple Cecil and advise the queen. I thought we could show her how to deal justly with the Scots queen, befriend the French and make alliances with Spain. I thought we could teach her how to live like a queen with pride, not like a usurper haunted with terror. I thought that we could give her such confidence in her right to the throne that she would marry and make an heir. But I was wrong. As Bess obligingly tells me: I was foolishly wrong.

Cecil is determined to throw all who disagree with him into the Tower. The queen listens only to him and fears treason where there was only dissent. She will not consult any one of the lords now, she mistrusts even Dudley. She would behead shadows if she could. Who knows what profit Cecil can make of this? Norfolk is driven from his own cousin's court, driven into rebellion; the Northern lords are massing on their lands. For me, so far, he reserves only the shame of being mistrusted and replaced.

Only shame. Only this deep shame.

I am beyond distress at the turn events have taken. Bess, who is frosty and frightened, may well be right and I have been a fool. My wife's opinion of me is another slur that I must learn to accept in this season of coldness and dark.

Cecil writes to me briefly that two lords of his choosing will come to remove the Scots queen into their safe-keeping and will take her away from me. Then I am to travel to London to face questioning. He says no more. Indeed, why should he explain anything to me? Does the steward explain to a copyholder? No, he simply gives his orders. If Queen Elizabeth thinks I cannot be trusted to guard the Scots queen then she has decided that I am unfit to serve her. The court will know what she thinks of me, the world will know what she thinks of me. What cuts me to my heart, my proud unchanging heart, is that now I know what she thinks of me.

She thinks badly of me.

Worse than this is a private, secret pain, of which I can never complain, which I can never even acknowledge to another living soul. The Scots queen will be taken away from me. I may never see her again.

I may never see her again.

I am dishonoured by one queen, and I will be bereft of the other.

I cannot believe that I should feel such a sense of loss. I suppose I have become so accustomed to being her guardian, to keeping her safe. I am so used to waking in the morning and glancing across to her side of the courtyard, and seeing her shutters closed if she is still asleep or open if she is already awake. I am in the habit of riding with her in the morning, of dining with her in the afternoon. I have become so taken with her singing, her love of cards, her joy in dancing, the constant presence of her extraordinary beauty, that I cannot imagine how I shall live without her. I cannot wake in the morning and spend the day without her. God is my witness, I cannot spend the rest of my life without her.

I don't know how this has happened, I certainly have not been disloyal to Bess nor to my queen, I certainly have not changed my allegiance either to wife or monarch, but I cannot help but look for the Scots queen daily. I long for her when I do not see her, and when she comes – running down the stairs to the stable yard, or walking slowly towards me with the sun behind her – I find that I smile, like a boy, filled with joy to see her. Nothing more than that, an innocent joy that she walks towards me.

I cannot make myself understand that they will come and take her away from me and that I must not say one word of protest. I will keep silent, and they will take her away and I will not protest.

They arrive at midday, the two lords who will take her from me, rattling into the courtyard, preceded by their own guards. I find a bitter smile. They will learn how expensive these guards are to keep: fed, and watered, and watched against bribery. They will learn how she cannot be guarded, whatever they pay. What man could resist her? What man could refuse her the right to ride out once a day? What man could stop her smiling at her guardian? What power could stop a young soldier's heart turning over in his chest when she greets him?

I go to meet them, shamed by their presence, and ashamed of the dirty little courtyard, and then I recoil, recognising their standards, and seeing the men that Cecil has chosen to replace me to guard this young woman. Dear God, whatever it costs me, I cannot release her to them. I must refuse.

'My lords,' I stammer, horror making me slow of speech. Cecil has sent Henry Hastings, the Earl of Huntingdon, and Walter Devereux, the Earl of Hereford, as her kidnappers. He might as well have sent a pair of Italian assassins with poisoned gloves.

'I am sorry for this, Talbot,' Huntingdon says bluntly as he swings down from his saddle with a grunt of discomfort. 'All hell is on in London. There is no telling what will happen.'

'All hell?' I repeat. I am thinking quickly if I can say that she is ill, or if I dare send her back in secret to Wingfield. How can I protect her from them?

'The queen has moved to Windsor for safety and has armed the castle for siege. She is calling all the lords of England to court, all of them suspected of ill-doing. You too. I am sorry. You are to attend at once, after you have helped us move your prisoner to Leicestershire.'

'Prisoner?' I look at Hastings' hard face. 'To your house?'

'She is no longer a guest,' Devereux says coldly. 'She is a prisoner. She is suspected of plotting treason with the Duke of Norfolk. We want her somewhere that we can keep her confined. A prison.'

I look around at the cramped courtyard, at the one gate with the portcullis, at the moat and the one road leading up the hill. 'More confined than this?'

Devereux laughs shortly and says, almost to himself, 'Preferably a bottomless pit.'

'Your household has proved itself unreliable,' Hastings says flatly. 'Even if you are not. Nothing proven. Nothing stated against you, at any rate not yet. Talbot, I am sorry. We don't know how far the rot has gone. We can't tell who are the traitors. We have to be on guard.'

I feel the heat rush to my head and for a moment I see nothing, in the intensity of my rage. 'No man has ever questioned my honour. Never before. No man has ever questioned the honour of my family. Not in five hundred years of loyal service.'

'This is to waste time,' young Devereux says abruptly. 'You will be questioned on oath in London. How soon can she be ready to come?'

'I will ask Bess,' I say. I cannot speak to them, my tongue is dry in my mouth. Perhaps Bess will know how we can delay them. My anger and my shame are too much for me to say a word. 'Please, enter. Rest. I will inquire.'

1569, October, Tutbury Castle: Mary

I hear the rattle of mounted men and I rush to the window, my heart pounding. I expect to see Norfolk in the courtyard, or the Northern lords with their army, or even – my heart leaps up at the thought, what if it is Bothwell, escaped from prison, with a hard-riding group of borderers, come to rescue me?

'Who is that?' I ask urgently. The countess's steward is beside me in my dining hall, both of us looking out of the window at the two travel-stained men and their army of four dozen soldiers.

'That's the Earl of Huntingdon, Henry Hastings,' he says. His gaze slides away from me. 'I will be needed by my lady.'

He bows and steps to the door.

'Hastings?' I demand, my voice sharp with fear. 'Henry Hastings? What would he come here for?'

'I don't know, Your Grace.' The man bows and backs towards the door. 'I will come back to you as soon as I know. But I must go now.'

I wave my hand. 'Go,' I say. 'But come back at once. And find my lord Shrewsbury and tell him that I want to see him. Tell him I want to see him urgently. Ask him to come to me immediately.'

Mary Seton comes to my side, Agnes behind her. 'Who are these lords?' she asks, looking down at the courtyard and then at my white face.

'That one is what they call the Protestant heir,' I say through cold lips. 'He is of the Pole family, the Plantaganet line, the queen's own cousin.'

'Has he come to set you free?' she asks doubtfully. 'Is he with the uprising?'

'Hardly,' I say bitterly. 'If I were dead he would be a step closer to the throne. He would be heir to the throne of England. I must know what he is here for. It will not be good news for me. Go and see what you can find out, Mary. Listen in the stable and see what you can hear.'

As soon as she is gone I go to my desk and write a note.

Ross – greetings to you and to the Northern lords and their army. Bid them hurry to me. Elizabeth has sent her dogs and they will take me from here if they can. Tell Norfolk I am in terrible danger. M

1569, October, Tutbury Castle: Bess

They can have her. They can take her and damn well have her. She has brought us nothing but trouble. Even if they take her now the queen will never pay us what she owes. To Wingfield and back, with a court of sixty people, perhaps forty more coming in for their meals. Her horses, her pet birds, her carpets and furniture, her gowns, her new lute player, her *tapissier*; I have kept her household better than I have kept my own. Dinner every night with thirty-two courses served, her own cooks, her own kitchens, her own cellar. White wine, of the best vintage, just to wash her face. She has to have her own taster in case someone wants to poison her. God knows, I would do it myself. Two hundred pounds a week she costs us against an allowance of fifty-two; but even that is never paid. Now it will never be paid. We will be thousands of pounds the poorer when this is finished and they will take her away but not pay for her.

Well, they can have her; and I shall manage the debt. I shall write it at the bottom of the page as if it were the lost account of a dead debtor. Better to be rid of her and us half-bankrupt, than she stays here and ruins me and mine. Better that I account of her as dead and there is no reckoning.

'Bess.' George is in the doorway of my accounting room, he is leaning against the door, his hand to his heart. He is white-faced and shaking.

'What is it?' I rise at once from the table, put down my pen, and take his hands. His fingers are icy. 'What is it, my love? Tell me. Are you ill?' Three husbands I have lost to sudden death. This, my greatest husband, the earl, is white as a corpse. At once I forget I have ever thought badly of him, at once dread of losing him clutches me like a pain of my own. 'Are you ill? Do you have a pain? My love, what is it? What's the matter?'

'The queen has sent Hastings and Devereux to take her away,' he says. 'Bess, I cannot let her go with them. I cannot send her. It is to send her to her death.'

'Hastings would not . . .' I start.

'You know he would,' he interrupts me. 'You know that is why the queen has chosen him. Hastings is the Protestant heir. He will put her in the Tower, or in his own house, and she will never come out. They will announce that she is in frail health, and then that she is worse, and then that she is dead.'

The bleakness in his voice is terrible to me.

'Or they will kill her on the journey and say she fell from her horse,' he predicts. His face is wet with sweat, his mouth twisted with pain.

'But if the queen commands it?'

'I cannot let her go out to her death.'

'If it is the queen's order . . .'

'I cannot let her go.'

I take a breath. 'Why not?' I ask. I dare him to tell me. 'Why can you not let her go?'

He turns away from me. 'She is my guest,' he mutters. 'A matter of honour . . .'

I turn a hard face to him. 'You learn to let her go,' I say harshly. 'Honour has nothing to do with it. You command yourself to let her go, even to her death. Bring yourself to it. We cannot stop them taking her, and if we protest we only look worse. They think you are disloyal already, if you try to save her from Hastings they will

173

be certain that she has turned you to her side. They will know you for a traitor.'

'This is to send her to her death!' he repeats, his voice breaking. 'Bess! You have been her friend, you have spent day after day with her. You cannot be so heartless as to hand her over to her murderer!'

I glance back to my desk to the figures in my book. I know to a penny what she has cost us so far. If we defend her against the queen we will lose everything. If the queen thinks we are overly fond of this other queen she will destroy us. If she charges us with treason we will lose our lands and every single thing we own. If we are found guilty of treason it is a hanging offence; we will both die for my husband's tender heart. I cannot risk it. 'Who cares?'

'What?'

'I said, who cares? Who cares if they take her and behead her in a field, and leave her body in a ditch? Who cares about her?'

There is a terrible silence in the room. My husband looks at me as if I am a monster. The Fool and the Monster face each other and I wonder at what we have become. Twenty-one months ago we were a newly married man and wife, well-pleased with the contract we had made, enjoying each other, the joint heads of one of the greatest families in the kingdom. Now we are ruined in our hearts and our fortunes. We have ruined ourselves.

'I'll go and tell her to pack,' I say harshly. 'We can do nothing else.'

Still he won't leave it. He catches my hand. 'You cannot let her go with Hastings,' he says. 'Bess, she is our guest, she has sewed with you and eaten with us and hunted with me. She is innocent of any wrongdoing, you know that. She is our friend. We cannot betray her. If she rides out with him, I am certain that she will never get to his house alive.'

I think of my Chatsworth, and my fortune, and that steadies me. 'God's will be done,' I say. 'And the queen has to be obeyed.'

174

'Bess! Have pity on her as a young woman! Have pity on her as a beautiful friendless young woman.'

'God's will be done,' I repeat, holding tight to the thought of my new front door and the portico with the plasterwork flowers, and the marble entrance hall; thinking of the new stable block that I want to live to build. I think of my children, well-married, and well-placed at court in good positions already, of the dynasties I will found, of the grandchildren I will have and the marriages I will make for them. I think of how far I have come and how far I hope to go. I would go to hell itself, rather than lose my house. 'Long live the queen.'

1569, October, Tutbury Castle: Mary

The countess comes into my rooms, her face as kindly as flint. 'Your Grace, you are going on a journey again. You will be glad to be away from here, I know.'

'Going where?' I ask. I can hear the fear in my voice, she will hear it too.

'Ashby-de-la-Zouche, Leicestershire,' she says shortly. 'With the Earl of Huntingdon.'

'I prefer to stay here, I will stay here.'

'It must be as the queen commands.'

'Bess . . .'

'Your Grace, I can do nothing. I cannot deny my sovereign's commands for you. You should not ask it of me. Nobody should ask it of me.'

'What will Huntingdon do with me?'

'Why, he will house you better than we can do here,' she says reassuringly, as if she is telling a fairy story to a child.

'Bess, write to Cecil for me, ask him if I can stay here. I ask you – no, I command you – to write to him.'

She keeps the smile on her face but it is strained. 'Now, you don't even like it here! You must have complained of the smell from the midden a dozen times. And the damp! Leicestershire will suit you far better. It is wonderful hunting country. Perhaps the queen will invite you to court.'

'Bess, I am afraid of Henry Hastings. He can wish me nothing but harm. Let me stay with you. I demand it. I command you. Write to Cecil and tell him I demand to stay with Lord Shrewsbury.'

But the way I say her husband's name, 'Chowsbewwy', suddenly triggers her rage.

'You have spent half my husband's fortune, my own fortune,' she spits out. 'The fortune I brought to him on my marriage. You have cost him his reputation with his queen; she doubts our loyalty because of you. She has ordered him to London for questioning. What do you think they will do to him? They think we favour you.' She pauses, and I see the evil flash of her jealousy, the envy of an older woman for my youth, for my looks. I had not thought that she felt this. I had not known that she saw how her husband is with me. 'They think that my husband favours you. It will not be hard to find witnesses to say that he favours you. Exceptionally.'

'*Alors*, Bess, you know very well . . .'

'No, I don't know,' she says icily. 'I don't know anything about his feelings for you, or yours for him, or your so-called magic, your so-called charm, your famous beauty. I don't know why he cannot say "no" to you, why he squanders his wealth on you, even my own fortune on you. I don't know why he has risked everything to try to set you free. Why he has not guarded you more closely, kept you to your rooms, cut down your court. But he cannot do it any more. You will have to resign yourself. You can try your charms on the Earl of Huntingdon and see how they work on him.'

'Huntingdon is Queen Elizabeth's man,' I say desperately. 'You know this. He is her kin. He courted her for marriage. He is the next heir to her throne after me and my boy. Do you think I can charm him?'

'God knows, you are welcome to try,' she says sourly, curtseys and walks backwards to the door.

'Or what?' I ask as she goes. 'Or what? What will become of me in his keeping? You are sending me to my death and you know it. Bess! *Bess!*'

1569, November, Tutbury Castle: George

I cannot sleep. I cannot eat either as it happens. I cannot sit quietly in my chair nor take any pleasure in riding out. I have bought four days of safety for her by arguing that they have not a strong-enough guard, that with the Northern army on the march – who knows where? – they dare not ride out with her. They could take her straight into an ambush. No-one knows how many men have joined the Northern lords. No-one knows where they are now. Hastings, grumbling, has sent for more of his men.

'Why bother?' Bess asks me, her brown eyes cold. 'Since she has to go anyway? Why see that Hastings has a strong guard? I should have thought you would have wanted her to be rescued.'

I want to tell her: 'Because I would say anything to keep her under the same roof as me for another day.' But that would make no sense at all. So I remark, 'The news from all around is that Westmorland and Northumberland are on the move and their army is more than two thousand strong. I don't want to send them out into trouble. It does us no good at all if they go from here into an ambush.'

Bess nods, but she does not look convinced. 'We don't want her trapped here,' she says. 'The army will swarm to her like wasps to a jam pot. Better she goes than they set siege to us here. Better that she goes sooner rather than later. We don't want her here. We don't want her army coming here for her.'

I nod. The newly wed husband and wife that we were only months ago did not want her here, interrupting our happiness. But us? Now we are divided in our wishes. Bess thinks only of how to get herself and her fortune safe through this dangerous time. And for some reason, I cannot think at all. I cannot plan at all. I think I must have a touch of the gout that I had before. I have never felt so light-headed and so weary and so sick. I seem to spend hours looking out of the window across the courtyard to where her shutters are closed. I must be ill. I can think of nothing but that I have only four days left with her under my roof, and I can't even devise a reason to go across the courtyard and speak to her. Four days and I may spend them like a dog sitting outside a shut door, not knowing how to get in. I am howling inside my head.

1569, November, Tutbury Castle: Bess

It is dawn when I hear the hammering on the great house gate. I am awake at once, certain that it is the Northern army come for her. George does not move, he lies like a stone, though I know he is wide awake; he never seems to sleep these days. He lies and listens with his eyes shut, he will not talk to me nor give me any chance to talk to him. Even now, with the hammering at the door, he does not move – he is a man who has had someone else to open his door for all his life. I get crossly out of bed, pull a robe around my nakedness, tie the strings, and run to the door and down the stairs to where the gatekeeper is swinging open the gate and a mud-stained rider clatters into the courtyard, his face white in the dawn light. Thank God it is a messenger from London and not a force from the North. Thank God they have not come for her and no-one here to face them but me in my nightgown and my husband left abed, lying like a gravestone.

'Name?' I demand.

'From Cecil.'

'What is it?'

'War,' he says shortly. 'Finally it is war. The North is up, the Lords Westmorland and Northumberland have declared against the queen, their men out, their banners unfurled. They are riding under the banner of the five wounds of Christ, every Papist in the country is

181

flocking to join them. They have sworn to restore the true religion, to pay proper rates to working men, and –' he nods to the royal lodgings '– free her and put her back on her throne.'

I clutch the robe to my throat; the chill air is as icy as dread. The mist coming off the water meadows is as wet as rain. 'They are coming here? You are sure?'

'For certainty. Here. Your orders,' he says, digging into his satchel and thrusting a crumpled letter at me. With a breath of relief, as if paper alone can save me, I recognise Cecil's writing.

'How far are they? How strong the army?' I demand, as he swings down from the saddle.

'I didn't see them, thank God, on my way here; but who knows?' he says tersely. 'Some say they will take York first, others Durham. They could take York and restore the kingdom of the North. It will be the great wars all over again, but worse. Two queens, two faiths on crusade, two armies, and a fight to the death. If the Spanish land their army for her, which they can do within days from the Spanish Netherlands, it will be all over, and we will be dead.'

'Get what you want from the kitchen, but say nothing to them,' I tell him and go back to my bedroom at a run. George is sitting up in bed, his face grim.

'Wife?' he asks.

'Read this,' I say, thrusting it at him and climbing on the bed.

He takes the letter and breaks the seal. 'What's happening?'

'The messenger says that the lords of the North have their army and are on the march,' I say briefly. 'They have declared war. They are coming here for her.'

He shoots a quick look at me and spreads the letter. 'This is from Cecil. He says we are to get away south immediately. We have to take her to the castle at Coventry at once for safe-keeping. He will command us from there. We have to get south before they rescue her. We must go at once.' He jumps from the bed. 'Sound the alarm,' he says. 'I shall have to rouse the guard and take her at once. And you go to her and tell her she has to make ready to leave at once.'

I pause at the doorway, struck by a bitter thought. 'I wager she knows all about it,' I say suddenly. 'They will have told her when they visited. When you let her talk with them in private. She will be in their confidence. She will have had secret letters. She has probably been waiting for them all this last week.'

'Just get her ready to leave.'

'What if she won't go?'

'Then I will have to tie her to her horse,' he says. 'An army of fifty could take this place in an hour. And half of our servants would free her for love, and open the gates for her. If they set a siege we are lost.'

I am so glad to hear of his planned brutality to her that I am halfway out of the door before the thought strikes me. 'But wait, my lord. Wait! What if they win?'

He checks in his rapid dressing, the laces for his riding trousers in his hands. 'If they win?'

'What if the army of the North takes and holds the North? What if Westmorland and Northumberland are victorious and march on London? What if the Spanish arrive to support them? What if Howard brings in the east of the country and the Cornish get up for the old religion, the Welsh too? What if they defeat Elizabeth, and we are imprisoning the future queen? What if you are tying the next Queen of England to her horse? Then we are traitors and will die in the Tower.'

My husband shakes his head, baffled. 'I serve the queen,' he says flatly. 'I have given my word as a Talbot. I have to do as my king commands. I don't serve the side that I guess might win. I serve the king. Whatever it costs me. If Mary Queen of Scots is victorious and becomes Mary Queen of England, then I will serve her. But till then, I serve the crowned queen, Elizabeth.'

He understands nothing but loyalty and honour. 'Yes, yes, once she is crowned queen you change sides and then it is the honourable thing to do. But how will we and our children and our fortunes be secure? Now? In these dangerous days? While everything hangs in the balance? When we cannot tell which queen will be crowned in London?'

He shakes his head. 'There is no safety,' he says. 'There is no safety for anyone in England now. I just have to follow the crown.'

I go then, and order them to wake the castle and turn out the guard. The great bell starts tolling like a heart booming with fear. I send them running to the kitchen to get all the stores loaded on wagons, I shout for my steward of the household to pack the most valuable goods as we will have to take them with us, and then I go to her quarters, to the other queen's rooms, shaking with anger that she should bring such dire trouble upon us this day, and so much more trouble to come in the days that will follow.

And as I run I open the little piece of paper that came for me, scribbled with my name, in the package from London. It is from Cecil.

If you are in danger of being captured by the army of the North, she must be killed. Hastings will do it, or if he is dead you must command your husband in the queen's name. Or anyone whose loyalty you trust, whose silence you can guarantee. If there is no-one left alive but you women, you will have to do it yourself. Carry a knife. Burn this.

1569, November, Tutbury Castle: Mary

At last! I think, Good God! At last! as I hear the bell tolling, and know at once that the war has started. At last they have come for me, and only a day to spare before I would have been kidnapped by that brute Hastings. I wake and dress, as fast as I can, my hands trembling with laces, and start to pack the things I must take with me, burning the letters from my ambassador, from my betrothed, from the Spanish ambassador, from his agent Ridolfi, from Bothwell. I wait for the countess or for Shrewsbury to come and beg me to hurry, hurry to run away from this castle that they cannot defend. I shall travel with them. I shall obey their orders. I dare not defy them and risk Hastings snatching me from them. My only safety is to stay with Shrewsbury until my army catches us.

I won't leave Shrewsbury until I am safe with my own army. I dare not. He has been my only friend in England, I have seen no other man that I can trust. And he has never been anything but kind to me. He has never been anything but honourable. A woman with a man like this at her side would be safe. God knows how much I long to be safe.

Westmorland has sworn to me he will come wherever I am. Only if they take the road to London and to the Tower must I make my escape. If Elizabeth, in her fear, tries to put me in the dungeon where she herself waited for her death sentence, I must get away.

I don't need to resist them, for while this war is waging, it does not matter where they take me. The lords will demand my freedom as part of their settlement with Elizabeth, wherever I am hidden. They will demand the right to our religion, and the right to my freedom, and with the North up in arms she will be forced to agree. The North has always been another kingdom, Elizabeth's rule has never run north of the Trent. No Tudor has ever ventured further than York. If the Northerners defy her she will have to make an agreement with them, whatever her preferences.

Beyond all this is a greater plan, an ambitious plan that I do not sanction. I dare not sanction it. I will not make war against a queen on her throne. But of course they all think that if a battle is joined, and it goes their way, then they can march on London. They can take me to the very throne of England itself. This is what Philip of Spain and his ambassador want. This is why his banker Roberto Ridolfi has paid over a fortune in Spanish gold. To put me not only on the throne of Scotland, but of England too. This is nothing more than my right. Elizabeth is a disowned bastard of the late King Henry, I am the granddaughter of his sister. I am the true heir and I should have the throne. I was raised to claim it as my own. They call it the 'great enterprise of England' and they swear it can be done. If the people of England rise to defend their faith shall they consent to a settlement that leaves a heretic on the throne to rule them? What is the point of rising against Elizabeth unless we throw her down forever? The people of England want a queen of their faith, one pledged to tolerance and fairness who will restore the church and the old ways of England.

This is not my plan, I do not plot treason. I would never encourage rebellion against an anointed queen, however badly she has betrayed me, however false her claim. But I have lived long enough to know that all things are decided by God. When the tide is running strongly it will carry all the boats. If God gives us a great victory and the army of the North rides on to take London, then it is God who gives

186

me the throne of England and I would be an ungrateful daughter to refuse it.

I think of Elizabeth, flying to Windsor Castle with double guards posted at the gates, the trained bands of London called to arms, scrambling to find their weapons, scouts racing up the North road, terrified that at any moment the army of the North will come marching south and demand her exile or her death, and I find myself hard-pressed not to laugh aloud at the thought of her fear.

Now she knows how it feels when your people turn against you. Now she knows the terror that I felt when I heard that they would dare to wage war against their own anointed queen. She let my people rise up against me, without punishment. She let them know that they could rebel against me, their God-given ruler, and throw me from my throne; and now the people rise against her, and if they throw her down who shall save her? She should have thought of that before now! I bet she is shaking in her shoes, looking out of her window at the river, straining her eyes for the first sign of the sails of the Spanish ships. She is prone to fear, by now she will be sick with terror. The French are sworn to support me, the Spanish are my loyal friends. The Holy Father himself prays for me by name and says I should be restored. But Elizabeth? Who is Elizabeth's friend? A rabble of Huguenots in France, a couple of German princes, who else? None! She is alone. And now she is facing her own coun- trymen, alone.

I do everything I am bidden, packing my clothes, boxing my books and my jewels, giving my new tapestry to Mary to carry for me, and running down the stone stairs to the stable yard with the bell tolling out a warning, the maids screaming and the dogs barking.

It is raining, a fine cold drizzle, which will mean the roads will churn into mud under our horses' hooves and travel will be painfully slow. The soldiers are pale-faced in the dawn light, fearing the powder for their pistols will be damp and they will have to face the horsemen of the North without weapons. Everyone but me looks half-sick with terror.

Anthony Babington, Bess's sweetest young page, comes to me as I am getting into my saddle and whispers to me the code word that tells me I can trust him. 'Sunflower.'

It is the *impresa* of my girlhood, my chosen badge, the sunflower which turns to light and warmth and hope. 'Send a message to them if you can, to tell them where I am going,' I whisper to him, hardly looking at him, as he tightens the girth on my horse, and straightens the reins for me. 'I don't know where they are taking me. South, somewhere.'

His honest boy's face beams up at me. Bless the child. His brown eyes are filled with adoration. 'But I know,' he says joyfully. 'I heard my lord talking. Coventry. I will tell them.'

'But you take care,' I warn him. 'Take no risks. You are too young to put your head in a noose.'

He flushes. 'I am eight,' he says stoutly, as if it were a great age. 'And I have been in service since I was six.'

'You are a young man of courage,' I say to him, and see his boyish flush.

All the way along the road, as we ride as fast as we dare in the grey light of a wintry dawn, I see the men looking to the left and to the right, listening for the sound of drums and pipes, fearfully alert for the great army of the men of the North. They fear that they will round a bend in the road and find a wall of men, waiting to take me. They fear that even now their horsemen are closing on us, coming up on us from the rear, gaining on us however fast we ride. They know that coming down the road behind us are men who have sworn to restore the true religion and the true queen, an army on the march under the very banner of Christ, in His very name, riding to revenge sacrilege against their church, treason against their queen, sin against their country's history. My captors know they are in the wrong, know they are outnumbered and defeated before they start.

They march at speed, almost at a run, their heads down and their faces grey; they are men in abject terror.

Agnes and Mary and I ride three abreast in silence, a secret smile passing between us from time to time, hard put not to laugh out loud. I look ahead and there is poor Shrewsbury, his face stony with worry, his eyes raking the horizon. Beside him rides my lord Hastings, his face grim, a sword at his side, an assassin's dagger hidden in his coat. He will not enjoy the experience of running before a greater force, he will hate the stink of panic that his men give off as they hurry along the road.

Bustling behind us, left far behind as usual, is the redoubtable countess Bess, organising stores to follow us, no doubt sending messengers to London for news, desperate to end up on the right side, desperate to know what the right side will be. I shan't have her in my household whatever side she decides to turn her coat. I don't forget she would have handed me over to Hastings. I don't forget she fears that I want her husband. I so despise a jealous wife and I have spent my life hounded by the fears of less beautiful women.

She was in the courtyard as we scrambled into the saddle, she was at my side as her husband lifted me up to my horse, trust her not to give us a moment together. She was there even before the pageboy Babington. She took my hand and raised her strained face to me. 'I swear you will be safe,' she promised quietly. 'If you are in danger I will come to you and set you free. If Cecil sends word that you are to be taken to the Tower, I shall get you safely away. I am on your side. I have always been on your side.'

I did not let her see my leap of joy. *Non, vraiment!* Of course, I have no expectation of her saving me, she is such a liar! This promise is nothing but her desperate bid to hold both sides at once. But what this tells me is that she thinks the Northern army will win. Whatever news she has from London, it warns her that things are going badly for Elizabeth's men, so badly that Bess wants me to know that she is my friend. She has the news from London in her pocket and now she wants to be my ally. I am watching Bess, Countess of Shrewsbury, turn her back on everything she believes in, desperate to be on the winning side. I don't laugh out loud, I don't even let her see my amusement. I press her hand gently in mine. 'You have been a good friend to me, Countess,' I say sweetly. 'I shall not forget you or your husband when I come to my own again.'

1569, November, on the road from Tutbury Castle: Bess

When a woman thinks her husband is a fool, her marriage is over. They may part in one year or ten, they may live together until death. But if she thinks he is a fool, she will not love him again.

So think I, jogging down the road south, my head bowed against a freezing sleety drizzle, Tutbury abandoned behind me, a battle or, worse, a defeat before me. A murder commanded of me, and a treason trial hanging over me. This tragedy has happened to me. Me, who thought that I had chosen so well, that I would end my life a countess, with a husband I admired, in a house that is one of the best in England. Now I am riding behind a train of wagons carrying my most valuable goods, desperate to get them stowed somewhere safe before we are plundered, trapped between two advancing armies. And all this because my husband is a fool.

A woman has to change her nature if she is to be a wife. She has to learn to curb her tongue, to suppress her desires, to moderate her thoughts and to spend her days putting another first. She has to put him first even when she longs to serve herself or her children. She has to put him first even when she longs to judge for herself. She has to put him first even when she knows best. To be a good wife is to be a woman with a will of iron that you yourself have forged into a bridle to curb your own abilities. To be a good wife is to enslave yourself to a lesser person. To be a good wife is to amputate your own power as surely as the parents of beggars hack off their children's feet for the greater benefit of the family.

If a husband is unfaithful, a good wife will wink at it. Men being who they are, she is not missing much: the quick thrill of being put up against a wall or being squashed on wet grass. If he is a gambler she can forgive him and pay off his debts. If he has a temper she can keep out of the way, or soothe him, or fight him. Anything that gets her safely through the day, until he apologises in tears – as violent husbands so often do. But if a husband jeopardises his wife's house, her fortune, her prosperity, if he puts at risk the very thing she has dedicated her life to amass, then I cannot see how she can ever forgive him. The only point in being a wife is to get a house and fortune and the children to inherit them. And the terrible danger in being a wife is that the husband owns all: everything that she brings to him on marriage, everything that she inherits or earns during that marriage. By the law of the land, a wife cannot own anything independently of her husband, not her house, not her children, not herself. On marriage she signs every single thing into his keeping. So if a husband destroys what she brings him – loses the house, spends the fortune, disinherits the children, abuses her – then she can do nothing but watch herself slide into poverty. He is a fool and I fear that she will never love him again. And she was a fool to choose him.

And, yes. This is the case for me. I allow him to gamble without reproach, I avoid his occasional moments of bad temper, I even turn a blind eye to his adoration of the young queen; but I cannot forgive him for putting my house at risk. If he is found guilty of treason they will behead him and take his possessions and I will lose Chatsworth and everything that my previous husbands and I gathered together. I cannot forgive him for taking this risk. I am more frightened by this than by the thought of his beheading. To lose Chatsworth would be to lose my life's work. To lose Chatsworth would be to lose my very sense of myself. He is a fool, and I am Mrs Fool, and he will make me Mrs Fool without a house, which is worse.

1569, November, on the road from
Tutbury Castle: Mary

Bothwell, Written in haste – they are taking me to Coventry. Our moment is now! I can promise you a fight to win. Come if you can, come whatever it costs you. Come now!

M

Westmorland has an army of more than a thousand at Brancepath Castle, and a note palmed to me when we stop for dinner tells me that they have already been joined by Northumberland's men. This makes them now two thousand strong. Two thousand – this is an army that can take the North, this is an army large enough to take London.

They are on their way to free me, Norfolk marching north to join them from Kenninghall and the three holy armies, his, Northumberland's and Westmorland's, carrying the banner of the five wounds of Christ, will unite and ride down the road to Coventry for me.

I don't even expect much of a battle. Shrewsbury has a couple of hundred men riding with us, and Hastings no more than forty. None of them has the stomach for a fight. Half of them are Catholic, many of them are sympathetic to my cause, I see it in their shy sideways grins when I ride among them, and in the way they duck their heads in a bow when I go by. When we march past a derelict wayside shrine half of them cross themselves and their officers look the other way. These are men who were christened in the Papist church, why should they want anything changed? Why should they die to defend a change that has brought them nothing but disappointment?

Dusk is falling on our first day of travel as Shrewsbury comes back to ride beside me. 'Not far now,' he says encouragingly. 'Are you not too tired?'

'A little,' I say. 'And very cold. Where are we to spend the night?'

'Ashby-de-la-Zouche,' he says. 'Lord Hastings' castle.'

I am seized with fear. 'I thought . . .' I begin and then I bite off what I thought. 'Do we stay here? I don't want to stay here. I don't want to be in his house.'

He puts out his hand and touches my glove. He is as gentle as a girl. 'No, no, we are here only for one night. Then we will go on.'

'He won't keep me here? Lock me up when we arrive?'

'He cannot. You are still in my charge.'

'You won't release me to him? Whatever he says?'

He shakes his head. 'I am to take you to Coventry and keep you safe.' He checks himself. 'I should not have told you where we are headed. You will not tell your ladies or your servants, please.'

I nod. We all know already. 'I promise I will not. And you will keep by my side?'

'I will,' he says gently.

The road turns ahead of us and we clatter towards the looming house, dark against the darkness of the winter afternoon. I grit my teeth. I am not afraid of Hastings, I am not afraid of anyone.

Shrewsbury comes to my rooms after dinner to see that I am comfortable and well-served. I half-expect him to offer me my freedom, to propose some kind of escape. But I wrong him. He is a man of determined honour. Even when he is losing he will not cut his losses. He is doomed tonight, and yet he smiles at me with his usual courtesy, and I see the affection in his weary face.

'You are comfortable?' he asks me, looking around at the rich furniture which Bess has hastily unloaded and assembled in the bare rooms. 'I am sorry for the poor accommodation.'

'I am well enough,' I say. 'But I don't understand why we have to ride so hard, nor where we are going.'

'There is some unrest in the Northern counties and we want to ensure your safety,' he says. He shifts his feet, he cannot meet my eyes. I could love this man for his hopeless honesty; I think he is the first man I have ever known who is incapable of telling a lie.

'There is some trouble,' he says reluctantly. 'The queen is troubled by the loyalty of the Northern lands. Nothing for you to worry about. But I shall stay with you until we reach our destination, and you are safe.'

'I am in danger?' I widen my eyes.

He flushes a dull red. 'No. I would never lead you into danger.'

'My lord Shrewsbury, if the Northern earls come for me, your dear friends and mine, will you let me go?' I whisper, going close to him, and putting my hand on his. 'Will you let me go to them, so I can be free? They are your friends, they are my friends too.'

'You know about this?'

I nod.

He looks at his boots, at the fire, at the wall. Anywhere but at me. 'Your Grace, I am bound by my word, I cannot betray the cause of my queen. I cannot let you go until she orders it.'

'But if I were in danger?'

Shrewsbury shakes his head, more in bafflement than refusal. 'I would rather die than let anyone hurt a hair of your head,' he swears. 'But I cannot betray my queen. I don't know what to do. Your Grace, I don't know. I don't know what to do. I cannot be false to my queen.

I have taken my oath to her. No man of my line has ever betrayed his king. I cannot betray my oath.'

'But you will not let Lord Hastings take me away? You won't let him kidnap me out of your keeping?'

'No, I won't allow that. Not now. Not in these dangerous days. I shall keep you safe. But I cannot release you.'

'What if he has orders to kill me?'

He flinches as if it were a knife to his heart rather than to mine. 'He would not do such a thing. No man could.'

'What if he has to? What if he is ordered?'

'The queen would never order such a crime. It is unthinkable. She told me, she intends to be your kinswoman, she wants to treat you fairly. She said to me herself that she would be your friend.'

'But Cecil . . .'

His face darkens. 'I will stay with you. I will keep you safe. I would lay down my life for you. I . . .' He chokes on what he wants to say.

I step back. So it is just as his wife fears, and she was fool enough to tell me. He has fallen in love with me and he is torn between his old loyalty to his old queen and his feelings for me. I take my hand from his. It is wrong to torment such a serious man. Besides, I have had enough from him. When the moment comes, I think he will let me go. I really think he will. Whatever he says now, I believe that he is so engaged in my cause that he will disobey his queen, dishonour his proud name, play traitor to his country when the moment comes. When the army of the North has us encircled and demands that I am released to them, I am certain he will let me go. I know it. I have won him. He is mine, through and through. He does not even know it yet. But I have won him from his queen and I have won him from his wife. He is mine.

1569, November, Ashby-de-la-Zouche Castle: Bess

It is impossible to get reliable news, the countryside is alive with gossip and terror, the villages empty of men who have run off to join the army of the North. The women left behind, their stupid faces bright with hope, swear that the good days will come again. These imaginary good days will be the end of me and the destruction of my fortune. If this other queen, Mary Stuart, conquers and becomes the only queen, then she will not look kindly on me. And the first thing she will do is restore the old church. They will want their buildings back, they will want their wealth restored. They will want their gold candlesticks returned from my table, their Venetian glassware, their forks, their gold ewer and ladle. They will want my lands, my mines, my quarries and my sheep runs. When the Scots queen is on the throne she will remember me well enough as the woman who pretended friendship but spat out jealousy one fatal night. My promises to be her saviour will make little impression when the whole of England is her best friend. If this Northern army conquers England and puts their queen on the throne, I will lose my houses and my fortune, my place in the world and everything I have ever striven for.

My husband cannot help me; he will fall too. My friends will not protect me; we are all Protestants, we are all newly arrived at wealth, we are all building on abbey lands, dining off church silver; we will all be forced to return our goods, and thrown down together. My poor children will be paupers and inherit nothing but debts. The old church and their new queen will take everything from me and I will be poorer than my mother; and I swore never to be brought so low.

I drive along the wagons with the goods and the provisions as fast as I can, feeling more like a poor peasant fleeing before an army than a countess moving from one beautiful castle to another.

And all the time I am fretting for my home and for my children. My mother and my sister are at Chatsworth, right in the line of march of the Northern army. No army led by noblemen like Westmorland or Northumberland would harm women; but they will be bound to take my cattle and my sheep, they will march through my wheatfields and camp in my woods. And Henry my son and Gilbert my stepson are at court with the queen, and wild for adventure. I pray that Robert Dudley absolutely forbids them to ride out. Henry in particular is a scamp, mad for any excitement, he will offer to scout for the queen, or join the citizens of London to defend her. Robert is my true friend, I know he will keep my boys safe. Pray God he keeps my boys safe. They are my inheritance as much as my houses and all are in danger tonight.

How I wish I could be with my husband the earl, my George. Fool or not, in this crisis I miss him bitterly. His loyal faith and his determination to do his duty by his queen steadies me when I could cry out in panic at the sudden change in our fortunes. He does not plan and foresee and twist and turn in terror as I do. He does not have wagon-loads of stolen goods to keep safe. He does not have false promises on his conscience and a knife in his bag. He has not promised the queen her safety and yet been ordered to kill her. He knows his duty and he does it, he does not even have to think about what he should do. He is not clever like me, he is not false-hearted like me.

Maybe he is in love with the Queen of Scots. Perhaps he has

enjoyed her looks, and who could blame him? I admit myself, I have never seen such a beautiful woman. Perhaps he has relished her company. Why not? She is as charming as any Frenchwoman raised in vanity and idleness. Perhaps like a man, like a foolish man, he has desired her. Well, he won't be the first to make that mistake.

But it does not go deep with him, God bless him. When Queen Elizabeth sent him an order he did at once as he was bid. He said he would tie the other queen to her horse if he had to. I love him for that alone. He has faith and loyalty. He has constancy; when all I have is a hunger for wealth and a terror of being poor again. He is a nobleman of honour and I am a newly made woman of greed. I know it.

And then of course it is easier for him; how should he be so plagued with fears like me? He does not have the hunger for land and the fear of loss that I have. He was not raised by a bankrupted widow, he did not have to scrape and serve his way into a good place. He never had to choose his friends on the basis of what they would do for him, he never had to sell himself to the highest bidder, yes, and run the auction too. He does not even know that these are the abbeys' gold candlesticks on his table and their flocks of sheep on his land. His purity is founded and protected by my greed and calculation. I do the hard and dirty work in this marriage and tonight, for once, I would like to be as clean as him.

We stop for the first night at the castle at Ashby-de-la-Zouche, one of Hastings' houses, and though Queen Mary is only here for a night she has to be royally served, and it is my task to make sure it is so. More than ever I want her to see that we are doing the best we can for her. I have to send outriders ahead of her guards to make sure that the house is ready for her arrival; Hastings had shut it down while he was at court, and so my servants have to open it and air the rooms and light the fires. Then I have to catch up with them as quickly as I can so that I can have the wagon of her special goods unpacked and in her room ready for her dinner, I have to have her bedroom fit for a queen before I dream of sitting down to eat. She has to have her special carpet from Turkey on the floor beneath her bed, she has to have her own linen sheets on her bed, lavender-scented, she has to have a change of clothes for the next day, two changes of linen, starched and ironed, and her little dog washed and walked.

Yet all the time that I am fussing about her missing Belgian lace handkerchiefs I am waiting for the news that the army is upon us and closing fast. My wagon train lumbers slowly in the rear, forever getting stuck in the thick mud or having to go round rivers swollen with winter rain, and I have to be with it as we scramble for Coventry. I am unprotected, all the guards are around her, two hours ahead of me. If the army of the North come upon us tomorrow it will be me they find first, with a wagon-load of Papist treasures, quite without defence. At any moment they could ride down on us and all I will have to protect myself is a Turkey carpet, a dozen linen sheets and the queen's stupid little dog.

1569, November, Ashby-de-la-Zouche Castle: George

One by one they are taking the towns of the North, raising their troops and manning each for a siege. The kingdom of the North is unrolling before them like a welcome mat, they would seem to be unstoppable. This is not a campaign, it is a triumphal progress. The army of the North is cheered everywhere that they march. The wet weather does not delay them, they are greeted as if they were spring itself. A brief note from Cecil to Hastings (for it seems that I am not to be trusted with news) warns us that they have taken the great city of Durham, without a shot being fired. They ordered Mass to be said in the cathedral, they threw down the Protestant prayer book and returned the altar to the right place. People flocked to be blessed and the priests blazed out in their vestments. The statues are re-appearing in the shrines, the candles are lit, the good times have come again, the country will be free. They have restored the old faith in the land of the Prince Bishops and once again the cathedral arches have rung to the true word of God in Latin. Hundreds came to hear Mass, thousands more were told of it and are filled with joy, flocking to their own parish churches to ring the bells backwards to show that the new order is turned upside down again, running to fetch their sickles and their pitchforks, desperate to fight a war on the side of the angels. The priests who were forced on pain of death to put out the Bible where anyone could see it, as if it were a common book, but hide the holy bread, can now follow the church's orders once again and take back the Bible into their keeping but show the holy bread to all who come to worship it. The stone altars are back, the stoops are filled once more with holy water, the churches are warm again, murmuring with prayers. Once again you can buy a Mass for the soul of a beloved, once again you can claim sanctuary. The old religion has returned and the people can have its comfort. Elizabeth's peace and Elizabeth's religion are tumbling about her ears together and Bess and I will fall over and over in the ruins.

Cecil writes with fragile bravado that Queen Elizabeth is sending an army north, they are mustered and marching as fast as they can. But I know they will be too few and too late. These will be men from Kent, men from Wiltshire, they will be tired by the time they get here, and they will be far from home. They will be disinclined to fight men of the North, on their own lands, proud of their own religion. The Southerners will be afraid. We of the North are known as hard men, men who take no prisoners. When the North rises, no-one can stand against us. Those who remember the stories of the bitter years of the war of York against Lancaster will prefer to stay home and let these rival queens battle it out between themselves. No-one wants to join in another war between the North and the South. Only the Northerners are eager for battle because they know that God is on their side, and they have nothing to lose and are certain to win.

Many – both Southerners and Northerners – will believe that Queen Mary has every right to her freedom and should fight for it. Some, I know, will think that she has a right to the English throne and will not join an army against her. They will not march against a legitimate heir to the throne; who would raise a sword against good King Henry's own kin? The grandchild of his beloved sister? Such a true Tudor should be defended by every Englishman. So hundreds, perhaps thousands will come north to fight for her and for the old religion, and for the ways that they love. Most of the country would go back to the old ways if they could, and this is their greatest chance. The earls have raised the banner of the sacred wounds of Christ. The people will flock to it.

Cecil has no news of Howard; and his silence to us shows the extent of his fear. When the duke brings his men into the battlefield he will outnumber any that Elizabeth could arm. He will turn out half of England with him. The Howard family have commanded most of the east of the country for generations, as princes in their own liberty. When the Howards declare for the king on the throne, half the country goes with them, as thoughtless as hounds to the horn. When the Howards reject a king, it is to announce a usurper. When Howard stakes his standard for Queen Mary, it will be over for Elizabeth.

Cecil is afraid, I would stake my honour on it. He does not say so; but he writes from Windsor, which means they have surrendered London, in order to arm the only castle they can hope to defend. This is worse than anything in living memory. King Henry never abandoned London. Nor did his father. Even Queen Mary, facing Wyatt and a mighty Protestant rebellion, never surrendered London. Little Queen Jane bolted herself into the Tower. But Queen Elizabeth has abandoned her capital city and is readying for a siege, with no hope of any relief from abroad. Worse: she has foreign armies massing against her. No king in Christendom will come to the aid of Elizabeth, they will let her fall and be glad to see her die. This is the harvest that Cecil reaps from his policy of suspicion. He and his queen have made enemies of the French, they hate the Spanish, they are divided from their own people, they are strangers in their own kingdom. She has aligned herself with pirates, with merchants, with Puritans and with their paid informers; and now she declares war on the nobility of her kingdom who should advise her.

I should be there at Windsor Castle, I should be there with my equals, with my queen. She should have the advice of her peers, men who have served the throne for generations, men who have taken arms for the safety of the English king for centuries. She should not be dependent on that clerk Cecil who comes from nowhere and was a nobody until yesterday. How can he counsel caution and good sense when he himself is filled with terror? How can he bring the people together when it is his fears and his spies who have driven us apart and made us enemies to each other? How can the lords advise her when she has accused most of them of treason? The best men in England are in the Tower or under house arrest.

God knows, I want to serve her now, at the time of her terror. God knows, I would tell her not to arm, not to raise the troops, I would tell her to send in friendship to the Scots queen and parley with her, promise to return her to Scotland, to treat her like a good cousin and not an enemy. More than anything else, I would advise her to listen no more to Cecil, who sees enemies everywhere and, in so seeing, makes enemies everywhere.

Well, I cannot serve the queen under siege in Windsor Castle, but I will serve her here. This is my task, and it is not a light one. I shall serve her here by guarding the woman who would take her throne, by avoiding, if I can, the army who would free her, by praying to my God in my own way – since truth be told I don't know any more if I am Papist or Protestant and I don't know how one knows, and I don't care – that this war may be, by a miracle, averted and that cousin shall not war with cousin in England again. And when I have formed that prayer I whisper another one, to the sweet queen's name-sake: 'Holy Mary, Mother of God, keep her safe. Keep your daughter safe. Keep your angel safe. Keep my dearest safe. Keep her safe.'

1569, November, Coventry: Mary

A note from my ambassador Bishop Lesley, balled up and held tight in the brown fist of little Anthony Babington, is dropped by him into my lap in our temporary quarters at Coventry, the best house in the town and a mean dirty little place at that.

> *I write in haste with great news. Our campaign is underway. Roberto Ridolfi is returned from the Spanish Netherlands, and has seen the armada. They are ready to sail to support you now. They will land at Hartlepool or Hull, either city will declare for you, and then the Spanish troops will march to free you. Elizabeth has raised a reluctant army from the merchants and apprentices of London but they are making slow progress, losing men at every stop, there is no appetite for battle.*
>
> *Your own army is triumphant, every city and town in the North is throwing open its gates, one after another. We have Elizabeth's Council of the North pinned down in York, unable to get out of the town, surrounded by our army. Their leader, the Earl of Sussex, stays faithful to Elizabeth but he does not have the men to break out of the city and the county all around is yours. Your army now dominates every town and village east of the Pennines. The true religion is restored in every parish church in the North, the kingdom of the North is yours to command, and you shall be freed within days and returned to Scotland, to your throne.*

I read in haste, I cannot stop myself smiling. He writes to me that the Northern earls have played a clever hand. They have declared that they will not rebel against Elizabeth, there is no question of treason, this is emphatically not a rebellion. The battle is against her evil councillors and their policies. They insist only that the church be restored, and the Roman Catholic religion freely practised in England again, and me returned to the throne of Scotland and acknowledged as heir in England. It is the moderation of these demands which attracts support as much as their righteousness. We are triumphant. Not a man in England would disagree with such a programme. All we lack is Elizabeth's herald under a white flag, asking to parley.

Bishop Lesley urges me to be patient, to do nothing that might lead Elizabeth and her spies to think that I am in touch with the Northern army. To be a jewel, carried silently from one place to another until it finds its final setting.

'*Deus vobiscum*,' he ends. 'God be with you. It cannot be long now.'

I whisper '*Et avec vous, et avec vous*, and also with you,' and I throw his letter into the fire that burns in the small fireplace.

I shall have to wait, though I long to be riding at the head of the army of the North. I shall have to be rescued, though I long to free myself. I shall find patience and I shall wait here, while poor Shrewsbury paces the walls of the town and forever looks north in case they are coming for me. I shall find patience and know that this cruel game of wait and fear which Elizabeth has played with me has suddenly turned in my favour and in days, in no more than a week, I shall ride back into Edinburgh at the head of the army of the North and claim my throne and my rights again. And now it is she who has to wait and fear; and I who shall judge whether I shall be kind to her. I am like a precious ship which has been waiting outside the harbour for so long, and now I can feel the tide has turned and the ship is pulling gently at the anchors, the current is flowing fast for me, and I am going home.

1569, November, Coventry: Bess

Just because we are far from our own lands does not mean that anybody eats any the less, but now everything has to be bought at market prices and the gold I brought with me is running perilously short. There are no fresh vegetables to be had, and no fruit because of the winter season, but even dried fruits and winter vegetables are priced beyond our means.

I write to Cecil to beg him to send me money to supply the queen's household, to send me news of the army of the North, and to send me the reassurance that he knows we are faithful. I write to Henry to ask him news of the court and to command him to stay with Robert Dudley. I command him as his mother not to dream of taking arms for the queen and not to come to me. If Cecil only knew the terror I am in, the smallness of my little hoard of coins, the depletion of my courage, he would take pity and write to me at once.

If my husband the earl is suspected, as half the lords of England are suspected, then my fate hangs in the balance with him, with the army of the North, with the destiny of the Queen of Scots. If the Northern army comes upon us soon, we cannot hope to win. We cannot even hold this little city against them. We will have to let them have the queen and whether they take her and put her on the throne of Scotland, or take her to put her on the throne of England, then George and I are alike lost. But equally, if the English army reach us first then they will take the Queen of Scots from us, since they don't trust us to guard her, and George and I are lost, dishonoured and accused.

My greatest regret, my deep, deep regret in these anxious days, is that we ever agreed to take the Scots queen, that I thought we could manage her, that I thought I could manage my husband with her in the house. My second sorrow is that when he said he would hand all my lands back to me to punish me for doubting his abilities, that I did not say quickly: 'Yes!' and get the deed signed then and there. For if – God forbid – if George is kidnapped by the Scots, or accused by the English, or killed in battle, or runs away with the Scots queen for love of her, then either way alike, I shall lose Chatsworth, my house at Chatsworth, my beloved house of Chatsworth. And I would almost rather die myself than lose Chatsworth.

I can hardly believe that having spent all my life marrying for advantage, gathering small parcels of land, storing small pieces of treasure, that at the end I should have one of the greatest houses in England and risk it on the whim of the good will of Elizabeth and the good behaviour of her cousin, the other queen. When did Elizabeth ever show good will to another woman? When did Mary ever behave well? My fortune rests on two women and I would trust neither of them. My fortune is in the keeping of a man who serves one and loves the other, and is a fool into the bargain. And I must be the greatest fool of all three of them to be sinking into a mire of their making.

1569, November, Coventry: George

News at last from Durham; but no good news for us. The army of the North is marching south. They heard their Mass in Durham cathedral and celebrated their triumph with a great *Te Deum*, and have now set out with their banners in their strength down the great north road. We must assume they are coming to free the queen. They were seen on the road at Ripon and are said to have four thousand footmen; but their greatest strength is their horse. They have nearly two thousand mounted men, and these are the dazzling young gentlemen of the houses of the North, hardened by years of border raids, trained in the joust, desperate for battle, passionate about their faith, and all of them in love with the Queen of Scots. They are led by Westmorland and Northumberland, even the Countess of Northumberland rides with the army, swearing that we all might as well die in battle than miss this one great chance to restore the true faith.

When I hear this, I truly waver. I feel my heart leap for a moment at the thought of the banners waving and the march of the army for the true church. If only I could be with them, my friends, if only I could have their conviction. If only I could release the queen and ride out with her to join them. What a day that would be! To ride out with the queen to meet her army! But when I imagine this, I have to bow my head and remember that I owe my duty to Queen

Elizabeth, I have given my word as a Talbot. I am incapable of dishonour. I would choose death before dishonour. I have to.

Meanwhile Hastings continues to assure me that Elizabeth's army is on the way north, but no-one can say why they are taking so long, nor where they are. My own men are restless, they don't like this dirty little town of Coventry; I have had to pay them only half their wages since we are desperately short of coin. Bess does her best but the food supplies are poor, and half of them are longing for their homes and the other half yearn to join our enemies. Some of them are already slipping away.

Lord Hunsdon – faithful cousin to the queen – is pinned down by Queen Mary's supporters in Newcastle, he can't get west to relieve York which is on the brink of desperation. The whole of the north-east has declared for Mary. Hunsdon is marching cautiously down the coast, hoping to get to Hull, at least. But there are terrible rumours that the Spanish might land in Hull, and the city would certainly declare for them. The Earl of Sussex is trapped in York, he dare not march out. All of Yorkshire has declared for the army of the North. Sir George Bowes alone has held out against them, and raised a siege at the little market town of Barnard Castle. It is the only town to declare for Elizabeth, the only town in the North of England to prefer her claims to those of the Queen of Scots; but even so, every day his men slip out of the castle gates and run away to join the Papists.

Every day that Elizabeth's army dawdles reluctantly towards us, the army of the North grows in numbers and confidence and marches onward, faster and faster, greeted as liberating heroes. Every day that Elizabeth's army delays, the army of the North marches closer to us, and every day increases the chance that the army of the North will get here first and take the Scots queen, and then the war is over without a battle, and Elizabeth is defeated in her own country by her own cousin without the rattle of a sword in her defence. A fine ending to a short reign! A quick conclusion to a brief and unsuccessful experiment with a spinster queen of the Protestant faith! This will be the third child of Henry who has failed to endure. Why should we not try the grandchild of his sister? This will be the second disastrous Protestant Tudor, why should we not go back to the old ways?

Against all this, Bess tells me a little gossip from her steward at Chatsworth, which gives me a tiny glimpse of hope in these hopeless times. He reports to her that half a dozen of the tenant farmers who ran off when the standard of the North was raised have come home, footsore but proud, saying that the rebellion is over. They say that they have marched under the banner of the five wounds of Christ, that they have seen the Host raised in the cathedral at Durham, that the cathedral has been re-consecrated and all their sins have been forgiven, that the good times are here, and wages will be raised and the Queen of Scots will take the throne of England. They have been greeted as heroes in their villages and now everyone believes that the battle is over, and the Queen of Scots has won.

This gives me a moment's hope that perhaps these simple trusting people will be satisfied with the capture of Durham and the establishment of the old kingdom of the North, and disband. Then we can parley. But I know I am whistling in the dark. I wish to God I had some reliable news. I wish I could be sure that I will be able to keep her safe.

Hastings predicts that the Northern lords are going to establish a kingdom of the North, and wait for Elizabeth's army on the ground of their own choosing. They have the advantage of numbers, they will choose the battlefield as well. They have cavalry and Elizabeth's army has next to no horse. The young riders of the North will cut the apprentices of London to pieces. Hastings is grim at this prospect; but anything that delays the battle is good news for me. At least I will not have to face my own countrymen, my friends Westmorland and Percy, in battle today or tomorrow. I am dreading the moment that I have to command men from Derbyshire to sharpen their sickles against men of Westmorland and Northumberland. I am dreading the day that I will have to command men to fire on their cousins. I am certain that my men will refuse.

I abhor the thought of this war. I thought that God might have called me to defend my home against the Spanish or the French; but never did I dream I would find myself in a battle against fellow Englishmen. To threaten a fellow countryman, led by a man I have known for all my life as my friend, will break my heart. Good God, Westmorland and Northumberland have been companions and advisors and kin to me for all my life. We are third cousins and in-laws and step-cousins to each other through five generations. If those two and their kin are out under the flag of the five wounds of Christ, it is unbelievable to me that I am not at their side. I am their brother, I should be beside them.

The battle will come and then I shall have to look over my horse's ears at their standards, at their beloved, familiar standards, and see them as the enemy. The day will come when I shall see the honest English faces of the other side, and still I shall have to tell my men to prepare to stand against a murderous charge; but it won't be today. Thank God it won't be today. But the only reason it is not today, is their choice. They are choosing their moment. We are defeated already.

1569, Christmas Eve, Coventry: Mary

My chaplain locks my door and my household and I celebrate Mass on this most special night, as if we were Christians in hiding in the catacombs of Rome, surrounded by the ungodly. And like them we know, with utter conviction, that though they seem so powerful, though they seem to dominate the world, it will be our vision that triumphs, and our faith that will grow until it is the only one.

He finishes with the bidding prayers and then he wraps up the sacred goods, puts them in a box, and quietly leaves the room. Only his whispered 'Merry Christmas' stirs me from my prayer.

I rise up from the kneeler and blow out the candles before the little altar. 'Merry Christmas,' I say to Agnes and Mary, and I kiss them on each cheek. The members of my household file out, one by one, pausing to bow or curtsey to me, and whisper their blessings. I smile as they go, and then the room is silent, warm.

'Open the window,' I say to Agnes, and I lean out. The stars are sharp as diamonds against the blackness of the sky. I look for the north star and think that my army will be sleeping beneath it, on its way to me. A story Bothwell once told me comes to my mind and I take in a breath of cold, cold air, and whistle a long cold whistle like the howl of a gale out into the night.

'What are you doing?' Mary asks, throwing a shawl around my shoulders.

'I am whistling up a storm,' I say, smiling at the thought of Bothwell who whistled up his own storm the night before Carberry Hill. 'I am whistling up a storm that is going to blow me all the way to my throne.'

1569, December, Coventry: Bess

A cold season and little chance of much joy at a Christmas feast for my household this year. This is the second Christmas for me and my lord that has been spoilt by this other queen. I wish to God I had never heard of her, never mind thinking I could make a profit from serving her. Far from my home, and separated from my children, with no news of my mother and sister or my house, we wait in anxiety for the arrival of the army of the North. Hastings sends out scouts three times a day to see if we can get at least some idea of where it is now, and when it will be upon us, but half the time they are riding blind in mist and rain and could be within feet of the Northern army and not see it.

The town is fortified as well as it can be but there is no doubt in anyone's mind that we cannot hold out a siege against an army of nearly six thousand men. We have a handful of men whose loyalty we cannot depend on, nor will the citizens of Coventry defend us. They want to see the queen freed too. We are not popular here, we are an army of occupation.

I cannot stop fretting for my mother and sister at Chatsworth. My girls are safe in the south, in service with friends, learning how to run great households and making the friendships which will serve them in later life, and my boy Charles is at school. But the Northern army could march through Chatsworth and though my mother has the determination and the courage to order them off my land, what if the soldiers take offence? I worry too for Henry, my son, and Gilbert, my stepson, who are both at court. I cannot stop thinking that they may take it into their heads to volunteer to march with the queen's army and come north against her enemies. If my Henry is in a battle with the Northern army I swear I will behead the Queen of Scots myself. I am sure Robert Dudley will not let him go, I am sure the queen would forbid it. But over and over again I start up in the night, certain that my boy will have volunteered for danger and is even now marching north to meet an unstoppable army of traitors.

Hastings has a letter from London, promising relief and pretending to optimism, but it brings the disastrous news that Barnard Castle has fallen to the army of the North. Sir George Bowes was holding out for the queen but his men risked their necks and jumped down from the castle walls to join the rebels. One of them even broke his leg in his determination to change sides, and the townspeople themselves threw open the gates and called the rebels in, singing the old anthems as they advanced. They held Mass in the parish churches, they brought out the hidden stoops for the holy water, the gold, the silver, even the pictures and the stained-glass windows. They declared the return of the faith at the market cross and all the farmers' wives brought their children to be properly baptised at last.

It will be as it was before, I know it: the church at the centre of life, the monasteries and the abbeys rich with their wealth, the faith restored. It is as if the world is knitting itself back together, like a skilled weaver repairing an unravelled cloth. I can hardly believe that I will not walk backwards myself, back past my third good husband, William St Loe, back past my second good husband, William Cavendish who gave me Chatsworth and stole the gold candlesticks from the abbey for me, past my first manor, all the way back to my childhood when I married my first husband to escape my life as a poor girl with no prospects at Hardwick and my mother did not even hold the deeds to our home.

I remark to the queen at dinner that every night in this terrible time of waiting, I dream that I am going backwards to my childhood, and her face lights up as if this were a wonderful prospect. 'If I could wish anything I would be back in France,' she says. 'I would be a little princess in France once again.'

I smile weakly, as if in agreement. God knows, I wish she was there too.

1569, December, Coventry: George

The queen is housed in the best house in town and that is not good enough for her. Bess and I are quartered next door, goods piled up in the rooms, servants sleeping on benches. The grooms are sleeping in the stables with the horses, Hastings' men pushed into the houses of poor people all around the town. The market has run out of food and the stink of the streets and the drains is unbearable. We will have to move on, whatever the danger, or illness will break out in these cramped quarters. Hastings has written to Cecil but the reply comes to me in our poor quarters, carried by yet another of his young nameless men. That I am now his chosen correspondent and Hastings is ignored tells me everything at once. Cecil must be in despair. Cecil has brought his queen to the brink of defeat and now he needs me to negotiate with the other queen.

> *Your friendship with the Queen of Scots must serve us now. I have certain information that the rebels have taken the port of Hartlepool to serve as a beachhead for a Spanish landing. The Spanish fleet will come from the Netherlands and land their army to support the army of the North. We have no force that can match them, nor can we raise one.*
>
> *In this event, you are to protect the Queen of Scots at all costs and start negotiations with her to reach a settlement. Tell Bess, Devereux and*

Hastings that they must keep her safe at all costs. Whatever plans we had before are now urgently changed – make sure that they understand this. Far from being our danger, she is now our only hope for a truce. She must be kept safe and if possible turned into a friend and future ally.

Find out what she will accept. We would support her return to the throne of Scotland, and guarantee her as heir to the throne of England, if we have to. She would have to guarantee freedom of religion but she could practise her own faith as queen. She would have to choose any future husband on the advice of her Privy Council. She can have Norfolk if she still wants him.

You see from this that I judge our situation to be grave, extremely grave. I am anticipating our defeat by the army of the North and we have to persuade Queen Mary not to overthrow Queen Elizabeth. We are counting on you to come to an agreement with her that leaves Queen Elizabeth on her throne. When the Spanish armada sails into our port and lands their army we are lost. We cannot muster a defence against such a force. We cannot even muster against the army of the North. Everything will depend on the agreement you can make with Queen Mary. Please use your best endeavours, Shrewsbury. We may have had our differences in the past but please put them out of your mind now.

This is to save the life of Queen Elizabeth and her throne, and everything we have done for her and for God.

This should come as no surprise. After all, I have been on the lookout for an overwhelming enemy for days; but even so, I am shocked, so shocked that I can hardly hold the letter in my hands. My fingers are trembling.

I shall have to do as he commands. As soon as the Spanish are landed I shall have to start to talk to Queen Mary as a supplicant talks to a victor. I shall have to beg her for the life and freedom of Queen Elizabeth. I shall have to see if I can persuade her to be generous. But, in all honesty, I cannot see why she would be merciful when no mercy has ever been shown to her.

When Queen Mary commands the army of the North and Spanish army together, then she commands England. I cannot think why she would not simply take her throne. And then she will be Queen Mary of England and Scotland, and Elizabeth will become the other queen and a prisoner once more.

1569, December, Coventry: Mary

I am trembling with excitement and I cannot hide it. I cannot make my face serene or my voice calm. I am a French princess, I should be under complete self-control, but I want to dance around the room and scream with delight. It seems that the storm I have summoned has broken on England like a great wave at sea. My army has won the whole of the North, and today captured the port of Hartlepool for the Spanish armada, which will land there. The Pope will declare for me, and order every Roman Catholic in England to take arms for me. I cannot hide my joy and my excitement, so I tell Mary Seton to announce that I am ill and that I must stay in my room. I dare not let anyone see me.

Hartlepool is a deep-water port, and the Spanish fleet has only to come the short voyage from the Netherlands. They could sail overnight and be here tomorrow. They could be at sea now, even now. When the Spanish army is landed it has only to march across country to me. I am now counting my time in captivity in days.

I hear a tap at the outer door of my rooms and a quiet voice outside. It is Shrewsbury, I would know his diffident tones anywhere. Mary Seton tells me he has come to inquire after my health.

'Let him enter,' I say, and rise from my chair and straighten my skirts. I glance in my looking glass. I am flushed and my eyes are bright. He will think I am feverish, rather than thrilled.

'Your Grace,' he says, and comes in and bows.

I give him my hand to kiss. 'My dear Shrewsbury.'

He smiles at my pronunciation of his name and he looks carefully into my face. 'I heard you were unwell. I was worried about you. But I see you are more beautiful than ever.'

'I have a slight fever,' I say. 'But I don't think it is anything serious.'

Mary Seton steps over to the window, out of our way.

'Would you wish to see a doctor? I could send to London for a physician.' He hesitates. 'No, I cannot promise that. I am not sure we could get someone to make the journey in these troubled times. May I see if there is a trustworthy local man?'

I shake my head. 'I will be well tomorrow, I am sure.'

'These are difficult times,' he says. 'It is not surprising that you are unwell. I have been hoping to take you back to Wingfield Manor for the twelve days of Christmas, you will be more comfortable there.'

'We can go to Wingfield?' I ask, wondering if he has new intelligence. Can he know where my army is now? Can he really hope to take me to a house that cannot be defended?

'I hope so,' he says, and in his uncertain tone I know that they are advancing on us, that he knows he is defeated, and Wingfield and Christmas is his dream of peace with me, not a real plan.

'Oh, it will be our second Christmas together,' I exclaim, and watch the colour slowly rise under his skin.

'I did not know then . . .' he starts and then falls silent. 'If you are taken,' he says, and corrects himself. 'When you are taken from me . . .'

'Are they close?' I whisper. 'Do you expect them?'

He nods. 'I may not say.'

'Don't resist,' I say urgently. 'I could not bear for you to be hurt for my sake. You will be hugely outnumbered, you know, and the men of Coventry won't take up arms for Elizabeth. Please, just surrender.'

He smiles, a little sadly. 'I have to do my duty to the queen. You know that.'

'I too cannot tell you some things,' I whisper. 'I have secrets too. But I do know that they are a force, an overwhelming force. When they arrive I want you to promise to come to me, come to my side, and I will protect you.'

'It is I who should be protecting you,' he says. 'That is my duty and also my . . . my . . .'

'Your what?' I think he will say 'desire', and then we will be on the very brink of a declaration. I know that I should not raise my eyes and my face to him; but I do, and I take a small step so that we are close as lovers.

'It is my habit,' he says simply. 'I have a habit of obedience to my queen. And I am obliged. It is my obligation to Queen Elizabeth.' And he steps back from me, his eyes down. 'I came only to see if you needed a physician,' he says, his gaze on his boots. 'I am glad to find you well.' He bows, and leaves.

I let him go. I have my safety in his unacknowledged love for me, he is mine, even if he does not know it. I have my rescue in the army which is coming ever closer. My future marches towards me, step by step, and the young men of the North on their fast beautiful horses are coming to save me from Elizabeth. The finest army in Europe is coming in their great ships. I am about to regain my own.

If Bothwell has escaped, he will be on his way to me, by land, by sea, by foot, by horse, by ship; if he has to crawl on his hands and knees, he will. This will be a battle he will not miss. He hates the English like a man possessed, he hates them like the borderer he is. His kin have raided the English lands and suffered English attack for centuries. He would do anything to threaten them. To defeat them in open battle would be the delight of his life.

We will meet again as we parted, on a battlefield. He left me, after the dreadful long day on Carberry Hill, and he told me, at the last, everything. He predicted that the rebellious Scots lords would give their word for my safety and for his; but they would betray their own oath the minute he was out of sight. He said they would post him as an outlaw and arrest me. He begged me to let him fight our way out, to run together. But I thought I knew better. I said they could not harm me, I was of blood royal. They dared not harm me, I was certain to be safe. No-one could touch me, my person was sacred, and he was my husband, they would never dare touch him.

He threw down his hat and swore at me, he said he might be damned but he knew they would harm me – my name and my crown would not protect me. He said I was a fool, had his own kidnap of me taught me nothing? Did I not see? Did I not know? The magic of royalty is an illusion that can be shattered by a man without a conscience. He shouted at me: did I think he was the only rapist in Scotland? Would I leave his protection now?

I lost my own temper in return. I swore he was wrong, that even the wickedest Scots lords know their king. I said they would never harm one of royal blood, they might be angry but they were not outright mad – they could not lay a hand on me.

And then he told me. He told me to my face the truth that I had sworn to discover but feared to hear. He told me that he and the rebel lords had made an alliance and sworn a covenant to kill Darnley, who had royal blood just as I do. They had joined together and signed a bond to kill Darnley, who was consort to a queen, father of the prince, and of blood royal himself. Bothwell put his heavy hands on my shoulders and said: 'Marie, listen, your body is not sacred. If it ever was – it is not sacred any more. I have had it. They all know that I had you, and without your consent. They all know you are a mortal woman. You can be raped, you can be seduced. You can be killed. You can be pushed into prison, you can be marched to the scaffold and your head can be laid on the block. I have taught them that. God forgive me, I did not realise that was the lesson they would learn. I thought I would make you safe by making you mine, but all I have done is break your spell. I have shown them what can be done. I have shown them a man can do what he wants with you, with or without your consent.'

I did not even hear him. In that moment he told me the truth as he had never spoken before, and I was not listening. I just said, 'Who? Tell me the names. Tell me the regicides that killed Darnley. They are dead men.'

In answer he reached into his doublet and brought out the very bond that they had sworn, folded carefully and kept for this moment. He said: 'This is for you. It may be the last thing I can do for you. This is for you. It proves your absolute innocence in his murder and our guilt. This is my parting gift to you.'

And then he rode away from me without saying goodbye. Not another word.

The paper was the bond, and on it was the name of almost every great lord at my court, the treacherous, rebellious murderers: including my half-brother James. They had sworn to join together to kill my husband, Darnley.

And – *voilà* – Bothwell's name was at the top. He was as guilty as any of them. That was what he was trying to tell me, on that day when he left me. That they could all bring themselves to kill a sacred royal person, just like me, one of sacred royal blood, like me. Any man without a conscience could do it. Bothwell too.

1569, December, Coventry: George

I cannot sleep in this dirty town. The noise of our soldiers goes on all night like a rumble of discontent, and the raucous squeals of the girls of the town pierce the night air like vixen calling.

I get dressed by candlelight, leaving Bess asleep. As I go quietly from the bedroom I see her stir and her hand goes across the bed to where I usually lie. I pretend not to see that she is stirring. I don't want to talk to Bess. I don't want to talk to anybody.

I am not myself. The thought checks me as I go down the creaking stairs and let myself out of the front door. A sentry in the doorway gives an awkward salute as he sees me and lets me go by. I am not myself. I am not the husband that I was, nor the servant of the queen. I am no longer a Talbot, famed for loyalty and steadiness of purpose. I no longer sit well in my clothes, in my place, in my dignity. I feel blown all about, I feel tumbled over by these great gales of history. I feel like a powerless boy.

If the Queen of Scots triumphs, as she is likely to do today, or tomorrow, I will have to negotiate a peace with her as my new queen. The thought of her as Queen of England, of her cool hands around mine as I kneel before her to offer her my vow of fealty, is so powerful that I stop again, and put my hand against the town wall to steady myself. A passing soldier asks: 'All right, my lord?' and I say: 'Yes. Quite all right. It's nothing.' I can feel my heart hammering in my chest at the thought of being able to declare myself as her man, in her service, in all honour sworn to her till death.

I am dizzy at the thought of it. If she wins the country will be turned upside down again, but the people will quickly change. Half of them want the old ways back, the other half will obey. England will have a young beautiful queen, Cecil will be gone, the world will be quite different. It will be like dawn. Like a warm spring dawn, unseasonal hope, in the middle of winter.

And then I remember. If she comes to the throne it will be by Elizabeth's death or defeat, and Elizabeth is my queen and I am her man. Nothing can change that until her death or surrender; and I have sworn to lay down my life if I can prevent either.

I have walked around the town walls to the south gate and I pause for a moment to listen. I am sure I hear hoofbeats, and now the sentry looks through the spyhole and shouts: 'Who goes there?' and at the shouted reply swings open one half of the wooden gate.

It is a messenger, off his horse in a moment, looking around. 'Lord Shrewsbury?' he says to the sentry.

'I am here,' I say, going slowly forward, like a man in no hurry for bad news.

'Message,' he says in little more than a whisper. 'From my master.'

I don't need to ask his master's name, and he will not tell me his own. This is one of the smartly dressed well-paid young men of Cecil's secret band. I put out my hand for the paper and I wave him to the kitchens which have been set up in the Shambles where already the fires are lit and the bread is baking.

Cecil is brief as always.

Enter into no agreement with the Scots queen as yet. But keep her safe. The Spanish fleet at the Netherlands is armed and ready to sail; but it has not sailed. It is still in port. Be ready to bring her to London as fast as you can travel, as soon as I send word. Cecil

1569, December, Coventry: Mary

'A letter came, while you were sleeping.' Agnes Livingstone wakes me with a gentle touch to my shoulder in the early morning. 'One of the soldiers brought it in.'

My heart leaps. 'Give it to me.'

She hands it over. It is a little scrap of paper from Westmorland, his pinched script blurred with rain. Not even in code. It says to keep my faith and my hopes high, he will not be defeated, he will not forget me. If not this time, then another. I will see Scotland again, I will be free.

I struggle to sit up, and wave to Agnes to move the candle closer so I can see if anything more is written on the paper. I was expecting him to tell me when they would come for me, of his rendezvous with the Spanish. This reads like a prayer, and I was expecting a plan. If it had been a note from Bothwell he would have told me where I should be and at what time; he would have told me what I should do. He would not have told me to keep my hopes high nor that he would not forget me. We never spoke so to each other.

But if it had been Bothwell's note there would have been no mournful tone. Bothwell never thought of me as a tragic princess. He thinks of me as a real woman in danger. He does not worship me as a work of art, a beautiful thing. He serves me as a soldier, he takes me as a hard-hearted man, he rescues me as a vassal serves a monarch in need. I don't think he ever promised me anything he did not attempt.

If it had been Bothwell there would have been no tragic farewell. There would have been a hard-riding party of desperate men, coming by night, armed to kill and certain to win. But Bothwell is lost to me, in prison at Malmö, and I have to trust to the protection of such as Shrewsbury, the determination of Norfolk, and the daring of Westmorland, three uncertain fearful men, God damn them. They are women compared to my Bothwell.

I tell Agnes to hold the candle close and I bring the note up to the flame, hoping that I will see the secret writing of alum or lemon juice turning brown in the heat. Nothing. I scorch my fingers and pull them away. He has sent me nothing but this note of regret, of nostalgia. It is not a plan; it is a lament, and I can't bear sentiment.

I don't know what is happening; this note tells me nothing, it teaches me nothing but dread. I am very afraid.

To comfort myself, without hope of reply, I write to the man who is utterly free of sentiment.

I fear that Westmorland has failed me and the Spanish have not sailed and the Pope's bull dethroning Elizabeth has not been published. I know that you are no saint, worse: I know that you are a murderer. I know you are a criminal fit for the scaffold and you will undoubtedly burn in hell.

So come. I don't know who will save me if you do not. Please come. You are, as before, my only hope.

Marie

1569, December, Coventry: Bess

Hastings comes upon me as I stand on the town walls, looking north, a bitter wind blowing into my face, making my eyes water as if I were weeping, feeling as bleak as the grey day itself. I wish that George was here to put his arm around my waist and make me feel safe once more. But I don't think he has touched me since the day at Wingfield when I told him that I am the spy that Cecil has placed in his household.

I wish to God I had news from Chatsworth and from my mother and my sister. I wish I had a note from Robert Dudley to tell me that my two boys are safe. I wish, more than anything in the world, I wish that I had a note, a line, a single word of encouragement from Cecil.

'News from Lord Hunsdon,' Hastings says briefly. A paper flutters in his hand. 'At last. Thank God we are saved. Dear God, we are saved. Praise God, we are saved.'

'Saved?' I repeat. I glance north again, it is a gesture we all make; one afternoon against the grey horizon I will see the darker grey of six thousand men marching towards us.

He waves his hand northwards. 'No need to look for them any more. They're not there!' he exclaims. 'They're not coming!'

'Not coming?'

'They turned back to meet the Spanish at Hartlepool and the Spanish failed them.'

'Failed them?' It seems all I can do is echo him, like a chorus.

Hastings laughs in his joy and snatches my hands as if he would dance with me. 'Failed them. Failed them, Madam Bess! The damned Spanish! Failures, as you would expect! Failed to meet them and broke their hearts!'

'Broke their hearts?'

'Some have given up and gone home. Westmorland and Northumberland are riding separately. Their army is dispersing.'

'We are safe?'

'We are safe.'

'It is over?'

'Over!'

Relief makes friends of us. He holds out his arms and I hug him as if he were my brother. 'Thank God,' I say quietly. 'And without a battle joined nor a drop of kinsman's blood spilled.'

'Amen,' he says quietly. 'A victory without a battle, a victory without a death. God save the queen.'

'I cannot believe it!'

'It is true. Cecil writes to me himself. We are saved. Against all the odds we are saved. The Protestant queen keeps her throne and the other queen is at our mercy. Her allies delayed, her friends dispersed, her army gone. Thank God, thank the God of our faith.'

'Why have the Spanish not come?'

Hastings shakes his head, still laughing. 'Who knows? Who knows? The main thing is they missed their rendezvous, she is ruined. Her army discouraged, her thousands of men melted away. We have won! Thank God who smiles on us, His own.'

He whirls me round and I laugh out loud.

'My God, there will be profits to be made out of this,' he says, going from piety to prospect in one swift leap.

'Land?'

'Westmorland's estates and Northumberland's lands must be confiscated and broken up,' he says. 'They will be charged with treason, their houses will be awarded to those who have been loyal. Who more loyal than you and me, eh, Countess? Shall you get another grand house from this, d'you think? How would half of Northumberland suit you?'

'It's no more than I've paid out already,' I say.

'Richly rewarded,' he remarks with intense pleasure. 'We will be richly rewarded. God blesses us, doesn't He? Praise Him.'

1569, December, Coventry: George

I should be glad, I should be singing an anthem, but I cannot delight in her defeat. It is clear to me now that my heart has been divided in these hard days, and I cannot seem to be a whole man again. I should be as happy as the others: the relief in Bess is palpable, Hastings has cracked his hard face into a smile. Only I have to pretend to happiness. I don't feel it. God forgive me, I feel such pity for her. I feel her defeat as if it were my own cause that is lost.

I go to her room and tap at the door. Mary Seton opens it and her eyes are red from weeping. I understand at once that the queen knows of her downfall; perhaps she knows more than I do. She has been receiving secret letters even here, even in Coventry, and I cannot blame her for that.

'You know, then,' I say simply. 'It is over.'

She nods. 'She will want to see you,' she says quietly and holds the door wide.

The queen is seated in her chair of state by the fireside, the cloth of estate is shining golden in the candlelight. She is as still as a painting as I come into the room, her profile outlined in gold by the glow from the fire. Her head is slightly bowed, her hands are clasped in her lap. She could be a gilded statue entitled 'Sorrow'.

I step towards her, I don't know what I can say to her nor what hope I can give her. But as I move she turns her face up to me and rises to her feet in one graceful movement. Without words she comes to me, and I open my arms and hold her. That is all I can do: wordlessly hold her, and kiss her trembling head.

1569, December, Coventry: Bess

So, it is over. Good God, I cannot believe that it is over, and I have my goods safe in my wagons and I can go home again. I have a home to go to. I cannot believe it; but it is true. It is over. It is over, and we have won.

I should have predicted this, I would have predicted it if I had kept my wits about me. But I am a vulgar farmer's daughter in very truth, and all I could think about was burying the silver, and not about the will and the wit of the rival armies. Elizabeth's army finally arrived on their sluggish march at Durham and sought an enemy to engage and found they had gone, blown away like mist in the morning. The great army of the North marched to meet the Spanish armada at Hartlepool and found nothing. At once they doubted every plan. They had sworn to restore the old church, so they held their Mass and thought that was done. They were for freeing the Scots queen but they were none of them sure where she had gone and they were counting on the Spanish pikemen and Spanish gold. They did not fancy facing Elizabeth's army without either; and to tell truth they wanted to slip off to their homes and enjoy the peace and prosperity that has come with Elizabeth. They did not want to be the ones to start another war between kin.

Alas for them. The Spanish doubted them and did not want to risk their army and their ships until they were certain of victory.

236

They delayed, and while they hesitated, the Northern army waited at Hartlepool, straining their eyes to see over the white wave tops for the whiter sails, and seeing nothing but the grey skyline and wheeling gulls with the cold spray of the North Sea blowing in their disappointed faces. Then they heard that the Duke of Norfolk had submitted to Elizabeth and written to Westmorland and Northumberland, begging them not to march against their queen. He dropped his head and rode to London though his own tenants hung on his horse's tail and stirrup leathers and begged him to fight. So there was no Spanish fleet, there was no great army led by the Duke of Norfolk; the Northern army had victory at their very finger-tips but they did not know it, and they did not grasp it.

Cecil writes to Hastings to be warned that the country is not at peace, to trust no-one; but Westmorland is fled to the Netherlands and Northumberland has gone over the border to Scotland. Most of the men have gone back to their villages with a great story to tell and memories for the rest of their lives and nothing, in the end, achieved. Let a woman, even a vulgar farmer's daughter, know this: half the time the greater the noise the less the deeds. And grand announcements do not mean great doings.

Let me remember also, in my own defence, that the vulgar farmer's daughter who buries the silver and understands nothing at least has her silver safe when the great campaigns are over. The army is dispersed. The leaders are fled. And I and my fortune are safe. It is over. Praise God, it is over.

We are to take the queen back to Tutbury for safe-keeping before she goes with Hastings to the Tower of London, or wherever he is commanded to take her; and the carters have broken some good Venetian glasses of mine and lost one wagon altogether, which held some hangings and some carpets; but worse than all of this, there is no note from Cecil addressed to us. We are still left in silence, and no word of thanks from our queen for our triumph in snatching the Scots queen from danger. If we had not rushed her away – what then? If she had been captured by the rebels would not the whole of the North have turned out for her? We saved Elizabeth as surely as if we had met and defeated the army of the North, fifty against six thousand. We kidnapped the rebels' figurehead and without her they were nothing.

So why does Elizabeth not write to thank my husband the earl? Why does she not pay the money she owes for the queen's keep? Why does she not promise us Westmorland's estates? Day after day I tally up her debt to us in my accounts book and this pell-mell rush across the country did not come cheaply either. Why does not Cecil write one of his warm short notes to send me his good will?

And when we are back in Tutbury with only a few broken glasses, one lost soup tureen, and a wagon full of hangings gone missing, to show for our terror-struck flight – why can I still not feel safe?

1570, January, Tutbury Castle: George

There is no peace for me. No peace at home, where Bess counts up our losses every day, and brings me the totals on beautifully written pages, as if mere accuracy means they will be settled. As if I can take them to the queen, as if anyone cares that they are ruining us.

No peace in my heart, since Hastings is only waiting for the countryside to be declared safe before he takes the other queen from me, and I can neither speak to her nor plead for her.

No peace in the country where I can trust the loyalty of no-one, the tenants are surly and are clearly planning yet more mischief, and some of them are still missing from their homes, still roaming with rag-tag armies, still promising trouble.

Leonard Dacre, one of the greatest lords of the North, who has been in London all this while, is now returned home, instead of seeing that the battle is over, and lost; even with Elizabeth's great army quartered on his doorstep, he summons his tenants, saying that he needs them to defend the queen's peace. At once, as always, guided by the twin lights of his fear and his genius at making enemies, Cecil advises the queen to arrest Dacre on suspicion of treason; and, forced into his own defence, the lord raises his standard and marches against the queen.

Hastings bangs open the door into my private room as if I am traitor myself. 'Did you know this of Dacre?' he demands.

I shake my head. 'How should I? I thought he was in London.'

'He has attacked Lord Hunsdon's army, and got clean away. He swears he will raise the North.'

I feel a sinking fear for her. 'Not again! Is he coming here?'

'God knows what he is doing.'

'Dacre is a loyal man. He would not fight the queen's army.'

'He has just done so, and is now an outlaw running for his life like the other Northern earls.'

'He is as loyal as –'

'As you?' Hastings insinuates.

I find that my fists are clenched. 'You are a guest in my house,' I remind him, my voice trembling with rage.

He nods. 'Excuse me. These are troubling times. I wish to God I could just take her and leave.'

'It's not safe yet,' I say swiftly. 'Who knows where Dacre's men might be? You can't take her away from this castle until the country-side is safe. You will raise the North again if they kidnap her from you.'

'I know. I'll have to wait for my orders from Cecil.'

'Yes, he will command everything now,' I say, unable to hide my bitterness. 'Thanks to you, he will be without rival. You have made our steward our master.'

Hastings nods, pleased with himself. 'He is without equal,' he says. 'No man has a better vision of what England can be. He alone saw that we had to become a Protestant country, we had to separate ourselves from the others. He saw that we have to impose order on Ireland, we have to subordinate Scotland, and we have to go outward, to the other countries of the world, and make them our own.'

'A bad man to have as an enemy,' I remark.

Hastings cracks a brutal laugh. 'I'll say so. And your friend the other queen will learn it. D'you know how many deaths Elizabeth has ordered?'

'Deaths?'

'Executions. As punishment for the uprising.'

I feel myself grow cold. 'I did not know she had ordered any. Surely there will be trials for treason for the leaders only, and . . .'

He shakes his head. 'No trials. Those who are known to have ridden out against her are to be hanged. Without trial. Without plea. Without question. She says she wants seven hundred men hanged.'

I am stunned into silence. 'That will be a man from every village, from every hamlet,' I say weakly.

'Aye,' he says. 'They won't turn out again, for sure.'

'Seven hundred?'

'Every ward is to have a quota. The queen has ruled that they are to be hanged at the crossroads of each village and the bodies are not to be cut down. They are to stay till they rot.'

'More will die by this punishment than ever died in this uprising. There was no battle, there was no blood shed. They fought with no-one, they dispersed without a shot being fired or a sword drawn. They submitted.'

He laughs once more. 'Then perhaps they will learn not to rise again.'

'All they will learn is that the new rulers of England do not care for them as the old lords did. All they will learn is that if they ask for their faith to be restored, or the common lands left free to be grazed, or their wages not driven down, that they can expect to be treated as an enemy by their own countrymen and faced with death.'

'They are the enemy,' Hastings says bluntly. 'Or had you forgotten? They are the enemy. They are my enemy and Cecil's enemy and the queen's enemy. Are they not yours?'

'Yes,' I say unwillingly. 'I follow the queen, wherever she leads.' And I think to myself: Yes, they have become my enemies now. Cecil has made them my enemies now; though once they were my friends and my countrymen.

1570, January, Tutbury Castle: Mary

My husband, Bothwell – I am returned to Tutbury, I am imprisoned without hope of release. My army has dispersed. I wish I could see you. Marie

I have not summoned my lord Shrewsbury since our return to this miserable place from miserable Coventry, when he comes to me without announcement, and asks me if he may sit with me for a moment. His face is so weary and so sad that for a second I am filled with hope that he has heard of a reverse for his queen.

'Is anything wrong, my lord?'

'No,' he says. 'No. Not for me and for my cause. But I have grave news for you.'

'Norfolk?' I whisper. 'Is he coming for me at last?'

He shakes his head. 'He did not rise with the Northern earls. He went to court. In the end he decided to obey his queen. He has submitted to her will. He is her liegeman and he has thrown himself on her mercy.'

'Oh,' I say. I bite my lip so that I say nothing more. Dear God, what a fool, what a coward, what a turncoat. Damn Norfolk for his stupidity that will be my ruin. Bothwell would never have threatened an uprising and then submitted early. Bothwell would have ridden out to battle. Bothwell never evaded a fight in his life. An apology would have choked him.

'And I am sorry to tell you that Lord Dacre has fled over the border to Scotland.'

'His rising is over?'

'It is all over. The queen's army controls the North, and her executioners are hanging men in every village.'

I nod. 'I am sorry for them.'

'I too,' he says shortly. 'Many of them will have been ordered to follow their liege lord, and done nothing more than their duty. Many of them will have thought they were doing the will of God. They are simple men who didn't understand the changes that have come to this country. They will have to die for not understanding Cecil's policies.'

'And I?' I whisper.

'Hastings will take you as soon as the roads are fit to travel,' he says, his voice very low. 'I cannot prevent him. Only the bad weather is holding him now; as soon as the snow clears he will take you away. I am under suspicion myself. Pray God I am not ordered to London to the Tower on a charge of treason as you are taken from me to Leicester.'

I find I am shaking at the thought of being parted from him. 'Will you not travel with us?'

'I won't be allowed.'

'Who will protect me when I am taken from your care?'

'Hastings will be responsible for your safety.'

I don't even mock this. I just give him a long fearful look.

'He will not harm you.'

'But, my lord, when shall I see you again?'

He gets up from his chair and leans his forehead against the high stone mantelpiece. 'I don't know, Your Grace, my dearest queen. I don't know when we shall meet again.'

'How will I manage?' I can hear how small and weak my voice

is. 'Without you . . . and Lady Bess, of course. How shall I manage without you?'

'Hastings will protect you.'

'He will incarcerate me in his house, or worse.'

'Only if they accuse you of treason. You cannot be charged with any crime if you were only planning to escape. You are only in danger if you encouraged rebellion.' He hesitates. 'It is essential that you remember this. You have to keep the difference clear in your mind, if anyone should ever question you. You cannot be charged with treason unless they can show that you were plotting the death of the queen.' He pauses, he lowers his voice. 'If you wanted nothing more than your freedom then you are innocent of any charge. Remember this if anyone asks you. Always tell them that you were only planning to be free. They cannot touch you if you insist that your only plan was escape.'

I nod. 'I understand, I will be careful what I say.'

'And even more careful of what you write,' he says, very low. 'Cecil is a man for written records. Never put your name to anything he can name as treason. He will be watching your letters. Never receive and never write anything that threatens the safety of the queen.'

I nod. There is a silence.

'But what is the truth?' Shrewsbury asks. 'Now that it is all over, did you plot with the Northern lords?'

I let him see my gleam of amusement. 'Of course I did. What else is there for me to do?'

'It is not a game!' He turns irritably. 'They are in exile, one of them charged with treason, and hundreds of men will die.'

'We might have won,' I say stubbornly. 'It was so close. You know it yourself, you thought we would win. There was a chance. You don't understand me, Chowsbewwy. I have to be free.'

'There was a great chance. I see that. But you lost,' he says heavily. 'And the seven hundred men who must die have lost, and the Northern lords who will be executed or exiled have lost, and the greatest duke in England, fighting for his life and his good name, has lost . . . and I have lost you.'

I rise and stand beside him. If he turned his head now he would see me, looking up at him, my face raised for his kiss.

'I have lost you,' he says again, and he steps away from me, bows and goes to the door. 'And I don't know how I will manage, how I will manage without you.'

1570, January, Tutbury Castle: Bess

You would not take us for a castle of victors. Hastings is surly and anxious to be home. He speaks of riding out and overseeing the hangings himself, as if the lives of our tenants were a matter of sport: another sort of kill when the weather is too snowy for hunting. The queen is pale and sickly, she complains of a pain in her side, in her leg, she has headaches and sits in the darkness of her rooms with the shutters closed against the cold wintry light. She is taking this hard, as well she might.

And my lord is as quiet and grave as if there was a death in the house, he goes quietly about his business almost on tip-toe. We hardly speak to one another except about the work of the house and family matters. I have not heard him laugh, not once, not since we were at Wingfield, when it was summer and we thought the queen would go back to her throne in Scotland within days.

Elizabeth's justice is clamping down on our lands like a hard winter. The news of the planned executions has leaked out and men are disappearing from the villages overnight, leaving nothing but their footsteps in the snow, leaving wives like widows with no-one to break the ice on the water of the well. It will not be the same here, not for a generation. We will be ruined if the strong young men run away and their sons are taken to the gallows in their place.

I don't pretend to know how to run a country, I am a woman of no education, and I care for nothing but keeping my lands in good heart and building my houses, keeping my books, and raising my children to the best estate I can find for them. But I do know how to run a farm, and I do know when a land is ruined, and I have never seen anything more sad and sorry than the estates of the North in this bitter, bitter year of 1570.

1570, January, Tutbury Castle: Mary

Babington, the sweet boy page Anthony Babington, brings me my little dog who insists on running away from my rooms to whore in the stable yard, where there is some kind of rough lady guard-dog to whom he is a most devoted swain. He is a bad dog and whatever the charms of the stable-yard bitch, he should show a little more discrimination. I tell him so, kissing the warm silky head as Babington holds him and says, his face scarlet, 'I washed him for you, and towelled him dry, Your Grace.'

'You are a kind boy,' I say. 'And he is a bad dog. You should have beaten him.'

'He's too small,' he says awkwardly. 'Too small to beat. He is smaller than a kitten.'

'Well, I thank you for bringing him back to me,' I say, straightening up.

Anthony's hand goes inside his doublet, pulls out a packet, tucks it under the dog and hands them both to me.

'Thank you, Babington,' I say loudly. 'I am indebted to you. Make sure you take no risks,' I say softly. 'This is a graver matter than bringing a naughty dog home.'

He flushes red, like the little boy he is. 'I would do anything . . .' he stammers.

'Then do this,' I caution him. 'Take no grave risks for me. Do only what you can do safely.'

'I would lay down my life for you,' he says in a rush. 'When I am grown to be a man I will set you free myself, you can count on me. I will make a plan, we will call it the Babington plot, everyone will know of it, and I will rescue you.'

I put my fingertips on his bright cheek. 'And I thank you for that,' I say quietly. 'But don't forget to take care. Think: I need you free and alive to serve me. I shall look for you when you are a man, Anthony Babington.'

He smiles at that and bows to me, a great sweep of a bow as if I were an empress, and then he dashes off, long-legged like a colt in a springing field. Such a sweet, sweet boy, he makes me think of my own son, little James, and the man that I hope he will be.

I carry the dog and the packet to my privy room where my two-winged altar stands. I lock the door and look at Babington's parcel. I see the unbroken seal of Bishop Lesley of Ross, writing from London.

I am grieved to my heart to tell you that my lords Westmorland and Northumberland and the Duke of Norfolk are all undone. Norfolk has given himself up, and is in the Tower under charge of treason, God help him. Northumberland will join him there as soon as they bring him in. He was raising an army for you in Scotland but your wicked half-brother captured him and sold him to Elizabeth for a ransom. It should have been thirty pieces of silver.

Westmorland has disappeared, and the word is that he has got away to Europe, perhaps France, perhaps the Netherlands, and the Countess of Northumberland with him. She rode at the head of your army, God bless her, and now she pays a heavy price. She will be a widow in exile. Westmorland's own wife has gone to their country house in despair and declares she knows nothing of the plot, and wishes only to live quietly in peace. She hopes that the Tudor lust for revenge will pass over her.

Your betrothed, Norfolk, is almost certain to be charged with treason, God be with him and you. Cecil will revel in this undoing of his enemies and we have to pray that King Philip of Spain or your French cousins exert themselves to ensure your safety while these brave men face accusation and die for you. You are the third point to this plot, and there is no doubt in my mind that any evidence brought against Norfolk will implicate you. Pray God they do not dare to come near you, though all who love you are in danger of their lives.

I am in constant contact with de Spes, the Spanish ambassador, for your protection. But your loyal servant Roberto Ridolfi, who loaned money to Norfolk and brought me the Spanish gold and the promise of support from the Holy Father, has disappeared off the face of the earth. I am deeply afraid for him. I think we will have to assume that he has been arrested. But why would they arrest him and not come for me? I pray that he is safe in hiding, and not captive or dead.

I myself am in fear of my own life and safety. The city is like a darkened courtyard at night, filled with spies, every footstep echoes, every passer-by is watched. No-one trusts his neighbour and everyone listens at every corner. Please God that the queen is merciful and Cecil does not destroy these poor men he has captured. Please God they leave you where you are, with your trustworthy guardian. I shall write again as soon as I can. I wish I had better news to send you and greater courage for myself but I remain, your faithful friend and servant, John Lesley.

I swear I will never fail you, not now, at this time of your need.

Slowly, I throw the pages one by one into the little grate. They blacken and flame and curl and I watch the smoke drift up the chimney, and my hopes with it. The Northern lords are defeated in my cause, Norfolk is in the Tower. His life will be in the hands of his cousin Elizabeth. I have to believe that she will never destroy her own kinsman, her own cousin. Surely she will not kill him for nothing more than the offence of loving me, of wanting me as his wife.

I take the diamond ring he sent to me and press it to my lips. We are betrothed to marry, he has given his word, and I mine, and I will not release him. He has sent me this valuable ring and we are sworn. Besides, if we get through this, if he survives the charge and escapes the scaffold, then our case is as good as ever. Why should she not support him as king consort of Scotland? Why should he not have sons with me? Why should they not inherit the thrones of England and Scotland? He is still my best choice. And, anyway, until Bothwell escapes, I have no other.

I take out the numbered code which is hidden in the Bible at the altar and start to write a letter to my husband, Norfolk. I shall send the letter to Bishop Lesley and hope that he can get it to my beloved. If he will stand by me now, and Elizabeth spares him, we still might get Scotland by agreement when we could not get it by battle.

Dearest Husband, I will pray for you daily, I shall fast once a week until you are freed. I am yours and you are mine and I shall be yours until death. May God forgive those who come against us, for I never will. Be brave, be faithful, and I will too. Perhaps our friends will rise up for us and we will conquer at last. Perhaps we will win our throne in peace. Perhaps you can persuade Elizabeth, as I will try, to let us marry and restore us, her loving cousins, to our throne. I will pray for that. I will pray for the day when you are my husband in deed as well as sworn promise; and I am Queen of Scotland again.

Your wife before God, Mary

I seal it and put it ready for a chance to smuggle it out, and then Agnes comes to prepare me for bed. My nightgown has been badly pressed and I send it away and choose another, then we pray together, then I dismiss her. All the time my thoughts are like a weasel in a cage, twisting this way and that, going round and round. I think of Bothwell, another animal in a cage. I think of him walking the length of his room, turning, and walking back again. I think of him looking out of his barred window at the moonlight on the dark water of Malmö Sound, watching the sky for storms, scratching another mark on the wall to show another night in captivity. This is the eight hundredth and eighty-seventh night we have been apart, more than two and a half years. He will know that tonight, as well as I do. He will need no scratch on the wall to know how long he has been parted from me. He will be a wolf caged, he will be an eagle pinioned. But he will be himself, they will not break him. The wolf is still there, still a wolf despite the cage. The eagle is ready to soar, unchanged. Before I sleep, I write to him, who is sleepless, thinking of me.

Bothwell, my star is in eclipse, my friends arrested or exiled, my spies in hiding, my ambassador afraid. But I don't despair. I don't surrender. I wait for you and I know you will come.

Don't expect a reward. Don't expect anything of me, we know what we are to each other, and it remains our secret.

I wait for you, and I know you will come.

Marie

1570, January, Tutbury Castle: George

The wintry days drag by. Hastings is still here, spending his time riding out to supervise the hangings of men named as rebels and given to the gallows as a pagan sacrifice to some ruthless god. I can hardly bear to leave the grounds of the castle, I cannot meet the accusing eyes of the widows in Tutbury. Inside, of course, there is nothing for me to do.

Bess keeps busy with the reports from her stewards and her endless books of accounts. She is anxious to get back to Chatsworth and summon Henry and her other children. But we cannot leave until Hastings takes the Scots queen, and we all wait upon our orders.

When they come, they are not what we expected. I go to find Bess in the little room she has commandeered for her records, with the letter from Cecil in my hand.

'I am ordered to court,' I say quietly.

She looks up at once from her desk, a ledger still open before her, ink drying on the quill pen, the colour draining from her face until she is as white as the page before her. 'Are you to be charged?'

'Your dear friend Cecil neglects to tell me,' I say bitterly. 'Have you heard from him privately? Do you know? Am I to go straight to the Tower? Is it a charge of treason? Have you provided him with evidence against me?'

Bess blinks at my savage tone and glances towards the door.

She too fears eavesdroppers now. The spies must be spying on the spies. 'He does not write to me any more,' she says. 'I don't know why. Perhaps he does not trust me either.'

'I have to go at once,' I say. 'The messenger who brought this rode with a guard of six men. They are eating in the kitchen and waiting to escort me to London.'

'You are under arrest?' she whispers.

'It is wonderfully unclear. He says I am to ride with an escort at once,' I say wryly. 'Whether this is to ensure my safety or to ensure my arrival they don't specify. Will you pack a saddlebag for me?'

At once she gets to her feet and starts to bustle towards our bedroom. I put my hand on her arm. 'Bess, if I go to the Tower, I will do my best to save your fortune from the wreck of my own. I will send for a lawyer, I will settle my fortune upon you. You will not be the widow of a dead traitor. You will not lose your house.'

She shakes her head and her colour rises. 'I don't think of my fortune now,' she says, her voice very low. 'I think of you. My husband.' Her face is strained with fear.

'You think of me before your house?' I say, trying to make a joke of it. 'Bess, this is love indeed.'

'It is love,' she emphasises. 'It *is*, George.'

'I know,' I say softly. I clear my throat. 'They say I am not allowed to say goodbye to the Queen of Scots. Will you give her my compliments and tell her that I am sorry I cannot say farewell?'

At once I feel her stiffen. 'I will tell her,' she says coldly, and she moves away.

I should not go on; but I have to go on. These may be my last words to the Queen of Scots. 'And will you tell her to take care, and warn her that Hastings will be a rigorous guardian. Warn her against him. And tell her that I am sorry, very sorry.'

Bess turns away. 'I will pack for you,' she says icily. 'But I can't remember all of that. I shall tell her that you are gone, that you may be tried for treason for your kindness to her, that she has cost us our fortune and our reputation and she may cost your life. I don't think I can bring myself to tell her that you are very, very sorry for her. I think the words would make me sick.'

1570, January, Tutbury Castle: Bess

I pack for him, throwing his things into saddlebags in a cold fury, and I send a manservant on a carthorse with food for the first day so he is not reliant on the poor fare of the Derbyshire inns. I see that he has his new hose and a change of linen in his bag, some good soap and a small travelling looking glass so he can shave on the road. I give him a sheet of paper with the latest accounts in case anyone at court chooses to see that we have been ruined by our care of the Scots queen. I curtsey to him and I kiss him goodbye as a good wife should, and all the time the words he wanted me to say to the queen, the tone of his voice when he spoke of her and the warmth in his eyes when he thought of her eat away inside me as if I had worms.

I never knew that I was a passionate woman, a jealous woman. I have been married four times, twice to men who clearly adored me: older men who made me their pet, men who prized me above all others. I have never in my life before seen my husband's gaze go past me to another, and I cannot reconcile myself to it.

We part coldly and in public, for he sets off from the courtyard and, though they were forbidden to see each other privately, the queen arrives as if by accident, as the guard is mounting. Devereux and Hastings come to see the little party off through the gates. But even if we had been quite alone I think it would have been no better.

I could cry out at the thought that this was my darling husband, the man I loved to call 'my husband the earl' only two years ago, and now he may be riding to his death and we part with a dry kiss and a chilly farewell.

I am a simple woman, not a trained clerk or a scholar. But whatever wrong they say Elizabeth has done to England, I can attest that these years of her reign have taken the very heart out of me.

1570, January, Tutbury Castle: Mary

I see from my window that Shrewsbury's big horse is saddled for a journey, and then I see there is an armed guard waiting for him. I throw a shawl over my head and go downstairs, not even changing my shoes.

I see at once that he is going alone. Bess is white and looks sick; Hastings and Devereux are not dressed for travelling, they are clearly to stay here. I am very afraid that he is summoned to court, perhaps even arrested.

'Are you going on a journey, my lord?' I ask, trying to sound easy and unconcerned.

He looks at me as if he would snatch me up before them all. He is desperate for me. He puts his hands behind his back as if to stop himself from reaching for me. 'I am summoned to court,' he says. 'My lord Hastings will keep you safe in my absence. I hope I shall be home soon.'

'I am to stay here until you return?'

'I believe so,' he says.

'And you will return?'

'I hope so.'

I feel my mouth quiver. I so want to cry out that he is not to go, or that I shall go with him. I cannot bear to stay here with his furious wife and with the cold Hastings. To tell the truth I am afraid of them both.

'I shall look for you,' is all I dare say in front of them all. 'And I wish you a safe and pleasant journey.'

The twisted smile that he gives me as he bows over my hand tells me that he does not expect either. I want to whisper to him to come back to me soon, but I don't dare. He presses my hand, it is all that he can do, and then he turns and mounts his horse quickly and in a second – it is all far too quick – there is a scramble of the guards and he is riding out of the gate, and I bite my lip so as not to call out.

I turn, and his wife is looking at me, her face hard. 'I hope he comes home safely to you, Bess,' I say.

'You know that I have lost him, whether he comes home or not,' she says, and she turns her back on me, which she should not do, and walks away, without a curtsey, which is worse.

1570, January, Windsor Castle: George

It is a long cold journey in winter, and poor company on the road. Behind me is an inadequate farewell and ahead of me the certainty of an unkind welcome. Parted from the Queen of Scots, not even knowing if she is safe, I arrive at the court of the Queen of England and know myself in disgrace.

Every morning and every night, my first and last thought is of her, my lost queen, the other queen, and I torture myself with blame. I feel as if I have failed her. Even though I know well enough that I could not have kept her with me, not when Hastings was there with orders to take her, not when Cecil was determined that she should be parted from me. But even so . . . even so.

When I told her I was going to London, her eyes went darker with fear, but in front of Bess, Hastings and Devereux she could say nothing but that she hoped I had a pleasant journey and a safe homecoming.

I thought I might go to her privately, while Bess was packing for me. I thought I might tell her how I feel, now that we are to be parted. I thought for once I might have spoken from the heart; but I could not. I am a man married to another woman, and sworn in fealty to another queen. How could I speak to the Scots queen of love? What have I got to offer her freely? Nothing. Nothing. When I was in the courtyard, ready to say my farewells, they were all there,

Bess and the two lords and every servant and spy in the place, anxious to see how I would leave her and how she would take it. Hopeless to try to say goodbye to her in any way other than a bow, and a formal farewell. What did I think I could say to her, before her ladies-in-waiting, with my own wife looking on? With Hastings trying to hide a smile, and Devereux looking bored and tapping his whip against his boot? I stumbled on wishing her well and she looked at me as if she would beg me to help her. She looked at me in silence, I would swear there were tears in her eyes, but she did not let them fall. She is a queen, she would never show her fears before them. I followed her lead, I was cool and polite. But I hope she knew that my heart was churning for her. She just looked at me as if I might save her, if I wanted to. And God knows I probably looked as I feel – a man who has failed the woman he swore to protect.

I could not even assure her that she will be safe. All the men who have ever spoken in her favour to Queen Elizabeth, who have tried to balance Cecil's counsel of fear and suspicion, are now disgraced. Some of them are in the Tower, some of them are exiled and will never show their faces in England again. Some of them are condemned to death and their wives will be widows and their houses will be sold. And I am summoned to see the queen, ordered to leave my prisoner, ordered to hand her over to her enemy. I have been commanded to court as if they don't trust me to go willingly. I am under shadow of suspicion and I count myself lucky to be ordered to report to the court and not directly to the Tower.

It takes us nearly a week to get there. One of the horses goes lame and we cannot hire another, some of the roads are impassable with snow drifts and we have to go round on the high ground where the winter winds cut like a knife. The snow flurries drive into my face and I am so miserable and so sick of my failure to be faithful and failure to be unfaithful that I would rather be on the long cold journey forever, than arrive at Windsor in the early winter dark to a chilly welcome and poor rooms.

The court is in sombre mood, the cannon still primed and pointing towards London. They are still recovering from their fear that the army of the North would come against them, they are ashamed of their panic. I have to kick my heels for three days while Cecil decides if the queen has time to be bothered by me. I wait in the royal presence chamber, ever alert for a summons, dawdling around with the other men she cannot be troubled to greet. For the first time I am not admitted as soon as my name is mentioned. My stock is low with my fellows too, even with those that I thought were my friends. I eat in the great hall, not in the privy chamber, and I ride out alone, no-one asks for my company. Nobody even stops to chat with me, no-one greets me with pleasure. I feel as if I carry with me a shadow, a stink. I smell of treason. Everyone is afraid and nobody wants to be seen with someone who is shady, who smells of suspicion.

Cecil greets me with his usual equanimity, as if he never in all his life suspected me of plotting against him, as if he never begged me to befriend the Scots queen and save us all, as if he is not now engineering my downfall. He tells me that the queen is much absorbed with the damage of the uprising, and she will see me as soon as she can do so. He tells me that Norfolk, the Scots queen's ambassador Bishop Lesley of Ross and the Spanish ambassador were hand in glove in planning and financing the uprising and that their guilt must be a guarantee of the complicity of the Scots queen.

I say, stiffly, that I think it most unlikely that Norfolk, Queen Elizabeth's own cousin and a man who has benefited from her rise to power, would do anything to bring his kinswoman down. He may have hoped to release his betrothed, but that is a long step from rebelling against his queen and cousin. Cecil asks me do I have any evidence? He would be most glad to see any letters or documents that I have so far failed to divulge. I can't even bring myself to answer him.

I go back to the lodgings they have given me at court. I could stay in our London house but I don't have the heart to open it up for such a short stay, and besides, I find I am reluctant to advertise my presence in the City. My house has always been a proud centre for my family, it is where we come to advertise our greatness, and now I have no sense of greatness: I am ashamed. It is as simple as that. I have been brought so low between the plots of these two queens and their advisors that I don't even want to sleep in my own bed with the carved coronet in the headboard. I don't even want to walk through my own stone pillars with my crest emblazoned on every stone. I would give away all this outward show if I could just be at peace with myself once more. If I could just feel that I know my own self, my own wife and my own queen once more. This uprising has, in the end, overthrown nothing but my peace of mind.

I see Bess's son Henry and my own son Gilbert, but they are awkward in my presence and I suppose they have heard that I am suspected of betraying my wife with the Scots queen. They are both big favourites with Bess, it is natural that they should take her side against me. I dare not defend myself to them and, after asking them both for their health and if they are in debt, I let them go. They are both well, they both owe money, I suppose I should feel glad.

On the third day of waiting, when they judge that I have suffered enough, one of the ladies-in-waiting comes and tells me that the queen will see me in her private rooms after dinner. I find I cannot eat. I sit in my usual place in the great hall at a table with my equals; but they do not speak to me and I keep my head down like a whipped page. As soon as I can, I leave the table, I go and wait in her presence room again. I feel like a child, hoping for a word of kindness; but certain of a beating.

At least I can be assured that I am not to be arrested. I should take a little comfort from that. If she was going to arrest me for treason she would do it in the full council meeting, so that they could all witness my humiliation as a warning to other fools. They would strip me of my titles, they would accuse me of disloyalty and send me away with my cap torn from my head and guards on either side of me. No, this is to be a private shaming. She will accuse me of failing her and though I can point to my deeds and prove that I have never done anything that was not in her interests, or as I was ordered, she can reply by pointing to the leniency of my guardianship of the queen, and to the wide and growing belief that I am half in love with Mary Stuart. And, in truth, if I am accused of loving her, I cannot honestly deny it. I think that I won't deny it. I don't even wish to deny it. A part of me, a mad part of me, longs to proclaim it.

As I thought, it is the gossip of that intimacy that upsets the queen more than anything else. When I am finally admitted into her privy chamber, with her women openly listening, and Cecil at her side, it is the first thing she raises.

'I would have thought that you of all men, Shrewsbury, would not be such a fool for a pretty face,' she spits out, almost as soon as I enter the room.

'I am not,' I say steadily.

'Not a fool? Or does she not have a pretty face?'

If she were a king, these sorts of questions would not be hurled out with such jealous energy. No man can answer such questions to the satisfaction of a woman of nearly forty years whose best looks are long behind her, about her rival: the most beautiful woman in the world and not yet thirty. 'I am sure that I am a fool,' I say quietly. 'But I am not a fool for her.'

'You let her do whatever she wanted.'

'I let her do what I thought was right,' I say wearily. 'I let her ride out, as I was ordered to do, for the benefit to her health. She has grown sick under my care, and I regret it. I let her sit with my wife and sew together for the company. I know for a fact that they never talked of anything but empty chit-chat.'

I see the gleam in her dark eyes at this. She has always prided herself in having the intelligence and education of a man.

'Women's chatter,' I hint dismissively and see her approving nod.

'And she dined with us most nights because she wanted the company. She is accustomed to having many people around her. She is used to a court and now she has no-one.'

'Under her own cloth of state!' she exclaims.

'When you first put her into my keeping you ordered me to treat her as a reigning queen,' I observe as mildly as I can. I must keep my temper, it would be death even to raise my voice. 'I must have written to you and to Cecil a dozen times asking if I could reduce her household.'

'But you never did so! She is served by hundreds!'

'They always come back,' I say. 'I send them away and tell her she must have fewer servants and companions but they never leave. They wait for a few days and then come back.'

'Oh? Do they love her so very much? Is she so beloved? Do her servants adore her, that they serve her for nothing?'

This is another trap. 'Perhaps they have nowhere else to go. Perhaps they are poor servants who cannot find another master. I don't know.'

She nods at that. 'Very well. But why did you let her meet with the Northern lords?'

'Your Grace, they came upon us by accident when we were out riding. I did not think any harm would come of it. They rode with us for a few moments, they did not meet with her in private. I had no idea what they were planning. You saw how I took her away from danger the minute that their army was raised. Every word I had from Cecil I obeyed to the letter. Even he will tell you that. I had her in Coventry within three days. I kept her away from them and I guarded her closely. They did not come for her, we were too quick for them. I kept her safe for you. If they had come for her, we would have been undone; but I took her away too quickly for them.'

She nods. 'And this ridiculous betrothal?'

'Norfolk wrote of it to me, and I passed on his letter to the queen,' I say honestly. 'My wife warned Cecil at once.' I do not say that she did so without telling me. That I would never have read a private letter and copied it. That I am as ashamed of Bess being Cecil's spy as I am of the shadow of suspicion on me. Bess, as Cecil's spy, will save me from the shadow of suspicion. But I am demeaned either way.

'Cecil said nothing of it to me.'

I look the liar straight in the face. His expression is one of urbane interest. He inclines forward as if to hear my reply the better.

'We told him at once,' I repeat smugly. 'I don't know why he would have kept it from you. I would have thought he would tell you.'

Cecil nods as if the point is well made.

'Did she think she would make a king of my cousin?' Elizabeth demands fiercely. 'Did she think he would rule Scotland and rival me here? Did Thomas Howard think to be King Thomas of Scotland?'

'She did not take me into her confidence,' I say, truly enough. 'I only knew that lately she hoped that they would marry with your permission, and that he would help her with the Scots lords. Her greatest wish, as far as I know, has always been only to return to her kingdom. And to rule it well; as your ally.'

I do not say – as you promised she should. I do not say – as we all know you should. I do not say – if only you had listened to your own heart and not to the mean imagination of Cecil, none of this would ever have happened. The queen is not a mistress who cares to be reminded of her broken promises. And I am fighting for my life here.

She gets up from her chair and goes to the window to look out over the road that runs down from the castle. Extra guards are posted at every door and extra sentries at the entrance. This is a court still fearing a siege. 'Men I have trusted all my life have betrayed me this season,' she says bitterly. 'Men that I would have trusted with my life have taken arms against me. Why would they do that? Why would they prefer this French-raised stranger to me? This queen with no reputation? This so-called beauty? This much-married girl?

I have sacrificed my youth, my beauty and my life for this country, and they run after a queen who lives for vanity and lust.'

I hardly dare to speak. 'I think it was more their faith . . .' I say cautiously.

'It is not a matter of faith.' She wheels around on me. 'I would have everyone practise the faith they wish. Of all the monarchs in Europe I am the only one that would have people worship as they wish. I am the only one who has promised and allows freedom. But they make it a matter of loyalty. D'you know who promised them gold if they would come against me? The Pope himself. He had a banker distributing his gold to the rebels. We know all about it. They were paid by a foreign and enemy power. That makes it a matter of loyalty, it is treason to be against me. This is not a matter of faith, it is a matter of who is to be queen. They chose her. They will die for it. Who do you choose?'

She is terrifying in her rage. I drop to my knee. 'As always. I choose you, Your Grace. I have been faithful to you since your coming to the throne, and before you, your sister, and before her, your sainted brother. Before him, your majestic father. Before them, my family has served every crowned King of England back to William the Conqueror. Every King of England can count on a Talbot to stand faithful. You are no different. I am no different. I am yours; heart and soul, as my family always has been to the Kings of England.'

'Then why did you let her write to Ridolfi?' she snaps. It is a trap and she springs it, and Cecil's head droops as he watches his feet, the better to listen to my answer.

'Who? Who is Ridolfi?'

She makes a little gesture with her hand. 'Are you telling me you do not know the name?'

'No,' I say truly. 'I have never heard of such a person. Who is he?'

She dismisses my question. 'It doesn't matter then. Forget the name. Why did you let her write to her ambassador? She plotted a

267

treasonous uprising with him when she was in your care. You must have known that.'

'I swear I did not. Every letter that I found I sent to Cecil. Every servant she suborned I sent away. My own servants I pay double to try to keep them faithful. I pay for extra guards out of my own pocket. We live in the meanest of my castles to keep her close. I watch the servants, I watch her. I never cease. I have to turn over the very cobblestones of the road leading to the castle for hidden letters, I have to rifle through her embroidery silks. I have to rummage through the butcher's cart, and slice into the bread. I have to be a spy myself to search for letters. And all this I do, though it is no work for a Talbot. And all of it I report to Cecil, as if I were one of his paid spies and not a nobleman hosting a queen. I have done everything you might ask of me with honour, and I have done more. I have humbled myself to do more for you. I have done tasks I would never have believed that one of my line could have done. All at Cecil's request. All for you.'

'Then if you do all this, why did you not know when she was plotting under your very roof?'

'She is clever,' I say. 'And every man who sees her wants to serve her.' At once I wish I had bitten back the words. I have to take care. I can see the colour rising under the rouge in the queen's cheeks. 'Misguided men, foolish men, those who forget what you and yours have done for them. They seek to serve her from their own folly.'

'They say she is irresistible,' she remarks idly, encouraging me to agree.

I shake my head. 'I don't find her so,' I say, tasting ugly words in my mouth before I speak them. 'I find her often sickly, often bad-tempered, often moody, not very pleasing, not a woman I could admire.'

For the first time she looks at me with interest, and not with hostility. 'What? You don't find her beautiful?'

I shrug. 'Your Grace, remember I am newly married. I love my wife. You know how smart and neat and steady is Bess. And you are my queen, the most beautiful and gracious queen in the world. I have never looked at another woman but you and my Bess these past three years. The Queen of Scots is a burden you asked me to carry. I do it to the best of my ability. I do it for love and loyalty to you. But there is no question of me enjoying her company.'

For a moment I can almost see her, my exquisite Queen Mary, as if I have summoned her with my lies. She is standing before me, her pale face downturned, the dark eyelashes against her perfect cheek. I can almost hear the third crowing of a cock as I deny my love for her.

'And Bess?'

'Bess does her best,' I say. 'She does her best for love of you. But we would both rather be at court with you, than living at Tutbury with the Scots queen. It is an exile for us both. We have both been unhappy.' I hear the ring of truth in my voice at that, at least. 'We are both very unhappy,' I say honestly. 'I don't think either of us knew how hard this would be.'

'The expense?' she jeers.

'The loneliness,' I say quietly.

She sighs as if she has come to the end of a piece of hard work. 'I was sure all along that you were faithful, whatever anyone said. And my good Bess.'

'We are,' I say. 'We both are.' I begin to think that I may walk out of this room a free man.

'Hastings can take her to his house until we decide what is to be done with her,' she says. 'You can go back to Chatsworth with Bess. You can start your married life all over again. You can be happy again.'

'I thank you,' I say. I bow low and walk backwards towards the door. There is no point in mentioning the huge debt she owes me for the queen's keep. There is no point in telling her that Bess will never forgive me for the loss of this fortune. No point in repining that we cannot start married life all over again, it is spoiled, perhaps forever. I should be glad just to get out of here without an escort of guards to take me to the Tower, where my friends wait for the death sentence.

At the door, I hesitate. 'Has Your Grace decided what is to become of her?'

The queen shoots me a hard suspicious look. 'Why would you care?'

'Bess will ask me,' I say feebly.

'She will be held as a prisoner until we can judge what to do,' she says. 'She cannot be tried for treason, she is no subject of mine, so she cannot be accused of treason. She cannot be returned to Scotland now, clearly she cannot be trusted. She has made my life impossible. She has made her own life impossible. She is a fool. I don't want to keep her imprisoned forever, but I don't see what else I can do with her. It is that or her death, and clearly I cannot kill a fellow queen and my cousin. She is a fool to force this dilemma upon me. She has raised the stakes to victory or death and I can give her neither.'

'She would make a peace agreement with you, I think,' I say cautiously. 'She would hold to a peace treaty with you. She always speaks of you with the deepest of respect. This uprising was none of her making and she was preparing to return to Scotland as an ally of yours.'

'Cecil says she cannot be trusted,' she says shortly. 'And she herself has taught me not to trust her. And hear this, Talbot, I would take Cecil's opinion before that of a man who permitted her to court, betroth herself, and plan a rebellion under his very roof. At the very least you were too trusting with her, Shrewsbury. I pray to God it is nothing worse. She has fooled you, I hope she has not seduced you.'

'I swear she has not,' I say.

She nods, unimpressed. 'You can go back to your wife.'

I bow. 'I am always loyal,' I say from the doorway.

'I know what you do,' she says bluntly. 'I know every single thing that you do, trust Cecil for that. But I don't know what you think any more. I used to know what you all thought, but now you are grown mysterious, all of you. You have all lost your fidelity. I don't know what you all want. You are opaque to me now, where once you were all so clear.'

I find I cannot answer her. I should be a clever courtier and have some words of reassurance or even flattery. But she is right. I no longer understand myself, nor the world that Cecil has made. I have grown mysterious to myself.

'You can go,' she says coldly. 'Everything is different now.'

1570, January, Tutbury Castle: Bess

My husband the earl comes home from London in tight-lipped silence. He is as white as if he was suffering from an attack of the gout again. When I ask him if he is ill he shakes his head in silence. I see then that he has taken a deep wound to his pride. The queen has humiliated him before the other nobility. She could have done nothing worse to this rightly haughty man than imply that he cannot be trusted; and this is what she has done to him.

She might as well have put him on the rack as tell him, before the others, that he no longer has her confidence. This is one of the greatest noblemen in Britain and she treats him as if he is some lying servant that she might dismiss from his place for stealing. This is a queen who uses torture indeed.

I don't know why Elizabeth should turn so cruel, making old friends into enemies. I know she is nervous, prone to deep fears; in the past I have seen her sick for fear. But she has always before been acute in knowing her friends, and she has always counted on them. I cannot think what has thrown her from her usual habit of using flattery and guile, desire and sweetness to keep her court around her, and the men dancing to her tune.

It has to be Cecil who has shaken her from her old, safest course. It has to be Cecil, who halted the proper return of the Scots queen to her throne, and who has imprisoned two lords, declared another a runaway traitor; and now tells the queen that my husband is not to be trusted. Cecil's enmity against the other queen, against all Papists, has grown so powerful that he is prepared to behead half of England to defeat them. If Cecil, my true and faithful friend, now thinks that my husband is against him, if he is prepared to use all his power against us, then we are in danger indeed. This return of my husband from London is nothing more than a temporary relief, and everything that I counted on is unreliable, nothing is safe.

I walk across the courtyard, a shawl over my head for warmth, the cold and damp of Tutbury creeping into my bones through my winter boots. I am summoned to the stables, where the stack of hay has fallen so low that we will not be able to get through the winter. I shall have to get more sent from Chatsworth or buy some in. We cannot afford to buy in fodder, I can barely afford to cart it across the country. But truly, I am thinking of nothing but how I shall manage if my husband is accused. What if Cecil recalls him to London, just as they released and then recalled Thomas Howard? What if Cecil arrests my husband, as he has dared to arrest Thomas Howard? What if he puts him in the Tower along with the others? Who would have thought that Cecil would have grown so great that he could act against the greatest lords of the land? Who would have thought that Cecil would claim that the interests of the country are different from those of her great lords? Who would have thought that Cecil could claim that the interests of the country are the same as his?

Cecil will stand my friend, I am sure of that. We have known each other too long for betrayal now; we have been each other's benchmark for too long in this life. We are cut from the same cloth, Cecil and me. He will not name me as a traitor and send me to the Tower. But what of my husband the earl? Would he throw down George?

I have to say that if Cecil knows for certain that George had joined with his enemies, he would act at once and decisively. I have to say that I would not blame him. All of us children of the Reformation are quick to defend what we have won, quick to take what is not ours. Cecil will not let the old lords of England throw him down for no better reason than he was a steward when they were nobility. Neither would I. We understand that about each other, at least.

My husband the earl does not understand either of us. He cannot be blamed. He is a nobleman, not a self-made man like Cecil. He thinks he needs only to decide something: and it shall be. He is used to raising his head and finding what he wants to his hand. He does not know, as Cecil and I know from our hard childhoods, that if you want something, you have to work at it night and day. Then, when you have it, you have to work night and day to keep it. Right now, Cecil will be working night and day towards the death of the Queen of Scots, the execution of her friends and the breaking of the power of the old lords who support her claim and hate him.

I shall write to Cecil. He understands what houses and land and fortune mean to a woman who was raised with nothing. He might listen kindly to a wife appealing for the safety of her beloved husband. He might listen with generosity to a newly married woman in distress. But if I beg him to save my fortune, he will understand that this is something more important than sentiment, this is business.

1570, January, Tutbury Castle: Mary

Bothwell, I have your letter. I know you would have come if you could. I did look for you at the time; but it is all over for me now. I see that it is over for you. We have been great gamblers and we have lost. I shall pray for you. Marie

It is so bitterly cold, it is so drear, it is so miserable here that I can hardly bear to get out of my bed in the morning. The old ache in my side has returned and some days I cannot eat nor even lie in my bed without crying for pain. It has been raining, sleety freezing rain, for days and all I can see from my poky windows are grey skies and all I can hear is the ceaseless drip, drip, drip from the roof to the mud below.

This castle is so damp that not even the biggest fire in the hearth can dry the patterns of damp from the plaster on the walls, and my furniture is starting to grow green with a cold wet mould. I think that Elizabeth chose this place for me hoping that I will die here. Some days I wish that I could.

The only event which has gone my way at all is the safe return of the Earl of Shrewsbury from Windsor Castle. I expected him to face death too; but Elizabeth has chosen to trust him a little longer. Better than that, she has even decided to leave me in his care. Nobody knows why this should be; but she is a tyrant, she can be whimsical. I suppose that once she had ordered her killings, her excessive fears were sated. She over-reacts, as she always does, and from sending me two extra jailors, banishing my household servants and companions, threatening me with house arrest, and the arrest of my host; now she restores me to the keeping of Shrewsbury, and sends me a kind letter inquiring after my health.

Shrewsbury delivers it; but he is so pale and drawn that I might have thought the letter was his order of execution. He hardly looks at me and I am glad of that, for I am huddled in rugs in my chair at the fireside, twisted around to try to spare the pain in my side, and I have never looked worse.

'I am to stay with you?' He must hear the relief in my voice, for his tired face warms in response.

'Yes. It seems I am forgiven for letting you meet the Northern lords, God save their souls. But I am on parole as your guardian, I am warned not to make mistakes again.'

'I am truly sorry to have brought such trouble to your door.'

He shakes his head. 'Oh, Your Grace, I know that you never meant to bring trouble to me. And I know you would not plot against an ordained queen. You might seek your freedom but you would not threaten her.'

I lower my eyes. When I look up again he is smiling down on me. 'I wish you could be my advisor as well as my guardian,' I say very quietly. 'I would have done better in my life if I could always have been kept by a man such as you.'

There is a silence for a moment. I hear the log shift in the grate and a little flame makes the shadowy room brighter.

'I wish it too,' he says, very low. 'I wish I could see you come to your own again, in safety and health.'

'Will you help me?' My voice is barely louder than the flicker of the fire.

'If I can,' he says. 'If I can without dishonour.'

'And not tell Bess,' I add. 'She is too good a friend of Cecil for my safety.' I think he will hesitate at this, I am asking him to ally with me against his wife. But he rushes forward.

'Bess is his spy,' he says, and I can hear the bitterness in his voice. 'Her friendship with him may have saved my life; but I cannot thank her for it. She is his friend and his ally, his informant. It was her reporting to him that saved me. It is his authority that sanctions everything. Bess is always friends with the most powerful. Now her choice lights on Cecil whereas it used to be me.'

'You don't think that they . . .' I mean to hint at a love affair. But Shrewsbury shakes his head before I need say more.

'It is not infidelity; it is worse than that,' he says sadly. 'It is disloyalty. She sees the world as he sees it: as a battle between the English and everyone else, as a battle between the Protestants and the Papists. The reward for the English Protestants is power and wealth, that is all they care for. They think that God so loves them that He gives them the riches of the world. They think that their wealth is evidence that they are doing the right thing, beloved by God.' He breaks off and looks at me. 'My confessor would have called them pagans,' he says bluntly. 'My mother would have called them heretics.'

'You are of the true faith?' I whisper incredulously.

'No, not now; but like every Protestant in England today, I was raised in the old church, I was baptised as a Papist, I was brought up to say Mass, I acknowledged the authority of the Holy Father. And I cannot forget the teachings of my childhood. My mother lived and died in the old faith. I cannot think another way for the convenience of the queen. I cannot believe, as Bess does, as Cecil does, that we have a private insight into the mind of God. That we don't need priests, or the Pope. That we know everything, all by ourselves, and that the proof of this is the blessing of our own greed.'

'If I am ever Queen of England I will let men worship as they wish,' I promise.

He nods. 'I know you will. I know you would be a most . . . a most gracious queen.'

'You would be my dearest friend and counsellor,' I say with a little smile. 'You would be my advisor. You would be my secretary of state and head of my Privy Council.' I name the titles that Cecil has usurped. I know how deeply Shrewsbury wants them.

'Get well quickly then,' he says, and I can hear the tenderness in his voice. 'You must be well and strong before you can hope for anything. Rest and get well, my . . . Your Grace.'

1570, January, Tutbury Castle: George

News from London which changes everything. What a world we live in now! Everything is turned about again, without warning, almost without reason. My letter comes from Cecil, so there is every reason for me to mistrust it. But this is news that not even he could conceal or invent. It must be the case. The Scots queen's luck has come good once more, and her star has shot into the ascendant. She is a queen whose fortune ebbs and flows like the tides and suddenly she is in full flood. Her half-brother, the usurper of her throne, her greatest enemy, Lord Moray, has been assassinated in Scotland and her country is once again without a leader. This leaves a gaping hole at the very head of the Scots government. They have no-one who can take the throne. They must take her back. There is no other. Amazingly, just when she was thrust down lower than she has ever been in her life, her luck has turned again and she will be queen. They have to take her back. Indeed, they want her back as queen.

Instead of hurrying to Bess with the letter, as I would have done only months ago, I go straight across the courtyard to find the queen. She is better, thank God. I find her dressed in her beautiful black velvet, turning out the contents of some trunks, which have moved from house to house with her and never been unpacked. She is holding a red brocade against her face to look at herself in a looking glass, and laughing. I don't think I have ever seen her more beautiful.

'My lord, will you look at this gown!' she starts, but then she sees my face and the letter in my hand, and she thrusts the gown at her friend Mary Seton and comes quickly towards me.

'George?'

'I am sorry to have to tell you that your half-brother, Lord Moray, is dead,' I say.

'Dead?'

'Assassinated.'

I cannot mistake the joy that lights up her face. I know at once that she has been hoping for this, and I know also my familiar dread of dealing with people who love secrets. Perhaps it was her dark plan and her wicked assassin who struck the blow.

'And my son? My James? Do you have news of my son?'

This is a mother's response. This is a true woman. I should not be so suspicious. 'He is safe,' I assure her. 'He is safe.'

'You are certain? He is safe for sure?'

'They say so.'

'How did you hear?'

'From Cecil. It must be true. He writes to tell me that shortly the queen will be writing to you. She will have some proposals to put before you that she hopes will resolve all. So he says.'

'Ah!' she breathes, taking my hands in her own and stepping close to me. She has grasped in an instant what this means. There is no woman in the world quicker than her. 'Chowsbewwy,' she says. 'This is the start of my new beginning. With Moray dead, the Scots will have to let me back to my throne. There is no-one else who can take power. There is no other heir. Elizabeth will have to support me – now she has no choice, there is no-one else. It is me, or no-one. She will have to support me. I shall go back to Scotland and I shall be queen again.' She chokes on a little laugh. 'After all!' she exults. 'After all we have been through. They will have me back.'

'Please God,' I say.

'You will come with me?' she whispers. 'Come as my advisor?'

'I don't know if I can . . .'

'Come with me as my friend,' she suggests so quietly that I can only hear her by bending my head so that her lips are at my ear and I can feel her breath on my cheek. We are as close as lovers.

'I need a man at my side. One who can command an army, one who will use his fortune to pay my soldiers. A loyal Englishman to deal with Cecil and Elizabeth for me. I need an English nobleman who will keep the Scots lords' confidence, who will reassure the English. I have lost my lord duke. I need you, Chowsbewwy.'

'I cannot leave England . . . I cannot leave the queen . . . or Bess . . .'

'Leave them for me,' she says simply, and the moment she speaks, it does all seem extraordinarily clear. Why not? Why should I not go with this most beautiful woman and keep her safe? Why should I not follow my heart? For a glorious moment I think that I could just go with her – as if Bess, and the queen, and England were of no importance. As if I had no children, no step-children, and no lands, as if I did not have a hundred kinsmen and -women, a thousand dependants, another thousand servants, and more tenants and workers than I can count. As if I could just run away like a boy might run to the girl he loves. For a moment I think that I should do this, that it is my duty to her, the woman I love. I think that a man of honour would go with her, and not stay at home. An honourable man, a noble man, would go and defend her against her enemies.

'Leave them all for me,' she says again. 'Come to Scotland with me and be my friend and advisor.' She pauses. She says the words I want to hear more than any other words in the world. 'Oh, George. Love me.'

1570, February, Tutbury Castle: Bess

This young woman, who it seems I must now endure as a rival for my husband as well as a constant drain on my accounts, has the cursed nine lives of a cat and the luck of the devil. She has survived the guardianship of Hastings, who rode off and left her to us, though he swore to me he would see her dead rather than live to destroy the peace of England, she has survived the rising of the North, though better men and women than her will die on a scaffold for lesser crimes than she has joyfully committed, and she has survived the disgrace of a secret betrothal, though her betrothed is locked up in the Tower and his servants are on the rack. She sits in my great chamber, sewing with the finest silks, as well as I do myself, before a fire blazing with expensive timber, and all the while messages are going from her to her ambassador, from him to William Cecil, from him to the queen, from Scotland to each of them, all to forge an agreement that she will be returned in glory to her throne. After all she has done, all these great powers are determined that she shall regain her throne. Even Cecil says that, in the absence of any other royal Scot, she must be restored.

The logic of this escapes me, as it must do everyone whose handshake is their bond and who drives a straight bargain. Either she is not fit to be queen – as certainly the Scots once thought, and we agreed. Or she is as fit now as she was when we held three inquiries into her conduct. The justice of this escapes me too. There is the Duke of Norfolk, waiting in the Tower for a trial for treason, there is the Earl of Northumberland executed for his part in the Northern Rising, there is the Earl of Westmorland in exile forever, never to see his wife or lands again, all for seeking the restoration of this queen; who is now to be restored. Hundreds died under the charge of treason in January. But now in February, this same treason is policy.

She is a woman accursed, I swear it. No man has ever prospered in marriage to her, no champion has survived the doubtful honour of carrying her colours, no country has been the better for her queenship. She brings unhappiness to every house she enters; and I, for one, can attest to that. Why should a woman like this be forgiven? Why should she get off scot free? Why should such a Jezebel be so damned lucky?

I have worked all my life to earn my place in the world. I have friends who love me and I have acquaintances who trust me. I live my life to a code which I learned as a young woman: my word is my bond, my faith is close to my heart, my queen has my loyalty, my house is everything to me, my children are my future, and I am trustworthy in all these things. In business I am honourable but sharp. If I see an advantage I take it; but I never steal and I never deceive. I will take money from a fool but not from an orphan. These are not the manners of the nobility; but they are the way that I live. How shall I ever respect a woman who lies, defrauds, conspires, seduces and manipulates? How shall I see her as anything other than despicable?

Oh, I cannot resist her charm, I am as foolish as any of these men when she promises to invite me to Holyroodhouse or to Paris; but even when she enchants me I know that she is a bad woman. She is a bad woman through and through.

'My cousin has treated me with great cruelty and injustice,' she remarks after one of my ladies (my own ladies!) has the stupidity to say that we will miss her when she returns to Scotland. 'Great cruelty, but at last she sees what everyone in the world saw two years ago: a queen cannot be thrown down. I must be restored. She has been both stupid and cruel but at last now she sees reason.'

'I would think she has been patient beyond belief,' I mutter irritably into my own sewing.

The Queen of Scots arches her dark eyebrows at dissent. 'Do you mean to say that you believe she has been patient with me?' she inquires.

'Her court has been divided, her own cousin tempted into disloyalty, her lords have plotted against her, she has faced the greatest rebellion of her reign, and her parliament calls for her to execute all those involved in the plot, including you.' I glare balefully at my own ladies, whose loyalty has been suspect ever since this glamorous young queen first appeared among us with her romantic stories of France and her so-called tragic life. 'The queen could have followed the advice of her councillors, and called in the hangman for every one of your friends. But she has not.'

'There is a gibbet at every crossroads,' Queen Mary observes. 'There are not many in the North who would agree with you that Elizabeth's mercy falls like the gentle rain.'

'There is a rebel at the end of each rope,' I say stoutly. 'And the queen could have hanged a dozen more for each one.'

'Yes, indeed, she has lost all her support,' Mary agrees sweetly. 'There was not a town or village in the North that declared for her. They all wanted the true religion, and to see me freed. Even you had to run before the army of the North, Bess. *Tiens!* How you laboured with your wagons and how you fretted for your goods! Even you knew that there was not a town or village in the North that was loyal to Elizabeth. You had to whip up your horses and get through them as quick as you could while your silver cups fell off the back.'

There is a ripple of sycophantic laughter from my ladies at the thought of me, struggling along with my Papist candlesticks. I bend my head over my sewing and grit my teeth.

'I watched you then,' she says more quietly, drawing her chair a little closer to me so that we can speak privately. 'You were afraid in those days, on the road to Coventry.'

'No blame in that,' I say defensively. 'Most people were afraid.'

'But you were not afraid for your own life.'

I shake my head. 'I am no coward.'

'No, you are more than that. You are courageous. You were not afraid for your life, nor for the safety of your husband. You were not afraid of the battle either. But you were terrified of something. What was it?'

'The loss of my house,' I concede.

She cannot believe me. 'What? Your house? With an army at your heels you were thinking of your house?'

I nod. 'Always.'

'A house?' she repeats. 'When we were in danger of our very lives?'

I give a half-embarrassed laugh. 'Your Grace, you would not understand. You have been queen of so many palaces. You would not understand what it is like for me to win a small fortune and try to keep it.'

'You fear for your house before the safety of your husband?'

'I was born the daughter of a newly widowed woman,' I say. I doubt she will understand me even if I could spell it out for her. 'On my father's death she was left with nothing. I mean that: nothing. I was sent to the Brandon family, as companion and upper servant in their household. I saw then that a woman must have a husband and a house for her own safety.'

'You were surely in no danger?'

'I was always in danger of becoming a poor woman,' I explain. 'A poor woman is the lowest thing in the world. A woman alone owns nothing, she cannot house her children, she cannot earn money to put food on the table, she is dependent on the kindness of her family, without their generosity she could starve to death. She could see her children die for lack of money to pay a doctor, she could go hungry for she has no trade nor guild nor skill. Women are banned

285

from learning and from trade. You cannot have a woman blacksmith nor a woman clerk. All a woman can do, without education, without a skill, is to sell herself. I decided, whatever it cost me, I would somehow win property and cling to it.'

'It is your kingdom,' she says suddenly. 'Your house is your own little kingdom.'

'Exactly,' I say. 'And if I lose my house I am thrown on the world without protection.'

'Just like a queen.' She nods. 'A queen has to have a kingdom and without it she has nothing.'

'Yes,' I say.

'And does your fear of losing your house mean that you see your husbands as providers, and nothing more?' she asks inquisitively.

'I loved my husbands because they were good to me and left me their fortunes,' I admit. 'And I love my children because they are my dearest own children and because they are my heirs. They will go on after I am gone. They will be heirs to my fortune, they will own my houses and wealth, please God they will add to them, and they will have titles and honour.'

'Some would say you are a woman without a tender heart,' she remarks. 'A woman with the heart of a man.'

'I am not a woman who relishes the uncertainty of a woman's life,' I reply stoutly. 'I am not a woman who glories in being dependent. I would rather earn my own fortune than curry the favour of a rich man and look to him for my safety.'

As she is about to reply the door opens behind me, and I know that it is my husband the earl. I know it before I even turn to see, because of the way her face lights up at the sight of him. I know that she would shine her smile on any man. She has all the discrimination of a whore. Any man or boy, from my eight-year-old pageboy Babington, to my forty-two-year-old husband: to them all she is equally delightful. She was even gaily flirtatious with Hastings in the days before he left.

I cannot say how galling it is for me to see the intimacy of her smile and the way she extends her hand, and how utterly infuriating to see him bow over her hand and kiss her fingers and hold them for a moment. There is nothing improper in her behaviour or his. Her gesture is queenly and he is a restrained courtier. God knows, there is far grosser flirtation between Queen Elizabeth and any new arrival to her presence chamber, more bawdiness in the court, too. Elizabeth can be downright lustful and her constant hunger for flattery is a by-word amongst her courtiers. In contrast, this queen, though far more desirable, never strays from the most enchanting manners.

But I suppose I am weary to my soul of seeing her in my rooms, seated in my best chair, curtained by her own cloth of state, with my husband bowing to her as if she were an angel descended to illuminate, rather than a most unreliable woman.

'A messenger has come from London,' he says. 'He carries letters for you. I thought you might want to see them at once.'

'Indeed I do.' She rises from her seat and so we all have to jump up too. 'I will read them in my rooms.'

She throws a smile at me. 'I shall see you at dinner, Lady Bess,' she dismisses me. But she turns to my husband. 'Will you come and look at what they say?' she invites him. 'I would appreciate your advice.'

I press my lips together to swallow words that I should not even think. Such as: what help could he possibly give you, since he thinks of nothing and plans ahead not at all? How could he ever choose any course when he does not know what he is worth, what it would cost him, and if he can afford it? Do either of you know that he is sliding into debt every day? What help would you seek from a fool? Unless you are a fool yourself?

My husband the earl, who now I inwardly call: my husband the fool, gives her his arm and they go out together, their heads close. He has forgotten either to greet me or say farewell. I feel the eyes of my ladies on me and I sit down on my stool and snap my fingers at them. 'Carry on,' I say. 'Sheets don't mend themselves, you know.'

1570, February, Tutbury Castle: Mary

Bothwell, you will laugh to read this as I laugh while I write. My half-brother Moray is dead, and they want me back as queen. I will be back on my throne this summer and have you freed the next day. I always was lucky, and the prison that could keep you has not been built. Marie

1570, April, Tutbury Castle: George

I have become, despite myself, Queen Mary's advisor. I have to: it is a duty of honour. She cannot be left without someone to talk to. She has no-one that she can trust. Her betrothed, the Duke of Norfolk, is imprisoned and can only write to her in secret, her ambassador, the bishop John Lesley, has been silent since the arrests, and all the time Cecil is pressing her to come to an agreement about her return to Scotland, on terms that even I can see are relentless.

'You are too hasty,' I scold her. 'You are too eager. You cannot agree to these terms.'

They want to impose on her Cecil's old Treaty of Edinburgh, which makes Scotland a subject nation, subservient to England, incapable of making its own alliances, banned from having a foreign policy at all. They want her to agree to make Scotland a Protestant country, where she may worship only in private, almost in hiding. They even want her to surrender her claim to the English throne, they demand that she disinherit herself. And like a queen in very truth she is prepared to accept this humiliation, this martyrdom, to win again her throne of Scotland and return to her son.

'These are impossible demands, they are wicked demands,' I tell her. 'Your own mother refused them for you, as she was dying. Cecil would have forced them on her, he should be ashamed to force them on you.'

'I have to agree,' she says. 'I know they are onerous. But I will agree.'

'You should not.'

'I will, because once I am there . . .' She shrugs, a gesture so utterly French that if I saw only the movement of her shoulders among a crowd of other women, I would know her at once. 'Once I am on my throne again I can do as I please.'

'You are joking. You cannot mean to sign an agreement and then renege?' I am genuinely shocked.

'No, *non, jamais*, no. Of course not. But who would blame me if I did? You yourself say these terms are wickedly unfair.'

'If they thought you would go back on your word, then they would never agree with you at all,' I point out. 'They would know that you could not be trusted. And you would have made your own word, the word of a queen, utterly valueless.'

She flicks a smile at me like a naughty child. 'I have nothing to put on the table,' she says simply. 'I have nothing to barter but my word. I have to sell it to them.'

'They will make you keep your word,' I warn her.

'Ah, bah!' she laughs. 'How can they? Once I am on my throne again?'

'Because of this last condition,' I say, pointing it out to her. The document is written in English, I fear that she has not fully understood it.

'They say that my son James shall be raised a Protestant?' she queries. 'It is unfortunate; but he will be with me, I can instruct him in private. He will learn to think one thing and say another as all clever kings and queens must do. We are not as normal people, my Chowsbewwy. We learn very young that we have to act a part. Even my little boy James will have to learn to deceive. We are all liars under our crowns.'

'He will be raised as a Protestant in England.' I point to the words. '*En Angleterre.*' Usually she laughs at my attempts to speak her language; but this time, as she understands me, the colour and the smile drain from her face.

'They think they can take my son from me?' she whispers. 'My boy? My little boy? They would make me choose between my throne and my child?'

I nod.

'Elizabeth would take him from me?'

I say nothing.

'Where would he live?' she demands. 'Who would care for him?'

Of course the document, drawn by Cecil under instructions from Elizabeth, does not trouble itself with this most natural question from a young mother. 'They don't say,' I tell her. 'But perhaps the queen would make a nursery for him at Hatfield Palace. That's the usual . . .'

'She hates me,' the Scots queen says flatly. 'She has taken my pearls and now she would take my son.'

'Your pearls?'

She makes a little dismissive gesture with her hand. 'Most valuable. I had a great string of black pearls and my half-brother sold them to Elizabeth the moment he forced me from the throne. She bought them. She outbid my mother-in-law. See what vultures I have around me? My own mother-in-law bid for my looted pearls while I was held in prison; but she was outbid by my cousin. Elizabeth wrote to me of her sorrow at the injustice that was being done to me and yet she bought my pearls. Now she would take my son? My own son?'

'I am sure you could see him . . .'

'She has no child of her own, she can have no child. She will soon be beyond childbearing years, if she is not dried up already. And so she would steal my son from his cradle. She would take my son and heir and make him her own. She would rob me of my heart, of all that makes my life worth living!'

'You have to think of it from her point of view. She would have

291

him as a hostage. She would hold him to make sure that you kept to this treaty. That is why, when you agree to it, you must realise that you will have to keep to it.'

She hears nothing of this. 'A hostage? Will she keep him in the Tower like the poor little princes? Will he never come out at all? Will he disappear as they did? Does she mean to kill him?'

Her voice breaks on the thought of it and I cannot bear her distress. I rise from my seat at the table and I go to look out of the window. In our rooms across the courtyard I can see Bess walking down the gallery, accounts books tucked under her arm. She feels a long way away from me now, her worries about rents and our costs are so trivial compared to the unfolding tragedy of the Scots queen. Bess has always been prosaic; but now I have the very heart of poetry beating wildly in my own house.

I turn back to the queen. She is sitting quite still with her hand shading her eyes. 'Forgive me,' she says. 'Forgive my emotion. You must wish you had a cold-hearted queen to deal with, like your own. And forgive my stupidity. I had not read it properly. I thought that they meant only to supervise James's education, to make him a good heir to the English throne. I did not realise that they want to take him from me altogether. I thought we were talking about a treaty – not about my destruction. Not about the theft of my child. Not about his kidnap.'

I feel too big and too awkward for the room. Gently, I stand behind her, and put my hand on her shoulder and with a sigh she leans back so that her head rests against my body. That little gesture, and the warmth of her head on my belly, fill me with tenderness, and an inevitable rising desire. I have to step away from her, my heart pounding.

'I was parted from my mother when I was just a little girl,' she says sadly. 'I know what it is to be homesick, and to miss one's mother. I wouldn't do that to my son, not for the throne of France, let alone Scotland.'

'He would be well cared for.'

'I was dearly loved in France,' she says. 'And my dearest papa, King Henri, loved me better than his own daughters. He could not have been more kind and tender to me. But I longed for my mother, and I could never go to her. She visited me once, just once, and it was as if I became whole again, as if something was restored that had long been missing; my heart perhaps. Then she had to go back to Scotland to defend my throne for me, and your Cecil, your great William Cecil, saw her weakness and her loneliness and her illness and he forced the treaty on her that he is now forcing on me. She died trying to defend my throne against Elizabeth and Cecil. Now I have to fight the same battle. And this time they want to take my child and break my heart. Elizabeth and Cecil together destroyed my mother and now they want to destroy me, and destroy my son.'

'Perhaps we can negotiate,' I say, then I correct myself. 'Perhaps you can negotiate. You could insist that the prince stays in Scotland, perhaps with an English guard and tutor?'

'I have to have him with me,' she says simply. 'He is my son, my little boy. He has to be with his mother. Not even Elizabeth can be so hard-hearted as to steal my right to the throne and then my own son from me.'

1570, May, Tutbury Castle: Mary

I try to stay courageous but some days I am exhausted by sadness. I miss my child and I am so fearful as to who is caring for him, and educating him, and watching over him. I trust the Earl of Mar, his guardian, to guide him and educate him, and his grandfather the Earl of Lennox should keep him safe if only for the sake of Darnley, his dead son, my boy's father. But Lennox is a careless man, dirty and rough, with no affection for me, and he blames me for the death of his son. What would he know about caring for a little boy? What would he know about the tenderness of a little boy's heart?

The warmer weather is coming and it is light at six o'clock in the morning and I am woken every dawn by birdsong. This is my third spring in England, my third spring! I can hardly believe I have been here for so long. Elizabeth promises I shall be returned to Scotland by the summer, and she has ordered Shrewsbury to let me ride out freely and receive visitors. I am to be treated as a queen and not as a common criminal. My spirits always used to lift at this time of the year, I was raised so long in France that I am accustomed to the warmth of those long beautiful summers. But this year I do not smile to see the primroses in the hedge, the birds flying, carrying straw and twigs for their nests. This year I have lost my optimism. I have lost my joy. The coldness and the hardness that my cousin Elizabeth embodies in her spinster rule seem to have drained my world of light and warmth. I cannot believe that a woman could be so cruel to me, and that I have to endure it. I cannot believe that she could be so unloving, so unmoved by my appeals to her. I have been the beloved of everyone who knows me, I cannot accept that she should remain so indifferent. I cannot understand unkindness. I am a fool, I know. But I cannot understand her hardness of heart.

I am writing at my desk when there is a tap at the door and Mary Seton comes flying into the room, her hood half-pushed off her head. 'Your Grace, you will never believe . . .'

'What?'

'Elizabeth has been excommunicated! The Holy Father himself has published a Papal Bull against her. He says she is a usurper with no right to the throne, and that no Christian need obey her. He says it is a holy duty to pull her down from her borrowed power. He is calling upon every Christian in the world to defy her. He is calling on every Roman Catholic to rebel! He is calling on every Roman Catholic power to invade! He is calling all Christians to destroy her. This is like a crusade!'

I can hardly breathe. 'At last,' I say. 'I was promised this. The Northern lords told me that Roberto Ridolfi had the Holy Father's word that this would be done. But when I heard nothing I thought it had all gone wrong. I even doubted Ridolfi.'

'No! He was true to you. The Bull was published last year,' Mary whispers, out of breath. 'In time for the uprising. But the Bull has only just arrived. Oh! If only it had come before! If it had come during the uprising! All of England would have turned against Elizabeth.'

'It's not too late now,' I say rapidly. 'Everyone of the true faith will know it is their duty to throw her down and that the Holy Father has named me as Queen of England. And besides, it will force my family in France, and Philip of Spain, to act. It is not only justice but now it is their holy duty to put me on my throne of Scotland, and England too.'

Mary's eyes are shining. 'I will see you wear your crown again,' she declares.

'You will see me wear the crown of England,' I promise her. 'This does not just mean my freedom, it means that the Pope recognises me as the true heir of England. If the Holy Father says that I am Queen of England, who can stand against me? And all the Papists in the world are bound by their faith to support me. Mary, I shall be Queen of England and Scotland. And I shall crown my son as Prince of Wales.'

'Thank God that the Holy Father has ruled in your favour!'

'Thank God for Ridolfi, who put my case to him,' I say quietly. 'He is a great friend to me. God keep him, wherever he is. And when I come to my own again he shall be among the men who can claim their reward for serving me.'

1570, May, Chatsworth: Bess

I hear them ringing the bells in the church at Chatsworth as I am ordering the linen for the Scots queen's bed. She is to come here within a few days, and my heart rushes in sudden terror. It can't be an uprising again. Pray God it is not the landing of the Spanish armada. I send one of the pageboys racing to discover what is amiss now. He comes back and finds me in the laundry room, a list of linen in my shaking hand, and tells me that the Queen Mary Stuart has been declared the true Queen of England and the Pope has called on all those of the old faith to destroy the bastard Elizabeth and put the true queen, Mary, in her place, and there is an uprising for her in Norwich and they say the whole of the east of England will turn out for the true queen and the true faith.

I am so shocked for a moment that I pretend I want some fresh air, and go out to the gallery and sink down on a bench among all the painted saints. I can hardly believe that this nightmare goes on, goes on and on, and we never achieve victory, and we never achieve peace. I look at my painted saints, as if they could tell me the answer to the purgatory of the times that we endure. God knows we are a small country and there are very few of us with a vision as to how the country should be. Now the old scarlet whore of Rome has called down on us the rage of the rest of Christendom: Philip of Spain, Madame Serpent in France – they will think that battle against us is a crusade, a holy war. They will think themselves commanded by God to destroy us. They will come against us, united they will master us.

'We are so few,' I whisper to myself. It is true. We are a little island, with enemies for neighbours in Ireland and France and the Spanish Netherlands just half a day's sail away. We are so few who really understand what destiny God has given us. We are so few who are prepared to serve as His saints to bring the purity of His true church to England, His chosen country. We are surrounded by enemies, we are tempted by Satan, we are besieged by the superstitions and lies of the old faith; they will destroy us if they can.

I tell the boy to run and order the vicar to stop them ringing the bells. Tell him it is my command. If they are pealing to sound a warning we none of us need to be reminded that we are on the edge of disaster. An old woman on the throne, no heir in the nursery, a faith under constant threat, a nation in the making which could be wiped out in a moment. On the other hand, if they are ringing the peal, as they did at Durham and York, at Ripon and even in the end at Barnard Castle, to say that the old faith will triumph, then they can silence the bells and go to hell while my word carries any weight in Derbyshire.

I am a Protestant. I will live and die a Protestant. My enemies will think that is because it has been a religion to profit me, cynics will point to my gold candlesticks and my lead mines and my coal mines and my stone quarries, and even these stolen painted saints in my gallery. But what the cynics don't understand is that these are the goods that God has given to me as a reward for the purity of my faith. I am a Protestant through and through. I don't acknowledge this Stuart Papist queen, I deny the wisdom of the priest of Rome, I deny the sanctity of the bread and wine. It is bread, it is wine. It is not Body and Blood of Christ. The Virgin Mary was a woman, like any of us, Jesus was a carpenter, a working man proud of his tables, as I am a working woman proud of my houses and lands. The kingdom of the saints will come when the world has earned purity, not when enough money has been poured into the collecting plate of the church. I believe in God – not in a wizard doled out at a price by the priests of the old church. I believe in the Bible, which I can read for myself in English. And more than anything else I believe in me, in my view of the world. I believe in my responsibility for my own destiny, guilt for my own sins, merit for my own good deeds, determination of my own life, and in my accounts books which tell me how well or ill I am doing. I don't believe in miracles, I believe in hard work. And I don't believe that Queen Mary is now Queen of England just because some old fool in Rome chooses to say so.

1570, May, on the road to Chatsworth: Mary

We are at our happiest, eccentric pair that we are, the greatest nobleman in England and the rightful queen, when we are on the road travelling together. I learned that he loved me when we were riding by night, on the way to Coventry. In the heart of danger, he thought only of me. But I had learned to value him long before then, on our first journey: when we were riding from Bolton Castle to Tutbury and I hoped that he would escort me back to Scotland within days. I learned, on those journeys, to enjoy a pleasure in his company that I have never felt with any other man. I do not desire him; the idea is laughable – no woman who has known Bothwell could settle for a safe man, an honourable man, or even a quiet man. But I feel that I can rest on him, I can trust him to keep me safe, I can be myself with him. He reminds me of my father-in-law Henri II, the King of France, who always cared for me so well, who treasured me as his little pearl, who always made sure that I was well served and honoured as the Queen of Scotland, the next Queen of France, and Queen of England. Shrewsbury's quiet constant care reminds me of being a treasured girl, the favourite of the wealthiest and most powerful man in Europe. With him, I feel like a young beauty again, the girl that I was: unspoiled, untroubled, filled with absolute confidence that everything would always go well for me, that everyone would always love me, that I would inherit my thrones one after another and become the most powerful queen in the whole world by right and without contradiction.

We ride side by side and he talks to me of the countryside and points out the features of the landscape. He is knowledgeable about birds and wildlife, not just the game, but the songbirds and the little birds of the hedgerows. He cares for the land, he loves it like a countryman, and can tell me the names of the flowers and laughs when I try to say their impossible names like 'ladies' bedstraw' and 'stitchwort'.

I am allowed to ride ahead of the guards these days. I am a queen with attendants once more, not a prisoner with jailors, and for once we ride in fresh air, untroubled by companions, and not surrounded by a crowd in a storm of dust. At every village, as ever, the common people come out to see me, and sometimes they gather around the gibbet at the crossroads where the body of a man, dead for my cause, swings in chains. Shrewsbury would take me quickly past these gruesome puppets but I pull up my horse and let the people see me cross myself, and bow my head to say a prayer for the soul of a good man who died for the true faith and the true queen.

At almost every village I see the quick half-hidden movement as the good men and women cross themselves too, and their lips whisper the words of a Hail Mary. These are my people, I am their queen. We have been defeated by Elizabeth and her traitorous army once; but we will not be defeated again. And we will come again. We will come under the flag of the Pope. We will be unbeatable. She can be very sure of that.

'We will go from Chatsworth on to Wingfield,' Shrewsbury says to me as we stop to dine on the side of a riverbank, a simple meal of roast meats, breads and cheeses. 'Chatsworth is so much Bess's house, she begrudges every penny she spends there if it is not on her eternal rebuilding and re-fashioning. I would rather have you under my own roof, and Wingfield Manor has been in my family for generations. And from Wingfield, if you can agree with the queen, I am to escort you to Edinburgh.'

'I will agree,' I say. 'How can I refuse her? She has me as her prisoner, there is nothing worse that she can do against me. We are both entrapped. The only way I can be free, and that she can be free of me, is for us to agree. I have nothing to bargain against her. I am forced to agree.'

'Even to her holding your son?' he asks.

I turn to him. 'I have been thinking of that, and there is a solution I would consider, if you would help me?'

'Anything,' he says at once. 'You know I would do anything for you.'

I savour the words for a moment then I go to the main question. 'Would you serve as his guardian? If Prince James were to live with you, in your house, would you care for him, as you have done for me?'

He is astounded. 'I?'

'I would trust you,' I say simply. 'And I would trust no-one else. You would guard him for me, wouldn't you? You would care for my boy? You would not let them corrupt him? You would not let them turn him against me? You would keep him safe?'

He slips from his stool and kneels on the carpet that they have laid on the riverbank under my chair. 'I would lay down my life to keep him safe,' he says. 'I would devote my life to him.'

I give him my hand. This is the last card in the pack that I have to play to get myself back to Scotland and ensure at the same time that my son is safe. 'Can you persuade Cecil that James shall come to you?' I ask. 'Propose it to him as your own idea?'

He is so in love with me that he does not stop to think that he should ask his wife first, nor that he should beware when an enemy of his country asks for a special favour.

'Yes,' he says. 'Why would he not agree? He wants a settlement, we all do. And I would be honoured to care for your son. It would be as if . . . to guard him for you would be like . . .' He cannot say it. I know he is thinking that to raise my son would be as if we had married and had a child together. I cannot encourage him to speak like this, I have to keep him carefully placed: in his marriage, in the esteem of his peers, in the trust of his queen, in his position in England. He is of no use to me if they think of him as disloyal. If they think too badly of him they will take me from him, and not trust him with my son.

'Don't say it,' I whisper passionately, and it silences him at once. 'Some things must never be said between us. It is a matter of honour.'

This checks him, as I knew it would. 'It is a matter of honour to us both,' I say to make sure. 'I cannot bear that men should accuse you of taking advantage of your position as my guardian. Just think how dreadful it would be if people should say that you had me at your mercy, and dishonoured me in your thoughts.'

He almost chokes. 'I would never! I am not like that!'

'I know. But it is what people would say. People have said terrible things about me, for all of my life. They might accuse me of trying to seduce you, so that I could escape.'

'No-one could think such a thing!'

'You know that is what they think already. There is nothing that Elizabeth's spies will not say against me. They say the worst things about me. They would not understand what I feel . . . for you.'

'I would do anything to protect you from slander,' he declares.

'Then do this,' I say. 'Persuade Cecil that you can guard my son James and I can get back to Scotland. Once I am back on my throne I will be safe from scandal and from Cecil's spies alike. You can save me. And you can keep James safe. Keep him safe for love of me. It can be our secret. It can be the secret of our two hidden hearts.'

'I will,' he says simply. 'Trust me, I will.'

1570, June, Chatsworth: George

It is agreed, thank God, it is agreed and will shortly be sealed and signed. The queen is to be returned to Scotland and I shall be guardian to her son. Nothing less than this duty would console me for the loss of her. But to stand as father to her boy will be everything. I shall see her beauty in him, and I will raise him as she would wish. My love for her will be invested in him, she will see a good young man will come from my care. She will be proud of him, he will be a boy of my making, and I will forge him into a good prince for her. I will not fail her in this. She trusts me and she will find me trustworthy. And it will be such a joy to have a little boy in the house, a boy whose mother is a woman of such beauty, a boy that I can love for his mother's and for his own sake too.

It seems that our troubles may be over. The riots in Norwich have been put down with rapid brutality and those Catholics who have heard of the Papal Bull against Elizabeth are not hurrying forward to put their heads into a noose. Norfolk is to be released from the Tower. Cecil himself argued that though his offence is great, his crimes do not amount to treason. He is not to face trial, nor the death sentence. I am more relieved by this than I show to Bess when she tells me.

'Are you not pleased?' she asks, puzzled.

'I am,' I say quietly.

'I thought you would have been delighted. If they do not accuse Norfolk then there can be no shadow over you, who did so much less.'

'It is not that which pleases me,' I say. I am irritated by her assumption that all I think of is my own safety. But I am always irritated by her these days. She cannot say a word that does not grate on me. Even when I know that this is unfair, I find that the way that she walks into a room sets my teeth on edge. She has a way of putting down her feet, heavily like a woman going to market, a way of carrying her eternal accounts books, a way of being always so busy, so hard-working, so efficient. She is more like a housekeeper than a countess. There is no grace about her. She utterly lacks any elegance.

I know, I know, I am wickedly unfair to blame Bess for lacking the charm of a woman raised in a court and born to greatness. I should remember that she is the woman I married for choice, and she has good looks, good health and good spirits. It is unfair to complain that she does not have the looks of one of the most beautiful women in the world or the manners of the queen of one of the finest courts in Europe. But we have such a being in our house, such a paragon smiles at me each morning, how can I help but adore her?

'So what pleases you?' Bess asks encouragingly. 'This is good news, I think. I expected you would be happy.'

'What pleases me is that I shall be spared his trial.'

'His trial?'

'I am still Lord High Steward of England,' I remind her, a touch sourly. 'Whatever your friend Cecil thinks of me, and would do against me if he could. I am still Lord High Steward and if a peer of the realm is to be tried for treason then I would be the judge who would sit on his case.'

'I hadn't thought,' she said.

'No. But if your good friend Cecil had brought my true friend Norfolk to trial for his life, it would have been me who would have been forced to sit with the axe before me, and bring in a verdict. I would have had to tell Norfolk, a man I have known from his boyhood, that I found him guilty, when I knew he was innocent, and that he was to be hanged and disembowelled while still alive and cut into pieces. D'you not think I have been dreading this?'

She blinks. 'I didn't realise.'

'No,' I say. 'But when Cecil attacks the old lords, this is the consequence. We are all torn by his ambition. Men who have loved each other all their lives are thrown one against the other. Only you and Cecil don't see this, for you don't understand that the old lords are as a family of brothers. Newcomers cannot know this. You look for conspiracies, you don't understand brotherhood.'

Bess does not even defend herself. 'If Norfolk had not engaged to marry the Queen of Scots in secret then he would not have been in trouble,' she says stoutly. 'It is nothing to do with Cecil's ambitions. It is all Norfolk's own fault. His own ambitions. Perhaps now that he has withdrawn, we can all be at peace again.'

'What d'you mean, withdrawn?' I ask.

She has to hide a smile. 'It seems your great friend is not very gallant to his lady-love. Not very chivalrous at all. Not only has he given her up, and broken off the betrothal, apparently he also suggested that she should take his place in the Tower, as surety for his good behaviour. It seems that there is one man at least who does not long to die for love of her. One who would happily see her in the Tower for treason. One man who is quite prepared to walk away from her and make a better life for himself without her at all.'

1570, June, Chatsworth: Bess

There is no peace for a woman who tries to run a proper household with a spendthrift guest and a husband who is a fool. The greater the queen's freedom, the greater the expense for us. Now I am told that she can entertain visitors; and every sensation-seeking gawper in the country comes to watch her dine, and help themselves to some dinner as they do. Her wine bill alone is more in a month than mine is in a year. I cannot begin to balance the accounts, they are beyond me. For the first time in my life I look at my books without pleasure but with absolute despair. The pile of bills grows all the time and she brings in no income at all.

Out goes the money on the queen: her luxuries, her servants, her horses, her pets, her messengers, her guards, the silk for her embroidery, the damask for her gowns, the linen for her bed, the herbs, the oils, the perfumes for her dressing table. The coal for her fire, the best wax candles which she burns from midday till two in the morning. She has them burning while she is asleep, lighting empty rooms. She has silken carpets for her table – she even puts my best Turkey carpets on the floor. She has to have special goods for her kitchen, sugars and spices all have to come from London, her special soap for her laundry, the special starch for her linen, the special shoes for her horses. Wine for the table, wine for her servants, and – unbelievably – best white wine for her to wash her face. My accounts for keeping the Scots queen are a joke, they have only one side: expenditure. On the income side of the page there is nothing. Not even the fifty-two pounds a week we were promised for her. Nothing. There are no pages of receipts, since there are no receipts. I begin to think there never will be, and we will go on like this until we are utterly ruined.

And I can now say with certainty we will be ruined. No house in the land could keep a queen with limitless numbers of servants, with numberless friends and hangers-on. To keep a queen you need the income of a kingdom and the right to set a tax; and that we do not have. We were once a wealthy couple, wealthy in land, rents, mines and shipping. But all of these businesses have a balance of money coming in slowly and quickly going out. It was a balance which I managed superbly well. The Scots queen has thrown this balance all wrong. Quickly, amazingly quickly, we are becoming poor.

I shall have to sell land on a great scale. The little borrowings and sales I have bodged together since she arrived will no longer suffice. I shall have to raise mortgages. I shall have to enclose and put up the rents for tenants who are already behind in their payments, having wasted the winter in chasing around with the Northern army, which was her fault too. I shall have to levy extra payments on houses that are still missing men – hanged or run away for Mary Stuart. She will force me to be a harsh landlord and I shall get the blame for it. I shall have to take common land away from good villages and enclose it for crops. I shall have to drive people from their fields and make their gardens into sheep runs. I shall wring cash from the land as if it were a damp rag. This is not how to run a good estate. This is not how to be a good landlord. I shall become greedy in my need for money, and they will hate me and blame me for it and say I am a hard landlord and a harsh money-grabbing woman.

And she is not just expensive. She is a danger. One of my servants, John Hall, comes to me, his eyes down but his palm eager. 'I thought you should know, my lady, I thought you would want to be informed.'

Will I ever again hear a muttered preamble like this and think it is going to be nothing more than a broken vase? Will I ever get back to the time when I feel only irritation? Now, and forever, I am going to feel my heart pound with dread, waiting for the news that she has escaped, or that she has sent out a letter, or received a guest who will ruin us.

'What is it?' I ask sharply.

'I thought you would be glad to know I was loyal.'

I itch to slap him. 'And you will be rewarded,' I say, though every bribe is just another cost. 'What is it?'

'It is the queen,' he says, as if I could not have guessed. 'There is a plot to release her. The gentlemen offered me a gold sovereign to bring her to the high moor and they would ride away with her.'

'And she agreed?' I ask.

'I haven't asked her yet,' he says. 'I thought I should come straight to you. I am loyal to you, my lady, whatever bribe I am offered.'

'You shall have two guineas for this,' I promise. 'So who are the gentlemen? What are their names?'

'Sir Thomas Gerard is the man,' he says. 'But it was his friend met me at the inn, a gentleman called Rolleston. But whether there is a greater man behind them, I don't know. I know another man who would be glad of the information.'

I wager you do, I think miserably; there are more spies than shepherds in England these days. The disloyalty of the people has become so intense that everyone keeps a servant to watch every other. 'Perhaps you could sell to another buyer. But you are my man, and serve me only. Go back to this Rolleston and tell him that you need to know who is in the plot. Say that it isn't safe to go ahead without knowing who is engaged. Tell him you will do it, and ask him for a keepsake to show to the queen. Then come back to me.'

'Lead them on?'

I nod.

'And you will entrap them?'

'If we have to. Perhaps they mean nothing. Perhaps it will all come to nothing.'

1570, June, Chatsworth: Mary

Husband Bothwell, I will be safe. Cecil himself is coming here to Chatsworth to make the agreement with me. I am to be restored to my throne in Scotland. I will ensure your release the moment I am back, and then they shall see what a neighbour they have. They will reap the whirlwind and we two shall be the storm that breaks on them. Marie

I spend my afternoons in the Chatsworth gardens, in a moated stone tower that stands alone, surrounded by a lake stocked with golden carp and dappled by overhanging willows. The stone steps lead down from my tower to the little stone bridge which reflects in the water beneath it, a dark green arch looking up at grey stone walls. Dragonflies hover over the water like blue arrowheads and swallows dip and drink.

Shrewsbury calls it my bower and says that it is my own kingdom till I have another. He has promised I shall spend my days here, quite undisturbed. He leaves a guard on the shore side of the bridge, not to keep me in, but to make sure no-one troubles me in the afternoons when I laze on a day bed in the shade of an arch where the white Tudor roses are just in bud, slowly unfurling white petals.

I lie on my silk cushions, listening to my lute player who sings me the dreamy songs of the Languedoc, songs of love and longing, impossible romantic stories of poor men adoring cruel mistresses, the birds singing with him. There are skylarks in the parkland, I hear them carolling with each wingbeat as they climb their way heavenwards. I would not even know that they were named skylark but for Shrewsbury. He showed me them in flight, pointed out the little bird on the ground, and then taught me to listen for their aspiring, soaring song. He told me that they sing as they fly upwards, each wingbeat bringing out another glorious burst of melody, and then they close their wings in silence and plummet to their nest.

There is nothing for me to do here at Chatsworth, this summer; nothing I can do. I need neither strive nor worry. I have only to wait for Elizabeth's agreement, for Cecil's permission, and at last I can be confident that their assent must come. They may not like it, but I have won, yet again, by simple inheritance. My half-brother is dead and there is nobody else but me for the throne of Scotland. Soon Elizabeth will die and there will be nobody but me for the throne of England. I will have my thrones by right since I am a queen born and bred, a sacred being with inalienable rights. They have fought against this inexorable progress and I have fought for it; but in the end it is my destiny. It is God's will that I shall be Queen of Scotland and Queen of England and *voilà*! His will be done.

I ride out in the morning in the beautiful woods, sometimes up to the hunting tower that clever Bess designed and built for its view all around this wildly beautiful countryside, and sometimes I ride out on to the moors. I am free to go where I please and I am accompanied only by a courtesy guard, and by Shrewsbury: my dearest companion and only friend. In the afternoon I lie in the sun and doze.

I dream. Not the nightmares that haunted me in Scotland but I dream that I am back in France, in the sunshine of my childhood. We are dancing in the gardens of Fontainebleau and the musicians – oh! there are fifty musicians to play for us four children! – the musicians are playing for us and we call for the same tune over and over again so that we can practise our dance.

311

We are rehearsing for the coming of the king, the King of France, the dazzling Henri II, my father-in-law, the only father I have ever known, the only man who ever loved me without exacting a price, the only man I can trust, have ever trusted.

He rides up and jumps from his horse, his bonnet aslant on his dark head, his chestnut beard and moustache sleek. He catches me in his arms – me before everyone, before his son and heir, before his daughters. 'My precious girl,' he says in my ear. 'Every day you are more beautiful, every day more exquisite. Say you will jilt little Francis and marry me.'

'Oh, yes!' I cry without a moment's hesitation. I bury my face in the silky hair of his beard and inhale the scent of his clean linen and the smell of his cologne. 'I would marry you tomorrow. Will you divorce Madame Serpent for me?'

This is very naughty of me but it makes him roar with laughter. 'Tomorrow, my darling, *ma chérie*. At once! Tomorrow I will do it. Now show me your dance.'

I smile in my sleep and turn to the sun. Someone, one of my maids, moves a curtain of damask so that the sun shall not shine on my face. My skin must stay as pale as cream. My beauty must not be made ordinary by daylight. He said I must always be shielded from the sun, always dressed in the best silks that could be had, always wearing the finest jewels; nothing but the best of the very best for the little dauphine.

'You will be Queen of France when I am dead, my little princess,' he says to me earnestly. 'I shall leave my kingdom in your care. You are the one with the wit and the will, I trust you.'

'Papa-Your-Grace, don't talk of it,' I whisper.

'You will be Queen of Scotland,' he reminds me. 'And when Mary Tudor dies you will be Queen of England.'

I nod. Mary Tudor is the last legitimate heir of Henry VIII, only daughter of his wife Katherine of Aragon. After her, since she has no child, comes me, the granddaughter of King Henry's sister.

'And you must take your throne,' he says to me. 'If I am gone, don't forget this. If I am alive I shall put you on the throne of England, I swear it. But if I am dead you must remember this. You are Queen of Scotland, France and England. You must claim your inheritance. I command it.'

'I will, Papa-King,' I say solemnly. 'You can depend on me. I will not forget, and I will not fail.'

He puts his finger under my chin and turns up my face to him. He bends his head and kisses me on the lips. 'Enchanting,' he says. His touch makes me feel faint and warm.

'You will be the finest queen the world has ever known. And you will win England and Scotland for France. You will create a kingdom greater than William of Normandy. You will be Queen of France, England and Scotland. You will have the greatest kingdom the world has ever known and I have raised you to be the greatest queen. Never, ever forget this. It is your destiny, it is the destiny that God has laid on you. You are to be the greatest queen in Christendom, perhaps in the world. It is God's will. Obey Him.'

1570, June, Chatsworth: George

I am about to mount up to ride out with the queen when I hear the clatter of a small guard of horses and a man with a small group of companions rides up the drive under the big arching trees. He comes to the stable entrance, without hesitation, as if he has studied a map of my house and knows where everything is.

Warily, I hand over the reins of my horse to the stable lad and go to meet him. 'Yes?'

He dismounts and pulls his hat from his head, and bows low to me. Not very low, I notice. 'My lord Shrewsbury?'

I nod. I recognise him as one of the men that I sometimes see at court, standing behind Francis Walsingham, when he, in turn, is standing behind William Cecil. So he is a spy, yet another spy. So he is an enemy to the freedom of the people of England, however plausible and charming he will try to be.

'I am Herbert Gracie. I serve Master Cecil.'

'You are welcome,' I say politely. I see by his clothes that he is a gentleman, this is one of the hidden men of Cecil's affinity. God knows what he wants here with me. 'Will you come into the house?'

'I won't delay you,' he says, nodding to my horse. 'Are you about to ride out with the queen?'

I smile and say nothing. I do not need to tell Cecil's servants what I do in my own house.

'Forgive me,' he says. 'I will not delay you. I wanted to speak with you for only a moment.'

'You have come a long way for only a moment,' I observe.

He has a rueful merry smile. 'When you serve my lord you soon get accustomed to long rides and scant results,' he says.

'Do you indeed?' The last thing I want to hear is the hardship of Cecil's service, and the rigours of life as a dirty spy.

'A word only,' he says. I go to the corner of the stable yard with him, and wait.

'A servant of your wife has met with three conspirators and plotted to release the queen,' he says flatly.

'What?'

'He reported back to her, and she gave him two guineas and told him to go on with the conspiracy.'

'This isn't possible.' I shake my head. 'Truly. Bess would never free the queen. *I* am more likely to free her than Bess.'

'Oh? Why is that?'

'Bess dislikes her,' I say unguardedly. 'Women's jealousy . . . They are like the sea and the shore, they cannot help but beat against each other. Two strong women under the same roof, you cannot imagine . . .'

'Only too well! Does she dislike her so much she would try to get rid of her by helping her run away?'

I shake my head. 'She would never plot against Queen Elizabeth, she would never go against Cecil . . .' As I protest, a truly horrible thought strikes me as to what Bess might be capable of. Would she, over-active, businesslike, spiteful as she is, try to entrap Queen Mary in an unsuccessful escape attempt? So that she would be taken from us? 'I had better speak to her.'

'I'll have to come too,' he says carefully.

I bristle at once. 'You can trust me, I should hope.'

'We can trust no-one,' he says simply. 'Your wife has taken some part in a plot with Sir Thomas Gerard to free the queen. It is my task to find out how far the plot has gone. I shall have to question her. It is a courtesy to you, my lord, and to Master Secretary Cecil's friendship with you and with your wife, that I come to you first. That I speak to you privately and that there are no immediate arrests.'

I try to hide my shock. 'There can be no need for arrests . . .' I protest weakly.

'I have the warrants in my pocket.'

I take a breath. 'Well, I shall see Bess with you,' I stipulate. 'She is not to be put to question.' Whatever she has done, I think to myself, they shall not see her without my protection. She is a determined woman and when she thinks that something is the right course she will do it, and damn the consequences. Damn her, actually.

'She'll be in the muniments room,' I say, and we are turning towards the house just as the queen comes through the garden door into the yard and calls gaily: 'Chowsbewwy!'

Before Cecil's man can say or do anything, I stride to her side. 'This is a spy from London,' I say rapidly in a whisper. 'Tell me quickly. Have you been plotting? Is there a plot for you to run away? Has a man called Gerard spoken to you? My life depends on this.'

She is so quick-witted, she sees at once the danger, the waiting man, my urgent tone. She replies at once, without prevarication, in a quick whisper. 'No. I swear. I have never even heard of him.'

'Bess did not speak to you of a plot to free you?'

'Bess? On my life, no.'

I bow. 'I shall have to delay our ride, if you will forgive me,' I say loudly.

'I shall walk him round the grounds until you are ready,' she says formally, and turns for her horse.

I wait till her horse is held steady before her, and I can lift her into the saddle. Even with Cecil's man waiting to question my wife, I cannot bear to let anyone else lift Queen Mary and hold her for that brief, spellbinding moment. She smiles down at me.

'*Soyez brave,*' she whispers. 'I am innocent of this. Elizabeth has no evidence against me, and she dare do nothing against me. We just have to be brave and wait.'

I nod, and she turns her horse and rides out of the yard. As she passes Cecil's spy she flicks him the most mischievous little smile and nods her head to his low bow. When he comes up she is gone; but his face is a picture.

'I didn't know . . .' he stammers. 'Good God, she is beautiful. My God, her smile . . .'

'Exactly,' I say grimly. 'And that is one of the reasons that I pay for double guards, why I never cease watching, and why I can promise you that there are no plots in my household.'

We find Bess, as I knew we would, in the room which should be the muniments room, the room to store the records of the family, pedigrees, peerages, records of the joust and standards, and the like. Under Bess's command all this history of honour has been discarded and the shelves and drawers are filled instead with records of the income and expenditure from Chatsworth, yields from the flocks of sheep, timber from the woods, lead from the mines, stone from the quarries, coal production, ship-building reports, and the travelling chest which she takes with her everywhere is filled with all the records of her other lands and estates. These are all mine now, they came to me on marriage. They are all in my name and ownership as her husband. But Bess was so perturbed at the thought that my stewards would manage the estates – though they would do it perfectly well – that she has gone on keeping the records of her old properties, while I merely collect the income. It makes no difference to me. I am not a tradesman whose pleasure is weighing his gold. But Bess likes to know how her lands are doing, she likes to be involved in the tedious business of shepherding, quarrying, mining and shipping. She likes to see all the business letters and reply to them herself. She likes to add everything up and see her profit. She cannot help herself. It is her great pleasure, and I allow it to her. Though I cannot help but find it very beneath the behaviour one would expect of a countess of England.

I can see that Herbert Gracie is a little taken aback to find Bess in her lair, surrounded with books written up in copperplate and with two clerks head down and scribbling to her dictation. So I take the moment of his discomfort to step towards her, take her hand and kiss her, and so whisper in her ear: 'Beware.'

She has not the quick understanding of the Scots queen. 'Why, what's the matter?' she asks, out loud like a fool.

'This is Herbert Gracie, he comes from Cecil.'

At once, she is all smiles. 'You are welcome,' she says. 'And how is the Master Secretary?'

'He is well,' he says. 'But he asked me to speak with you in private.'

She nods to the clerks who pick up their pens, ready to go. 'Here?' she asks, as if a countess should do business at a clerk's office.

'We'll go to the gallery,' I interrupt and so I get a chance to lead the way with Bess, and try to warn her again: 'He is inquiring after a plot to free the queen. He says you are in it. With a man called Thomas Gerard.' Her little gasp tells me everything. 'Wife,' I almost groan. 'What have you done?'

She doesn't answer me, she ignores me, though I am risking my own neck by whispering to her. She spins around to young Mr Gracie, standing on the stair below her, and puts out her hand to him, with her frank honest smile.

'My husband tells me that Cecil knows of the Gerard plot,' she says quickly. 'Is this why you are here?'

I stifle my horror at this plain dealing. If only she would take advice from me, if only she would not act as she does, always so independently.

He takes her hand as if she were sealing a bargain with him, and nods, watching her intently. 'Yes, it is about the Gerard plot.'

'You must think me very foolish,' she says. 'I was trying to do the right thing.'

'Indeed?'

'I was going to tell my husband today, he knows nothing of this.'

A quick glance from Mr Gracie's brown eyes to my horror-struck face confirms this well enough, and then he is back to Bess.

'My servant, John Hall, came to tell me that someone had tried to bribe him to lead the Scots queen riding on to the moor where she would be met by her friends and taken away.'

Cecil's man nods again. It strikes me that all this is old news to him, he knows all about it already; what he is listening for is to hear Bess lie. This is not an inquiry, this is an entrapment.

'Tell the truth, wife,' I warn her. 'Don't try to protect your servants. This is important.'

She turns her pale face to me. 'I know,' she says. 'I will tell Mr Gracie the whole truth, and he will tell my good friend Mr Cecil that I am honest and loyal as I ever was.'

'What did you do, when your servant John Hall came to you?' Mr Gracie asks her.

'I asked him who else was in the plot, and he named a Mr Rolleston, and Sir Thomas Gerard, and said that there might be another, greater man behind it all.'

'And what did you do?'

Bess looks at him with her frank smile. 'Now, I daresay that you will think me a scheming woman; but I thought that if I sent John Hall back to the men with word that the plot could go ahead, he could discover the names of the plotters and if there was a greater man behind them. And then I could tell Master Cecil the whole plot, and not a small worthless strand of it.'

'And has he reported back to you?'

'I have not seen him today,' she says and then she looks at him in sudden understanding. 'Oh, have you taken him up?'

Gracie nods. 'And his confederates.'

'He came straight to me though they had bribed him,' she says. 'He is loyal. I would vouch for him.'

'He will be questioned but not tortured,' Gracie says. He is matter-of-fact, I note that torture is now a routine part of Cecil's questioning, and it can be mentioned in front of a lady in an earl's own house without remark. We have come to this: that a man can be taken without warrant, without a word from a justice of the peace, without the permission of his master, and he can be tortured on the say-so of Cecil. This is not how it was. This is not English justice. This is not how it should be.

'And your intention was only to discover the full plot before you alerted your husband or Secretary Cecil?' he confirms.

Bess widens her eyes. 'Of course,' she says. 'What else? And John Hall will tell you, those were my exact instructions to him. To lead them on and report to me.'

Herbert Gracie is satisfied, and Bess is plausible. 'Then I must ask you to forgive my intrusion and I shall leave.' He smiles at me. 'I promised it would only be a moment.'

'But you must eat!' Bess presses him.

'No, I must go. My lord expects me back at once. I was only to ascertain what you have kindly told me, take the relevant men into custody, and bring them back to London. I do thank you for your hospitality.' He bows to Bess, he bows to me, he turns on his heel and he has gone. We hear his riding boots clatter away down the stone steps before we realise that we are safe. We never even got as far as the gallery, this interrogation all took place on the stairs. It started and was completed in a moment.

Bess and I look at each other as if a storm has blown through our garden destroying every blossom, and we don't know what to say.

'Well,' she says with pretended ease. 'That's all right then.'

She turns to leave me, to go back to her business, as if nothing has happened, as if she was not meeting with plotters in my house, conspiring with my own servants, and surviving an interrogation from Cecil's agents.

'Bess!' I call her. It comes out too loudly and too harshly.

She stops and turns to me at once. 'My lord?'

'Bess, tell me. Tell me the truth.'

Her face is as yielding as stone.

'Is it how you said, or did you think that the plot might go ahead? Did you think that the queen might be tempted to consent to the escape, and you would have sent her out with these men into certain danger and perhaps death? Though you knew she has only to wait here to be restored to her throne and to happiness? Bess, did you think to entrap her and destroy her in these last days while she is in your power?'

She looks at me as if she does not love me at all, as if she never has done. 'Now why would I seek her ruin?' she asks coldly. 'Why would I seek her death? What harm has she ever done me? How has she ever robbed me?'

'Nothing, I swear, she has not harmed you, she has taken nothing from you.'

Bess gives a disbelieving laugh.

'I am faithful to you!' I exclaim.

Her eyes are like arrow slits in the stone wall of her face. 'You and she, together, have ruined me,' she says bitterly. 'She has stolen my reputation as a good wife, everyone knows that you prefer her to me. Everyone thinks the less of me for not keeping your love. I am shamed by your folly. And you have stolen my money to spend on her. The two of you will be my ruin. She has taken your heart from me and she has made me see you with new, less loving eyes. When she came to us, I was a happy wealthy wife. Now I am a heart-broken pauper.'

'You shall not blame her! I cannot let the blame fall on her. She is innocent of everything you say. She shall not be falsely accused by you. You shall not lay it at her door. It is not her doing . . .'

'No,' she says. 'It is yours. It is all yours.'

1570, August, Wingfield Manor: Mary

My darling Norfolk, for we are still betrothed to marry, copies to me the playscript of the charade he must act. He has to make a complete submission to his cousin the queen, beg her pardon, assure her that he was entrapped into a betrothal with me under duress, and as a fault of his own vanity. The copy that he sends me of his submission, for my approval, is so weepingly guilty, such a bathetic confession of a man unmanned, that I write in the margin that I cannot believe even Elizabeth will swallow it. But, as so often, I misjudge her vanity. She so longs to hear that he never loved me, that he is hers, all hers, that they are all of them, all her men, all of them in love with her, all of them besotted with her poor old painted face, her bewigged head, her wrinkled body, she will believe almost anything – even this mummery.

His grovelling makes its own magic. She releases him, not to return to his great house in Norfolk, where they tell me that his tenants would rise up for him in a moment, but to his London palace. He writes to me that he loves this house, that he will improve and embellish it. He will build a new terrace and a tennis court, and I shall walk with him in the gardens when we pay our state visits as king consort and Queen of Scotland. I know he thinks also of when we will inherit England. He will improve this great house so that it will be our London palace, we will rule England from it.

He writes to me that Roberto Ridolfi is thankfully spared and is to be found in the best houses in London again, knowing everyone, arranging loans, speaking in whispers of my cause. Ridolfi must have nine lives, like a cat. He crosses borders and carries gold and services plots and always escapes scot free. He is a lucky man, and I like to have a lucky man in my service. He seems to have strolled through the recent troubles, though everyone else ended up in the Tower or exile. He went into hiding during the arrests of the Northern lords and now, protected by his importance as a banker and his friendship with half the nobles of England, he is at liberty once more. Norfolk writes to me that he cannot like the man, however clever and eager. He fears Ridolfi is boastful and promises more than he can achieve, and that he is the very last visitor my betrothed wants at Howard House, which is almost certainly watched day and night by Cecil's men.

I reply that we have to use the instruments that come to hand. John Lesley is faithful but not a man of action, and Ridolfi is the one who will travel the courts of Europe seeking allies and drawing the plots together. He may not be likeable – personally, I have never even laid eyes on him – but he writes a persuasive letter and he has been tireless in my cause. He meets with all the greatest men of Christendom and goes from one to another and brings them into play.

Now, he brings a new plan from Philip of Spain. If these present negotiations to return me to my throne break down again, then there is to be an uprising by all of the English lords – not just those of the North. Ridolfi calculates that more than thirty peers are secret Papists – and who should know better than he who has the ear of the Pope? The Pope must have told him how many of Elizabeth's court are secretly loyal to the old faith. Her situation is worse than I realised if more than thirty of her lords have secret priests hiding in their houses, and take Mass! Ridolfi says they only need the word to rise, and King Philip has promised to provide an army and the money to pay them. We could take England within days. This is 'the Great Enterprise of England' re-made afresh, and though my betrothed does not like the man, he cannot help but be tempted by the plan.

'The Great Enterprise of England', it makes me want to dance, just to hear it. What could be greater as an enterprise? What could be a more likely target than England? With the Pope and Philip of Spain, with the lords already on my side, we cannot fail. 'The Great Enterprise', 'the Great Enterprise', it has a ring to it which will peal down the centuries. In years to come men will know that it was this that set them free from the heresy of Lutheranism and the rule of a bastard usurper.

But we must move quickly. The same letter from Norfolk tells me the mortifying news that my family, my own family in France, have offered Elizabeth an alliance and a new suitor for her hand. They do not even insist on my release before her wedding. This is to betray me, I am betrayed by my own kin who should protect me. They have offered her Henri d'Anjou, which should be a joke, given that he is a malformed schoolboy and she an old lady; but for some reason, nobody is laughing and everyone is taking it seriously.

Her advisors are all so afraid of Elizabeth dying, and me inheriting, that they would rather marry her to a child and have her die in childbirth, old as she is, old enough to be a grandmother – as long as she leaves them with a Protestant son and heir.

I have to think that this is a cruel joke from my family on Elizabeth's vanity and lust; but if they are sincere, and if she will go through with it, then they will have a French king on the throne of England, and I will be disinherited by their child. They will have left me in prison to rot and put a rival to me and mine on the English throne.

I am outraged, of course, but I recognise at once the thinking behind this strategy. This stinks of William Cecil. This will be Cecil's plan: to split my family's interests from mine, and to make Philip of Spain an enemy of England forever. It is a wicked way to carve up Christendom. Only a heretic like Cecil could have devised it; but only faithless kin like my own husband's family are so wicked that they should fall in with him.

All of this makes me determined that I must be freed before Elizabeth's misbegotten marriage goes ahead, or, if she does not free me, then Philip of Spain's armada must sail before the betrothal and put me in my rightful place. Also, my own promised husband, Norfolk, must marry me and be crowned King of Scotland before his cousin Elizabeth, eager to clear the way for the French courtiers, throws him back in the Tower. Suddenly, we are all endangered by this new start of Elizabeth, by this new conspiracy of that arch plotter Cecil. Altogether, this summer, which seemed so languid and easy, is suddenly filled with threat and urgency.

1570, September, Chatsworth: Bess

A brief visit for the two of them to Wingfield – the cost of the carters alone would be more than her allowance if they ever paid it – and then they are ordered back to Chatsworth for a meeting which will seal her freedom. I let them go to Wingfield without me; perhaps I should attend on her, perhaps I should follow him about like a nervous dog frightened of being left behind; but I am sick to my soul at having to watch my husband with another woman, and worrying over what should be mine by right.

At Chatsworth at least I can be myself, with my sister and two of my daughters who are home for a visit. With them I am among people who love me, who laugh at silly familiar jokes, who like my pictures in the gallery, who admire my abbey silver. My daughters love me and hope to become women like me, they don't despise me for not holding my fork in the French style. At Chatsworth I can walk around my garden and know that I own the land beneath my boots, and no-one can take it from me. I can look out of my bedroom window at my green horizon and feel myself rooted in the country like a common daisy in a meadow.

Our peace is short-lived. The queen is to return and my family will have to move out to accommodate her court and the guests from London. As always, her comfort and convenience must come first, and I have to send my own daughters away. William Cecil himself is coming on a visit with Sir Walter Mildmay, and the Queen of Scots' ambassador, the Bishop of Ross.

If I had any credit with the merchants or any money in the treasure room I would be bursting with pride at the chance to entertain the greatest men of the court, and especially to show Cecil the work I have done on the house. But I have neither, and in order to provide the food for the banquets, the fine wines, the musicians and the entertainment I have to mortgage two hundred acres of land and sell some woodland. My steward comes to my business room and we look at each parcel of land, consider its value and if we can spare it. I feel as if I am robbing myself. I have never parted with land before but to make a profit. I feel as if every day the fortune that my dear husband Cavendish and I built up so carefully, with such determination, is squandered on the vanity of one queen who will not stop spending and will repay nothing, and the cruelty of another who now delights in punishing my husband for his disloyalty by letting his debts rise up like a mountain.

When William Cecil arrives with a great entourage, riding a fine horse, I am dressed in my best and at the front of the house to greet him, no shadow of anxiety on my face or in my bearing. But as I show him around and he compliments me on everything I have done to the house, I tell him frankly that I have had to cease all the work, lay off the tradesmen, dismiss the artists, and indeed I have been forced to sell and mortgage land, to pay for the cost of the queen.

'I know it,' he says. 'Bess, I promise you, I have been your honest advocate at court. I have spoken to Her Grace as often and as boldly as I dare for you. But she will not pay. All of us, all her servants, are impoverished in her service. Walsingham has to pay his spies with his own coin and she never repays him.'

'But this is a fortune,' I say. 'It is not a matter of some bribes for traitors and wages for spies. This is the full cost of running a royal court. Only a country paying taxes and tithes could afford her. If my lord were a lesser man she would have ruined him already. As it is he cannot meet his other debts. He does not even realise how grave is his situation. I have had to mortgage farms to cover his debts, I have had to sell land and enclose common fields, soon he will have to sell his own land, perhaps even one of his family houses. We will lose his family home for this.'

Cecil nods. 'Her Grace resents the cost of housing the Scots queen,' he says. 'Especially when we decode a letter and find that she has received a huge purse of Spanish gold, or that her family have paid her widow's allowance and she has paid it out to her own secret people. It is Queen Mary who should be paying you for her keep. She is living scot free on us while our enemies send her money.'

'You know she never will pay me,' I protest bitterly. 'She pleads poverty to my lord; and to me she swears she will never pay for her own prison.'

'I will speak to the queen again.'

'Would it help if I sent her a monthly bill? I can prepare the costs for every month.'

'No, she would hate that even worse than one bigger demand. Bess, there is no possibility that she will fully repay you. We have to face it. She is your debtor and you cannot force her to pay.'

'We will have to sell yet more land then,' I say gloomily. 'Pray God you can take the Scots queen off our hands before we are forced to sell Chatsworth.'

'Good God, Bess; is it that bad?'

'I swear to you: we will have to sell one of our great houses,' I say. I feel as if I am telling him that a child will die. 'I will lose one of my properties. She will leave us with no choice. Gold drains away in the train of the Scots queen and nothing comes in. I have to raise money from somewhere, and soon all we will have left to sell is my house. Think of me, Master Cecil, think of where I have come from. Think of me as a girl who was born to nothing but debt and has risen as high as the position I now enjoy; and now think of me having to sell the house that I bought and rebuilt and made my own.'

1570, September, Chatsworth: Mary

> B –
> *I will not fail now. This is my chance. I will not fail you. You will see*
> *me on my throne again and I shall see you at the head of my armies.*
> M

This is my great chance to seduce Cecil and I prepare as carefully as a general on campaign. I do not greet him as he arrives, I let Bess supervise the dinner and so wait until he has rested from his journey, dined well, drunk a little, and then I plan my entrance to the Chatsworth dining hall.

The doorway faces west, so that when I enter, the great doors thrown open behind me, the sun comes in with me, and he is dazzled by the light. I am wearing my signature black and white, the white veil that suits my face so well, sitting square on my forehead, just a few tendrils of hair curling around my face. My gown is cut tight, so tight I can hardly breathe – these months in prison have made me fatter than I like – but at least I have the exaggerated curves of a fertile young woman, I am not a spinster stick like the queen he serves.

I wear a ruby crucifix at my throat, it demonstrates the pure whiteness of my skin, and will please the Bishop of Ross. My slippers are ruby red too, as is the discreet half-hidden petticoat that Cecil will see as I lift my gown over the step and show the prettiness of my ankles and my embroidered stockings. The mixture of devotion with the ruby-red cross and provocation with the ruby-red heels and scarlet petticoat should be enough to muddle most men into a slight fever of lust and respect.

Cecil, Mildmay, Ross and Shrewsbury all rise and bow low as I enter. I greet Shrewsbury as my host first – it gives me such confidence to feel his hand tremble at my touch – and then I turn to Cecil.

He is weary – that's the first thing that strikes me about him, weary and clever. His dark eyes are set deep in a lined face, he looks like a man who keeps his own counsel. And he does not look impressed by either the ruby cross or the pretty shoes. I smile at him but he does not respond. I see him taking me in, studying me like a secret message, and I see the rise of a little colour to his sallow cheeks.

'I am so pleased to meet you at last,' I say in French, my voice very low and sweet. 'I have heard so much about the good counsel that you give my cousin, I have wished for so long that I had a wise advisor for myself.'

'I do my duty,' is all he says, coldly.

I move on to Sir Walter Mildmay and then I greet my bishop with affection. Sometime in this visit we will seize a moment for him to tell me, face to face, the progress of Ridolfi's plot, 'the Great Enterprise of England', and the news of my betrothed and my supporters. But in the meantime I have to pretend that we write nothing, that we plan nothing, that great deeds do not shimmer between us like exciting ghosts. I greet him like a queen quietly pleased to see her ambassador after a long silence.

They have papers for me to sign and seal, and Shrewsbury suggests that we go to the smaller family room so that we can be more private.

I take Cecil's arm and let him lead me to the privy chamber.

I smile up at him and laugh at his remarks about the journey. I tell him of my own ride to Wingfield and back again and how much I love to ride out. I tell him that my pantaloons for riding have scandalised Bess but that she allows me out in them after I told her that they are worn by my mother-in-law, Catherine de Medici herself. This makes him laugh, reluctantly, like a man who seldom does so. I ask him attentively after the health of the queen, and I look surprised and interested when he tells me of the Anjou proposal.

He asks me what I think of the bridegroom and I twinkle at him and let him see that I am laughing at the thought of it, and yet I answer him seriously enough and say that I know nothing against young Henri. Indeed, he was offered once to me, though I found it possible to refuse the honour. He smiles down at me, I know I have amused him. I slide my hand a little further into his arm. He bends his head to say something quietly to me, and I look up at him from under my eyelashes, and I know that this man is for the winning, and I can win him.

And all the while I am thinking in his doublet he carries the document that will set me free. All the while I am thinking this is the man that killed my mother. All the while I am thinking I have to make him like me, I have to make him trust me. Best of all if I could make him hopelessly besotted with me.

1570, October, Chatsworth: Bess

'So what did you think of her?' I ask Cecil when they have met half a dozen times to talk and finally all the documents are signed and sealed and the horses at the door and Cecil is ready to leave.

'Most beautiful,' he says. 'Most charming. A real heart-stealer. I wouldn't blame you if you wanted her gone from your door, even if she were not prohibitively expensive.'

I nod.

'Clever,' he says. 'Not educated like our queen; no scholar, no tactician; but clever and with a constant eye to her own interests. Cunning, I don't doubt; but not wise.'

He pauses, smiles at me.

'Elegant,' he says. 'In her mind as well as her stature. Perfect on a horse, paradise on a dance floor, sweet as a nightingale when she sings, beautiful as a portrait. A delight. A very picture of a queen. As a woman, a pleasure to watch, a lesson in charm. The men who say there is no more beautiful queen in Europe speak nothing but the truth. More than that, I think she is the most beautiful woman I have ever met. Engaging, desirable. Perhaps perfection. And so young, and such a radiance about her – a woman who could turn your heart right over.'

I blink. Then to my embarrassment I feel hot tears rise under my eyelids and I blink again and brush them away like dust. I have seen my own husband fall in love with this damned siren, but I thought that Cecil, with his incorrigible hatred of Papists, of the French, of female vanity, would be immune. But it seems that even he can be seduced by a smile and an upward glance. The way she looks up at a man would make any honest woman want to slap her. But even in my jealousy I cannot deny her beauty.

'She is,' I admit. 'She is perfection.' I am aware I have gritted my teeth and I unlock my jaw and smile at this new and most unlikely recruit to the huge circle of men who are in love with Mary Queen of Scots. 'I must say, I did not expect you, of all people, to fall for her too.' I try to speak cheerfully but I feel very heavy in my heart at this sudden new suitor.

'Oh, she is irresistible,' Cecil says. 'I feel the magic. Even I, with so many reasons to dislike her, feel her peculiar powerful charm. She is a queen beyond queens. But Bess, not so fast, ask me what else would I say of her?'

He smiles at me, understanding everything. 'Let me think. What else do I see in this perfect princess? She is untrustworthy, an unreliable ally but a frightening enemy. A determined Papist and foe to everything we have done and hope to do in England. She would bring back the church and drive us back into superstition. There is no doubt in my mind that she would burn us Protestants until all opposition to her was ashes. And she lies like a bargee, and deceives like a whore. She sits like a spider at the centre of a web of plots that corrupts or ensnares almost every man in the country. I would call her the most dangerous enemy to the peace of the commonwealth that we have ever faced. She is enemy to the peace of England, she is enemy to our queen, she is my enemy. I will never forget the danger that she poses nor forgive her for the threat that she is to my queen and to my country.'

'You will get rid of her to Scotland soon?' I ask urgently. 'You will make her queen and restore her?'

'Tomorrow,' he says grimly. 'She might as well be in Scotland as here. She is as great a danger to us in Scotland as here, I don't doubt. Wherever she is she will be surrounded by men so far gone in love with her that they are ready to die for her, she will be a focus for Spanish plots and French betrayal. Whether she goes to Scotland or to hell, I have to get her out of our country, or out of this life, before she costs the lives of more innocent men, before her plots take the queen's life, before she destroys us all.'

'I don't think she would take the queen's life,' I observe. It is hard for me to be just to her; but I have to say it. 'She has a great respect for the sanctity of royal blood. There is no doubt in her mind that an ordained monarch is sacred. She would oppose Elizabeth; but she would never have her killed.'

Cecil shakes his head. 'The men she plots with would see both women dead, to serve their cause. That is why she is so dangerous. She is an active, energetic fool in the hands of wicked men.'

1570, October, Chatsworth: Mary

They try to make sure that I have no time alone with Bishop Lesley, but I need only a moment and I seize that moment when he is mounting his horse in the stable yard, and Bess deep in conversation with her great friend William Cecil.

'This agreement will send me back to Scotland with an army for my protection,' I say quickly to him. 'You will watch that Cecil and Elizabeth hold to it. This is my future. You will ensure that they don't double cross us.'

'Trust me,' he says. He hauls himself into the saddle. 'If you are not back in Scotland by next spring then Philip of Spain himself will come to restore you to your throne. I have his word on it.'

'His own word?'

'As good as,' he says. 'Ridolfi has his promise, Ridolfi is the centre of the Great Enterprise and will bring everything together. He won't fail you, and nor will I.'

1570, Winter, Sheffield Castle: George

Places that I find hidden and treasonous letters to the Queen of Scots:

1. Under a stone in the garden, brought to me by the gardener's lad who is too simple to understand that the shilling stuck on the outside of the letter was payment to take it in secret to her.

2. Baked inside special Christmas bread for her from my own pastry maker.

3. Sewn inside a gown of silk as a gift from friends in Paris.

4. Pasted into the leaves of a book from a spy in the Spanish Netherlands.

5. Folded into a bolt of damask from Edinburgh.

6. Flown in by one of her own homing pigeons from God knows where, but I am especially worried by this, for the bird was not spent from a long flight: whoever sent it out must be close at hand.

7. Tucked into her saddle where I find it as I lift her up to go riding. She laughed, as if it does not matter.

8. In the collar of her lapdog. These two last must be men in my household acting as couriers for her friends. The homing bird she trained herself, pretending to me that she wanted tame doves. I gave them to her myself, more fool I.

'This must stop,' I tell her. I try to sound stern but she has been washing her dog and she has a linen apron over her gown, her head-dress is laid aside and her hair is falling down from its pins. She is as beautiful as a laundry-maid in a fairy story and she is laughing at the dog splashing in the bathwater and wriggling as she tries to hold him.

'Chowsbewwy!' she exclaims with pleasure at seeing me. 'Here, Mary, take little Pêche, he is too naughty, and too wet.'

With a lunge the little dog struggles to be free and shakes himself vigorously, drenching us all. The queen laughs. 'Take him! Take him! Vite! Vite! And get him dry!'

I regain my solemn expression. 'I daresay you would not like it if I took him away from you for good?'

'Not at all,' she replies. 'But why would you dream of doing such a cruel thing? How has Pêche offended you?'

'Or if I refused to give you books, or new material for a gown, or did not let you walk in the garden?'

She rises to her feet and strips off her linen apron, a gesture so domestic and ordinary that I almost catch her hand and kiss it as if we were newlyweds in our own little house. 'My lord, are you offended with me for something?' she asks sweetly. 'Why do you threaten me so? Is something wrong? Has Bess complained of me?'

I shake my head. 'It is your letters,' I say. 'You must authorise men to write to you. I find letters everywhere. The guards bring me one practically every day.'

She shrugs, a typical gesture which says, in her French way: 'I don't know, and I don't care.' 'Pouf! What can I do? England is full of people who want to see me free. They are bound to write to me to ask if they can help.'

'This will ruin us,' I say urgently to her. 'Ruin you, as well as me. D'you not think that Cecil has a spy in this very castle? D'you not think he knows that you write every day, and that people write to you? D'you not think he reads what you have written and all the letters that come for you? He is the spy-master of England, he will know far more than I do. And even I know that you are in constant correspondence with the French and with the Spanish and that men, whose names I don't know, write in code to you all the time, asking you if you are safe, if you need anything, if you are going to be set free.'

'I am a queen,' she says simply. 'A princess of the blood. The King of Spain and the King of France, the Holy Roman Emperor are my kinsmen. It is only right and proper that the kings of Europe should write to me. And it is a sign of the criminal kidnap that I endure that any of their agents should think it better to send to me in secret. They should be free to write to me openly; but because I am imprisoned, for no reason, for no reason at all, they cannot. And as for the others – I cannot help that loyal hearts and reverent minds write to me. I cannot prevent them writing, nor should I. They wish to express their love and loyalty and I am glad to have it. There can be nothing wrong in that.'

'Think,' I say urgently to her. 'If Cecil believes that I cannot stop you plotting, he will take you away from me, or replace me with another guardian.'

'I should not even be here!' she exclaims with sudden bitterness. She draws herself up to her full height, her dark eyes fill with sudden tears. 'I signed the document for Cecil, I agreed to everything. I promised to give up my son to Elizabeth, you were there, you saw me do it. Why then am I not returned to Scotland as agreed? Why does Cecil not honour his part of the bargain? Pointless to tell me: don't write to my friends. I should not have to write to them, I should be among them as a free woman. You think of that!'

I am silenced by her temper and by the justice of what she says. 'Please,' I say weakly. It is all I can say. 'Please don't endanger yourself. I have read some of these letters. They come from varlets and fools, some of the most desperate men in England, and none of them has a penny to rub together and none of them could plan an escape if his own life depended on it. They may be your friends but they are not dependable. Some of them are little more than children, some of them are so well known to Cecil that they are on his pay-roll already. He has turned them to his service. Cecil's spies are everywhere, he knows everybody. Anyone who writes to you will be known to Cecil and most of them will be his men trying to entrap you. You must not trust these people.

'You have to be patient. You must wait. As you say, you have an agreement with the queen herself. You have to wait for her to honour it.'

'Elizabeth honour a promise to me?' she repeats bitterly. 'She has never done so yet!'

'She will,' I say valiantly. 'I give you my own word she will.'

1571, February, Sheffield Castle: Bess

My good friend William Cecil is to be Baron Burghley; and I am as glad of it as if I had been ennobled myself. This is nothing more than he deserves for years of loyal service to the queen, a lifetime of watching her, and planning for England. God only knows what dangers we would be in now, what terrible perils we would face – even worse than those that now haunt us – if it had not been for Cecil's wise advice and steady planning, ever since the queen came to her throne.

That the danger is very real cannot be doubted. In his letter to announce his ennoblement Cecil adds a warning: that he is certain that the Queen of Scots is planning a new uprising.

Dear Bess, beware. It may be that you can detect the plot by watching her, though it has escaped us watching her associates in London. I know that Norfolk, while swearing utter loyalty to Her Grace the Queen, is selling his gold and silverware at a knock-down price to the London goldsmiths. He has even parted with his own father's jewel of the Garter to raise cash. I cannot believe that he would sacrifice his father's greatest honour for anything other than the opportunity of his life. I can think of nothing that would be worth such a sacrifice to him but some terrible rebellion. I fear very much that he is planning to finance another war.

All my pride and joy in my new position is nothing if the peace of England is destroyed. I may be a baron now, and you may be a countess, but if the queen we serve is thrown down or murdered, then we are no better off than when we were children of landless fathers. Be watchful, Bess, and let me know all that you see, as always. – Burghley.

I smile to see his new signature, but the smile drains from my face as I tear his letter into little pieces and feed it into the fire in my muniments room. I cannot believe that a sensible man such as Norfolk would risk everything again – not again! – for the Queen of Scots. But Cecil – Burghley, I should say – is seldom wrong. If he suspects another plot, then I should be on my guard. I will have to warn my husband the earl, and watch her myself. I had hoped they would have taken her back to Scotland by now. God knows, I am at the point where I wish they would take her anywhere at all.

1571, February, Sheffield Castle: Mary

I am hopeful, I am so hopeful. Weeks now, I think, and we will both be free.

Marie

I dress with particular care in black and white, sober colours, but I wear three diamond rings (one is my betrothal ring from Norfolk) and a band of rich bracelets just to demonstrate that though my crown has been taken from me and my rope of black pearls stolen by Elizabeth, I am still a queen, I can still look the part.

Lord Morton is visiting me from Scotland and I want him to go back with the news that I am ready and fit to take my throne. He is due at midday but it is not till the mid-afternoon and it is growing dark and cold that he comes riding into the courtyard.

Babington, my faithful pageboy, comes dashing into my rooms, his nose red from the cold and his little hands frozen, to tell me that the nobleman from Scotland has finally arrived and his horses are being stabled.

I seat myself in my chair, under my cloth of estate, and wait. Sure enough, there is a knock at the door and Shrewsbury is announced with Morton. I do not rise. I let him be presented to me and when he bows low I incline my head. He can learn to treat me as a queen again; I don't forget that before he was as bad as any of them. He can start as I intend we shall go on. He greets me now as a prisoner, he will next see me on my throne in Edinburgh. He can learn deference.

Bess comes in behind the two men and I smile at her as she curtseys. She dips the smallest of bows, there is little love left between us these days. I still sit with her on most afternoons, and I still give her hopes of her prospects when I am returned to the throne; but she is weary of attending on me, and beggared by the expense of my court and the guards. I know it, and there is nothing I can or would do to help her. Let her apply to Elizabeth for money for my imprisonment. I am hardly going to pay my own jailors for incarcerating me.

The worry has put lines on her face and a grimness about her that was not there when I first walked into her house more than two years ago. She was newly married then, and her happiness glowed in her face. Her pride in her husband and her position was fresh for her. Now she has lost her fortune in entertaining me, she may lose her house, and she knows she has lost her husband already.

'Good day to you, my lady countess,' I say sweetly and watch her murmur a reply. Then the Shrewsburys take themselves off to the corner of the room, I nod to my lute player to play a tune, and to Mary Seton to see that wine and little cakes are served, and Morton sits on a stool beside me and mutters his news in my ear.

'We are ready for your return, Your Grace,' he says. 'We are even preparing your old rooms at Holyrood.'

I bite my lip. For a moment I see again, in my mind, the dark red stain of Rizzio's blood on the floor of my dining room. For a moment I think what a return to Scotland will mean to me. It will be no summer of French roses. The Scots were ill-suited to me before, and matters will not have improved. I shall have to live with a barbaric people and dine with a bloodstain on my floor. I shall have to rule them with my will and all my political skills. When Bothwell comes

343

we can dominate them together, but until he arrives I will be in constant danger again of kidnap and rebellion.

'And the prince is being prepared for his journey,' he says. 'He is looking forward to going to England, we have explained to him that this will be his home for the future, and he will be King of England one day.'

'He is well?'

'I have reports for you from his nurse and from his governor,' he says. 'Also, from his tutor. He is well and forward. He is growing strongly and learning his lessons.'

'He speaks clearly now?' Early reports had been of him drooling and failing to close his mouth in eating and in speech. A prince who is to command two kingdoms, perhaps three, has to be beautiful. It is harsh: but this is the way of the world.

'Much improved, as you will see.'

I take the package of reports and hand them to Mary Seton for reading later.

'But I have a request,' he says quietly.

I wait.

'We hear from the English ambassador that you are in correspondence with the King of Spain.'

I raise my eyebrows and say nothing. It is surely not Morton's business who writes to me. Besides, I am not directly in touch with the King of Spain. He is meeting my emissary Ridolfi, who is travelling to the Duke of Alva in the Netherlands, to the Pope himself, and then to Philip of Spain. The joke is that Elizabeth gave him a pass of safe conduct out of the kingdom, having no idea that he was my emissary, touring her enemies to raise a campaign against her.

'And also with the King of France.'

'And?' I ask frostily. '*Et puis?*'

'I have to ask you, while matters are so sensitive, that you don't write to them,' he says awkwardly. His Scots accent, always rather thick to my ears, grows more impenetrable as he is embarrassed.

'We are making agreement with Baron Burghley on behalf of the English court –'

'Baron Burghley?'

'Lord William Cecil.'

I nod, the ennoblement of my enemy can only make things worse for me and the old aristocracy – my friends.

'We are making an agreement, but when Lord Cecil finds secret letters to and from enemies of the state and you, he does not trust you. He cannot trust you.'

'The French are my kin,' I point out. 'He can hardly blame me for writing to my family when I am far from home and utterly alone.'

Morton smiles. He does not look overly concerned at my loneliness.

'And Philip of Spain? England's greatest enemy? Even now he is building ships for an invasion. He calls it an armada, to destroy England.'

'I do not write to him,' I lie readily. 'And I write nothing to my family which Cecil cannot read.'

'Actually, Your Grace, you probably write *nothing* at all that he does not read,' he emphasises. 'He probably sees every letter that comes and goes, however clever you think you have been with your secret couriers and number codes and invisible ink.'

I turn my head away from him to indicate my irritation. 'I have no state secrets,' I say flatly. 'I must be allowed to write to my friends and family.'

'And Ridolfi?' he asks suddenly.

I hold my face quite still, I do not show the smallest flicker of recognition. He could stare at me as if I were a portrait and he still would not see my secret. 'I know nothing of any . . . Ridolfi,' I say as if the name is strange to me. 'I know nothing of any letters.'

'I beg of you,' Morton says awkwardly, all flushed with sincerity and embarrassment at being forced to call a lady and a queen a downright liar. 'I will not quibble with you over who you know, or who you write to. I am not a spy. I am not here to entrap you. Your Grace, I am your true friend and I am here to make the arrangements to return you to Scotland and to your throne. And so I beg of you not to set any plots in motion, not to write to any conspirators, not to trust anyone but myself and Lord Shrewsbury here, and the Queen of England herself. We are all determined to see you returned to your throne. You have to be patient; but if you will be patient and honourable as the great queen that you are, then we will see you restored this year, perhaps this Easter.'

'This Easter?'

'Yes.'

'You give me your word?'

'Yes,' he says; and I believe him. 'But will you give me yours?'

'My word?' I repeat icily.

'Your word, as a queen, that you will not plot with the enemies of England.'

I pause. He looks hopeful, as if my safe return to Scotland and all his plans are hanging on this moment. 'Very well. I promise,' I say solemnly.

'Your word as a queen?'

'I give you my word as a queen,' I say firmly.

'You will not receive or send secret letters? You will not engage in any conspiracy against the peace of England?'

'I give you my word that I will not.'

Morton sighs and glances over at Shrewsbury as if he is much relieved. Shrewsbury comes closer and smiles at me. 'I told you she would promise,' he says. 'The queen is determined to return to her throne. She will deal with you and with all of your loyal countrymen with spotless honour.'

1571, March, Sheffield Castle: George

The queen and I ride home in the bright midday spring sunshine, a wagon following behind us with two roe deer for Bess's flesh kitchen. The queen is in light-hearted mood; she loves hunting and rides better than any woman I have ever met, she could outride most men.

When we come through the great gate for the stable yard my heart sinks to see Bess waiting for us, hands on her hips, the very portrait of an offended wife. The queen gives a little ripple of suppressed laughter and turns her head so Bess cannot see her amusement.

I dismount and lift the queen down from the saddle, and then the two of us turn to Bess like children waiting for a reprimand.

She gives an unwilling curtsey. 'We are to go to Tutbury,' she says, without preamble.

'Tutbury?' the queen repeats. 'I thought we were to stay here and then go to Scotland?'

'A letter from the court,' Bess says. 'I have started packing again.'

She hands over the sealed letter to the queen, nods distantly at me and strides off to where the travelling wagons are being made ready for another journey.

All the joy is wiped from the queen's face as she hands the letter to me. 'Tell me,' she says. 'I cannot bear to read it.'

347

I break the seal and open the letter. It is from Cecil. 'I don't quite understand,' I say. 'He writes that you are to go back to Tutbury for greater safety. He says there have been some incidents in London.'

'Incidents? What does he mean?'

'He doesn't say. He says nothing more than he is watching the situation and he would feel happier for your safety if you were at Tutbury.'

'I would be safer if I were in Scotland,' she snaps. 'Does he say when we are to go?'

'No,' I say. I pass the letter to her. 'We will have to go as he bids. But I wish I knew what is in his mind.'

She slides a sideways glance at me. 'Do you think Bess will know? Might he have written to her separately? Might he have told her what he fears?'

'He might have done.'

She slips off her red leather glove and puts her hand on my wrist. I wonder if she can feel my pulse speed at the touch of her fingers. 'Ask her,' she whispers. 'Find out from Bess what Cecil is thinking, and tell me.'

1571, March, on the road from Sheffield Castle to Tutbury: Bess

As always, they ride ahead and I labour behind with the wagons laden with her luxuries. But once they are arrived at the castle and my lord has seen her safe into her usual rooms, he leaves her, and rides back to meet me. I see his surprise at the amount of wagons, there are forty on this trip, and at my weariness and dustiness as I ride at their head.

'Bess,' he says awkwardly. 'What a number, I did not . . .'

'Have you come to help them unload?' I ask acidly. 'Did you want me, my lord?'

'I wondered if you had news from Gilbert, or Henry, or anyone else at court,' he says hesitantly. 'Do you know why they have sent us back here?'

'Does she not tell you?' I ask sarcastically. 'I would have thought she would have known.'

He shakes his head. 'She is afraid that they are going to renege on their promise to send her back to Scotland.'

We turn up the lane towards the castle. It is muddy as usual. I have come to hate this little castle. It has been my prison as well as hers. I will tell him everything I know, I have no taste for torturing him, nor the queen.

'I don't know anything about that,' I say. 'All I know from Henry is that the queen seems likely to accept the French prince in marriage.

Cecil is advising her to take him. In those circumstances I imagine Cecil thought it best to have the Queen of Scots somewhere that he could prevent her persuading her family against the match, which she is certain to do, or stirring up any other sort of trouble.'

'Trouble?' asks my husband. 'What trouble could she cause?'

'I don't know,' I say. 'But then, I have never been very good at predicting the trouble she can cause. If I had foreseen the trouble she could cause I would not be here now; riding before forty wagons to a house I hate. All I know is that Cecil warned me that he feared there was a plot but could find no evidence.'

'There is no plot,' he says earnestly. 'And Cecil can find no evidence because there is none. She has given her word, don't you remember? She gave her word as a queen to Lord Morton that there would be no plots and no letters. She will be returned to Scotland. She swore on her honour she would not conspire.'

'Then why are we here?' I ask him. 'If she is as innocent and honourable as you say?'

1571, April, Tutbury Castle: George

'This is a most unnatural thing, I am sure, a most illegal thing. A damned wicked and dishonourable thing. Wrong, against custom and practice, another innovation, and another injustice.'

I come to my senses and find I am muttering to myself as I walk along the outer wall of Tutbury Castle, gazing out, but not really seeing the fresh greenness of the spring landscape. I don't think I will ever look out to the north again without fearing that I may see an army coming to besiege us.

'Illegal surely, and in any case wrong.'

'What is the matter now?' Bess says, coming to my side. She has thrown a shawl over her head and shoulders and she looks like a farmer's wife run outside to feed the hens. 'I was just in the garden and I saw you striding about and muttering to yourself like a man driven insane. Is it the queen? What has she done now?'

'No,' I say. 'It is your great friend, Cecil.'

'Burghley.' She corrects me just to irritate me, I know. That nobody is now a baron and we must all call him 'my lord'. And for what? For persecuting a queen of the blood until she is driven halfway to treason?

'Burghley,' I say mildly. 'Of course, my lord Cecil. My lord Cecil the baron. How glad you must be for him. Your good friend. How grand he has become, what a pleasure for all who know and admire

351

him. And he is building his grand house still? And he has substantial money from the queen, posts and preferments? He grows wealthier every day, does he not?'

'What's the news? Why are you so angry?'

'He has pushed a bill through parliament to disinherit the Queen of Scots,' I say. 'Disinherit her. Now we see why he ordered us here where she could be so closely guarded. If ever the country would rise for her, you can see they might rise now. Declaring her invalid to inherit! As though parliament can determine who is the heir to the throne. As though it does not go by blood. As though a bunch of commoners can say who is a king's son! It makes no sense, apart from anything else.'

'Burghley has achieved this?'

'She must see this as false dealing to her. In the very month when she is due to go back to Scotland as queen, Cecil sends us here, and pushes through a bill that says that no-one of the Roman Catholic faith can ever be a monarch of England. Their faith is to disbar them as much as if they were . . .' For a moment I am speechless, I cannot think of an example. It has never been like this in England before. 'A Jew . . .' I manage. 'If one can imagine such a thing as a Tudor Jew, a Stuart Jew. A Mussulman, a Hindoo pretender. They are treating her as if she were a Turk. She is a child of the Tudor line – Cecil is saying she is a foreigner to us.'

'It makes Elizabeth safe from a Papist assassin,' Bess says shrewdly. 'There is no point in any hidden priest making a martyr of himself by killing her if it does not put a Papist on the throne.'

'Yes, but that's not why he's done it,' I exclaim. 'If he cared so much to protect the queen he would have rushed the bill through last year when the Pope excommunicated Elizabeth and commanded every Papist criminal in the country to murder her. No. This is just to attack the Queen of Scots at the very moment when we have a complete agreement. This is to drive her into rebellion. And I will have to be the one who has to tell her what he has done. It was to be an act of absolute faith between the two queens; and I am the one who has to tell her that she has been cheated of her inheritance.'

'You can tell her that her plotting has all been for nothing then.' There is a vindictive pleasure lilting in my wife's voice. 'Whatever she has written to Norfolk or to her foreign friends, if she is debarred from the throne she can promise what she likes but they will know her to be a liar without friends in England.'

'She is no liar. She is the heir,' I say stubbornly. 'Whatever anyone says, whatever Cecil says in parliament. She has Tudor blood, she is nearest to the throne, whether they like it or no. She is the next heir to England. What else do we say? That we pick and choose the next king or queen depending on our preference? Are monarchs not chosen by God? Are they not descended one from another? Besides, all the Kings of England before this one have been Papist. Is the religion of the fathers of the Kings of England now to be an obstacle to their being king? Has God changed? Has the king changed? Has the past changed too? Has Cecil – I beg your pardon, Baron Burghley – has he the power to disinherit Richard I? Henry V?'

'Why should you be so upset?' she asks unpleasantly. 'Has she promised you a dukedom as reward when she is Queen of England?'

I gasp at the insult on my own castle wall from my own wife. But this is how things are now. A land steward is a baron, a queen is disinherited by the House of Commons, and a wife can speak to her husband as if he were a fool.

'I serve the Queen of England,' I say tightly. 'As you know, Bess. To my cost.'

'My cost too.'

'I serve the Queen of England and none other,' I say. 'Even when she is ill-advised. Woefully ill-advised by your friend.'

'Well, I am glad that your loyalty is unchanged and nothing is wrong,' she says sarcastically, since it must be clear to everyone that everything is all wrong in England today. She turns to go back down the stone stairs to the mean little herb garden in the castle yard.

'And when you tell her, be sure she understands that this is the end of her ambition. She will be Queen of Scotland again as we have agreed; but she will never rule in England.'

'I serve the Queen of England,' I repeat.

'You would do better to serve England,' she says. 'Cecil knows that England is more than the king or the queen. All you care about is who is on the throne. Cecil has a greater vision. Cecil knows it is the lords and the commons too. It is the people. And the people won't have a burning persecuting wicked Papist queen on the throne ever again. Even if she is the true heir ten times over. Make sure you tell her that.'

1571, August, Tutbury Castle: Mary

I am like a fox in a trap in this poor castle and like a fox I could chew off my own foot for rage and frustration. Elizabeth promises to return me to my throne in Scotland but at the same time she is doing everything she can to see that I will never inherit the greater prize of England.

She has taken to courtship like a woman who knows that her last chance has finally come. They all say that the old fool has fallen in love with Anjou, and is determined to have him. They say she knows that this is her final chance to wed and bed and breed. At last, with me on her doorstep and her lords all for my cause, she realises that she has to give them a son and heir to keep me from the throne. At last she decides to do the thing that everyone said must be done: take a man as her husband and lord and pray that he gives her a son.

That my family in France could so far forget themselves and their honour as to betray me and my cause shows me how great an enemy Catherine de Medici has always been to me. At this very moment, when they should be ensuring my safe return to Scotland, they are spending all their time and trouble trying to marry little Henri d'Anjou to the old spinster of England. They will side with her against me and my cause. They will agree with her that my needs can be forgotten. Elizabeth will leave me here in miserable

Tutbury, or bundle me into some other faraway fortress, she will stick me in Kimbolton House, like poor Katherine of Aragon, and I will die of neglect. She will have a son and he will disinherit me. She will be married to a French prince and my kin, the Valois, will forget I was ever one of theirs. This marriage will be the last time anyone thinks of me and my claims. I must be free before this wedding.

Cecil has forced a bill through parliament, which says that no Roman Catholic can inherit the English throne. This is obviously directed at me, designed to disinherit me, even before the birth of the Protestant heir. It is an act of such double-dealing falsehood that it leaves me breathless. My friends write to me that he has even worse to come: plans to disinherit all Papists from inheriting their fathers' lands. This is an open attack on all of my faith. He plans to make us all paupers on our own lands. It cannot be borne. We have to move now. Every day my enemies become more determined against me, every day Cecil becomes more vindictive to us Papists.

This is our time, it must be our time. We dare not delay. The Great Enterprise of England must be launched this month. I dare not delay. Cecil has disinherited me in law and Elizabeth will divide me from my family. I am promised a journey to Scotland and yet I am in Tutbury again. We have to launch the enterprise now. We are ready, our allies are sworn to our service, the time is set.

Besides, I long to act. Even if this was going to fail, I would relish the joy of trying. Sometimes I think that even if I knew it would fail for a certainty I would still do it. I write to Bothwell of this sense of wild desperation and he writes back:

Only a fool rides out to fail. Only a fool volunteers for a forlorn hope. You have seen me take desperate risks but never for something I thought was doomed. Don't be a fool, Marie. Only ride out if you can win.

Riding out for death or glory benefits only your enemy. Don't be a fool, Marie, you have only once been a fool before. B

I laugh as I read his letter. Bothwell counselling caution is a new Bothwell. Besides, it is not going to fail. At last we have the allies we need.

A message from the French ambassador tells me that he has delivered to my beloved Norfolk three thousand crowns in gold coin – enough to finance my army. Norfolk will send it on to me by a secret courier in his own service. Ridolfi reports that he has seen the Spanish commander in the Netherlands, the Duke of Alva, who has promised to lead an assault by the Spanish troops from the Low Countries on the English channel ports; he has been blessed by the Pope, who has even promised his financial backing too. As soon as Spanish troops set foot on English soil the power and wealth of the Vatican will be behind them. Now Ridolfi is on his way to Madrid to confirm that Spain will back the scheme with all its power. With the Pope's support and with the Duke of Alva's advice, Philip of Spain is certain to give the order to go ahead.

I write to John Lesley, the Bishop of Ross, for his latest news and to my old servant now in his service, Charles Bailly. Neither has replied yet, and this is troubling. Bailly could well be on a secret mission for the bishop and away from his lodgings; but my ambassador should have answered me at once. I know he is in London awaiting news of the 'Great Enterprise'. When I hear nothing from him I write to Norfolk to ask him for news.

Norfolk replies in code, and his letter comes to me hidden in a pair of hollow heels to a pair of new shoes. He says that he has sent a letter to Lesley, and also sent a trusted servant to his house, but the house was closed and he was not at home. His servants say that he is visiting a friend but they don't know where he is, nor did he take any clothes with him, nor his personal servant.

Norfolk says that this sounds less like a visit, more like capture, and he fears the bishop has been arrested by Cecil's spy ring. Thank God at least they cannot torture him, he is a bishop and an accredited ambassador, they dare not threaten him or hurt him; but they can keep him from writing to me or to Norfolk, they can keep him from the network of information that we need. At this most important moment we are without him, and – worse than that – if Cecil has arrested him it must be that he suspects that something is being planned, even if he does not know what it is.

Cecil never does anything without good reason. If he has picked up Bishop Lesley now, when he could have arrested him at any time, then he must know we are planning something of importance. But then I comfort myself by thinking that we have driven him from the shadows where he works. Bothwell always used to say: get your enemies out in the open where you can see their numbers. Cecil must be afraid of us now, to act so openly.

As if this were not trouble enough, Norfolk writes to me that he has sent out the three thousand crowns of French gold by means of a draper from Shrewsbury who has served one of his servants by running errands in the past. They have not told the man what he is carrying. Norfolk decided it was safer to tell him it was only some sealed papers and a little money, and to ask him to deliver them on his way, at his own convenience. This is a risk, it is a terrible risk. The messenger, not knowing the value of what he is carrying, might well not take enough care. If he is curious, he can simply open the bag. I suppose my lord's thinking is that if he did know the value of the package, he might simply steal the gold – and there would be no way we could complain of him or arrest him for theft. We are in danger whichever way we turn but I have to wish that Norfolk could have chosen someone – anyone – from all his thousands of servants who could have been trusted with this great, this crucial secret. These are the wages to pay my army for the uprising and Norfolk has sent them out by a Shrewsbury draper!

I have to bite my tongue on my impatience. For the love of God! Bothwell would have given it to a bondsman, or someone sworn to lifetime fealty. Norfolk must have such men, why does he not use them? He acts as if he has no sense of his own danger when we are about to make war against a sovereign queen. He behaves as if he were safe. But we are not safe. We are about to take on the greatest power in England, we are about to challenge her on her own land. We are about to take on Cecil and his spy ring and he is already alert and suspicious. God knows, we are not safe. We are none of us safe.

1571, September, Sheffield Castle: Bess

It is the dusty hot weather at the end of the English summer, the leaves of the trees like crumpled gowns at the end of a masque. We have been sent back to Sheffield Castle. Whatever crisis they feared seems to be over and the summer is sunny once more. The court is on progress and Lady Wendover, writing to me from Audley End, tells me that Elizabeth has turned gracious to her cousins the Howards, is staying in their house, is speaking sweetly of her love for her cousin Thomas, and they are going to ask her to forgive him and restore him to his place at court and his house at Norfolk. The poor Howard children who left their home in the hands of the royal assessors are now asking Elizabeth for her favour and are getting a kindly hearing. The court is hopeful that this will end happily. We all want to see a reconciliation.

Elizabeth has no family but the Howards; she and her cousin have been brought up together. They may quarrel as cousins do; but no-one can doubt their affection. She will be seeking to find a way to forgive him, and this progress and this hospitality by his young son, in his father's house, is her way to allow him back into her presence.

I let myself hope that the danger and the unhappiness of these last two miserable summers is finished. Elizabeth has ordered us back to Sheffield Castle, the fears that drove us to Tutbury are passed.

Elizabeth will forgive her cousin Norfolk, perhaps she will marry Anjou and we can hope that she will have a son. The Scots queen will be sent back to Scotland, to manage as well or as ill as she can. I will have my husband restored to me and slowly, little by little, we will regain and recoup our fortune. What has been sold is lost and gone and we can never have it back. But the loans can be repaid, the mortgages settled, and the tenants will get used to paying higher rents in time. Already, I have made plans for mortgaging a coal mine and selling some packages of land that should take my lord out of the hands of the moneylenders within five years. And if the Scots queen honours her promises, or if Elizabeth pays some share, even half her debt to us, we should survive this terrible experience without the loss of a house.

I am going to settle my lord and the queen here in Sheffield Castle and then I will go on a visit to Chatsworth. I pine like a lover to be there, I have missed most of this summer, I want to catch the leaves turning sere. We cannot afford to rebuild or improve this year, nor the next, perhaps not for a decade; but at least I can plan what I would like to do, at least I can enjoy the work I have done. At least I can ride around my own land, and see my friends, and be with my children as if I were a countess and a woman of substance and not a cipher at a young woman's court.

This autumn, my husband the earl and I will escort the queen to Scotland, and if she rewards him as richly as she should, we shall have Scottish lands and perhaps a Scottish dukedom. If she gives him the rights to the harbour dues of a port, or the taxes on the import of some restricted goods, or even the tolls of the border roads, we might make our fortune again from this painful vigil. If she plays us false, and gives us nothing, then, at the very least, we are rid of her, and that alone is worth a barony to me. And when we are rid of her there is no doubt in my mind that he will return to me in his heart. We did not marry for passion but for a mutual respect and affection, and our interests run together now, as they

361

did then. I put my lands into his keeping, as I had to; he put his children and his honourable name into mine. Surely, when she is gone, and he has recovered from his foolish adoration of her, he will come back to me and we can be once more as we were before.

So I comfort myself, hoping for a better future, as I walk from the rose garden to the garden door. Then I pause, as I hear the worst sound in the world: the sound of galloping hooves, rapid like an anxious heartbeat, and I know at once, without a moment's doubt, that something terrible has happened. Something truly terrible is happening again. Some terror is coming into my life carried by a galloping horse. She has brought some horror to our door and it is coming as fast as it can ride.

1571, September, Sheffield Castle: George

I am in the mews, tending to my favourite hawk, when I hear Bess screaming my name at the same time as I hear the tolling of the castle bell.

The hawk bates off my wrist and tries to fly in terror at the noise, and there is a moment of flapping wings and confusion and me hollering for the falconer, as if the world is ending. He comes at the run and hoods the frightened bird, scoops her into his steady hands, and takes her from me as I unwind the leash and hand her over to him, and all the time the terrible bell is tolling and tolling, loud enough to wake the dead, too loud for the living.

'God save us, what is it?' he demands of me. 'Have the Spanish landed? Is it the North up again?'

'I don't know. Get the bird safe. I have to go,' I say, and I set off at a run for the front of the house.

I am not strong enough for these alarms. I cannot run, even though my heart is pounding in terror. I drop to a walk, cursing my lungs and my legs, and when I get to the front of the house I see Bess there, white as a sheet, and a man collapsed on the ground before her, with his head between his knees, having fainted from exhaustion.

She hands me the letter he has brought, without a word. It is Cecil's handwriting, but scrawled as if he has lost his mind. My heart sinks as I see it is addressed to me, but on the outside he has written, '5th of September, 1571, at 9 of the night. Haste, post haste. Haste, haste, for life, life, life, life.'

'Open it! Open it! Where have you been?' Bess screams at me.

I break the seal. The man on the ground whoops for his breath, and begs for water. No-one attends to him.

'What is it?' Bess demands. 'Is it the queen? Never say she is dead?'

'The Spanish are coming,' I say. I can hear my own voice tight and cold with fear. 'Cecil writes that the Spanish are to land an army of six thousand men. Six thousand. Six thousand. They are coming here to free her.'

'What are we to do? Are we to go to Tutbury?'

The man raises his head. 'No use,' he croaks.

Bess looks blankly at me. 'Are we to ride south?'

'Are you in Cecil's confidence?' I ask him.

He gives me a wry smile as if to say that no-one is in that position. 'It's too late to get her away. I have my orders,' he says. 'I am to discover all that she knows and get back to my lord. You are to stay here and wait for the invasion. You can't outrun them.'

'Dear God,' Bess says. 'What are we to do when they come?'

He says nothing; but I know the answer is: 'Kill her.'

'Is the queen safe?' I demand. 'Our queen, Elizabeth?'

'When I left she was safe,' he says. 'But my lord was sending guards to Audley End to bring her back to London.'

'They plan to capture Queen Elizabeth,' I say briefly to Bess. 'It says here. They have a great plan. Kidnap the Queen of England, free the Queen of Scots, raise the people. The Spanish will march through us.' I turn to the man. 'Was London ours when you left?'

He nods. 'Please God, we are ahead of them by a matter of days. The Queen of Scots' spy, a man called Ridolfi, blabbed the whole plan to an English merchant in Madrid. Thank the lord he knew what he was hearing and sent word to Cecil, as fast as his messenger could travel. Cecil sent me to you. We think the Spanish will be upon us in days. Their armada is launched, the Spanish Netherlands is armed, and the Pope is sending his wealth to arm traitors and calling out all the English Papists.'

I glance down the letter. 'Cecil says that I am to interrogate the queen and prevail upon her to tell me all she knows.'

'I am to be with you,' he says. He staggers to his feet and brushes the dirt from his breeches.

I bristle at the suggestion that I cannot be trusted. He falls back against the portals of the front door from sheer exhaustion.

'This is a matter beyond pride,' he says, seeing that I want to refuse him admission to the queen. 'I have to see her, and search her room for papers. The Scots queen may know where the Spanish are landing. We have to muster our army and get ready to meet them. This is life or death for England, not just her.'

'I'll speak to her.' I turn to Bess. 'Where is she?'

'Walking in the garden,' she says, her face grave. 'I'll send a girl to fetch her.'

'We'll go now,' the young man decides; but his legs buckle beneath him as he tries to walk.

'You can barely stand!' Bess exclaims.

He grabs on to the pommel of his saddle, and hauls himself upright. The look he shoots at Bess is desperate. 'I can't rest,' he says. 'I don't dare rest. I have to hear what the queen will tell us and get it back to my lord. If she knows at which port the Spanish are landing, we might even be able to intercept the armada at sea, and drive them off. Once they land, with six thousand, we won't have a chance; but if we can hold them at sea . . .'

'Come then,' I say. 'Walk with me.' I give him my arm and the two of us, me weak with gout and him with exhaustion, hobble towards the gardens.

She is there, like a girl waiting for her lover, at the gate. 'I heard the bell,' she says. Her face is bright with hope. She looks from the young man to me. 'What is happening? Why did they ring the alarm?'

'Your Grace, I must ask you some questions, and this gentleman –'

'Sir Peter Brown.' He bows to her.

'This gentleman will listen. He has come from Lord Burghley with most disturbing news.'

Her gaze that meets my eyes is so honest and true that I am certain that she knows nothing of this. If the Spanish land, they will do so without her knowledge. If they come for her and take her from me, it will be without her consent. She gave her word to Lord Morton and to me that she would not plot with anyone, any more. She plans to get back to Scotland by Elizabeth's treaty, not by destroying England. She gave her word there would be no more plots.

'Your Grace,' I begin trustingly. 'You must tell Sir Peter all that you know.'

She droops a little, like a flower, heavy-headed in a shower of rain. 'But I know nothing,' she says gently. 'You know that I am cut off from my friends and my family. You know yourself that you see every letter that comes for me and that I see no-one without your consent.'

'I am afraid that you know more than I do,' I say. 'I am afraid that you know more than you tell me.'

'You don't trust me now?' Her dark eyes widen as if she cannot believe that I would betray the affection I have for her, as if she cannot imagine that I would accuse her of being false, especially in front of a stranger, and an adherent of her enemy.

'Your Grace, I dare not trust you,' I say clumsily. 'Sir Peter here has brought me a message from Lord Burghley that commands me to question you. You are implicated in a plot. I have to ask you what you know.'

'Shall we sit?' she asks distantly, like the queen she is, and turns her back on us and leads us into the garden. There is a bench in an arbour with roses growing around the seat. She spreads out her gown and sits, like a girl interviewing suitors. I take the stool that her lady-in-waiting was using, and Sir Peter drops to the grass at her feet.

'Ask,' she invites me. 'Please, ask me whatever you want. I should like to clear my name. I should like everything to be above board with us.'

'Will you give me your word that you will tell me the truth?'

Queen Mary's face is as open as a child's. 'I have never lied to you, Chowsbewwy,' she says sweetly. 'You know I have always insisted that I be allowed to write privately to my friends and to my family. You know I have admitted that they are forced to write to me secretly and I to reply. But I have never plotted against the Queen of England, and I have never encouraged rebellion of her subjects. You can ask me what you wish. My conscience is clear.'

'Do you know a Florentine named Roberto Ridolfi?' Sir Peter says quietly.

'I have heard of him, but I have never met him nor had any correspondence with him.'

'How have you heard of him?'

'I have heard that he lent the Duke of Norfolk some money,' she says readily.

'D'you know what the money was for?'

'For his private use, I think,' she says. She turns to me. 'My lord, you know I do not have letters from the duke any more. You know he has abandoned our betrothal and sworn allegiance to the queen. He broke his betrothal to me and deserted me, on the command of his queen.'

I nod. 'That's true,' I say aside to Sir Peter.

'You have had no letters from him?'

'Not since he broke his promise to me. I would not receive a letter from him if he wrote it, not since he rejected me,' she says proudly.

'And when did you last hear from the Bishop of Ross?' Sir Peter asks her.

She frowns, trying to remember. 'Lord Chowsbewwy would recall, perhaps. His letters are always delivered to me by Lord Chowsbewwy.' She turns to me. 'He wrote to say he was safely back in London after visiting us at Chatsworth, didn't he?'

'Yes,' I confirm.

'And you have not heard from him since?'

Again she turns to me. 'I don't think so. Have we? No.'

Sir Peter gets to his feet, and puts his hand against the warm stone wall as if to steady himself. 'Have you had any letters from the Pope or from Philip of Spain or any of their servants?'

'Do you mean ever?' she asks, a little puzzled.

'I mean this summer, I mean in the past few months.'

She shakes her head. 'Nothing. Have they written to me and their letters gone astray? I think Lord Burghley spies upon me and steals my messages, and you can tell him from me that it is wrong to do so.'

Sir Peter bows to her. 'Thank you for your courtesy in talking with me, Your Grace. I will leave you now.'

'I have a question for you,' she tells him.

'Yes?'

'I am a prisoner, but that does not guarantee my safety. I was alarmed when I heard the bell ringing, and your questions have not reassured me. Please tell me, Sir Peter, what is happening? Please reassure me that my cousin the queen is safe and well.'

'Do you think she might be in danger?'

She glances down as if the question is an embarrassment. 'I know there are many who disagree with her rule,' she says, shamefaced. 'I am afraid there are those who would plot against her. There may even be those who would plot against her in my name. But that does not mean that I have joined with them. I wish her nothing but good, and I always have done. I am here in her country, in her power, imprisoned by her, because I trusted to the love that she promised me. She failed that love, she failed the bond that should be between queens. But even so, I would never wish her anything but good health and safety and good fortune.'

'Her Grace is blessed with such a friendship,' Sir Peter says and I wonder if he is being ironic. I look at him quickly, but I can tell nothing. He and the queen are equally bland. I cannot tell what either of them is truly thinking.

'So, is she safe?' she asks.

'When I left London the queen was on progress in the country and enjoying the warm weather,' he says. 'My lord Burghley has uncovered a plot in time to destroy it. All those who were party to it will go to the scaffold. Every one of them. I am here only to ensure that you are safe also.'

'And where is she?' Queen Mary asks him.

'On progress,' he replies levelly.

'This plot concerns me?' she asks.

'I think many plots concern you,' he says. 'But luckily my lord Burghley's men are thorough. You are safe here.'

'Well, I thank you,' she says coolly.

'A word,' Sir Peter says to me as he turns away from her, and I follow him to the garden gate. 'She is lying,' he says bluntly. 'Lying like a trooper.'

'I dare swear she is not . . .'

'I know she is,' he says. 'Ridolfi was carrying a letter of introduction from her to the Pope himself. He showed it to Cecil's man. He boasted of her support. She told the Pope to trust Ridolfi as he would trust her own self. Ridolfi has a plan he calls 'the Great Enterprise of England' to destroy us all. It is this plot which is coming to us now. She has called down six thousand fanatical Papist Spaniards on us. And she knows where they are landing, and she has organised for their payment.'

I hold on to the gate to conceal the weakness in my knees.

'I can't question her,' he goes on. 'I cannot interrogate her as I would any ordinary suspect. If she was anyone else she would be in the Tower now and we would be piling rocks on her chest till her ribs broke and her lies were squeezed out with her last gasping breath. We can't do that to her, and it is hard to tell what other pressure we can bring to bear. To tell truth, I can hardly bear to speak to her. I can hardly look into her false face.'

'There is no more beautiful woman in the world!' bursts from me.

'Oh aye, she's lovely. But how can you admire a face which is two-faced?'

For a moment I am about to argue, and then I remember the sweetness of her inquiry after her cousin's health and I think of her writing to Philip of Spain, bringing the Spaniards in on us, summoning the armada and the end of England. 'Are you certain she knows of this plot?'

'Knows of it? She has made it!'

I shake my head. I cannot believe it. I will not believe it.

'I have asked her as much as I can. But she might be more honest with you or the countess,' the young man says earnestly. 'Go back to her, see if you can find out any more. I shall eat and rest here tonight, and leave at dawn.'

'Ridolfi could have forged his letter which said that she recommended him,' I suggest. 'Or he could be lying about it.' Or, I think, in the mess we are in since I can be sure of nothing, you could be lying to me, or Cecil lying to us all.

'Suppose we start with the presumption that it is she who is lying,' he says. 'See if you can get anything out of her. The plans of the Spanish especially. We have to know what they are going to do. If she knows, she must tell you. If we had the slightest idea where they would land we could save hundreds of lives, we might save our country. I will see you before I leave. I am going to her rooms. My men will be turning them upside down right now.'

He sketches a little bow and walks away. I turn back to her. She is smiling at me as I walk across the grass and I know that heart-stopping mischievous gleam. I know it, I know her.

'How pale you are, dear Chowsbewwy,' she remarks. 'These alarms are bad for us both. I nearly fainted when I heard the bell.'

'You know, don't you?' I ask wearily. I don't sit down on the stool at her feet, again, I remain standing, and she rises from the seat and comes beside me. I can smell the perfume in her hair, she stands so close that if I stretched out my hand I could touch her waist. I could draw her to me. She tilts back her head and smiles at me, a knowing smile, one that would be exchanged between warm familiar friends, a lovers' smile.

'I don't know anything,' she says with her naughty confiding gleam.

'I have just been telling him that this Ridolfi might have used your name without your leave,' I say. 'He doesn't believe me, and I find I don't even believe myself. You know Ridolfi, don't you? You authorised him, didn't you? You sent him to the Pope, and to the duke in the Netherlands, and to Philip of Spain, you ordered him to plan an invasion? Even though you are sworn to a new agreement with Elizabeth? Even though you signed your name to her peace treaty? Even though you promised Morton that you would weave no plots and send no letters? Even though you promised me privately, between the two of us, at my request, that you would take care? Even though you know that they will take you away from me if I don't guard you?'

'I cannot live like a dead woman,' she whispers, though we are alone and there is no sound in the garden but the haunting late afternoon song of the thrush. 'I cannot give up on my own cause, on my own life. I cannot lie like a corpse in my coffin and hope that someone is kind enough to carry me to Scotland or to London. I have to be alive. I have to act.'

'But you promised,' I insist like a child. 'How can I trust anything, if I hear you promise on your honour as a queen, if I see you sign your name and place your seal, and then I find that it means nothing? You mean none of it?'

'I am imprisoned,' she says. 'Everything means nothing until I am free.'

I am so angry with her and I feel so betrayed that I turn my back on her and take two hasty steps away. It is an insult to a queen, men have been banished from court for far less than turning their back. I check when I realise what I have done, but I don't turn to face her and kneel.

I feel like a fool. All this time I have been thinking the best of her, reporting to Cecil that I have intercepted messages and she has not received them. I have told him I am sure she has not invited them, that she attracts conspiracies but does not conspire herself; and all this time he has known that she was writing treasonous rebellious instructions, planning to overthrow the peace of the country. All this time he has known that he was right and I was wrong, that she was an enemy and my tenderness towards her was itself a folly, if not treason. She has played the part of a devil and I have trusted her and helped her against my own interests, against my own friends, against my fellow Englishmen. I have been a fool for this woman, and she has abused my trust and abused my household and abused my fortune and abused my wife.

'You have shamed me,' I burst out, still turned away from her, my head bowed and my back to her. 'Shamed me before Cecil and the court. I swore that I could keep you safe and away from conspiracy and you have made me false to my oath. You have done whatever wickedness you pleased and you have made a fool of me. A fool.' I am out of breath, I end in a sob of mortification. 'You have played me for a fool.'

Still she says nothing and still, I don't turn to look at her.

'I told them that you were not plotting, that you could be trusted with greater freedom,' I say. 'I told them that you had entered into a treaty with the queen and made a promise to Morton and you had sworn these on your honour. I said that you would never break your word. Not your word of honour as a queen. I promised this on your behalf. I said that you had given your word. I said that was as good as a gold coin. I told them that you are a queen, a queen *par excellence*; and a woman incapable of dishonour.' I take a shuddering breath. 'I don't think you know what honour is,' I say bitterly.

'I don't think you know what honour means. And you have dishonoured me.'

Gently, like a petal falling, I feel her touch. She has come up behind me and put her hand on my shoulder. I don't move and gently she lays her cheek against my shoulder blade. If I turned, I could take her in my arms and the coolness of her cheek would be like a balm on my red and angry face.

'You have made a fool of me before my queen, before the court, and before my own wife,' I choke out, my back tingling under her touch. 'You have dishonoured me in my own house, and once I cared for nothing more than my honour and my house.'

Her hand on my shoulder grows firmer, she gives a little tug on my jacket and I turn to look at her. Her dark eyes are filled with tears, her face twisted with grief. 'Ah, don't say so,' she whispers. 'Chowsbewwy, don't say such things. You have been a man of such honour to me, you have been such a friend to me. I have never had a man serve me as you have done. I have never had a man care for me without hope of return. I can tell you, that I love –'

'No,' I interrupt. 'Don't say another word to me. Don't make another promise to me. How should I hear anything you say? I cannot trust anything you say!'

'I don't break my word!' she insists. 'I have never given my true word. I am a prisoner, I am not bound to tell the truth. I am under duress and my promise means noth—'

'You have broken your word and with it, you have broken my heart,' I say simply, and I pull away from her grip and walk away from her without looking back.

1571, October, Sheffield Castle: Bess

A cold autumn, and the leaves falling early from the trees, as if the weather itself will be hard on us this year. We have escaped disaster by a whisper, a whisper, nothing more. The Queen of Scots' spy and plotter, Roberto Ridolfi, had every great power in Christendom in alliance against us. He had visited the Pope in Rome, the Duke of Alva in the Netherlands, the King of Spain and the King of France. They all sent either gold or men or both, ready for an invasion which was to murder Queen Elizabeth and put Queen Mary on the throne. Only Ridolfi's boastful whisper of the plot reached the keen ears of William Cecil and saved us.

Cecil took the Queen of Scots' bishop to stay with the Bishop of Ely as a house guest. It must have been a merry party. He took his servant to the Tower and broke him on the rack, under the stones, and by hanging him from the wrists. The man – an old servant of the Queen of Scots – told the torturers everything they asked, and probably more besides. Then Norfolk's men were taken into the Tower and sang their songs as their fingernails were pulled out. Robert Higford showed them the hiding place for the letters, under the tiles of the roof. William Barker told them of the plot. Lawrence Bannister decoded the Queen of Scots' letters to her betrothed, Norfolk, filled with love and promises. Then finally they took the Queen of Scots' friend and ambassador, Bishop John Lesley, from his stay in Cambridgeshire to the harsher hospitality of the Tower and gave him a taste of the pain that had broken lesser men, and he told them everything.

Another round of arrests of men named as traitors and Norfolk himself was thrown back in the Tower again. It is unbelievable, but it seems that after giving his complete submission to our Queen Elizabeth, he went on writing and plotting with the other queen and was deep in the toils of the Spanish and the French, planning the overthrow of our peace.

I do believe we were within a day of a Spanish invasion that would have destroyed us, murdered Elizabeth, and put this most true heir to Bloody Mary Tudor – Bloody Mary Stuart – on the throne of England, and the fires in Smithfield would have been burning hot for Protestant martyrs once more.

Thank God Ridolfi was a braggart, thank God the King of Spain is a cautious man. Thank God the Duke of Norfolk is a fool who sent out a fortune in gold by an unreliable courier and the plotters betrayed themselves. And thank God Cecil was there, at the centre of the web of his spies, knowing everything. For if the other queen had her way, she would be in Whitehall now, Elizabeth would be dead, and England, my England, would be lost.

My husband the earl has grown dark along with the colder nights, and drawn in as they have done, into silence. He visits the queen in her rooms only once a week and asks her with bleak courtesy if she is well, if she has everything she needs, and if she has any letters that she would like dispatched by him, if she has any requests or complaints for him or for the court.

She replies with equal coldness that she is unwell, that she requires her freedom, that she demands Elizabeth honour the agreement to send her home to Scotland, and that she has no letters to send. They part as formally as enemies forced to dance together and joined for a moment by the movement of the dance and then released again.

I should be rejoicing that their friendship has ended so abruptly and so badly, I should be laughing in my sleeve that the faithless queen should have been faithless to him. But it is hard to take pleasure in this prison. My husband the earl has aged years in these last few days, his face is grooved with sorrow and he hardly speaks. She is lonely, now that she has lost his love, and once again she comes to sit with me in the afternoons. She comes quietly, like a maidservant in disgrace, and I must say I am surprised that his disapproval should hit her so hard. Anyone would think that she had cared for him. We have working candles lit by five o'clock and she says that she is dreading the darker nights and grey mornings. The midsummer tide of her good fortune has quite drained away, her luck has run dry. She knows that she will spend another winter in captivity. There is no chance now that they will send her back to Scotland. She has destroyed her own hopes and I am afraid that my house will be cursed with this sad ghost forever.

'Bess, what is happening in London?' she asks me. 'You can tell me. I can hardly make any use of the information. I should think everyone knows more than me already.'

'The Duke of Norfolk is arrested, again charged with plotting with the Spanish, and returned to the Tower of London,' I say to her.

She goes white. Aha, I think meanly, so for once you are not ahead of us all. Her spies and informants must be lying low. She did not know of this.

'Bess, no! Is this true?'

'He is accused of being part of a plot to release you,' I say. 'You would know more of this than I.'

'I swear . . .'

'Don't,' I say coldly. 'Save your breath.'

She falls silent. 'Ah Bess, if you were in my shoes you would have done the same thing. He and I –'

'Did you really persuade yourself that you loved him?'

'I thought he would save me.'

'Well, you have led him to his death,' I say. 'And that's a thing I wouldn't have done. Not even in your shoes.'

'You don't know what it is to be queen,' she says simply. 'I am a queen. I am not like other women. I have to be free.'

'You have condemned yourself to a lifetime of imprisonment,' I predict. 'And him to death. I would not have done that in your shoes, queen or not.'

'They can prove nothing against him,' she says. 'And even if they forge evidence, or torture false testimony from servants, he is still the queen's cousin. He is of royal blood. She will not condemn her own family to death. A royal person is sacred.'

'What else can she do?' I demand, driven to irritation. 'All very well for you to say that she can't do it; but what choice does she have? What choice does he leave her? If he will not stop plotting, after making a full submission and being forgiven, if you will not stop plotting, after giving your sworn word, what can she do but end it? She cannot spend the rest of her life waiting for your assassin to arrive and kill her.'

'She cannot kill him; he is her cousin and of royal blood. And she will never be able to kill me,' she declares. 'She cannot kill a fellow queen. And I would never send an assassin. So she can never end this.'

'You have become each other's nightmare,' I say. 'And it is as if neither of you can ever wake.'

We sit in silence for a moment. I am working on a tapestry of my house at Chatsworth, as accurate as a builder's drawing. Sometimes I think this will be all I have left of Chatsworth when I have to sell my pride and my joy to a buyer at a breakdown price. All I will have left of the years of my happiness is this tapestry of the house I loved.

'I have not heard from my ambassador for weeks,' the queen says quietly to me. 'John Lesley, Bishop of Ross. Is he arrested? Do you know?'

'Was he part of the plot?' I ask.

'No,' she says wearily. 'No. There was no plot that I know of. And certainly he was not part of it. And even if he had received a letter from someone, or met with someone, then he cannot be arrested, since he is an ambassador. He has rights, even in such a kingdom as this, where spies make proclamations and commoners pass laws.'

'Then he has nothing to fear,' I say unkindly. 'And neither do you. And neither does the Duke of Norfolk. He is safe, and according to you, so are you and the ambassador: all of you untouchable in either the sanctity of your bodies or the innocence of your conscience. That being so: why are you so pale, Your Grace, and why does my husband not ride with you in the mornings any more? Why does he never seek you out and why do you not send for him?'

'I think I'll go back to my rooms now,' she says quietly. 'I am tired.'

1571, November, Sheffield Castle: Mary

I have to wait for long months in silence, guarding my tongue, afraid even to write to my own ambassador for news, imprisoned in anxiety. In the end I hear from Paris, in a letter that has been opened and read by others, that Norfolk is arrested and will be charged with treason.

Last time he was in the Tower it was Cecil himself who argued that the duke was imprudent but not treasonous and had him released to his London house. But this time it is all different. Cecil is leading the duke's accusers, and has the duke and all his household under arrest. Undoubtedly the servants will be tortured and they will either confess the truth, or make up lies to escape the pain. If Cecil is determined that the duke will face a charge of treason then he will find the evidence to prove it, and the luck of the Howards will turn bad in this generation, as it has done so often before.

There is worse news on the second page. Bishop John Lesley, my faithful friend who chose exile in my service rather than his comfortable palace at home, is a broken man. He has turned up in Paris resolved to live the rest of his days as an exile in France. He will say nothing of what took place in England nor why he is now in France. He is dumb. The gossip is, that he turned his coat and told Cecil everything. I cannot believe it, I have to read and re-read the report but it assures me that John Lesley has abandoned my cause and gave the evidence which will condemn Norfolk. They say that Lesley told Cecil everything he knew; and of course, he knew everything. He knew all about Ridolfi – why, he was the joint author of the plot. The world now believes that the duke, the banker, the bishop and I sent a mission around Europe begging the French, the Spanish and the Pope to assassinate Elizabeth and to attack England. The world knows that I chose as my conspirators a braggart, a weakling and a fool. That I am a fool myself.

Shrewsbury will never forgive me for dishonouring my parole with him, for lying to Cecil, to Morton, to him. He has hardly spoken to me since that day in the garden when he said I had broken my word and his heart. I have tried to speak to him but he turns away, I have put my hand on his but he quietly withdraws. He looks ill and tired but he says nothing to me of his health. He says nothing to me of anything any more.

Bess is drained by worry about money, and by fear of the future, and by long bitter resentment of me. We are a remorseful household in this autumn season. I have to hope that the Scots will come to me once more and ask me to return, I have to believe that a fresh champion will write to me with a plan to release me, I have to believe that Philip of Spain will not be discouraged by this disastrous end to the plan that we swore could not fail. I cannot find in myself the courage to write once more, to start again, to stitch again the tapestry of conspiracy.

I think of Shrewsbury saying that I have dishonoured my word as a queen and I wonder if anyone will ever trust me in the future, or think it safe to rely on my judgement. I think I am truly defeated this time. My greatest champion and only friend Bothwell is still imprisoned in Denmark without hope of release, and he writes to me that he will go mad in confinement. My codes are all broken, my friends are imprisoned, the ambassador has left my service, my betrothed is facing a charge of treason and the man who loved me, without even knowing it, will no longer meet my eyes.

1571, December, Sheffield Castle: George

I thought I was in pain before. I thought that I had lost the love and duty of my wife who had decided that I was a fool. I pledged myself, in silence, always in silence, to a woman so far above me as to be more than a queen: an angel. But now I find there is a new hell, below the one I knew. Now I find that the woman to whom I had given my secret loyalty is a traitor, a betrayer of herself, forsworn, a liar, a person of dishonour.

I could laugh to think that I used to look down on my Bess for coming from a farmhouse, for having an accent which cracks into Derbyshire, for claiming to be Protestant while knowing no theology, for insisting on the Bible in English while being unable to read Latin, for decorating her walls and furnishing her rooms with the spoils of a destroyed church. For being, at worst, little more than the widow of a thief, the daughter of a farmer. I could laugh at myself now for the sin of false pride; but it would be a sound like a death rattle in the throat.

Despising this wife of mine, this straightforward vulgar lovable wife of mine, I set my heart and spent my fortune on a woman whose word is like the wind; it can blow wherever it wants. She can speak three languages but she can tell the truth in none of them. She can dance like an Italian but she cannot walk a straight line. She can embroider better than a sempstress and write a fair hand; but her seal on the bottom of a document means nothing. Whereas my Bess is known throughout Derbyshire for fair trading. When Bess shakes on a deal it is sealed and you could stake your life on it. This queen could swear on a fragment of the True Cross – and it would still be provisional.

I have spent my fortune on this will-of-the-wisp of a queen, I have put my honour on this chimera. I have squandered Bess's dowry and the inheritance for her children on keeping this woman as a queen should be served; never knowing that under the cloth of state was seated a traitor. I let her sit on a throne and command a court in my own house, and order things just as she would have them, because I believed, deep in my faithful heart, that this was a queen like no other had ever been.

Well, in that I was right. She is a queen as no other has ever been. She is a queen with no kingdom, a queen with no crown, a queen with no dignity, a queen with no word, a queen without honour. She has been ordained by God, and anointed by His holy oil; but somehow He must have forgotten all about her. Or maybe she lied to Him too.

Now it is I who will have to forget all about her.

Bess comes tentatively to my privy chamber and waits on the threshold, as if she is not sure of a welcome.

'Come in,' I say. I mean to sound kind but my voice is cold. Nothing sounds right between Bess and me any more. 'What d'you want of me?'

'Nothing!' she says awkwardly. 'A word, only.'

I raise my head from the papers I have been reading. My steward insisted that I see them. They are long lists of debts, money that we have borrowed to finance the keeping of the queen, and they fall due next year. I know of no way to pay them except by selling my lands. I slide a sheet of paper over them so that Bess cannot see, there is no point in worrying her too; and I slowly get to my feet.

'Please, I didn't mean to disturb you,' she says apologetically.

We are always saying sorry to each other these days. We tiptoe around as if there is a death in the house. It is the death of our happiness; and this is my fault too.

'You don't disturb me,' I say. 'What is it?'

'It is to say I am sorry, but I cannot see how we can have open house this Christmastide,' she says in a rush. 'We cannot feed all the tenant farmers and their families, not as well as all the servants. Not this year.'

'There is no money?'

She nods. 'There is no money.'

I try to laugh but it sounds all wrong. 'How much can it cost? Surely we have coin and plate in the treasure room enough for a dinner and ale for our own people?'

'Not for months and months.'

'I suppose you have tried to borrow?'

'I have borrowed all that I can, locally. I have already mortgaged land. They don't accept it at full value any more, they are starting to doubt our ability to repay. If nothing improves, we will have to go to the London goldsmiths and offer them plate.'

I wince. 'Not my family goods,' I protest, thinking of my crested plates being melted down as scrap. Thinking of the goldsmiths, weighing my silverware, and seeing my family crest, and laughing that I have come to this.

'No, of course not. We will sell my things first,' she says levelly.

'I am sorry for this,' I say. 'You had better tell your steward to tell your tenants that they cannot come for their dinner this year. Perhaps next.'

'They will all know why,' she warns me. 'They will know we are struggling.'

'I imagine everyone knows,' I say drily. 'Since I write to the queen once a month and beg her to pay her debts to me, and the letter is read in public to her. The whole court knows. All of London knows.

Everyone knows we are on the brink of ruin. No-one will offer us credit.'

She nods.

'I will put this right,' I say earnestly. 'If you have to sell your plate I will get it back for you. I will find a way, Bess. You will not be the loser for marrying me.'

She bows her head and bites her lip so she does not blurt out the reproach that is on her tongue. I know she is already the loser for marrying me. She is thinking of her husbands who carefully amassed their fortunes for her. Men I have sneered at as upstarts, with no family to speak of. She gained from marrying them, they founded a fortune. But I have squandered it. I have lost her fortune. And now I think I have lost my pride.

'Will you go to London this season?' she asks me.

'Norfolk's trial is delayed until after Christmas,' I say. 'Though I doubt they will be very merry at court, with this ghost at their feast. I shall have to serve at his trial. I'll go down to London then, after twelfth night, and when I see Her Majesty, I will speak again about her debt to us.'

'Perhaps she will pay us.'

'Perhaps.'

'Is there any plan to send the Queen of Scots home?' she asks hopefully.

'Not now,' I say quietly. 'They have sent her bishop into exile in France, and her spy, Ridolfi, has fled to Italy. The Spanish ambassador has been ordered to leave in disgrace, and everyone else is in the Tower. The Scots won't want her – seeing the company she keeps and how faithless she has been, breaking her parole, and her word, and her promise to Lord Morton. And Cecil must be certain that Norfolk's evidence will incriminate her. The question can only be: what will he do with evidence that damns her?'

'Will they put her on trial? What could be the charge?'

'If they can prove that she invited Spain to invade or plotted the queen's death then she is guilty of rebellion against a lawful monarch. That would carry the sentence of death. They can't execute her, of course; but they can find her guilty and put her in the Tower forever.'

Bess is silent, she cannot meet my eyes. 'I am sorry,' she says awkwardly.

'The punishment for raising a rebellion is death,' I say steadily. 'If Cecil can prove that she tried to assassinate Elizabeth then she would face a trial. She would deserve a trial, and lesser men have died for what she has done.'

'She says that Elizabeth will never kill her. She says that she is untouchable.'

'I know it. She is sacred. But a guilty verdict will see her in the Tower forever. And no power in Europe would defend her.'

'What could Norfolk say against her that would be so very bad?'

I shrug. 'Who knows what she has written to him, or what she wrote to the Spanish, or to her spy, or to the Pope? Who knows what she promised them?'

'And Norfolk himself?'

'I think it will be a treason trial,' I say. 'I shall have to be chief justice. It hardly seems possible. That I should sit as judge on Thomas Howard! We practically grew up together.'

'He will be found innocent,' she predicts. 'Or the queen will pardon him after the verdict. They have quarrelled as cousins do, but she loves him.'

'I pray that it is so,' I tell her. 'For if I have to turn the axe towards him and read out the death sentence, then it will be a dark day for me, and a worse one for England.'

1571, December, Chatsworth: Mary

I am hobbling painfully in the courtyard, as my legs are so stiff and painful I can hardly walk, when I see a stone flung in an arc over the wall from the outside, and it falls near my feet. A piece of paper is wrapped around it and, disregarding the twinge in my knees, I step over it at once, hiding it with my skirts.

My heart races, I can feel my lips smile. Ah, so now it begins again, another proposal, another plot. I had thought that I was too hurt and defeated for any more conspiracies; but now one has fallen at my feet and I feel my hopes leap up at the prospect of another chance of freedom.

I glance around, no-one is watching me except the little pageboy, Anthony Babington. Quick as a lad playing football, I kick the stone towards him, and he bends and snatches it up and puts it in his pocket. I stagger another few steps, wearily, as if my knees are worse, and then I call him to me.

'Lend me your shoulder, boy,' I say. 'My legs are too weak for walking today. Help me to my room.'

I am almost certain that no-one is watching us; but it is part of the delight of the plot to wait until we are on the turn of the stair and to say urgently to him: 'Now! Now!' and he slips his little hand into his breeches' pocket, unwraps the stone and gives me the crumpled paper.

'Good boy,' I whisper. 'Come and see me at dinner time and I will have a sugared plum for you.'

'I serve you for faith alone,' he says. His dark eyes are bright with excitement.

'I know you do, and God Himself will reward you for it; but I would like to give you a sugar plum as well,' I say, smiling at him.

He grins and helps me to the door of my chamber and then bows and leaves me. Agnes Livingstone helps me in.

'Are you in pain? The countess was coming to sit with you this afternoon. Shall I tell her not to come?'

'No, let her come, let her come,' I say. I shall do nothing to let them know that a fresh plot has started, a new war is beginning.

I open a book of devotional poems and spread the paper out over the leaves. The door opens, and Bess comes in, curtseys and sits at my invitation. From her stool, placed low, she cannot see my letter. To my amusement, she settles down to sew with me while I have this letter, this new invitation to the undoing of her queen and herself, open before me.

I let myself glance at it, and then gasp in horror. 'Look at this,' I say suddenly to her. 'Look! Look at this, which was flung over the courtyard wall!'

It is a drawing of me as a mermaid, a bare-breasted whore, and beneath it is a filthy poem listing my husbands, and remarking that they all die, as if my bed were a charnel house. It says that poor Francis of France was poisoned by me, Darnley was murdered by Bothwell, and I took him to my bed as a reward. It says Bothwell is kept as a lunatic in a barred cave facing the North Sea. It calls me his French whore.

Bess tosses it into the fireplace. 'Filth,' she says simply. 'Think nothing of it. Someone must have got drunk on Christmas ale and sung a little song and scribbled a picture. It is nothing.'

'It is directed at me.'

She shrugs. 'News of the Ridolfi plot will spread throughout the

387

kingdom and you will be blamed for it. You have lost the love that people had for you when they thought you were a princess tragically ill-treated by the Scots. Now they think you bring us nothing but trouble. Everyone fears and hates the Spanish. They will not quickly forgive you for inviting them in against us. Even the Catholics blame you for inciting the Pope against Elizabeth. They wanted to live in peace, we all want to live in peace, and you are spoiling it.'

'But this is not about the Spanish and all that,' I say. 'It says nothing about Ridolfi or the Duke of Norfolk. It is all about Darnley, and Scotland, and Bothwell.'

'Men in an ale house will repeat anything filthy. But it cannot matter to you what they say. They will say anything, and this is old scandal.'

I shake my head, as if to clear my thoughts, and I pick up my little dog and hug him for comfort. 'But why this old scandal? Why now?'

'They gossip about what they hear,' she says steadily. 'Isn't it perennial news? An old scandal?'

'But why speak of it now?' I demand. 'Why don't they blame me for inciting the Pope, or calling in the Spanish? Why this old story in preference to the new? Why now?'

'I don't know,' she says. 'I hear no gossip here. And I don't know why it would come up again now.'

I nod. I think I know what is happening, and I am certain who is doing it. Who else would slur my name but him? 'Do you think perhaps, Bess, that the men sent out to spy in the ale houses and markets for your queen can talk as well as listen? When they listen for any threat against her, do you think that they also supply scandal about me? About all her enemies? Do you not think, that as they listen at keyholes, they also drip fear and poison into the minds of ordinary people? Do you not think that they abuse me, that they spread fear of strangers, terror of war, accusations about Jews and Papists? Do you not think that this whole country is loyal to Elizabeth because she makes them terrified of anything else? That she has agents whose job is to go around spreading terror to keep her people loyal?'

'Well, yes,' Bess agrees, a child of Elizabeth's England where truth is a thing for sale in the market and scandal is priced to sell. 'But why would anyone tell old scandals about you? And why now?'

'That is the very question,' I say simply. 'Why now? At this particular, useful moment? Just before Norfolk comes to trial? Could it be that he has refused to say anything against me? Could they fear that they will take him to the very steps of the scaffold and he will not accuse me of treason? Because he knows he is innocent of a rebellion against Elizabeth and I am innocent too. All we wanted was to be married and for me to be released to my country. All we conspired to do was to free me. But they want to hang Norfolk and destroy me. Don't you know that's true?'

Bess's needle is still above her tapestry. She knows I am right and she knows my enemy. She knows how he works and she knows how he succeeds. 'But why traduce you with an old scandal?'

'I am a woman,' I say quietly. 'If you hate a woman, the first thing you destroy is her reputation. They will name me as a woman of shame; unfit to rule, unfit to marry. If they ruin my reputation then they make Norfolk's crime seem even worse. They make him look like a man who was ready to marry an adulteress and a murderess. They make him look insane with ambition and me lower than a whore. Who would follow Norfolk or serve me? No loyal Scotsman, or even Englishman would ever want me on the throne. They would think I was guilty of treason against Elizabeth because they believe I am a whore and a murderess.'

Bess nods reluctantly. 'To dishonour you both equally,' she says. 'Even if they cannot get you both to trial.'

'And who would whisper such a thing? Who do you think, Bess Talbot? Who do you know who uses rumour and false accusation and terrible slanders to destroy another's reputation? To finish them forever? When he cannot prove them guilty in an inquiry, but when he is determined to give them the reputation of guilt in the world? Who would do this? Who has the men already in his service, and the power that he could do this?'

I see in her stricken face that she knows full well who runs the spies, and that it is the same man who runs the slander-makers. 'I don't know,' she says stoutly. 'I don't know who would do such a thing.'

I let it rest. I have heard worse ballads than the one we have just burned on the fire, and seen worse portraits too. I let Bess cling to her denial rather than force her to name her friend Cecil as a spy and a pitcher of filth. 'Well, well,' I say lightly. 'If you do not know, having lived at court as you have done, having seen who rules and who has power, then I am sure that I do not know either.'

1572, January, Cold Harbour House, London: George

As I get to London, after a bad journey in terrible weather, and open up a few rooms of my London house, I learn that Cecil, having kept the terrible letters of the Scots queen as a state secret on the command of Elizabeth for over three years, has now seen fit to publish this odd and obscene collection of poetry, threat and evil.

Having refused to see them as a secret document, and insisted that they were presented as evidence in court or not shown at all, I now find these most secret papers, which we all agreed were too dreadful to be discussed by an official inquiry, are now available at the stationers as a little booklet, priced for sale, and the poor people are writing ballads and posting drawings based on this filth. The supposed author of these vile and lustful scribbles, the Queen of Scots, is unanimously reviled in London by everyone who has bought and read them; and even the common people throughout England seem to have learned of the letters and now claim to know, with the absolute certainty of the ignorant, that she is Bothwell's lover and Darnley's murderer, the poisoner of her first husband and the lover of her French father-in-law, and in league with the devil to boot. They are creating ballads and stories and more than one vile riddle. She, who I first saw as a creature of fire and air, is now notorious; she is become a figure of fun.

Of course this makes Norfolk look even more of a fool in the eyes of everyone. Before he stands his trial we all think that he must have been drunk with ambition to have been seduced by such an obvious Jezebel. Before a word of evidence has been posted, before he has even walked into court, every right-thinking man in England condemns him for stupidity and lust.

Except me. Except me. I do not condemn him. How can I? She took me in, as she took him in, I desired her, as he desired her. He, at least, had the sense to think that though she might have been a bad woman, she might still be Queen of Scotland and make him king. He had at least had the old Howard sense of ambition. I was a greater fool than he was. I just wanted to serve her. I didn't even want a reward. I didn't even mind the cost. I just wanted to serve her.

1572, January, Sheffield Castle: Bess

We have to wait for the verdict on Thomas Howard from London and there is nothing we can do to speed this time of waiting. Queen Mary is impatient for news and yet dreads to hear. One would almost have thought her truly in love with him. One would almost think that the man she loved is on trial.

She walks on the battlement and she looks south, where he is, instead of north. She knows that no army will come for her from the North this year. Her dupe Norfolk and her pander Ross are imprisoned and her spy is run away, she is a woman alone. Her master-plotter Ridolfi has conspired only to win his own safety. Her last husband, Bothwell, will never be released from his prison in Denmark; both the Scots lords and the English are determined that such a dangerous enemy shall never be set free. He can be of no help to her any more. Her besotted admirer and only loyal friend, my husband, is nursing a broken heart and finally remembering his duty to his queen and his country, and his promises to me. None of the men she has enchanted can help her now. There is no army of rescue for her, there is no man sworn to be hers till death, there is no network of friends and liars, gathering secretly and silently in a dozen hidden places. She is defeated, her friends are arrested, screaming on the rack, or run away. She is finally a true prisoner. She is quite in my power.

Odd then, that I should take such little joy in it. Perhaps it is because she is so roundly defeated: her beauty is dissolving into fat, her grace is made clumsy by pain, her eyes swollen with crying, her rosebud mouth now permanently folded into a thin line of suffering. She, who always looked so much younger than me, has suddenly aged like me, grown weary like me, grown sorrowful like me.

We form a quiet alliance, we have learned the hard way that the world is not easy for women. I have lost the love of my husband, my last husband. But so has she. I may lose my home and she has lost her kingdom. My fortunes may come good again, and so may hers. But in these cold grey winter days we are like two hangdog widows who cling together for warmth, and hope for better days though doubting they will ever come.

We talk of our children. It is as if they are our only prospect of happiness. I talk of my daughter Elizabeth, and she says that she is of an age to match with Charles Stuart, her husband Darnley's younger brother. If they were to marry – and this is a game to play over our sewing – their son would be heir to the English throne, second only to her son James. We laugh at the thought of the consternation of the queen if we were to make such an ill-starred ambitious match, and our laugh is like that of old ill-natured women, plotting something bad, as revenge.

She asks me about my debts and I tell her frankly that the costs of her lodging have taken my husband to the very brink of ruin, and that he has drawn on my lands and sold my treasure to save his own. The fortune that I brought him on marriage has been mortgaged, bit by bit, to meet his debts. She does not waste her time or mine in regret, she says that he should insist that Elizabeth pays her debts, she says that no good king or queen ever lets a good subject be out of pocket: how else can they rule? I tell her, and truly, that Elizabeth is the meanest sovereign that ever wore a crown. She gives her love and affection, she gives her loyalty, she can even give honours and sometimes (more rarely) money-earning positions; but she never hands over cash from her treasury if she can possibly help it.

'But she will need his friendship now,' she points out. 'To get the verdict of guilty on the duke? She must realise that she should pay her debts to him now, he is the master of the judges, she must want him to do her will.'

I see from this that she does not know him at all, she does not begin to understand him. I find I love him for his proud folly, even though I rail at him for being a proud fool. 'He won't bring in a verdict that depends on whether she pays her debt to him,' I say. 'He's a Talbot, he can't be bought. He will look at the evidence, weigh the charge and come to the just sentence; whatever he is paid, whatever it costs.' I hear the pride in my own voice. 'That is the sort of man he is. I would have thought you would know that by now. You can't bribe him, and you can't buy him. He's not an easy man, not even a very sensible man. He does not understand the way of the world and he is not a very clever man. You might even call him a fool, certainly he was a fool over you; but he is always, always a man of honour.'

1572, January, Sheffield Castle: Mary

The night that they start the trial I send my women to bed and sit beside my fire and think, not of the Duke of Norfolk, who faces the judges tomorrow for my sake, but of Bothwell, who would never have turned himself in to arrest, who would never have let his servants confess, who would never have written state secrets in a breakable code, who would never have let those codes be found. Who – God knows, above all other – would never have trusted a turncoat such as Ridolfi. Who – God forgive me – would never have trusted my assurance that Ridolfi was the man for us. Bothwell would have seen at once that my ambassador John Lesley would break under questioning, Bothwell would have known that Ridolfi would brag. Bothwell would have guessed that the plot would fail and would never have joined in it. Bothwell – it makes me laugh to think of it – would never have sent a queen's ransom in an unmarked bag by a Shrewsbury draper, trusting to luck. Bothwell was a thief, a kidnapper, a rapist, a murderer, a wicked man, a despicable man; but never a victim. No-one has ever held Bothwell for long, or cozened him, or tricked him, or had him serve against his own interests. Not until he met me, that is. When he fought for himself he was unbeatable.

I think of my palace at Holyrood in the early days of my marriage to Darnley. Within weeks I had discovered that the beautiful boy I had fallen in love with was a foul young man whose only charms were in appearance. As soon as we were married he let me see what everyone else knew, that he was a drunk and a sodomite with a burning ambition to put me aside from rule and take the power himself as king consort.

I blamed my distaste for him on my discovery of the sort of man he was; but the truth was worse than that – far worse. I remember Bothwell coming to my court at Holyrood, the shabby ladies and the uncouth men of my Scottish court falling back to make way, as they always did, for Bothwell, who came forward, unsmiling and powerful, head and shoulders above everyone else. Someone gave a little hiss of distaste, and someone left slamming the door, and three men drew away and fingered their belts where their swords should be, and instead of being angered at the disrespect I just caught my breath at the scent of a man who was at least a man and not a half-peasant, like these Scots lords, nor a half-girl, like my lightweight husband; but a man who would stand to look a king in the face, a man like my father-in-law, the King of France, who knew himself to be the greatest man in the room, whoever else was there.

I see him and I want him. It is as simple and as sinful as that. I see him, and I know he can hold this throne for me, defeat these lickspittle turncoats for me, confront John Knox and the men who hate me, knock these warring lords together, command my allowance from France, defend me from England, and make me queen here. No-one else can do it. They fear no-one but him. And so I want no-one but him. He is the only man who can keep me safe, who can save me from these barbarians. A savage himself, he can rule them. I look at him and I know he is the man who will take me to my destiny. With him I will command Scotland, with him I could invade England.

Does he know this, the minute he sees me – composed and beautiful on my throne? I am not such a fool as to let my desire show in my face. I look at him calmly and I nod my head at him and remark that my mother trusted him above all the other lords and he served her with honour. Does he know that as I am speaking so coolly I can feel my heart pounding underneath my gown and my body prickle with nervous sweat?

I don't know, even later, I still don't know. He will never tell me, not even when we are lovers whispering in the night, he won't tell me then, and when I ask, he laughs lazily, and says: 'A man and a maid . . .'

'Hardly a maid,' I say.

'Far worse,' he says. 'A married woman, a much-married woman, and a queen.'

'So did you know I wanted you?'

'Sweetheart, I knew you were a woman, so you would be bound to want somebody.'

'But did you know it was you?'

'Well, who else was there?'

'Will you not say?'

'There were you, clinging to your throne, desperate for help. Someone was going to kidnap you and marry you by force. You were like a wild bird waiting for the net. There was I, longing for wealth and position and the chance to settle some old scores and rule Scotland. Would you not say we were born for each other?'

'Do you not love me? Did you never love me?'

He pulls me into his arms and his mouth comes down on mine. 'Not at all. Not at all, you French whore, you precious vixen, mine own, all mine own.'

'No,' I say as his weight comes down on me. It is what I always say to him. It is the word which means desire to me, to us. It is the word which means yes: 'No.'

January 16th, 1572, Westminster Hall, London: George

London is like a city in mourning, I have never seen anything like it since the young Elizabeth was taken from the Tower to imprisonment in the country and we were so afraid that she would never come home safe again. Now her cousin makes another fearful journey, from the Tower to the Star Chamber at Westminster Hall. But this time it is ordered by us, the Protestants, the Englishmen, against another Protestant and an Englishman. How has this happened?

It is a cold morning, still dark – for God's sake, why are people not still in their beds? Or going about their business? Why are they here, lining the streets, in a miserable silence, filling the lanes with foreboding? Cecil has ordered the queen's guards and the mayor's men to keep order, and behind their broad shoulders, the white faces of ordinary men and women peep out, hoping to see the queen's cousin go by, hoping to call out to him their prayer that he will be saved.

They don't get a chance to do even that. Of course Cecil trusts no-one, not even the sorrowful good nature of the English crowd. He has ordered the guards to take Norfolk to Westminster Hall by royal barge along the river. The oars cut through the water to the drum beat, there is no flag at the pole. Norfolk is travelling without his standard, without his herald, without his good name: a stranger to himself.

This must be his darkest time, he must be lonelier than any man in the world. His children are banned from seeing him, Cecil will

399

not allow him any visitors. He has not even had a lawyer to advise him. He is as solitary as a man already on a scaffold. More so, for he does not even have a priest at his side.

There is not one of us, not one of the twenty-six of us peers called to judge him, who does not imagine himself in his place. So many of us have lost friends or kin to the scaffold in these last few years. I think of Westmorland and Northumberland – both gone from me, both driven from me and from England, the wife of one in exile, a widow to a dead traitor, and the wife of the other in hiding on her lands, swearing she wants to know nothing of anything. How can this have happened in England, in my England? How can we have fallen so quickly into such suspicion and fear? God knows we are more fearful and more faithless to each other now, while Philip of Spain threatens our coast, than we were when he was married to our old queen and sitting on our throne. When we had a Spaniard as our king consort, ruling over us, we were less fearful than we are now. Now we are terrified of him and his religion. How should that be? A man who does not know who his friends are, does not know what the world is, a man who does not know his servants, his allies, is a man utterly alone.

I shall have to sit in judgement on my friend and fellow peer Thomas Howard, the Duke of Norfolk, and I shall have to listen to some dirty stuff. I don't trust evidence which has been racked out of prisoners screaming with pain. When did torture become something that happens as a matter of course in the prisons, with the silent complicity of the judge? We are not in France, where torture is a legal practice, we are not Spanish with an artistry of cruelty; we became Protestant so that religion should be a private matter: not imposed by fire and the stake. We are Englishmen, and such savagery is illegal except at the specific request of the monarch in the gravest of times. This is how it is in England.

Or at any rate, it should be.

Or at any rate, it once was.

But since the queen is advised by men who do not flinch from a little barbarism I find all sorts of evidence is now presented to me and I am expected to wink at it. Men I have counted as my friends for years can be declared treasonous and led to the scaffold, their road lined with confessions from their broken servants. This is the new justice of England, where stories are crushed out of men by piling stones on their bellies, and the judge is told beforehand what verdict to bring in. Where we break the spirits of pageboys so that we can break the neck of their master.

Well, I don't know. I don't know. It was not for this that we prayed, when we longed for our Elizabeth. This is not the new world of peace and reconciliation that we thought the new princess would bring to us.

I mutter all this to myself as I go, sluggishly enough, in my own barge down the river to the Westminster steps, to alight from a rocking boat on a dark river and to walk up the damp steps and through the terrace of the palace towards the hall, never more down-hearted than now, as Cecil's great plan to make England safe from Papists, from the Spanish, from the Scots queen, reaches its powerful final act. My fortune destroyed, in debt to my own wife, my own peace in wretched scraps, my wife spying on me, the woman that I love dishonoured by her own lies, a traitor to my liege lord and queen, the other once-beloved queen my ruin. I lift my head and walk into the hall as a Talbot should walk, like a lord among his peers, as my father would have walked, and his father before him, all of us in a long line; and I think, dear God, none of them can ever have felt as I do: so uncertain, so very uncertain, and so lost.

I have the highest seat, and on either side of me are the other lords who will try this miserable case with me, God forgive them for serving here. Cecil has picked this court well for his purposes. Hastings is here: the Scots queen's inveterate enemy; Wentworth, Robert Dudley and his brother Ambrose: every one of them Norfolk's friend in the good times, not one of them ready to risk his reputation for him now, none would dare defend the Scots queen. All of us, who whispered against Cecil just three years ago, are huddled together now, like frightened schoolboys, to do whatever he says.

Cecil is here himself – Burghley, as I must remember to call him. The queen's newest and freshest creation: Baron Burghley, in his bright new robes, his ermine collar all white and fluffy.

Below us lords are the judges of the Crown, and before us all, a draped stage where Howard will stand to answer the charges. Behind him, seats for the nobility and behind them, standing room for the thousands of gentry and citizens who have come to London to enjoy the unique spectacle of a royal cousin on open trial for treason and rebellion. The royal family turning on itself once again. We find we are no further forward at all.

It is still dark and cold at eight when there is a stir at the door and Thomas Howard comes in. He exchanges a quick look with me and I think these last three years have not been kind to either of us. I know my face has lines of worry from my care of the queen and the destruction of my peace, and he is grey and fatigued. He has that terrible prison pallor which comes to a man whose skin has been burnished from being out in all weathers, every day, and then has been suddenly confined. The tan is on the skin like dirt but the healthy colour beneath has faded. It is the pallor of the Tower, he will have seen it on his father, on his grandfather. He stands on the dais and to my shock, I see his stance – always haughty, always over-proud – has become bowed. He stands like a man weighed down with false accusation.

The duke raises his head as the clerk of the Crown reads the charge, and he looks around, as a weary hawk will scan the mews, always alert, always ready for danger; but there is no bright Howard pride in his eyes any more. They imprisoned him in the room where they kept his grandfather charged with treason. He can overlook the green where they executed his father for offences against the Crown. Howards have always been their own greatest danger. Thomas must feel his line is accursed. I think if his cousin the queen could only see him now she would forgive him from sheer pity. He may have been wrongly advised, he may have done wrong, but he has been punished. This man is at the end of his strength.

He is asked for his plea but instead of answering guilty or no, he asks the court for a counsel, a lawyer to help him answer the charge. I don't have to look to Cecil for his refusal; the Chief Justice Catline is already there before us all, up on his feet like a little moppet, explaining that in trials for high treason no lawyer is allowed. Howard may answer only if he has been treasonous or not. And there is no mitigation either; in a trial for high treason, if he answers guilty he is saying he wants to die.

Thomas Howard looks at me, as an old friend that he thinks will deal with him fairly. 'I have had very short warning to answer so great a matter. I have not had fourteen hours in all, both day and night. I am hardly handled. I have had short warning and no books, neither a book of statutes, not so much as the breviate of statutes. I am brought to fight without a weapon.'

I look down at my hands, I shuffle my papers. Surely, we cannot hound this man to the scaffold without giving him time to prepare a defence? Surely, we will allow him a lawyer?

'I stand here before you for my life, lands and goods, my children and my posterity and that, which I esteem most of all, for my honesty,' he says eagerly to me. 'I forbear to speak of my honour. I am unlearned, let me have what the law would allow, let me have counsel.'

I am about to command the justices to withdraw and rule on his request. We were his friends, we cannot hear him ask us for something so reasonable and refuse it. The man has to have advice. Then a note from Cecil, further down the table, is passed along and slid under my hand.

1. If he has a lawyer then the full detail of the Queen of Scots' promises to him will be revealed. I assure you that her letters to him are not those that you would want read out in your court. They show her as a scandalous whore.

2. All this occurred under your guardianship, which must then be called into question. How could you have allowed such a thing to happen?

3. The trial will be prolonged, and the Queen of Scots' honour and reputation utterly destroyed.

4. Her Grace, our queen, will be held up for contempt before everyone, by what these two say of her. We will make a thousand traitors while prosecuting one.

5. Let us have the decency to get to judgement quickly and let Her Grace the queen deal mercifully with the sentence. She can always pardon him once this trial is over.

I read this and then I rule. 'You must make your answer to the charge,' I say to Howard.

He looks at me with his dark honest eyes. One long look, and then he nods. 'Then I must question the charge,' he says.

I consent; but we all know there is no avoiding a charge of treason. Cecil's new laws have so enlarged the definition of treason that it is not possible to live in England today without being guilty almost daily, almost hourly. To speculate as to the queen's health is treason, to suggest she might one day die is treason, to suggest that she might not be Queen of France is certain treason, though it is nothing but the most obvious truth: none of us will ever see an English Calais again. Even to think, in one's innermost secret heart, any criticism of the queen, is now treason. Thomas Howard must be guilty of treason, as indeed we all must be, every day of our lives, even Cecil.

They nag at him, as hounds will bait a tired bear. He so reminds me of a bear, chained with one leg to a post, while fresh dogs dash in and take a snap and shy away again. They take him back to the inquiry at York, and accuse him of favouring the Queen of Scots. They accuse her of claiming the throne of England, and imply that he would have married her and made himself King of England. They say that he plotted with the Scots lords, with his sister Lady Scrope, with Westmorland and Northumberland.

They take him through every moment of the inquiry at York; they have evidence that the Scots lords met him and suggested the marriage. This cannot be denied for it is true. It was no secret and we all approved it. Robert Dudley, now sitting at my side as a fellow judge, his face stony, had a hand in it too. Shall he be tried for treason alongside Howard? William Cecil, the chief playwright and choreographer of this trial, knew all about it as well. I know this, for my own wife reported to him, spying on me. Shall Cecil be on trial? Shall my wife? Shall I? But all of us are eager now to forget our parts in the courtship. We watch Howard shake the dogs from his flank and say that he cannot remember everything, that he admits he has neglected his duty to the queen, he has not been the subject and cousin that he should have been – but this does not make him guilty of treason.

He is trying to tell the truth in this masque of mirrors and costumes and false faces. I could laugh if I were not bowed down with my own sorrows, and sick to my heart for him. He is trying to tell the truth to this court of spies and liars.

We are all weary and about to stop for dinner when Nicholas Barham, the queen's sergeant and Cecil's instrument, suddenly produces a letter from John Lesley, the Bishop of Ross, to the Queen of Scots. He submits it as evidence and we all obediently read it. In it, the bishop tells Queen Mary that her betrothed, Norfolk, has betrayed his own queen to the Scots lords. It says that all of Queen Elizabeth's plans, all the advice of her councillors, all her innermost counsels, have been reported by Norfolk in full to the enemies of England. It is a most shocking letter, and proof, complete proof, that he was on the side of the Scots against England, and working for Queen Mary. It is an incredible document. It shows Norfolk, without doubt, as a complete and convinced traitor.

Damning indeed, utterly damning. Except that someone asks Nicholas Barham if this letter was intercepted on its way to the Scots queen or taken from her rooms? Everyone looks at me, of course, who should have caught such a letter. I am in the wrong now, for I did not catch this letter. I shake my head and Barham smoothly reports that this extraordinary letter was somehow lost, mislaid. It was not sent and I did not intercept it. The Queen of Scots never saw it. He tells us, straight-faced, that a copy of this most incriminating letter was hidden in a secret room, found as if by a miracle, years later, by James, Earl of Moray, and handed by him to the Queen of England shortly before his death.

I cannot help but look incredulously at Cecil, that he should expect men – not children enjoying fairytales – but men of the world, and his fellow lords, to accept this complicated fable. The look he returns to me is smilingly blank. I am a fool to expect something more convincing. To Cecil it does not matter if none of this makes sense; what matters is that the letter is entered on the record, that the record is part of the trial, that it will serve as evidence to justify the verdict to the world, and that the verdict will be guilty.

'Shall we have our dinner now?' he asks pleasantly.

I rise and we go out. I am so foolish that I look for Norfolk as we lords go for our dinner, and think I will put my arm around his shoulders for a moment, and whisper: 'Be of good courage, there is no escaping the verdict; but the pardon will follow.'

Of course, he does not dine with us. I had forgotten. We all go to eat our dinner in the great hall, he goes alone, to eat alone in his cell. He cannot dine with us, he is banished from our company, and I will never put my arm around his shoulders again.

1572, January, Sheffield Castle: Bess

I have no great love for the Scots queen, God knows, but it would take a woman with a harder heart than mine not to defend her against our new house guest and temporary jailor: Ralph Sadler. He is a hard-hearted bad-tempered old man, utterly immune to any form of beauty, whether it be the white hoar frost on the trees here at Sheffield Castle, or the pale strained beauty of the Scots queen.

'I have my orders,' he says hoarsely to me after she has withdrawn from the dinner table, unable to bear him slurping his pottage for another moment. She whispers of a headache and takes herself from the room. I could wish I could escape so easily, but I am the mistress of a great house, and I must do my duty by a guest.

'Orders?' I ask politely, and watch him spoon up another great swallow in the general direction of his big mouth.

'Aye,' he says. 'Defend her, protect her, prevent her escape, and if all else fails . . .' He makes a horrible gesture with his flat hand, a long cutting movement across his own throat.

'You would kill her?'

He nods. 'She cannot be allowed to get free,' he says. 'She is the greatest danger this country has ever faced.'

I think for a moment of the Spanish armada that they say Philip is building right now in his fearsome shipyards. I think of the Pope demanding that all of the old faith disobey Queen Elizabeth, authorising them to kill her. I think of the French and the Scots. 'How can she be?' I ask. 'One woman alone? When you think of all that we face?'

'Because she is a figurehead,' he says harshly. 'Because she is French, because she is Scots, because she is Catholic. Because none of us will ever sleep sound in our beds while she is free.'

'Seems a bit hard that a woman should die because you can't sleep,' I say waspishly.

It earns me a hard look from this hard old man, who is obviously unaccustomed to a woman with opinions. 'I heard that she had won you over, and your lord,' he says nastily. 'I heard that he, in particular, was very taken.'

'We are both of us good servants to the queen,' I say staunchly. 'As Her Grace knows, as my good friend Lord Burghley knows. No man has ever doubted my lord's honour. And I can be a good servant to Her Grace and yet not want to see the Scots queen murdered.'

'You might be able to,' he says gloomily. 'But I cannot. And in time, I expect there will be more who think like me than think like you.'

'She might die in battle,' I say. 'If, God forbid, there was a battle. Or she might be killed by an assassin, I suppose. But she cannot be executed, she is of blood royal. She cannot be charged with treason, she is a consecrated queen. No court can judge her.'

'Oh, who says?' he asks suddenly, dropping his spoon and turning his big face on me.

'The law of the land,' I stammer. He is almost frightening in his bulk and with his temper. 'The law of the land which defends both great and small.'

'The law is what we say it is,' he boasts. 'As she may yet discover, as you may one day see. The law will be what we say it should be. We shall make the laws and those who threaten us or frighten us will find that they are outside the protection of the law.'

'Then it is no law at all,' I maintain. After all I am the wife of the

408

Lord High Steward of England. 'The law must defend the high and the low, the innocent, and even the guilty until they are shown to be criminal.'

Sadler laughs, a rough loud laugh. 'That may have been so in Camelot,' he says crudely. 'But it is a different world now. We will use the laws against our enemies, we will find evidence against our enemies, and if there is neither law nor evidence then we will make it fresh, specially for them.'

'Then you are no better than they,' I say quietly, but aloud I turn to my server of the ewery and say: 'More wine for Sir Ralph.'

1572, January, Sheffield Castle: Mary

My betrothed is fighting for his life in a courtroom judged by men as fearful as he. My son is far from me. The only man who could save me now is far, far away, himself imprisoned, and I don't expect ever to see him again. My worst enemy is my new keeper and even Bess, the falsest friend a woman ever had, is repelled by his harshness towards me.

I am starting to feel afraid. I would not have believed that Elizabeth could put me in the charge of such a man. It is to dishonour me, to make such a man my custodian. She would know this, she has been a captive herself. She would know how a harsh jailor destroys a prisoner's life. He will not let me walk in the park, not even in the frozen snow in the morning, he will not let me ride out, he will allow me no more than ten minutes' walk in the cold yard, and he has been talking to Bess about reducing my household once more. He says I cannot have my luxuries from London, I may not have letters from Paris. He says I should not have so many dishes for dinner, nor fine wines. He wants to take down the cloth of estate which marks my royal status. He wants me to have an ordinary chair, not a throne; and he sits without invitation, in my presence.

I would not have believed that this could happen to me. But neither would I have believed that Elizabeth would put her own cousin, her closest kin, on trial for treason, especially as she must know that he is guilty of nothing but his ambition to marry me – which, though disagreeable to a woman of Elizabeth's gross vanity, is hardly a crime. He rode out in no rebellion, he sent no money of his own to any rebellious army – why, he lost the French gold he was supposed to send. He obeyed her order to go to court though his followers hung on to the leathers of his stirrups and the tail of his horse and begged him not to go. He surrendered Kenninghall, his own great house, disinheriting his own children: just as she asked. He stayed obediently at his London house and then went, as ordered, to the Tower. He met Ridolfi, several times, it is true. But I know, as they must know, that he would not have laid a plot with him to murder Elizabeth and overthrow her country.

I am guilty of that – good God yes, I don't deny it to myself though I will never confess it to them. I would see Elizabeth destroyed and the country free of her illegal, heretical rule. But Thomas Howard would never have done so. To be cruelly frank – he is not the man for it, he has not the stomach for it. There is only one man I know who would plan it and see it through, and he is in a well-guarded room with bars on the window, facing the sea in Denmark, thinking of me; and will never throw his life down on a gamble again.

'I have no prospects,' I say gloomily to Mary Seton as we sit over our own private dinner in my chamber. I will not dine with Ralph Sadler, I would rather starve.

Around us, about forty companions and servants sit down to dine, and the servers bring dish after dish for me to take a small helping and send them out around the hall. They still bring in more than thirty different dishes, a tribute to my importance as a queen. I would be insulted by less.

Mary Seton is not gloomy like me, her dark eyes are dancing with mischief. 'You always have prospects,' she whispers in French. 'And now you have another Sir Galahad ready to serve you.'

'Sir Galahad?' I ask.

'I don't know,' she says. 'Maybe he is more a Sir Lancelot. Certainly a nobleman ready to risk everything for you. One who has come in secret. One whose name you know. One that you don't expect, and one who has a plan to get you out of here before the end of the trial. Before the shame of having your business discussed in open court.'

'Bothwell,' I breathe at once. I have an instant certainty that he has got away from Denmark. For what prison could hold him? Bothwell, free and coming to my side, will have me out of here and on a horse to Scotland in a moment. Bothwell will raise an army in the borders, turn the country upside down. Bothwell will take Scotland as if the country were a reluctant woman and make her know her master. I could laugh aloud at the thought of him free. What a fox among a hen coop he will be when he is on his horse with his sword drawn once more. What a nightmare for the English, what a revenge for me. 'Bothwell.'

Thank God she does not hear me. I would not want Mary to think that his name ever comes to my mind. He was my undoing. I never to speak of him.

'Sir Henry Percy,' she says. 'God bless him. He sent this, it came to me from the hand of young Babington. Sir Ralph watches you so close we did not dare try to get it to you till now. I was going to hold it till bedtime if I had to.'

She hands me a little note. It is brief and to the point.

Be ready at midnight. Put a candle at your bedroom window from ten of the clock if you are ready to come tonight. At midnight tonight, blow out the candle, and let yourself down from the window. I have horses and a guard and will have you away to France at once. Trust me. I would give my life for you. Henry Percy

'Do you dare?' Mary asks me. 'Your closet window faces outwards over the garden, that must be the one he means. It is a drop of forty feet. It is no worse than Bolton Castle and you would have got away then but for the rope breaking on that girl.'

'Of course I dare,' I say. At once the candles burn brighter and the smell of dinner is so appetising that I feel my mouth water. My companions in the room are dear friends who will miss me when I am gone but who will delight in my triumph. At once, I am alive again, alive and with hopes. I think of Sir Ralph Sadler's consternation and Bess's destruction when I get away from their guardianship, and I cannot help but giggle at the thought of their faces when they find I am gone in the morning. I shall get to France and I shall persuade the king and his mother that they must send me home to Scotland with an army great enough to dominate the Scots lords. They will command that Bothwell be freed to lead my army. They will see the advantages of it, and if they do not, I shall apply to Philip of Spain for help. I could go to him, or to the Pope, or to any one of a dozen wealthy Papists who would help me if I were away from here and free from the wicked imprisonment of my cousin.

'Oh no! Did you not promise the Earl of Shrewsbury that you would not escape while he was away from home? He asked for your word of parole and you gave it.' Mary is suddenly aghast at the memory. 'You cannot break your word to him.'

'A promise under duress is worth nothing,' I say cheerfully. 'I will be free.'

1572, January, London: George

I almost fall asleep straining my eyes in candlelight, trying to read the notes I have made during the day of Norfolk's trial. The words that I have scribbled merge and go hazy before my eyes. The evidence from Bishop Ross is enough to destroy Norfolk but it has come from a man so terrified that he cannot even make up a convincing story. Half of the evidence has clearly been dictated by Cecil and attested by men out of their mind with terror and pain. The other half of it has no support from anyone, no witnesses, no evidence. It is nothing but Cecil's lies, undiluted shameless lies.

I am weary to my soul at the thought that if I were a better man I would stand up and denounce Cecil for a false advisor, demand that the lords stand with me and that we go to the queen and insist that she listen to us. I am the greatest man in England, I am the Lord High Steward, it is my duty and honour to defend England against bad advisors.

But to my shame, I know, I am not that man. As my wife would be quick to explain I have neither the wit nor the courage to state and defend a case against Cecil. I do not have the prestige with my peers, I do not have the ear of the queen. Worst of all: I no longer have pride in myself.

The last man to challenge Cecil is before us now on a charge of treason. If we had stood against Cecil when he first took sway over the mind of the young princess, or if we had backed Dudley against him in those early days, or if we had even backed Howard against him only months ago . . . But we are like a besom of sticks; if we stood together we would be unbreakable, but Cecil will snap us off one by one. There is no-one here who will rise to save Thomas Howard. There is no-one here who will rise to overthrow Cecil. Not even I, who know of Cecil's spying, and his lies, and the quiet men who do his bidding all around the country, the men who are trained in torture, the men who have taken the laws of this country and said that they shall not stand, that Cecil's imaginary dangers are greater than the law, the men who lie for him, and care nothing for the truth. I know all this, and I dare not stand against him. Actually, it is because I know all this that I dare not.

1572, January, Sheffield Castle: Mary

The little candle-flame bobs at my window, and at midnight, when I bend down to blow it out, I hesitate as I see an answering wink from a quickly doused lantern, down in the shadows of the garden where the dark trees overhang the dark grass. There is a small new moon, hidden by scudding clouds, throwing no light on the stone wall below me. It is black as a cliff.

I did this three years ago at Bolton Castle when I trusted in my luck, I thought no walls could keep me in, I thought some man would be bound to rescue me. Elizabeth would not be able to resist my persuasion, or my family would rise up for me, Bothwell would come for me. I could not believe that I would not once again be at a beautiful court, beloved, enchanting, at the heart of everything.

Now it is not the same. I am not the same. I am weary from three years in prison. I am heavier, I have lost my wiry strength, I am no longer tireless, undefeated. When I climbed down the wall at Bolton Castle I had spent a week on the run from my enemies, I was hardened. Here, in the three years of luxurious imprisonment, I have been over-fed and bored, inflamed with false hopes and distracted by my own dreams, and I am never well.

I am a different woman in my heart. I have seen the North rise and fall for me, I have seen my men swinging as picked-off bones on the gibbets at the village crossroads. I have accepted a man in marriage and learned of his arrest. And I have waited and waited for Bothwell, certain that he would come to me. He does not come. He cannot come. I have realised that he will never come to me again, even if I order him not to. Even if I send to tell him I never want to see him again, even though he would understand the prohibition is an invitation, he cannot come.

Courage! I bend my head and blow out the little flame. I have nothing to lose by trying, and everything to gain. As soon as I am free again I shall have everything restored to me, my health, my beauty, my fortune, my optimism, Bothwell himself. I check that the sheets are knotted around my waist, I hand the end to John my steward, I smile at Mary Seton, and give her my hand to kiss. I will not wait for her, this time, I will not take a maid. I shall start running the moment that my feet touch the ground.

'I will send for you when I am in France,' I say to her.

Her face is pale and strained, tears in her eyes. 'God speed,' she says. *'Bonne chance!'*

She swings open the lattice window and John winds the rope of sheets around the strong wooden post of the bed, and braces himself to take my weight.

I nod my thanks to him and step up to the windowsill, bend my head to get out of the window, and at that very moment there is a hammering on my door and Ralph Sadler's gruff voice hollering: 'Open up! In the name of the queen! Open up!'

'Go!' John urges me. 'I have you! Jump.'

I look down. Below me at the foot of the wall I see a gleam of metal; there are soldiers waiting. Hurrying from the main house come a dozen men with torches.

'Open up!'

I meet Mary Seton's appalled gaze and I shrug. I try to smile, but I feel my lip tremble. *'Mon dieu,'* I say. 'What a noise! Not tonight, then.'

'Open in the name of the queen, or I will break down this door!' Sadler bellows like a bull.

I nod to John. 'I think you had better let him in,' I say.

I put out my hand to Mary and let her help me down from the window. 'Quickly,' I say. 'Untie the rope. I don't want him to see me like this.'

She fumbles as he hammers with the hilt of his sword. John throws open the door and Sadler falls inwards. Behind him is Bess, white-faced, her hand tugging at his sleeve, holding back his sword arm.

'You damned traitor, you damned treasonous, wicked traitor!' he hollers as he stumbles into the room and sees the knotted sheets on the floor and the open window. 'She should take your head off, she should take your head off without trial.'

I stand like a queen, and say nothing.

'Sir Ralph . . .' Bess protests. 'This is a queen.'

'I could damned well kill you myself!' he shouts. 'If I threw you out of the window now I could say that the rope broke and you fell.'

'Do it,' I spit.

He bellows in his rage and Mary dives between us and John moves closer, fearing this brute will lunge at me in his temper. But it is Bess who prevents him, tightening her grip on his arm. 'Sir Ralph,' she says quietly. 'You cannot. Everyone would know. The queen would have you tried for murder.'

'The queen would thank God for me!' he snaps.

She shakes her head. 'She would not. She would never forgive you. She does not want her cousin dead, she has spent three years trying to find a way to restore her to her throne.'

'And look at the thanks she gets! Look at the love which is returned her!'

'Even so,' she says steadily, 'she does not want her death.'

'I would give it her as a gift.'

'She does not want her death on her conscience,' Bess says, more precisely. 'She could not bear it. She does not wish it. She will never order it. A queen's life is sacred.'

I feel icy inside, I don't even admire Bess for defending me. I know she is defending her own house and her own reputation. She doesn't want to go down in history as the hostess who killed a royal guest. Mary Seton slips her hand in mine.

'You will not touch her,' she says quietly to Sir Ralph. 'You will have to kill me, you will have to kill us all first.'

'You are blessed in the loyalty of your friends,' Sir Ralph says bitterly. 'Though you yourself are so disloyal.'

I say nothing.

'A traitor,' he says.

For the first time I look at him. I see him flush under the contempt of my gaze. 'I am a queen,' I say. 'I cannot be named as a traitor. There can be no such thing. I am of the blood royal, I cannot be accused of treason, I cannot be legally executed. I am untouchable. And I don't answer to such as you.'

A vein throbs in his temple, his eyes goggle like a landed fish. 'Her Majesty is a saint to endure you in her lands,' he growls.

'Her Majesty is a criminal to hold me against my consent,' I say. 'Leave my room.'

His eyes narrow, I do believe he would kill me if he could. But he cannot. I am untouchable. Bess tugs gently at his arm and together they leave. I could almost laugh: they go backwards, step by stiff step, as they must do when they leave a royal presence. Sadler may hate me, but he cannot free himself from deference.

The door closes behind them. We are left alone with our candle still showing a wisp of smoke, the open window, and the knotted rope dangling in space.

Mary pulls in the rope, snuffs the candle and closes the window. She looks out over the garden. 'I hope Sir Henry got away,' she says. 'God help him.'

I shrug. If Sir Ralph knew where to come and at what time, the whole plot was probably penetrated by Cecil from the moment that Sir Henry Percy first hired his horses. No doubt he is under arrest now. No doubt he will be dead within the week.

'What shall we do?' Mary demands. 'What shall we do now?'

I take a breath. 'We go on planning,' I say. 'It is a game, a deadly game, and Elizabeth is a fool for she has left me with nothing to do but to play this game. She will plot to keep me, and I will plot to be free. And we shall see, at the very end, which one of us wins and which of us dies.'

1572, March, Chatsworth: Bess

I am bidden to meet my lord, his lawyer and his steward in his privy chamber, a formal meeting. His lawyer and clerks have come from London, and I have my chief steward to advise me. I pretend to ignorance; but I know what this is all about. I have been waiting for this all the weeks after the verdict of guilty on Howard and my lord's silent return home.

My lord has served his queen as loyally as any man could do but even after the verdict she wanted, she has not rewarded him. He may be Lord High Steward of England but he is a great lord only in reputation. In reality he is a pauper. He has no money left at all, and not a field that is not mortgaged. He has returned from London as a man broken by his own times. Howard is sentenced to death and it will be Cecil's England now, and my lord cannot live in peace and prosperity in Cecil's England.

Under the terms of our marriage contract my lord has to give me great sums of money at my son's coming of age. Henry is now twenty-one years old and Charles will soon be twenty and my lord will owe me their inheritance and the money for my other children on the first day of April, as well as other obligations to me. I know he cannot pay it. He cannot get anywhere near to paying it.

In addition to this I have been lending him money to pay for the queen's keep for the past year, and I have known for the past six months that he won't be able to repay me this either. The expense of housing and guarding the Queen of Scots has cost him all the rents and revenues of his land, and there is never enough money coming in. To settle his debt to me, to fulfil his marriage contract, he will have to sell land or offer me land instead of the money he should pay me.

He finally realised what a crisis he was in when he could not hold his usual open house at Christmas. He finally realised that he could not go on pouring his fortune at the feet of the Scots queen. When I told him that there was nothing left in the treasure room, no credit available for us in the whole of Derbyshire, he finally saw the disaster that has been building every day for the past three years, and of which I have warned him, every time that we sent out our bill to the queen and received no payment. I have been thinking every day for three years about what we should do about this unbearable expense, every day for the past three years it has nagged at me like a pain; and so I know what I want. His poverty has come as a surprise to him; to me it is an old enemy.

I have not been idle. Indeed, I have deliberately shifted his debt from the money lenders to myself: securing his borrowings with my own funds, knowing that he would not be able to repay. Knowing what I want. I know what I will settle for, and I know what I will absolutely reject.

I sit on a straight-backed chair, hands in my lap, attentive, as the lawyer stands before me and explains that the earl's financial position is straitened through no fault of his own. He has had expenses beyond what any lord could bear, in his service to the queen. I bow my head like an obedient wife and listen. My husband looks out of the window as if he can hardly bear to hear his folly described.

The lawyer tells me that in view of the earl's obligations in terms of our marriage contract, and his later obligations from his borrowing from me, he is prepared to make a proposal. My chief steward glances at me. He has been frightened by my loans; I can feel his hopeful look on my face, but I keep my eyes down.

The lawyer proposes that all the lands that I brought to my lord on marriage shall be restored to me. All the lands that were gifted to me by my dearest husband William St Loe, and my careful husband before him William Cavendish, will be returned to me. In return I must forgive my husband his debt to me for the cash loans I have made him, and I must forgive him the support of my children, which he promised on marriage. The agreement we made on marriage is, in effect, to be dissolved. I shall have my own again and he will be responsible neither for me, nor for my children.

I could cry with relief, but I say nothing and keep my face still. This is to regain my inheritance, this is to restore to me the fortune I made with husbands who knew the value of money and knew the value of land and kept them safe. This restores to me: myself. This makes me once more a woman of property, and a woman of property is a woman in charge of her own destiny. I will own my house. I will own my land. I will manage my fortune. I will be an independent woman. At last I shall be safe again. My husband may be a fool, may be a spendthrift, but his ruin will not drag me down.

'This is a most generous offer,' his lawyer says, when I say nothing.

Actually, no; it is not a generous offer. It is a tempting one. It is designed to tempt me; but if I were to hold out for the cash I am owed my husband would be forced to sell most of these lands to clear his debts, and I could buy them at rock-bottom prices and show a profit. But, I imagine, this is not the way of an earl and his countess.

'I accept,' I say simply.

'You do?'

They were expecting more haggling. They were expecting a great repining about the loss of money. They expected me to demand coin. Everyone wants money, nobody wants land. Everyone in England; but me.

'I accept,' I repeat. I manage a wan smile at my lord who sits in a sulk, realising at last how much his infatuation with the Scots queen has cost him. 'I would wish to help my husband the earl in this difficult time. I am certain that when the queen is returned to Scotland she will favour him with the repayment of all debts.' This is to rub salt in a raw wound. The queen will never return to Scotland in triumph now, and we all know it.

He smiles thinly at my optimism.

'Do you have a document for me to sign?' I ask.

'I have one prepared,' the lawyer says.

He passes it over to me. It is headed 'Deed of Gift' as if my husband the earl had not been forced into repaying me my own again. I will not quibble at this, nor at the value of the lands that are overpriced, nor at the value of the woodland which has not been properly maintained. There are many items I would argue if I were not eager to finish this, desperate to call my own lands my own again.

'You understand that if you sign this you must provide for your own children?' The lawyer hands me the quill, and I am hard put not to laugh aloud.

Provide for my children! All my husband the earl has ever done is provide for the Queen of Scots. His own children's inheritance has been squandered on her luxuries. Thank God he will no longer be responsible for me and mine.

'I understand,' I say. 'I will provide for myself, and for my family, and I will never look to the earl for help again.'

He hears the ring of farewell in this, and his head comes up and he looks at me. 'You are wrong if you blame me,' he says with quiet dignity.

'Fool,' I think but I do not say it. This is the last time I shall call him fool in my thoughts. I promise myself this, as I sign. From this day if he is wise or if he is a fool, he cannot cost me my lands. He can be a fool or not as he pleases, he will never hurt me again. I have my lands back in my own hands and I will keep them safe. He can do what he wants with his own. He can lose all his own lands for love of her, if he so chooses, but he cannot touch mine.

But he is right to hear dismissal in my voice. This was my husband. I gave him my heart, as a good wife should, and I trusted him with the inheritance of my children, and all my fortune, as a good wife must. Now I have my heart and my fortune back safely. This is goodbye.

June 1st, 1572, London: George

The queen has finally screwed herself to the point that none of us dreamed she would ever reach. She has ordered the death of her cousin and it is to be tomorrow. She summons me to Westminster Palace in the afternoon and I wait among the other men and women in her presence chamber. I have never known the mood so sombre at court. Those who have had secret dealings with the other queen are fearful, and with good reason. But even those whose consciences are clear are still nervous. We have become a court of suspicion, we have become a court of doubt. The shadows that Cecil has feared for so long are darkening the very heart of England.

Queen Elizabeth crooks her finger towards me and rises from her throne and leads me to a window overlooking the river where we can stand alone.

'There is no doubt of her guilt,' she says suddenly.

'Her guilt?'

'His, I mean his. His guilt.'

I shake my head. 'But he did nothing more than send the money and know of the plans. He did submit himself to you. He did not take arms against you. He obeyed.'

'And then plotted again,' she says.

I bow. I take a little sideways glance at her. Under the white powder her skin is lined and tired. She holds herself like a queen unbowed but for once anyone can see the effort.

'Could you pardon him?' I ask. It is a risk to raise this, but I cannot let him face his death without a word.

'No,' she says. 'It would be to put a knife in the hand of every assassin in the country. And what is to stop him plotting again? We cannot trust him any more. And, God knows she will weave plots till the very moment of her death.'

I feel myself freeze at the threat to her. 'You would not accuse her next? You would not allow Cecil to accuse her?'

The queen shakes her head. 'She is a queen. She is not subject to my laws unless I know that she has conspired to kill me. There is no evidence that she plotted my death. No other accusation can stand against her.'

'If she could be set free . . .'

'She will never be free,' she says bluntly. 'This plot with Ridolfi has cost her that, at least. The Scots would not have her back now if I begged them, and I can release her to no-one. She has shown herself as my enemy. I shall keep her imprisoned forever.'

'In the Tower?'

The face she turns to me is hard like a basilisk's. 'I shall leave her with you for the rest of her life,' she says. 'That can be your punishment as well as hers.'

I stumble from her presence chamber before she can curse me with worse, and I go home to my London house. I cannot sleep. I get up from my bed and walk the quiet streets. No-one is about but whores and spies and neither of them trouble me tonight.

I find my way to the Tower. The thick walls are black against the silver quietness of the river, and then I see the royal barge coming swiftly downriver with the royal standard discreetly lashed. The queen too is restless tonight.

The barge goes silently in the watergate, where she herself once went in as a traitor and cried in the rain and said she would go no further. I walk to the little barred gate in the great wall, and a porter recognises me and lets me in. Like a ghost I stand in the shadow of the great walls and see the queen go quietly into the Tower. She has come to see the duke, her cousin, her closest kin, on the very eve of his death. There is no doubt in my mind that she will forgive him. No-one could send Thomas Howard to his death if they had seen his pride humbled, and his handsome face lined with pain; but at the very door of his chamber, she shies away. She cannot bear to see him; but she decides to spend the night under the same roof as him: he in his cell, she in the royal chamber. He will never even know that she is there, sharing his agony. She knows he will be awake: praying and preparing for his death at dawn, writing to his children, begging them to care for each other. He has no idea that she is so close to him as he readies himself for death on her orders. But she is housed beside him, sleepless as he is sleepless, watching for dawn through the windows of the same building, hearing the light rain drizzle on the same roof. God knows what is going through her mind; she must be in an agony of indecision to undertake such a vigil with him.

She knows that he has to die. All her advisors say that she must harden her heart and have him executed. He may be her cousin and beloved to her; but he is a known and declared rebel. Alive, he would be a figurehead for every traitor, every day, for the rest of her reign. Forgiven, he would make every spy hope for forgiveness, and how would Cecil rule by terror if we were known to have a merciful queen? Cecil's England is darkened by apprehension. He cannot have a queen who turns kind. Howard is a challenge to the rule of terror whether he likes it or not. He has to die.

But this is her cousin that she has loved from childhood. We all know and love him. We all have a story about his temper or his wit, about his absurd pride and his wonderful taste. We have all relished his lavish hospitality, we have all admired his great lands, the fidelity of his servants, the devotion that he showed to his wives; this is a man I have been proud to call my friend. We all care for his children who will be orphans tomorrow, another generation of heartbroken Howards. We all want this man to live. Yet tomorrow I will stand before his scaffold and witness his execution and then go down the river and tell his cousin the queen that he is dead.

I am thinking of all this as I walk along the cold lane around the White Tower and then I check as two women are coming the other way. In the flicker of the torchlight I see the queen, walking with a lady-in-waiting behind her, a yeoman of the guard behind the two of them, his torch smoking in the cold air from the river.

'You here too?' she says quietly to me.

I take my hat from my head and I kneel on the wet cobbles.

'Sleepless too, old man?' she says with a ghost of a smile.

'Sleepless and sad,' I say.

'I too,' she says with a sigh. 'But if I forgive him, I sign my own death warrant.'

I stand up. 'Walk with me,' she says and puts her hand in my arm. We go together, slowly, the white stonework of the Tower beside us gleaming in the moonlight. Together we walk up the steps to the open grass of Tower Green, where the scaffold is new-built and smelling of fresh wood, like a stage waiting for players, expectant.

'Pray God it stops here,' she says, looking at the scaffold where her own mother put down her head. 'If you can stop her plotting, Shrewsbury, this can be the last man who dies for her.'

I cannot promise. The other queen will go to her grave demanding her freedom, asserting the sanctity of her person, I know this now, as I know her, she is a woman I have loved and studied for years.

'You would never execute her?' I say, very low.

The white face Elizabeth turns to me is that of a gorgon in her cold forbidding beauty, a dangerous angel. The torch behind her gives her a halo of gold like a saint, but the flicker of smoke smells of sulphur. The sight of her, a queen triumphant, ringed with fire, strange and silent, fills me with wordless terror as if she were some kind of portent, a blazing comet, foretelling death.

'She says her person is sacred but it is not sacred,' she says quietly. 'Not any more. She is Bothwell's whore and my prisoner, she is not a sanctified queen any more. The common people call her a whore, she has destroyed her own magic. She is my cousin but – see here – tonight she has taught me to kill my own kin. She has forced me to put my own family on the block. She is a woman and a queen as I am, and she herself has shown me that a woman and a queen is not immune from assassins. She herself has shown me how to put a knife to the throat of a queen. I pray that I will not have to execute her. I pray that it stops here, with my cousin, with my beloved cousin. I pray that his death is enough for her. For if I am ever advised to kill her, she herself has shown me the way.'

She sends me away with a small gesture of her hand and I bow and leave her with her lady-in-waiting and the yeoman of the guard with his torch. I go from the darkness of the Tower to the darker streets and walk to my home. Behind me all the way, I hear the quiet footsteps of a spy. Someone is watching me all the time now. I lie down on my bed, fully clothed, not expecting to sleep, and then I doze and have the worst nightmare I have ever suffered in my life. It is a jumble of terrible thoughts, all mistaken, a wicked roil from the devil himself; but a dream so real that it is like a Seeing, a foreshadowing of what is to come. I could almost believe myself enchanted. I could believe myself accursed with foresight.

I am standing before the scaffold with the peers of the realm but it is not Norfolk that they bring before us from an inner room; but the queen's other treacherous cousin: my Mary, my beloved Mary, the Queen of Scots. She is wearing her velvet gown of deepest black and her face is pale. She has a long white veil pinned to her hair and an ivory crucifix in her hand, a rosary around her slim waist. She is in black and white, like a nun in orders. She is as beautiful as the day I saw her first, ringed with fire, at bay, under the walls of Bolton Castle.

As I watch, she puts her top gown aside and hands it to her maid. There is a ripple of comment in the crowded great hall for her under-gown is scarlet silk, the colour of a cardinal's robe. I would smile if I were not biting my lips to keep them from trembling. She has chosen a gown which slaps the face of this Protestant audience, telling them that she is indeed a scarlet woman. But the wider world, the Papist world, will read the choice of colour very differently. Scarlet is the colour of martyrdom, she is going to the scaffold dressed as a saint. She is proclaiming herself as a saint who will die for her faith and we who have judged her, and are here to witness her death, are the enemies of heaven itself. We are doing the work of Satan.

She looks across the hall at me and I see a moment of recognition. Her eyes warm at the sight of me and I know my love for her – which I have denied for years – is naked on my face for her to see. She is the only one who will truly know what it costs me to stand here, to be her judge, to be her executioner. I start to raise my hand; but I check myself. I am here to represent the Queen of England, I am Queen Elizabeth's Lord High Steward; not Mary's lover. The time when I could reach out for the queen that I love has long gone. I should never even have dreamed that I might reach out for her.

Her lips part, I think she is about to speak to me, and despite myself I lean forward to hear, I even take a step forward which takes me out of the line of the peers. The Earl of Kent is beside me; but I cannot stand with him if she wants to say something to me. If this queen calls my name as she says it, as only she says it: 'Chowsbewwy!', then I will have to go to her side, whatever it costs me. If she stretches out for me I will hold her hand. I will hold her hand even as she puts her head on the block if she wishes. I cannot refuse her now. I will not refuse her now. I have spent my life serving one queen and loving the other. I have broken my heart between the two of them; but now, at this moment, at the moment of her death, I am her man. If Queen Mary wants me at her side, she shall have me. I am hers. I am hers. I am hers.

Then she turns her head and I know that she cannot speak to me. I cannot listen for her. I have lost her to heaven, I have lost her to history. She is a queen through and through; she will not spoil this, her greatest moment, with any hint of scandal. She is playing her part here in her beheading as she played her part in her two great coronations. She has gestures to make and words to say. She will never speak to me again.

I should have thought of this when I went to her chamber to tell her that her sentence had come, that she was to die the next day. I did not realise it. So I did not say goodbye to her then. Now I have lost my chance. Lost it forever. I may not say goodbye to her. Or only in a whisper.

She turns her head and says a word to the dean. He starts the prayers in English and I see that characteristic irritable shrug of the shoulders and the petulant turn of the head that means that she has not had her own way, that someone has refused her something. Her impatience, her wilfulness, even here on the scaffold, fill me with delight in her. Even at the very doorway of death she is irritated at not getting her own way. She demands that her will is done as a queen; and God knows it has been my joy to serve her, to serve her for years – many, many years, for sixteen years she has been my prisoner, and my beloved.

She turns to the block and she kneels before it. Her maid steps forward and binds her eyes with a white scarf. I feel a sharp pain in my palms and I find I am clenching my fists and driving my fingernails into my own flesh. I cannot bear this. I must have seen a dozen executions in my time but never a queen, never the woman I love. Never this. I can hear a low groan like an animal in pain and I realise it is my voice. I clench my teeth and say nothing while she finishes her prayer and puts her head gently down, her blanched cheek against the wood.

The headsman lifts his axe and at that moment . . . I wake. The tears are wet on my cheeks. I have been crying in my sleep. I have been crying like a child for her. I touch my pillow and it is damp with my tears and I feel ashamed. I am unmanned by the reality of Howard's execution, and my fears for the Scots queen. I must be very tired and very overwhelmed at what we are going to do today that I should cry like a child in my sleep.

I shake my head and go to the window. This is no good. I am not a fanciful man, but I cannot shake off this dream. It was not a dream, it was a foreknowing. The details were so clear, my pain was so strong. This is not simply a dream, it is how it will be, I know it. For me; for her.

It is dawn. It is the very day of Howard's death. After such a terrible night, the terrible day has come. Today we are going to behead the Duke of Norfolk and I must be a man today, and servant to a queen who can do no other but kill her own kin. God save me from such dreams. God save the Queen of Scots from such an end. God save my beloved, my darling, from such an end; and God spare me from being a witness to it.

433

February 8th, 1587 and thereafter,
Hardwick Hall: Bess

God save them both today, and all days.

I have no cause to love either of them and no cause to forgive them either; but I find I do forgive them, this day of her death and this day of his final heartbreak.

She was an enemy to my queen, to my country, to my faith, and to me, certainly to me. And he was a fool for her, he laid down his fortune for her and in the end, as most of us think, he laid down his reputation and his authority for her as well. She ruined him, as she ruined so many others. And yet I find I can forgive them both. They were what they were born to be. She was a queen, the greatest queen that these days have known; and he saw that in her, knight errant that he was, and he loved her for it.

Well, today she paid for everything. The day that he dreaded, that she swore could never come, turned out to be a cold wintry morning when she came down the stairs at Fotheringhay to find a stage built in the great hall and the great men of England, my husband among them, to witness her death.

The final plot that could not be forgiven, that could not be over-looked, that she could not blame on others, was a plot to murder Queen Elizabeth and take her throne. The Scots queen, fatally, signed her name to it. Anthony Babington, now a young man, who had been little

Babington, my darling pageboy, was the chief deviser of this treasonous scheme and he paid for it with his life, poor young man. I wish to God I had never put him in her way, for she took his heart when he was just a child, and she was his death, as she was for so many others.

After all the thousands of letters that she had written, after all the plots she had woven, despite her training and being so well warned, she was finally careless; or else she was entrapped. She signed her own name to the plan to murder Queen Elizabeth and that was her death warrant.

Or they forged it.

Who knows?

Between a prisoner as determined on freedom as her, and jailors as unscrupulous as Cecil and Walsingham, who will ever know the truth of it?

But in a way today, despite them all, the Scots queen has won the battle. She always said that she was not a tragic figure, not a queen from a legend, but she saw in the end that the only way she would defeat Elizabeth – fully and finally defeat her – was to be the heroine that Elizabeth could not be: a tragic heroine, the queen of suffering, cut down in her beauty and her youth. Elizabeth could name herself the Virgin Queen and claim great beauty, surrounded by admirers; but Mary Queen of Scots will be the one that everyone remembers as the beautiful martyr from this reign, whose lovers willingly died for her. Her death is Elizabeth's crime. Her betrayal is Elizabeth's single greatest shame. So she has won that crown. She lost in their constant rivalry for the throne of England, but she will win when the histories are written. The historians, mostly men, will fall in love with her, and make up excuses for her, all over again.

They tell me that my husband watched her execution with the tears pouring down his face, speechless with grief. I believe it. I know he loved her with a passion that cost him everything. He was a prosaic man to be overwhelmed by love – and yet it was so. I was there and I saw it happen. I believe no man could have resisted her.

She was a tidal queen, a force of the moon, irresistible. He fell in love with her and she broke his fortune, his pride and his heart.

And her? Who knows with her? Ask anyone who has loved a beautiful princess. You never know what she may be thinking. The nature of a princess is enigmatic, contrary, just like the sea. But it is my honest opinion that she never loved anyone at all.

And I? I saved myself from the storm that was Mary Queen of Scots and I know myself to be like a cottager who fastens his shutters and bolts the door and sees the gales blow over. George and I parted, he to his houses and me to mine. He guarded the queen and tried to keep her safe, and tried to hide his love for her, and tried to meet her bills; and I made a life for myself and for my children and I thanked God that I was far away from the two of them, and from the last great love affair of Mary Queen of Scots.

The years have gone by but my love of houses and land has been constant. I lost Chatsworth to my husband the earl when we quarrelled and he turned against me; but I built a new house, a fabled house at Hardwick near the home of my childhood, with the greatest windows in the North of England, the most phenomenal stretches of glass that anyone has ever seen in great stone frames that look everywhere. The children even made a nursery rhyme about it: *Hardwick Hall, more glass than wall*, they sing. I have built a legend here.

I had my initials stamped on every side of the house in stone. *ES* it says, in stone at the edge of the towering roof, carved against the sky, so that from the ground, looking up, you can see my initials stamped on the clouds. *ES* the coronet bellows at the countryside, as far as the eye can see, for my house is set on a hill and the topmost roofs of my house shout: *ES*.

Elizabeth Shrewsbury my house declaims to Derbyshire, to England, to the world. *Elizabeth Shrewsbury* built this house from her own fortune, with her own skill and determination, built this house: from the strong foundations into Derbyshire rock to the initials on the roof. Elizabeth Shrewsbury built this house to declare her name and her title, her wealth, and her dominance over this landscape. You cannot see my house and not recognise my pride. You cannot see my house and not know my wealth. You cannot see my house and not know that I am a woman self-made, and glad of it.

I have made my children secure in their fortunes, I have done what I set out to do for them. I have founded dynasties: my children own the titles of the Earls of Shrewsbury, Devonshire and Lennox. My son William is the first Earl of Devonshire, my daughter Mary will be the Countess of Shrewsbury. And my granddaughter Arbella is a Stuart, as I planned with Queen Mary. The half-joking scheme that we dreamed over our sewing, I made real, I brought it about. Against the odds, against the will of Queen Elizabeth, in defiance of the law, I married my daughter to Charles Stuart and their child, my granddaughter, is heir to the throne of England. If luck goes with her – my luck, by which I mean my utter determination – she will be queen one day. And what woman in England but me would have dreamed of that?

I say it myself: not bad – not bad at all. Not bad at all, for the daughter of a widow with nothing. Not bad at all for a girl from Hardwick, who was born into debt, and had to earn everything she owns. I have made myself, a new woman for this new world, a thing that has never been before: a woman of independent means and an independent mind. Who knows what such women will do in the future? Who knows what my daughters will achieve, what my granddaughters might do? The world of Elizabeth is full of venturers: both those who travel far away to distant lands, and those who stay at home. In my own way, I am one of them. I am a new sort of being, a new discovery: a woman who commands herself, who owes her fortune to no man, who makes her own way in the world, who signs her own deeds, and draws her own rents, and knows what it is to be a woman of some pride. A woman whose virtue is not modesty, a woman who dares to boast. A woman who is glad to count her fortune, and pleased to do well. I am a self-made woman and proud of it.

And nobody in this world will ever call me Mrs Fool.

Bibliography

Bindoff, S. T., *Pelican History of England: Tudor England*, Penguin, 1993

Brigden, Susan, *New Worlds, Lost Worlds: The Rule of the Tudors 1485–1603*, Penguin, 2001

Cheetham, J. Keith, *Mary Queen of Scots: The Captive Years*, J. W. Northend, 1982

Childs, Jessie, *Henry VIII's Last Victim*, Jonathan Cape, 2006

Cressy, David, *Birth, Marriage and Death: Ritual Religions and the Life-cycle in Tudor and Stuart England*, OUP, 1977

Darby, H. C., *A New Historical Geography of England before 1600*, CUP, 1976

De Lisle, Leanda, *After Elizabeth*, HarperCollins, 2004

Dixon, William Hepworth, *History of Two Queens*, vol. 2, London, 1873

Drummond, Humphrey, *The Queen's Man: Mary Queen of Scots and the Fourth Earl of Bothwell – Lovers or Villains?*, Leslie Frewin Publishers Ltd, 1975

Dunlop, Ian, *Palaces & Progresses of Elizabeth I*, Jonathan Cape, 1962

Dunn, Jane, *Elizabeth and Mary: Cousins, Rivals, Queens*, HarperCollins 2003

Durant, David, N., *Bess of Hardwick: Portrait of an Elizabethan Dynast*, Peter Owen Books, 1999

Edwards, Francis, *The Marvellous Chance: Thomas Howard and the Ridolphi Plot*, Rupert Hart-Davis, 1968

Eisenberg, Elizabeth, *This Costly Countess: Bess of Hardwick*, The Derbyshire Heritage Series, 1999

Elton, G. R., *England under the Tudors*, Methuen, 1955

Fellow, Nicholas, *Disorder and Rebellion in Tudor England*, Hodder & Stoughton, 2001

Fletcher, Anthony and MacCulloch, Diarmaid, *Tudor Rebellions*, Longman, 1968

Guy, John, *My Heart is My Own*, Fourth Estate, 2004

Guy, John, *Tudor England*, OUP, 1988

Haynes, Alan, *Invisible Power: The Elizabethan Secret Services 1570–1603*, Sutton, 1994

Haynes, Alan, *Sex in Elizabethan England*, Sutton, 1997

Hogge, Alice, *God's Secret Agents*, Harper Perennial, 2006

Hubbard, Kate, *A Material Girl: Bess of Hardwick 1527–1608*, Short Books Ltd, 2001

Hutchinson, Robert, *Elizabeth's Spy Master: Francis Walsingham and the Secret War that Saved England*, Weidenfeld Nicolson, 2006

Kesselring, K. J., *Mercy and Authority in the Tudor State*, CUP 2003

Loades, David, *The Tudor Court*, Batsford, 1986

Lovell, Mary, S., *Bess of Hardwick: Empire Builder*, W. W. Norton & Company Ltd, 2005

Mackie, J. D., *Oxford History of England, The Earlier Tudors*, OUP, 1952

Masters, Brian, *The Dukes*, Blond & Briggs, London, 1975

Perry, Maria, *Sisters to the King: The Tumultuous Lives of Henry VIII's Sisters – Margaret of Scotland and Mary of France*, André Desutsch Ltd, 1998

Plowden, Alison, *The House of Tudor*, Weidenfeld & Nicolson, 1976

Plowden, Alison, *Tudor Women, Queens and Commoners*, Sutton, 1998

Plowden, Alison, *Two Queens in One Isle,* Sutton, 1999

Randall, Keith, *Henry VIII and the Reformation in England,* Hodder, 1993

Robinson, John Martin, *The Dukes of Norfolk,* OUP, 1982

Routh, C.R.N., *Who's Who in Tudor England,* Shepheard-Walwyn, 1990

Smith, Lacey Baldwin, *Treason in Tudor England: Politics & Paranoia,* Pimlico 2006

Somerset, Anne, *Elizabeth I,* Phoenix Giant, 1997

Starkey, David, *Elizabeth,* Vintage, 2001

Thomas, Paul, *Authority and Disorder in Tudor Times 1485–1603,* CUP, 1999

Tillyard, E. M. W., *The Elizabethan World Picture,* Pimlico, 1943

Turner, Robert, *Elizabethan Magic,* Element, 1989

Warnicke, Retha M., *Mary Queen of Scots,* Routledge, 2006

Watkins, Susan, *Mary Queen of Scots,* Thames and Hudson, 2001

Weatherford, John W., *Crime and Punishment in the England of Shakespeare and Milton,* McFarland, 2001

Weir, Alison, *Britain's Royal Families: The Complete Genealogy,* Pimlico, 2002

Weir, Alison, *Elizabeth the Queen,* Pimlico, 1999

Weir, Alison, *Mary, Queen of Scots and the Murder of Lord Darnley,* Pimlico, 2004

Williams, Neville, *A Tudor Tragedy: Thomas Howard, Fourth Duke of Norfolk,* Barrie and Jenkins, 1964

Youings, Joyce, *Sixteenth-Century England,* Penguin, 1991

Author's Note

Mary Queen of Scots is one of the great iconic characters of history and the
research for this book has been a revelation to me, as I hope it will be to the
reader. Recent work on the queen suggests a very different picture of her
from the romantic and foolish woman of the traditional version. I believe
she was a woman of courage and determination who could have been an
effective queen even in a country as unruly as Scotland. The principal difference between her and her successful cousin Elizabeth was good advisors and good luck, not – as the traditional history suggests – one woman
who ruled with her head and the other who was dominated by her heart.

Of course, a character who lives as long and in such dramatically contrasting
circumstances as Queen Mary experienced will be interpreted in different
ways by different writers, as in my version she suggests: 'A tragic queen with
a beautiful childhood in France and then a lonely widowhood in Scotland.
A balladeer would describe me married to the beautiful weakling Darnley,
but longing for a strong man to rescue me. A troubadour would describe me
as doomed from the moment of my birth, a beautiful princess born under
a dark star. It doesn't matter. People always make up stories about princesses.
It comes to us with the crown. We have to carry it as lightly as we can. If a
girl is both beautiful and a princess, as I have been all my life, then she will
have adherents who are worse than enemies. For most of my life I have been
adored by fools and hated by people of good sense, and they all make up
stories about me in which I am either a saint or a whore.'

My version of Queen Mary's story focuses on her years in captivity when
she was held by one of the most fascinating women of the Elizabethan era:

Bess of Hardwick. Interestingly, Bess is another woman whom popular history has defined in terms of her husbands. The new biography by Mary S. Lovell shows Bess laying the foundation of her fortune less as a gold-digger and more and more as a businesswoman and developer with an eye to good investment and management. Her last husband, George Talbot, the Earl of Shrewsbury, is not a man who features much in the history books but there is strong evidence to suggest that he was in love with Mary Queen of Scots, with whom he lived as her host and jailor for sixteen years and whose death he did indeed oversee with tears pouring down his cheeks.

The story of these three is a tragedy at the very heart of dramatic times. Their hopes and disappointment in each other is set against the great rising of the North which aimed to free Mary Queen of Scots, restore her to her throne in Scotland, guarantee her inheritance of the throne of England, and provide freedom of religion for Roman Catholics. If they had triumphed – as they looked certain to do – then Elizabethan England would have been a different place.

The Northern rebellion has been portrayed as the greatest challenge to the reign of Elizabeth; and yet it hardly features in the history books and fades into insignificance besides the excited descriptions of the less threatening armada. Indeed, the Northern army amassed a fighting force strong enough to take the kingdom, far greater than that of Henry VII at Bosworth, and their defeat was, as I relate here, a failure of conviction rather than military strength.

The defeat of the Northern army proved to be the final blow in the decline of the North which was always feared and hated by the Tudors and which still bears the scars today.

I am indebted as always to the fine historians whose works are listed in the bibliography, and the novel is heavily built on the historical record. But, also as always, when matters of fact are in dispute I make up my own mind based on the evidence as I understand it, and when there is a gap in the historical record I invent, as a novelist should, a fiction which accounts for the known facts.

For more background to this and all my other novels, for discussion with readers, and for many other features, please visit my website, www.PhilippaGregory.com.